GW00357317

THE
SEVENTH
PASSENGER

ANGIE ROWE

POOLBEG

This book is a work of fiction. References to real people, events, establishments, organisations, or locales are intended only to provide a sense of authenticity, and are used fictitiously. All other characters, and all incidents and dialogue, are drawn from the author's imagination and are not to be construed as real.

Published 2023
by Poolbeg Press Ltd
123 Grange Hill, Baldoyle
Dublin 13, Ireland
E-mail: poolbeg@poolbeg.com
www.poolbeg.com

© Angie Rowe 2023

© Poolbeg Press Ltd. 2023, copyright for editing, typesetting, layout, design, ebook

The moral right of the author has been asserted.
A catalogue record for this book is available from the British Library.

ISBN 978-1-78199-692-8

www.poolbeg.com

UNCORRECTED PROOF COPY.
NOT FOR RESALE.

About the Author

Angie Rowe has lived all her life in Dublin, first in Artane and for forty years in Ballymount. She is a qualified librarian and worked in a psychiatric hospital for many years.

Angie hadn't ever thought that writing fiction was something she could attempt, but when she was given a voucher for a writing class in 2017 she decided to give it a go. Three years later she submitted her first book, *Eaten Bread,* to Poolbeg Press. To her amazement and joy they liked it enough to offer her a three-book deal. She says she's still not quite over the shock of it.

Angie is about to start her third book and looks forward to what the future may bring.

Acknowledgements

Very many thanks to the talented people in Poolbeg Press for all their help in pulling this book together, especially editor Gaye Shortland.

Thanks to the Libraries of Ireland and their wonderful librarians who helped me source research and who were always cheerful, kind and went that extra mile. Particular thanks to the staff in South Dublin County Library in Tallaght.

To Jessica Phelan from the Garda Museum in Dublin Castle for providing information on the history and function of the Royal Irish Constabulary – much appreciated.

To Helene Forde who gave so much of her time reading early drafts and provided so much encouragement.

Thanks to my talented writing friends, the York Tribe, who provide a constant stream of support.

To my family – Chris, Graham, Jennie, Darren, Marianna – and Alexander to whom this book is dedicated. Thank you all for your love and support.

Dedication

For Alexander

PART ONE

PROLOGUE

Later, when asked, not one of them could remember much about the woman. They'd been aware of her in a vague sort of way, and all agreed that a mourning veil covered her face, but their attention had been on the ship.

Seven first-class passengers disembarked at Queenstown that day.

As the tender cast off, the young priest and the boy focused their lenses on the ship. The April sun bounced on the sea, making it glitter like diamonds. The tender slowly pulled away and the water between them and the vessel widened. The priest and the boy clicked their shutters, trying to fit the giant ship into a small frame.

The last photographs.

The boy's mother and aunt waved at the passengers on the ship's deck. The woman with the mourning veil raised her arm and waved to someone. They didn't notice to whom.

At the wharf, helping hands reached out to steady them.

A group of men ambled toward them. Cameras and notebooks in their hands. They wore the disinterested air of men who'd seen it all before. Reporters. They asked questions of the seven passengers. Had they enjoyed the *Titanic*? Why had they come to Ireland? They scribbled answers in their notebooks.

One of them tipped his well-worn bowler hat as he approached her.

'Your name, please? For the newspaper,' he said.

She was aware of glances from the other passengers. She felt trapped.

'Amelia Nelson,' she said, her voice low.

He licked the tip of his pencil and took a step closer, almost touching her.

'And you're travelling alone, Miss Nelson?' The hint of a smirk on his round face.

She felt her temper rise. '*Mrs.* Nelson,' she corrected him.

'And you're here for —'

'To join my husband.' The words were out before she could stop herself. She knew instantly it was a mistake.

'And his name would be?'

She took a breath. 'Mr. Frederick Nelson.'

A porter arrived with her bag. She took it from him and pretended she didn't hear the reporter say he had another question. She felt his eyes on her back as she walked away.

It'll be all right, she told herself. It's of no consequence. In a few days, the *Titanic* will be in New York. That's where the newspapers will focus their stories.

No one will remember who got off the ship in Queenstown.

CHAPTER ONE

Youghal, County Cork, Ireland, April 12, 1912

He knew. Sergeant Mulcahy's quick footsteps came toward his office and he knew something had happened. Probably something bad. The sergeant barely waited for him to say 'Come in' before he opened the door.

A boy's voice hollered from the front desk. '*Me da says he's got to come quick!*'

Sergeant Mulcahy jerked his head toward the boy's voice. 'Ned Dangan's lad Danny, sir. There's a body in the harbour and –'

'I know. I've got to come quick.' O'Dowd pushed the pile of paperwork on his desk to one side. 'Who's on this morning?'

'Flanagan, sir. I've told him to get ready.'

'Tell him to meet me out front in five minutes.'

A drowning. Inspector Lorcan O'Dowd hated drownings, but anything was preferable to updating the Register of Chimney Sweepers, or the Register of Public Houses, or the one he hated most, the Register of Evicted Farms. He was keen to go to the scene – but he was not a man to be rushed and certainly not one to jump at a

3

summons from a local fisherman. He forced himself to wait five minutes before he pulled his long body out of the chair, put on his tweed overcoat and dug his fingers deep into its pockets in search of a cigarette that he knew wasn't there. He hoped Constable Flanagan smoked.

Eager, broad-faced with a snub nose, Constable Flanagan stood to attention when O'Dowd walked past. He didn't look like a smoker.

'Sir,' he said, still standing to attention, 'should I bring my carbine?'

O'Dowd paused, pursed his lips, and pretended to consider this for a moment. 'No, constable, I think we'll be safe enough to attend this incident unarmed. Pencil and notebook will be our only weapons today.'

They stepped out into the morning drizzle. It was less than a five-minute walk to the harbour. He could tell Flanagan was eager; they were all eager in the beginning, inclined to walk too quickly. All those hours marching does that to a man.

'Steady, constable.' O'Dowd spoke quietly. 'It won't do to arrive breathless and flustered. Rule Number One: You must always look as if you're in complete control. Even if you're not, as long as you *look* like you have everything in hand, you'll earn the confidence of the people you're dealing with.'

'Yes, sir.' The constable took a deep breath and measured his pace.

It could be a pleasant walk on a summer's day, but this was only the middle of April. The sharp sea air and cold drizzle made their eyes water as they progressed along the quays toward the small harbour. This was where the River Blackwater and the sea merged and rippled in swirling currents across the bay.

A cluster of men at the far end of the harbour came into view. He could feel their eyes on him. O'Dowd slowed and looked down into vessels tied to heavy metal rings embedded in the grey stone harbour walls. He feigned interest in the contents of the boats. No harm in reminding the fishermen they could be searched at any time – gunrunning was rife along this coast.

O'Dowd knew he would never be accepted by the locals. No policeman would. He'd never be forgiven for being a member of the Royal Irish Constabulary. The locals saw the R.I.C as being at the bidding of the gentry, the largely absent landowners. That was unforgivable. Except on days like this when they needed the R.I.C. Then they had to, at least, be civil. The fact that he was from Dublin, a so-called 'jackeen', somehow made everything worse. He expected they would be suspicious of his questions. There would be a narrowing of the eyes, a pause as the answer was weighed. The whole trick of it, for them, was to answer a question with another question – that would give the most pleasure to the locals and the most vexation to the officer.

It was like getting blood from a stone.

The sea licked the harbour wall as they continued to the farthest boat. The one with flaky pale-blue paint and a faded name on its bow. Gulls circled and screeched at the group of fishermen beside the boat in their thick hand-knit jumpers, sleeves rolled to their elbows.

The men stood aside and lit cigarettes as though preparing for an entertainment to unfold. O'Dowd breathed in the smell of salt and tobacco and tried not to bite his lip from the sheer want of a cigarette.

'Morning, Ned,' said the constable to the boat's owner who stood smoking, a young boy beside him.

O'Dowd raised an eyebrow. Constable Flanagan was here only a couple of months and already seemed to be on friendly terms with the locals. He'd have to watch that.

'Morning, constable,' said the big wiry-haired man, his eyes taking in the inspector. 'You didn't need to bring anybody with you. There was no foul play here.'

'I'll be the judge of that,' said O'Dowd. 'What have you got?'

5

Dangan pointed his cigarette at an innocent-looking blanket behind baskets of open-mouthed mackerel.

O'Dowd's stomach tightened. He'd seen many revolting sights under innocent-looking blankets in the past. He stepped forward. Keeping his back to the onlookers, he got down on one knee and peeled the wet material from the corpse. A soggy, pale, puckered face looked unseeing to the sky.

Constable Flanagan blessed himself. 'God rest him, whoever he is.'

The men on the wharf removed their hats and made the sign of the cross too.

O'Dowd never ceased to wonder at the respect for the dead from those who wouldn't give the living the time of day.

He cast his eyes over the body and gently covered the man's face with his handkerchief. Something about the staring eyes of the dead always made O'Dowd uneasy. The man looked taller than average, dark-haired, mid-forties, he guessed, but it was hard to tell. His face was puffy from the water; mercifully, it looked like he hadn't been in it too long. At least the eyes were still in their sockets. O'Dowd checked the hands: perfectly shaped nails were still there. His clothes were intact and of good quality. White shirt with three pearl buttons and tiny pleats down the front. The studded collar was still attached, though no longer stiff. His waistcoat was buttoned, and O'Dowd checked the small pockets. They were empty, as were the trouser pockets. He turned his attention to the man's feet. Good leather shoes by the look of them. He checked the man's wrists and turned slightly towards Dangan.

'And this is exactly how you found him? No jacket or coat of any kind?'

Dangan narrowed his eyes. ''Tis.'

The weathered men on the quayside nodded and muttered.

The inspector replaced the blanket. No jacket probably meant no wallet, no means of identification. But something else was missing.

'Is there anything you want to tell me?' he asked Dangan.

The fisherman shook his head.

'In that case, I'll need you to come down to the station and make a statement about how and where you found him.'

'Four miles out, I'd say.'

'We need to make it official,' said O'Dowd.

Dangan looked at his feet, the cigarette dangling from the side of his mouth as he spoke. 'I've got to unload the catch. I'll call in after. It's Friday, you know.'

'I know what day it is,' said O'Dowd. He'd already seen the fishwives carrying baskets, fidgeting and watching from the corner of the street. Fish on a Friday. 'Have you any idea where he could have gone in?'

Dangan shrugged. 'Could be anywhere. Will you send the cart down now before the catch is ruined?'

Clouds gathered, the morning sky darkened, the drizzle turned to a light shower. The women pulled their shawls over their heads and started to edge along the quay wall toward them. Not one of them had a coat.

O'Dowd looked Dangan in the eye. 'I can get the constable to send for the cart as soon as you give me the cufflinks you took from him.'

Dangan looked up quickly; the ash fell from his cigarette and was scattered by the wind. He looked from the fish baskets to the women and muttered under his breath. He fumbled in his trouser pocket. 'I forgot. I looked to see if there was anything that could, you know, identify him.' He produced a pair of shiny cufflinks and dropped them into the inspector's waiting hand.

O'Dowd held them up to his eyes. The initials 'T.B.' were engraved into the gold.

'Constable, alert the coroner and the mortuary,' he said, 'and get the cart sent down as fast as you can.'

The constable made his way back through the growing crowd.

The inspector turned to Dangan. 'Make sure you come in later to make that statement for the record.'

He had taken just a few steps when he heard the boy whisper audibly, 'You forgot to show him the thing from his pocket, Da.'

The inspector stopped dead, turned, and caught the look on Dangan's face as he glared at his son.

'Was there something else, Mr. Dangan?' he said.

The fisherman said nothing, just looked at the policeman, a challenge in his eyes.

'I can wait here all day, Mr. Dangan. I've plenty of time.' O'Dowd made a show of pulling out his pocket watch.

Ned Dangan's shoulders drooped a fraction. 'I wish to God I'd tossed him back in. I was only trying to do the decent thing, and this is the thanks I get. I'll know in future.'

O'Dowd almost felt sorry for him but, then again, he'd robbed a dead man. He swung his watch by its chain.

'All right, all right,' said Dangan. 'When I looked in his pockets, I found something else. He again fumbled around in his trouser pocket and produced a small black-leather box. He handed it grudgingly to the inspector.

The fishermen jostled closer to see the inspector open the box and reveal a shiny blue-and-gold enamelled badge.

Inscribed across the badge was R.M.S. *Titanic*.

CHAPTER TWO

An hour later, Inspector O'Dowd was back in the police barracks, home to several policemen and their families. From his office, he could hear the chatter and laughter of the women in the washhouse. He sometimes wondered if he might be the topic of some speculation. A single man, the wrong side of forty, presented a challenge to the men's wives, which was one of the main reasons he tried not to get into conversation with them. It was always the same: once they realized he was unattached, he found he was introduced to their unmarried sister or friend, or cousin twice removed. He caught his reflection in the window and tried to see himself as they perceived him. He couldn't describe himself as handsome, his face being a little too thin, but he still had a good head of black hair with only an odd grey intruder visible. He held himself upright, as an officer should. True, there were several lines around his eyes and mouth but, even so, women sometimes flirted with him – so not quite ready to write me off, he thought, and caught his slight grin in his reflection.

There was a polite tap at the door. Constable Flanagan came in and proffered yet another piece of paper to add to the mountain on the desk.

O'Dowd suppressed a sigh, took it from the young man's hand, and sat down to read the short report.

The constable watched him anxiously. It seemed he couldn't stop himself from speaking.

'I've logged the *Titanic* badge and the cufflinks in the records, sir,' he said.

O'Dowd nodded.

'I thought you might want to see them again?' Flanagan placed them on the O'Dowd's desk. 'There's a bit of weight in the badge, sir. Might be of value.'

'Ned Dungan thought so,' said the inspector. 'But it's likely that the cufflinks are worth more, both in value and the information we can glean from them. He hadn't a notion of handing anything in, that's for sure. Probably gave young Danny a belt around the ear for his trouble.'

'Yes, sir. We've had word the coroner will examine the body later today.' Flanagan paused as if weighing up a question. 'Sir, do you think he was on the *Titanic*?'

'He might have been. But he could have got the badge from anywhere. Despite Ned's hopes, I'd say it cost only a couple of shillings. They probably sell them in all the White Star buildings. He might never have set foot on the *Titanic*.'

The constable wasn't making a move to leave.

O'Dowd looked up at him.

Flanagan took a breath. 'Sir, I was there yesterday morning in Queenstown when it passed through.'

The inspector raised his eyebrows. 'You kept that very quiet. I didn't have you down as an admirer of ocean liners, constable.'

Flanagan grinned. 'I'm not, as a rule, but my brother went on it. The family saved up for the ticket. He's the youngest, eighteen he is. I went to Queenstown so he wouldn't be on his own and he'd have someone to wave him off. He's never been anywhere and my mother was worried that he'd miss the boat. Would be just like him too.' His grin was a little uneven, and he looked down at the floor for a moment. 'Anyway, I could see him on the wharf with all the others, and I waved to him when he got in the tender to take them out to the ship.' He took a shaky breath. 'He has a job waiting for him in New York, and he'll be able to send a few shillings to my mother.'

O'Dowd became slightly alarmed as he listened to the young constable. He could see the lad was upset and searched for something comforting to say. He was never good at consoling.

'I'm sure he'll do very well in New York. I hope he'll write to your mother regularly.' Even to his own ears, it sounded cold.

Flanagan didn't appear to notice and nodded enthusiastically. 'He will. I made him promise.' His young face flushed.

O'Dowd wasn't quite sure if he was finished. He reached for a pen and hoped the slight incursion was over.

'Sir, when I was waiting to see him off, I saw a few passengers get off the *Titanic*.'

'And?'

'Well, I wondered if they might know the man, might have seen him on board. I was wondering if we showed them the man's photograph …'

The inspector leaned back in his chair and regarded the eager young constable. He reminded him of Michael, his brother – half-brother, he mentally corrected himself. He tried to ignore the unsettling pang of guilt and tapped his pockets, absently searching for tobacco.

'That would be a bit of a long shot, constable. After all, there are hundreds of people on board and, despite what you may think, the first-class passengers wouldn't all know each other. That's assuming our man was a first-class passenger, although his clothes certainly indicate he was.'

The constable looked crestfallen. 'Yes, sir. Sorry, sir.'

'Don't apologize, constable. And we have to start somewhere. We could get in touch with the White Star Office in Queenstown for a list of the people you saw disembark.' O'Dowd stood and reached for his coat; he couldn't go another day without a cigarette. 'Find out if we can get in touch with the *Titanic* before it reaches New York. We're looking for a missing passenger with the initials T.B. Once everyone gets off in New York, it'll be almost impossible to trace them.'

Flanagan followed him out of the office as far as the desk where Sergeant Mulcahy was writing in the station diary.

'Sergeant, contact the coroner and request some photographs of the drowned man,' said O'Dowd. 'I've asked Constable Flanagan to find out about getting a message to the *Titanic*.'

He glanced out the window: the earlier dark clouds were gone, and a promising-looking blue sky had appeared.

The constable and the sergeant exchanged glances and then looked at the telephone on the counter with mistrust. O'Dowd knew precisely what they were thinking. Telephone lines were unreliable, and neither favoured shouting police business into the mouthpiece for all to hear, never mind trying to decipher the crackly voice at the other end.

Flanagan hesitated. 'Sir, would it be all right if I went myself? I can get the train to Queenstown and be back in a couple of hours.'

'That all right with you, Mulcahy?' said O'Dowd.

Sergeant Mulcahy seemed relieved. 'I'll add the man's description to the missing person notices and see if there's anyone that sounds like him.'

O'Dowd looked again at the patch of clear blue sky. 'On second thoughts, it might speed things up if I went myself. You can accompany me, Flanagan. You might need to take notes. Rule Number One, always take careful notes.'

Queenstown always seemed to have an air of hustle and bustle that wasn't so evident in Youghal. Houses and inns were crammed into the hills above the town. The deep-water harbour town was the last port before the Atlantic and, as such, had importance more significant than its size. Colourful street stalls selling food and trinkets stretched along the seafront. Hawkers tried to make a sale to passengers arriving and departing, everything from hand-made lace to loaves of bread. Carts and wagons rumbled along the streets, piled with people and baggage.

They walked the short distance from the train station down the sloping road toward the town. The spire of the new cathedral looked out over the harbour, unfinished but rising steadily.

'French Gothic, sir,' Flanagan informed O'Dowd. 'One of the stonemasons told me. And flying buttresses too. There's a mighty view from up there. You can see right out to Spike Island and the naval base.'

O'Dowd made a mental note of this information. Always useful to drop in that sort of comment at a dinner party. As District Inspector, O'Dowd was often invited to the 'big houses' for social occasions. He had learned to ride reasonably well during his training and was a decent shot. The local gentry valued those attributes, and he was happy to accept invitations to dinner, the Hunt Ball, or shooting weekends. He was a single fellow, useful to have around when the dancing started. The gentry seemed willing to overlook the fact that he was a Catholic. Or at least he thought they had – until he met Penelope.

He stopped to admire the view out to sea. 'And where was the *Titanic*?' he said.

'That was out at Roches Point, sir. We couldn't see it from here. The passengers came and went on tenders from the wharf, just down there, at the White Star Line building. It was done very quickly, sir. I'd say she was only here about an hour and a half. I heard the tenders tooting goodbye and then the foghorn from the *Titanic* itself. They have a fierce mournful sound – foghorns, I mean.'

They called in to Queenstown police barracks and spoke with the duty officer. There were no recent reports of a missing man, but they'd be sure to let him know if they heard anything. O'Dowd didn't mention the *Titanic* connection; he knew it would raise eyebrows and probably make him a bit of a laughingstock. He could just imagine the rolling of the eyes and comments about the fanciful jackeen looking for notice.

They made their way along the wharf to the White Star Line building. A short flight of steps led to the open doors. Third-class passengers with bags and tickets were directed straight to the broad wooden wharf. First and second-class passengers left their luggage with porters and were accommodated in waiting rooms on the second floor.

O'Dowd asked to see the person in charge. Mr. Martin, a small, neat man with thinning hair and an air of busy importance, led them into his office and invited them to sit down.

Mr. Martin watched Constable Flanagan take out his notebook and pencil and immediately sat up straighter. His eyes flitted between the two men as though guilty of something, but not sure what.

'Mr. Martin, has the *Titanic* reported a missing passenger?' said O'Dowd.

'What on earth makes you think a passenger is missing? No, of course not. I've heard no such report. Why, the very idea!' He thumped his chest with his fist and belched loudly.

14

'And you would have heard if there was?'

'Of course I would. We, I mean the White Star Line, are in constant touch with the ship. Radio contact, you know.' He looked as pleased as though he'd invented it himself. 'Telegrams over and back. Extraordinary technology. They would have let us know as soon as something like that happened. Do you mean a third-class passenger? It was mostly third-class passengers that boarded here.'

'I can't go into too much detail at the moment.' O'Dowd used his gravest voice. 'Constable, would you show the item to Mr. Martin?'

Flanagan reached into his pocket, produced the black-leather box and handed it to Mr. Martin.

'Can you take a look at this, sir, and tell me what you can about it?' said O'Dowd.

'*Titanic* badge.' Mr. Martin shook his head and looked at the policeman. 'All the ships have their badges.'

'Are they for sale here, or at the other White Star Line offices?'

'No, they would only be available on board the ship. How did you get this?' His brow furrowed as he turned it over in his hand. 'As a matter of fact, I popped over to the *Titanic* for half an hour yesterday morning. Extraordinary ship! These badges are on sale in the souvenir shop. Well, it's actually in the first-class barbershop on C Deck. They sell these badges and postcards and souvenirs, small toys, that sort of thing.' He handed the badge back to Flanagan. 'They should be docking in New York on Wednesday, but if you like I'll ask the head office to radio them and check for any missing passengers.'

'As soon as you can, Mr. Martin.' O'Dowd caught Flanagan's eye. 'Mr. Martin, my young constable was here yesterday and noticed several passengers disembark. Would you have a list of their names and addresses by any chance?'

'Yes, there weren't too many. I'll get it for you.'

Mr. Martin went and retrieved the list from the outer office. He handed it over with a flourish. 'All seven were first-class passengers. Five are from one family, the Odells, here on holiday. They're touring around West Cork and Killarney for a week.' He leaned closer. 'In a motor car, would you believe?'

'And the others?'

'Father Francis Browne – his uncle is the Bishop of Cloyne. He's staying with him there. The seventh passenger was a Mrs. Amelia Nelson. I'm afraid I don't know anything about her.'

'Do you have the full passenger list here? I should like to take a look at it.'

Mr. Martin pushed his spectacles up to the bridge of his pointy nose. 'No, not the complete passenger list. You'd have to check with the Southampton office.'

'We will need to take a look at that, Mr. Martin. Can you arrange for a copy to be sent to me at Youghal Barracks – as soon as possible?'

Mr. Martin drew in a breath through his teeth. 'I can request it, but a document that size will take some time to combine and copy. There are several registers. More than thirteen hundred passengers are on board, not to mention hundreds of crew.'

'I'd be much obliged, Mr. Martin, as soon as possible.'

O'Dowd and Flanagan stood to leave.

'I trust you will be discreet, Mr. Martin,' said O'Dowd. 'We wouldn't want rumours circulating about missing passengers, now would we?'

Mr. Martin saw them out and assured them he'd get a message to the *Titanic* to check for a missing passenger.

They blinked in the sharp sunlight as they came out of the building and started toward the train station.

The sea mirrored the bright blue of the sky as they settled into the first-class compartment, quietly pleased that they didn't have to share with other passengers. The train creaked as they pulled out of the station.

'Amazing technology, Flanagan, don't you think?' said O'Dowd. 'If the *Titanic* responds to the telegram quickly, we will know straight away if they're missing a passenger. We might even know by tomorrow. As Mr. Martin says – extraordinary!'

CHAPTER THREE

The next day, Saturday the 13th of April, the *Titanic* was halfway through its journey.

Patrick Flanagan, brother of Constable Liam Flanagan, ate an enormous breakfast of porridge, herrings and potatoes and then lay down on one of the benches on the poop deck to have a nap.

He felt a tap on his shoulder. Reluctantly he opened his eyes and found himself facing a stern-looking young woman who pointed to his feet and asked him to move them so she could sit down.

'The seats are for everyone, you know.'

He apologized profusely, rubbed the place where his feet had been with the elbow of his jacket and, when she sat down, asked her name and where she was from – that was the opening question used by everyone in third-class. Maggie, she told him, and they spent the next hour talking about home and families, where they intended to go in America and how different everything would be for them.

The ship's telegraph office was busy. The two young operators sent and received messages from other craft as well as from New York and London; it was one of their busiest times. At 11.00 pm, a fault in the line stopped the messages to and from the ship. The two telegram operators stayed up all night until the fault was found and repaired at 5.00 am.

That same evening in Queenstown, Mr. Martin and his wife hosted a dinner party for a few close friends. Wine and stories flowed; spirits were high. At one point, Mr. Martin remembered the visit from the policemen. He decided against sharing the story of the body and the badge. He'd been cautioned to be discreet but, in any case, it would ruin the ambiance. A missing passenger. Ridiculous to think that someone could have fallen off that ship. Certainly not a first-class passenger. Something niggled at the back of his mind. He took a long draught from the red wine and closed his eyes briefly. The niggle formed into a realization that he'd forgotten to send the telegraph. He grinned around the room. How silly of me, he thought, but what of it? I'll do it on Monday. They'll still be two days out from New York. Plenty of time to ask the stewards to check for empty cabins.

He hiccupped. Monday would be plenty time.

Patrick went to Mass next morning, it being Sunday. He kept an eye out for Maggie but didn't see her among the crowd or later at lunch. It was chilly. He wrapped his arms around himself and walked along the poop deck, and there she was, coming toward him, wrapped up in her warm coat, hands in her pockets. It was too cold to stay on deck, so they went to the general area and had a cup of tea. They remarked that they could have a cup of tea anytime, and it didn't cost a penny.

There was no moon that night, but the stars sparkled cold and clear against the midnight-blue sky. The *Titanic* was making steady progress toward New York. The passengers could barely believe they would set foot in America in a few days. Spirits were high, and a party had begun in the third-class general room. Patrick danced with Maggie. He thought he couldn't be happier. He wanted the voyage to never end.

The first-class passengers enjoyed coffee and listened to the orchestra in the reception room outside the dining saloon. Several card games began in the smoking room. Many second-class passengers had spent the evening singing hymns organized by Reverend Ernest C. Carter, a London vicar.

Jack Phillips struggled with the backlog of passenger telegram messages in the telegram office. A telegram arrived from the *Mesaba*, warning of heavy ice. Jack put it to one side – he'd already sent up three other ice-warning messages to the bridge. The exhausted wireless operator continued to work on the passenger messages.

The sea was calm; no waves splashed the iceberg, and no tell-tale white foam gave away its position.

At 9.30 pm, Second Officer Lightoller asked the two men in the crow's nest to 'keep a sharp lookout for ice'.

At 10.00 pm, the party in third class ended when the crew turned out the lights in the public rooms. The passengers, including Patrick Flanagan, went to bed. He couldn't sleep; his mind was full of the girl from Mayo.

At 11.39 pm, Frederick Fleet in the crow's nest rang the warning bell three times and telephoned the bridge. '*Iceberg right ahead.*'

At 2.17 am on Monday, 15th April, the ocean swallowed the *Titanic*.

Over 1,500 people died.

Seven hundred and six people survived.

CHAPTER FOUR

Beads of sweat decorated Sergeant Mulcahy's creased forehead as he shouted into the phone.

'*Yes, I'll tell him. What's that?*'

O'Dowd stood waiting. Mulcahy's agitated eyes went from the phone to the inspector.

'Tomorrow, yes.' Mulcahy hung the earpiece on the hook where it swung as innocent as a child's plaything. '*Blasted thing!* I'll never get used to it.'

'Was that the coroner by any chance?'

Mulcahy wiped his forehead. ''Twas, sir. He's requested a post mortem on the drowned man and it'll be carried out later today. You should have the results tomorrow or the next day.'

O'Dowd was about to reply when the phone rang.

The sergeant put his hand on his chest. 'It'll give me a heart attack if it keeps doing that.' He picked up the earpiece and shouted into the mouthpiece. '*Youghal Police Barracks!*'

The inspector watched, slightly bemused, as the sergeant rolled his

22

eyes and listened. He saw the expression on the sergeant's face change to a puzzled look.

Mulcahy leaned on the wooden counter, looked at the earpiece, and then turned his eyes to the inspector.

O'Dowd could hear the bodiless voice was still talking. Then a clicking noise followed by a whirring sound. He reached across, took the earpiece from Mulcahy, and replaced it on the hook.

The blood had drained from the sergeant's face and his hand shook slightly as he covered his mouth with the tips of his fingers.

'What is it, man?' said O'Dowd.

Mulcahy looked at him as though he'd forgotten who he was.

'That was the Queenstown station, sir. It's the *Titanic*, sir. There's a report that the ship has sunk.'

'That can't be true,' said O'Dowd. 'There must be a mistake, a hoax even.' He waited for Mulcahy to regain his composure.

'I don't think so, sir. They seem to be taking it seriously.'

'It's unbelievable – there's been so much talk about that ship –' The inspector broke off suddenly as the realization hit him. 'Where's Flanagan?'

'I think he's outside at the washhouse. He's not due on till two o'clock, sir.'

'Find him and send him to me. Now, this minute.'

O'Dowd wasn't sure he was doing the right thing, but he couldn't have the young policeman hear the awful news, however vague it might be, without warning. He knew he wasn't the best person in a situation like this, but the least he could do was afford the man a little privacy. When Flanagan arrived, the inspector pointed at the chair, and the constable sat on the edge of it.

'I thought you should hear it from me. I'm sorry to tell you this – there's a report that the *Titanic* has sunk. We don't have any details yet.' He watched the young man's face absorb the words. 'I think perhaps you should go home and wait for news with your mother. Where is home, constable?'

Flanagan swallowed. He looked at the inspector as though a huge joke had been played on him and he was waiting to be told it was all right, that nothing terrible had happened. 'Delgany in Wicklow, sir.'

The inspector took glasses and a bottle of whiskey from a drawer, poured two small measures, and offered one to the constable.

Flanagan shook his head. 'If I went to my mother smelling of whiskey she'd batter me.' The boy stood up from the chair. 'Thank you for telling me, sir.'

At the door, he halted then turned.

'Yes, constable?'

'Actually, sir … I'd rather stay here until we know more, if that's all right?'

O'Dowd nodded. 'Yes, of course. Let me know as soon as you hear anything.'

Flanagan left, and O'Dowd looked at the whiskey he'd poured. Pity to waste it, he thought. It's not that early, and I've no mother to batter me, God rest her. He downed the tot and picked up the measure he'd poured for the young constable. For the shock, he told himself, and took a cigarette from the new pack he'd bought together with some pipe tobacco.

He knew why Flanagan didn't want to go home. He wouldn't be safe; it could be held against his family that one of them had taken the King's Shilling. He poured himself another tot – this was not the day to worry about incidentals like giving up tobacco and whiskey.

The next day the coroner called in to see O'Dowd. Both were still unwilling to believe that such a disaster could befall the *Titanic*, the 'unsinkable' ship.

'That drowned man of yours turned out not to be drowned after all. Post-mortem results show the cause of death was alcohol and opium, basically laudanum. If the body had been in the water longer we might not have picked that up at all.'

'And you don't think he could have taken laudanum and fallen into the sea?' O'Dowd asked.

'Not a chance. There was no water in the lungs, he was already dead. And, even if he did take the laudanum knowingly, a second party had to be involved in getting him overboard. At the very least there was aiding and abetting. I'll put it in the official report. Just wanted to give you a heads-up that there was foul play involved.'

O'Dowd pulled Constable Flanagan to one side and asked if he'd had news of his brother.

'We haven't heard one way or the other, sir, so we're hopeful. It might take weeks to get word officially.'

'And your mother?'

'One of my sisters wrote to say they're all there with her and the neighbours are in and out. There are decades of the rosary all hours of the day and night. As I say, we've not given up. If it's bad news, she'll never get over it. Patrick is the youngest – he'll always be the baby. You know how it is.'

'You could take some time, constable, in the circumstances.'

'No, sir, thank you.' He bent his head as though to hide the guilty look on his face. 'I can't be there, sir. I can't be in the house and do nothing. I can't comfort them … the crying and wailing and the fact that there isn't a body, nor any news. They're living in limbo. I couldn't sit there and listen to it. It's the uncertainty that gets me, sir, and that's the truth of it.'

He looked tired and washed out. O'Dowd guessed the boy hadn't slept since he'd heard. He'd be useless in the barracks, but he hadn't the heart to send him away.

CHAPTER FIVE

He lay on the deck of the *Carpathia*, not quite conscious, aware of wind on his face, murmuring voices getting closer. Someone had tucked a blanket around him, but he felt he would never be warm again.

The voices grew louder or nearer – he couldn't tell which. He thought he might be dead. He could feel nothing. Empty, exhausted.

He didn't try to open his eyes when the male voice said, 'And what about this man?'

'Yes, I know who this is,' a woman's voice answered. 'This is Terrence Bennett. He was in cabin nineteen. I never spoke to him, but I saw him going into his cabin once or twice.'

He couldn't bring himself to open his eyes. The voices drifted away, and he surrendered to the exhaustion that offered peace.

⊷◈⊶

'Mr. Bennett?' The voice was near his ear. He felt someone take his hand. 'Mr. Bennett, are you awake? You need to have something hot in your stomach.'

There was no icy breeze. He was indoors. Soup. He smelled soup. The voice seemed to require that he open his eyes, so he did. His throat was on fire, but he was hungry.

The young woman rewarded him with a smile as she pulled the chair closer. 'Open wide,' she said, holding the dripping spoon near his lips.

He did as he was told.

He glanced around the long room filled with beds, their occupants covered by blankets. He began to remember what had happened. He closed his eyes and kept them firmly shut, but the memories still came rushing in. He opened his eyes wide.

'My coat?' His voice was a whisper.

'It's here, Mr. Bennett. I've dried it out and all your belongings are here in this box. See?'

The woman held up a box and a jacket. She smiled and cried at the same time. 'You poor man!'

'I'm not ...'

'Don't try to talk now. Let's get some more of this nice hot soup into you.'

Just a week after the sinking, an investigation started in New York. A separate investigation was planned for London shortly, but there was no information about it yet.

Relatives of the victims from towns and farms all over the country waited for news. Families watched the postman's progress daily and read the lists of survivors printed in the newspaper's columns pasted up in shop windows. Rumours that travellers survived and completed their journey to New York flew around the town. There was talk of fishing boats from Halifax in Canada picking up survivors. The partial lists of survivors in the newspapers changed from day to day and relatives prayed that tomorrow the name of their loved one would somehow appear among the living. But as weeks went on and the reality of their loss seeped into their hearts, grief spread from village to village like a plague.

O'Dowd's head ached. He'd not slept well. He wondered how anyone *could* sleep if everyone's mind was taken over by the daily newspaper articles – accounts of survivors, deaths, and reports of the inquiry.

Sergeant Mulcahy followed O'Dowd into his office and waited while he hung up his coat and indicated to him to sit down. O'Dowd lifted his pipe from his desk then remembered he'd smoked the last of the tobacco the previous night. He put it in his mouth for comfort and nodded at Mulcahy.

'Well, what is it?'

'The mortuary sent these. They want to know if there's anybody to claim him?' He placed photographs of the dead man's face on the desk.

'Not yet,' said O'Dowd. 'Until we get a copy of the full passenger list, my hands are tied.' He picked up one of the photographs. 'These bloody things. I'm not sure how useful they are. We could show them to the passengers who disembarked at Queenstown. I have a list of them here.' He opened the top drawer of his desk and produced a slim file. 'I'll show them this God-awful photograph and see if they know anything. There's not much else we can do yet.'

'There might be,' said the sergeant. 'There's talk about town that a man smuggled himself off the *Titanic*. A crewman by the name of John Coffey. I could go as far as Queenstown and have a word with him. I'll take the photograph. You never know.'

'He might even have been involved in the murder,' said O'Dowd.

O'Dowd remembered what Mr. Martin had said about one of the passengers, a Father Francis Browne. Staying at the Bishop's Palace in Cloyne, not twenty miles from Youghal. It was too far to cycle, so he saddled up the horse who shared his stable with several bicycles, and set out.

O'Dowd always found the term '*palace*', used for all bishops' residences, to be a bit of an overstatement. There was never anything palatial about them, and the one in Cloyne did nothing to change his mind. The house itself was a large square grey building, three storeys high. It looked cold, even on this bright spring day. He shivered as he trotted into the large garden and past the well-tended lawn to the front door.

The young man with fair hair and kind eyes must have been waiting, for he opened the door quickly. He ushered O'Dowd into one of the parlours, invited him to sit and said he'd be back in a moment with some tea for him. True to his word, he returned a few minutes later, followed closely by an unsmiling woman bearing a tea tray. She put down the tray, then disappeared out the doorway without a word, let alone a smile.

'Ethel,' he said as though that were an explanation in itself. 'I'm afraid we've interrupted her routine.' He grimaced like a naughty schoolboy and poured the tea.

'Thank you for seeing me, Father Browne.'

'Actually, I'm not a 'Father' yet. I'm still studying. Please call me Francis.' He handed O'Dowd a cup of tea and sat down. 'I'm intrigued, inspector. What can I do for you?'

O'Dowd told him about the unidentified body and asked him to look at the photograph.

He studied it for a few moments. 'Interesting,' he said. 'I mean the photograph itself is interesting. The poor man,' he crossed himself, 'I hope he didn't suffer.'

'Do you recognize him? We suspect he was on the *Titanic*.'

'Good heavens, was he?' He peered more closely at the image. 'I'm sorry, I don't remember him, but perhaps he's in one of my photographs. I took quite a few. Would you care to look?'

He led O'Dowd over to a round table where there were some piles of photographs. 'These are just the first roll. I haven't had time to develop the other two rolls.' He pushed several photographs across the table. 'These were taken at Southampton. That's the first-class dining room, the gymnasium and here's poor Captain Smith before we departed.' He blessed himself.

They stood at the table and looked through the piles of photographs, to no avail.

'Do you always take so many?' O'Dowd asked.

'I'm afraid I'm addicted. I'm lucky that my uncle has been kind enough to allow me the use of one of the small rooms to develop the negatives.'

'We believe that this man's death was not an accident. I'm trying to find out anything I can about him. So far, all I know is that his initials are probably T.B. – the letters engraved on his cufflinks.'

'I see. I don't remember the face, and I'm usually good at remembering faces. Sorry. I'll develop the rest of the negatives as soon as possible and go through them.'

'I'd very much appreciate that.'

They returned to the armchairs and their tea.

'Of course, I wasn't the only one taking photographs,' Francis then said in his soft voice.

'Naturally, but presumably the other cameras will have gone down with the ship."

'Not all. I mean the Odell family who landed with me that day in Queenstown. Two of them had cameras. They might have snapped the man. It's worth asking the question, isn't it?'

'It certainly is. Thank you. Can you ring me if you find any photograph that shows the dead man?'

'Of course. I'll start straight away.'

'Appreciate that.' O'Dowd leaned back in the armchair. 'How did you happen to be travelling on the ship? It's not the most direct, nor the cheapest way to cross from England to Ireland.'

Francis Browne grinned. 'My uncle gave me a present of a ticket for the crossing. He's very good to me and I'd done well in my exams in Milltown.'

'Milltown?'

'In Dublin. The Institute of Theology and Philosophy. I travelled from Dublin to Southampton. Very generous of my uncle – and he saved my life, inspector.'

O'Dowd raised his eyebrows. 'You mean figuratively, of course?'

'No, I mean actually saved my life.' He swirled the tea in his cup. 'You see, I was rather taken with the *Titanic* – the people, the luxury of it all. As it happened, I was seated for dinner with a lovely couple – American millionaires. Quite elderly but so interesting and interested in everything. We hit it off, that's all I can say – we enjoyed each other's company. As we left the dining room the man said he couldn't remember when he'd had such a delightful dinner and said he hoped we'd have many more over the course of the journey. I told them it was my only dinner on the *Titanic* and that I'd be getting off the next morning. They were quite crestfallen and straight away offered to pay for the rest of the journey to New York. Their only condition was that I would have dinner with them each evening. Well, inspector, that would have been no hardship. We got on so well together that I had no qualms and, of course, I'd never been to New York.' The young man sat back in his chair and looked toward the ceiling, his face traced with sadness. 'I've prayed for them every day since it happened.'

'But how did your uncle save your life?'

Francis Browne's face brightened. 'Oh yes. There and then I skipped off to send a telegram to my uncle asking if I could stay on board, fully expecting him to agree.' He took a telegram from his pocket and handed it over. 'This was his reply.'

O'Dowd read the words, written in capital letters: 'GET OFF THAT SHIP – PROVINCIAL'

It was late evening when O'Dowd returned to the barracks in Youghal. He called in to see if Mulcahy had spoken with John Coffey.

'No luck with the photo,' said Mulcahy. 'In fact, he laughed when I showed him. You see, he was a boiler-room fireman and as such he had no contact with the passengers whatsoever.'

'Of course not.'

'He's saying now that he had a bad feeling about the ship. Though there was no mention of a premonition when he first came to Queenstown. He was telling people he'd just hitched a ride on the *Titanic* as a fireman and had no intention of crossing the Atlantic. He had finished a stint on the R.M.S. *Olympic* that ended in Southampton, and he wanted to get to Queenstown to visit his family.'

'So he's changed his story to what? A premonition!' O'Dowd shook his head. 'That doesn't wash – looks to me like the first version he told was nearer the truth. How did he get off?'

'The *Titanic* had to deliver mail and take on 1,300 bags of mail that day, as well as 123 passengers, but they only had two tenders – the *Ireland* and the *America*,' said Mulcahy. 'After the new passengers were boarded – and those seven passengers taken off – they used the tenders to transport the mailbags. The captain wanted it done as quickly as possible. Several volunteers, including Coffey, offered to help. He says he was able to carry a few mail sacks onto the tender and slip in between them. He might have had help, I don't know, but he was brought ashore on the *Ireland* and slipped away while it was being unloaded.'

'Fair enough, we can exclude him as a person of interest. After all, if he were involved in the murder, deserting ship and drawing attention to himself all over Queenstown would be the last thing he'd do.'

He took out the list and put a tick next to Francis Browne's name. Passenger Number 1. He could do no more here. All the other passengers had addresses in London. There was nothing else for it. He'd have to convince the County Inspector to let him go there to see this through.

CHAPTER SIX

County Inspector Patterson listened to O'Dowd's report on the victim. He raised his eyebrows when O'Dowd said he was requesting permission to go to London to interview the rest of the people on the list.

'I had a phone call from Francis Browne this morning. He's developed all his photographs and gone through them looking for the murdered man. No success, I'm afraid.'

'You could pass all this on to Scotland Yard, O'Dowd. Why would you want to drag yourself all the way over there? Isn't there enough going on here for you?'

'Of course I'd be happy to inform Scotland Yard, but I'd rather like to carry out the interviews myself.' He sat back in the chair. 'Truth is, I've been putting off a trip to London for quite a while. I have family there that I haven't seen for quite a few years. I never seem to have the time.' He heard his accent mirror the tone of the County Inspector's. Those years living in London, listening to English voices, had a lasting effect on him that became a little more pronounced when talking to his superiors or the gentry.

'Oh, yes. A brother, isn't it?' C.I. Patterson offered him a cigarette from the Indian carved box on his desk.

'Half-brother.' O'Dowd took a cigarette and lit up. He blew smoke toward the ceiling and felt a little light-headed. 'Thought I'd kill two birds and all that. I'll be happy to pass it on to the Yard if they want it, but my guess is that they're swamped with people trying to find out what happened to their relatives on the *Titanic*. I expect this will seem very small fry to them, more a nuisance than anything else. Probably be delighted that they don't have to take it on. Though I could probably do with a bit of help.'

Patterson nodded absently. 'You can sort that out over there – you'll have to shift for yourself. I'll give you a letter of introduction. See if that makes a difference.' He peered through the cigarette smoke. 'Has there been any activity in your neck of the woods? Have you heard anything since the Home Rule bill was presented? What are the locals saying?'

O'Dowd wasn't going to admit that he didn't know what the locals were saying. He could only repeat what Mulcahy had told him. 'They're cautious, sir. They say they'll believe it when they see it. But it seems to have calmed them down. I can't say there's no activity – you know what the terrain is like there. So many places they could use to continue manoeuvres. I'd think that's what they'll do in case the bill doesn't go through.'

'There's every chance it won't go through,' said Patterson. 'The Unionists will block it again. They certainly don't want to be ruled by a government of farmers, not after everything they've done to make Belfast a centre of commerce. I don't think that Carson chap will stand by and let it happen.'

'You're probably right, sir. Looks as though it's a wait-and-see game. It won't be clear until it's passed into law. I believe that could take two years.'

'Two years isn't long to wait,' said Patterson. 'Should be all done and dusted by 1914, unless something goes drastically wrong.'

CHAPTER SEVEN

He lifted his weary head as the train chugged the last few hundred yards into Euston Station and came to its resting place with a final jolt. The platform was full of porters and passengers, steam and smoke, trolleys, cases, tired whimpering children, and snappy adults. Never a good traveller, O'Dowd had a headache, stiff joints, and pain in his back. He stood slowly and winced as he rolled his shoulders. He struggled into his overcoat, picked up his hat and case, and joined the melee.

As he approached the guard gate, he saw Michael, his half-brother, neck strained, eager eyes scanning the crowds, wearing his constable's uniform. For a split second, O'Dowd wished he hadn't got in touch, had just slipped over and back without a word. And he would have done, except that his mother's voice came to haunt him and told him to 'make an effort'.

He waved his hat above his head and saw a look of relief sweep across Michael's face. He walked toward him and, for an uncomfortable moment, thought that Michael might try to hug him – he was always demonstrative as a child. O'Dowd hoped he'd grown out of it, but he approached with his hand out just in case. Michael grabbed it and shook it enthusiastically.

'I couldn't believe it when I got your letter, Lorcan. Come on, Gracie is dying to meet you. It's good to see you. I hope you're hungry. She's got in enough food to feed ten of you.'

'Sorry, I'm too tired to be hungry. The crossing was a bit rough, maybe later.' Why am I apologising, he thought, but couldn't help himself.

Michael picked up his brother's bag and slapped him on the shoulder. 'Don't worry. Whatever you want. Though you look like you could do with feeding.'

Michael jostled along at London pace, and O'Dowd managed to keep up.

'I'd forgotten how busy this city is.' He puffed out the words into the sooty London air.

It was a forty-minute train journey to his brother's home. The house his mother had brought him to all those years ago. Mr. Sudbury's house. He'd lived there before Michael was even born. The train journey to Forest Hills made him feel like he'd somehow fallen backward in time as familiar scenes swept past. It looked as though London hadn't changed over the thirty years since he'd crossed the water for the first time.

After the initial flush of greeting, the conversation petered out. Michael mentioned people that O'Dowd didn't remember, and they were both glad to reach their station and walk home. The streets looked the same, the trees in the gardens a little taller, but the road to the neat red-bricked Victorian house on Fields Road hadn't changed. The garden gate still squeaked. Before Michael could retrieve his key, the door was flung open, and a small plump dark-haired woman beamed at both of them.

She looked flushed and happy and reached up to kiss Michael on the cheek before turning to O'Dowd, arms wide. He realised there was no escape. She hugged him, despite the fact that her hands were covered in flour, and planted a kiss on his cheek.

He stepped across the threshold into his past.

The house was different, brighter, noisier, and untidier than he remembered. He let Gracie shepherd him into the warm kitchen. He swallowed hard at the sight of the kitchen table. He was sure it was the same one. He couldn't stop himself from running his fingers along the grain of it. He glanced at his mother's empty chair beside the hearth and then his eyes took in the rest of the room – the new sink and a shiny gas cooker that hadn't been there in his mother's time.

Two young children were staring at him from behind a chair. Gracie shooed them out. She picked up the youngest one then pulled the other from behind her voluminous skirts and patted his head as she waited for the approval of their uncle, who smiled and nodded and wished he'd brought something for them. The truth was he'd completely forgotten that they existed. He tried in vain to remember names, but Gracie came to his rescue.

'This here is Henry, and this is Daisy. Say hello to your Uncle Lorcan, children!'

She put the little girl down again and both children immediately ran back behind the chair and peered at him through the wooden slats.

'Never mind, they'll get used to you. Now, you must be tired, or do you need to eat?'

A look at his exhausted face gave her the answer. 'There's a bed made up for you in your old room – we thought you'd be comfortable there. Come along.'

She led him up the stairs, as though he wouldn't remember the room that had been his for eight years, and opened the door. The room smelled of lavender and paint. The plump bed was covered by a patchwork quilt he didn't recognize. A low fire glowed in the small grate. An unexpected lump came to his throat as Gracie walked past him and plumped up the pillow that didn't need plumping. She smoothed non-existent creases on the quilt and looked around the room with pride.

'And I've put a table there in case you need to write letters. And the matches for the lamp are here.'

He coughed before he could trust his voice.

'It's lovely, Gracie, thank you for this.'

She gave a deep sigh of satisfaction. 'I'll leave you to it. Come down whenever you like. I've got a nice stew that can be ready in a jiffy whenever you're hungry.'

'Thank you.'

The door clicked closed, and her footsteps faded down the stairs.

He went to the window and viewed the row of Victorian terrace houses opposite, precisely as he'd left them. The street was still and quiet. Children in school, fathers out at work, mothers in their kitchens with their babies in prams in the postage-stamp-sized gardens outside the door.

He lay on the bed and noticed the whiteness of the ceiling. They'd gone to a lot of trouble to make him welcome, and he felt guilty at his reluctance to visit them for many years.

He didn't think he'd sleep, but somehow two hours passed before he opened his eyes.

He made his way back to the kitchen, which smelled of bread and boiled meat, and was directed to the table and told not to move a muscle, that the food was just ready. Gracie dished up the lamb stew and, while they ate, asked him about his journey over, where he lived, how long it was since he'd been back to London, and whether he had missed it much.

O'Dowd's worries about long silences and reproaches for not coming to visit his stepfather in his later years had come to nothing. Michael mentioned his father briefly but didn't talk much – mainly because his wife didn't give him a chance.

Gracie's question about missing London took him by surprise. It had never occurred to him to miss it. He had spent most of his time in London wishing himself back in Dublin. He'd never considered London to be his home.

'I missed my mother.' He noticed a shadow passing across his half-brother's face. 'And of course Michael.' He knew he'd been a beat too late.

When they finished eating, Gracie put a mug of tea in front of him and asked the questions that Michael wouldn't.

'I believe your mother was a lovely woman. I never met her, you know. Michael says he doesn't know much about her life before she came to London.'

'Oh, it's not a very exciting story, really it isn't.' O'Dowd stirred his tea and tapped the spoon on the side of the mug.

'That's not the point, Lorcan, if you don't mind me saying so,' said Gracie. 'These two young ones will grow up and ask questions about their grandmother and grandfather, and what am I to tell 'em? Knowing where you've come from is important.'

'Well, I've never thought about it like that.' He smiled across the table at Gracie and caught the look of relief on Michael's face.

'All right, if you like.' He put the spoon down. 'My father was a policeman – a rank-and-file constable. Honest through and through, a good man. Though I suppose every boy thinks his father is a hero.'

Henry pulled at Michael's arm – he picked him up and put him on his knee. The child stuck his thumb in his mouth, laid his head on his father's chest, and watched his mysterious uncle's face as his eyes drooped. Little Daisy was already asleep under a blanket on the settle.

'I wasn't told the how or the why of it. Not then, but over the years I pieced it together. That night, I mean the night he died, he wasn't even on duty. He'd gone out – I never found out why. On his way back, he passed a group of men. Whatever it was that was said, he couldn't let go. It started with pushing and shoving and ended with my father cracking his skull on the corner of the path. Simple as that. Not in the line of duty, just a stupid remark and he saw red. If he'd kept walking, pretended he hadn't heard …'

He coughed to hide the catch in his voice and drank some tea.

'I was ten and thought I should be the man of the house. I was all for leaving school and getting a job until I could join the force. But she'd have none of it, I was to stay in school. There was a small pension, and she took a job cleaning.' He nodded toward Michael. 'That's how she met your father. Now and then she'd mention Mr. Sudbury, but I never dreamed that he was anything more than the man whose house she cleaned.'

Michael nodded. The child in his arms fought a losing battle with sleep.

O'Dowd weighed up how much he should say. He didn't want to hurt Michael's feelings. Not a good way to start the visit.

'You must have been upset when she told you.' Gracie reached over and patted his arm.

'I'm afraid I gave them both a bit of a hard time, and I regret it now. It wouldn't have mattered *who* she married – in my eyes, it was a betrayal of my father. Just before you were born she and your father asked if I'd like to change my name to Sudbury. My mother thought it would look odd that I had a different name to her and her husband and to you. I couldn't bring myself to do it. My father's name was all I had left of him. It wasn't meant to be an insult to your father.'

'Maybe it wasn't meant as an insult,' said Michael, 'but it hurt all the same. I know it did.'

'What age were you when she remarried?' said Gracie, cutting across.

'Twelve. Thought I knew everything.' O'Dowd shifted a little in his seat as the guilty feeling he usually succeeded in repressing began to rise in his heart. 'Your father was a good man, Michael, though at the time I wouldn't admit it even to myself. I wasn't happy leaving my friends, everything I knew, to come here, and I'm afraid I blamed him. Nothing would do me only to go back to Dublin and join the force as a constable. Your father took me aside and sat me down. He'd found out that I could take the entrance exam for cadet training a year early at eighteen because my father was a member of the constabulary. Your dad was generous in providing me with a good education. God, when I think about how ungrateful I was! He talked me into studying until I was eighteen and then taking the exam. Thanks to him, I did very well and got a place. I don't think I ever thanked him. I'm sorry about that. I wish I had.'

'I'm sure he knew,' said Michael.

O'Dowd was too ashamed to admit that he'd left them behind without a thought. When he was training he seldom returned to visit; there was always an excuse he could invent. But when he did visit, Michael latched on to him again, delighted with his big brother in a police uniform. O'Dowd wondered if that was why Michael had joined the London Police Force.

Gracie watched the two men avoid each other's eyes. 'Why don't you two go to the Dog and Duck for a drink?'

O'Dowd realized that Gracie was wiser than he'd given her credit for.

They walked to the pub two streets away. O'Dowd had been there once before – the day of his mother's funeral. It seemed ageless: the panelled windows, dark wooden counter, the smell of paraffin lamps and the murmur of whispering men.

Michael pointed him toward an empty table while he went to the bar. O'Dowd watched him lean on the counter as he was greeted by name and nodded and smiled in return. He didn't introduce O'Dowd.

Michael brought two pints of cloudy pale ale to the table and set one in front of his brother. An uneasy silence grew as they both studied their surroundings. Michael lifted his glass, nodded toward O'Dowd and took a deep swallow. O'Dowd followed suit, and grimaced as the liquid hit his throat. He put the glass down quickly.

'I never thought about how hard it must have been for you coming to London,' said Michael eventually. He gave a little chuckle. 'It must have come as a bit of shock to you when I was born.'

'Just a bit,' said O'Dowd.

He had decided not to say too much to Michael about that time. He'd been quietly furious with his mother for bringing him here and producing a baby brother. When he thought of Michael as a child, he was always smiling, all blue-eyed and rosy-cheeked, seeming to fill the house and take everyone's attention. As he grew, Michael followed his big brother around, constantly questioning him, mimicking his movements, and trying to engage him, but thirteen years is a breach too big to bridge. His mother was engrossed in the baby. He'd told himself she wouldn't even notice if he was gone, but he knew it wasn't true. He'd said it to hurt himself and give himself permission to turn his back on his family.

'Now I understand why you wanted to settle in Ireland. I never fully appreciated how difficult it must have been for you. But you were happy when you went back, weren't you?'

O'Dowd smiled. 'Yes, of course. Very happy.'

But that wasn't quite the truth. He visited the old neighbours who remembered him as a child. 'You've picked up the accent,' they said. 'We wouldn't have known you in your uniform, and you're going to be an officer. Isn't that grand? Your father would have been proud.' They took out their best teacups: that said it all. He didn't belong there anymore.

He couldn't explain all that to Michael, so he began to tell him about the case, the link to the *Titanic*, and the people he was trying to contact. Michael listened attentively, but O'Dowd felt there was something not being said. His brother, half-brother, seemed to be waiting for something else.

'So that's why you're here. You're on a case.' He seemed surprised.

'Well, yes. I hope that's all right. I'd have stayed in a hotel. I can if you'd prefer? Look, I know I should have come to see your father before he died. I'm sorry – it was a bad time. I just couldn't get away ...'

Michael sat back. 'It's all right. I'm happy to have you stay. We're family, after all. Tell me more about the case.' He looked at his brother's beer glass. 'You've barely touched your ale.'

O'Dowd felt obliged take another sip then began to talk about the drowning and the inquest, and he could tell his brother was interested. But there was something not quite right. Michael had relaxed and listened attentively, but O'Dowd had seen the look between him and Gracie before they left. Something was left unsaid; he suspected he knew what it was. He'd wait until they were both there so there'd be no misunderstanding. It was time to put the past to rest.

45

CHAPTER EIGHT

The next day O'Dowd was up early. Gracie had brought up hot water and towels and later fed him a good breakfast, though he noted the flavour of the sausages hadn't improved over the years.

He reported to Scotland Yard and was led to the office of Chief Inspector Atkinson, who took the letter that the County Inspector had written and read it slowly.

'I remember old Patterson. So, he's ended up in Ireland.' He glanced over the top of the page. 'What did he do to deserve that?'

O'Dowd wasn't sure if the Chief Inspector thought the posting was a reward or a punishment, so he left the question unanswered.

The C.I. waved him to a seat. 'You know there's a bureau set up to trace the relatives of the victims and survivors. They may be able to help you.'

'Yes, sir. The body hasn't been identified yet and, the thing is, the people I'm trying to trace are neither relatives nor victims nor survivors. They were on the *Titanic* but disembarked at Queenstown.'

'So, basically, what you've got is an unidentified body, no crime scene, no witnesses, just a notion that he might have been on the *Titanic*. It says here it's a murder inquiry. You're sure he didn't drown himself on purpose?'

'Yes, sir – the post mortem confirmed poison as the cause of death and, if I may say, his presence on the ship is more than a notion. It would narrow things down considerably if I could search the passenger list. I also have the man's cufflinks with his initials. And we have evidence – a badge that was sold only on board the *Titanic*.'

The C.I. lit a cigar, leaned back, and puffed smoke at the ceiling. 'I can't spare anyone to help you, O'Dowd. But I can give you access to the passenger list and a desk, telephone, that sort of thing. Just remember you're on my turf. If it is a murder, I want no cock-ups, no arrests until you've spoken to me. I'm not having an Englishman dragged across to Ireland to face a murder trial without making sure you've got the right man. Am I clear?'

'Absolutely, sir.'

The C.I. called to his assistant, who came in quickly.

'Barker, this is D.I. O'Dowd. Sort him out with everything he needs, find him a corner in with the *Titanic* bureau people. Make sure the desk sergeants know he's here – they may need to take messages for him. He's to be given every assistance – as much as can be spared. Understand?'

O'Dowd followed Barker to a large room with lines of desks and telephones. He was led to a space in the corner, given the keys to a small cabinet, and Barker told him to get in touch if he needed anything else.

That was it. O'Dowd looked around the room. Every desk was occupied, and the teams seemed to be working through lists. No one came to enquire as to what he was doing there. He was, more or less, on his own.

He took the cufflinks from his pocket and rubbed one of them between his finger and thumb as he looked around the crowded room. Everyone was busy, phones ringing, the door constantly opening and closing. He thought of the barracks in Youghal, a world away from this centre of activity.

He asked the officer at the next desk how he would request a copy of the first-class and second-class passengers.

'Ask one of the constables – they'll bring it to you.'

Within half an hour, he was sitting at his desk going through the lists. There were only three entries for male passengers with the initials T.B. The only details were the names and where they'd boarded the *Titanic*. He wrote them down:

> *Mr. Thomas Byles, Southampton*
> *Mr. Terrence Bennett, Southampton*
> *Mr. Theodore Brailey, Southampton*

He gave the list to a young constable and asked him to find the address and any up-to-date information on whether or not they'd survived, then went outside into the sunshine for a breath of fresh air. There was none to be had; the stench of the Thames drove him back inside just as the constable came to find him.

'Here you are, sir. Thomas Byles is, or rather was, a Roman Catholic priest. Travelled second class. Survivors remember him helping people onto the lifeboats, but he didn't get into one. He's listed as missing.'

'But he was seen that night?' O'Dowd thought it most unlikely that a priest would wear the sort of clothes in which the body in Youghal was dressed.

'Yes, he was mentioned by several of the survivors. As was Mr. Theodore Brailey. He wasn't a passenger, he was on board as a member of the band. He was seen on the night the ship went down.'

'What about Terrence Bennett?'

'There's some confusion there, sir. Terrence Bennett was included in the first list of survivors, but in the second and subsequent lists he's listed as "missing". I'm not sure what to make of that, sir.'

'Nor am I, constable. Only that it must have been chaotic there and it would be easy to tick the wrong name. Can you contact the centre in New York to get the name of the man they thought was Terrence Bennett. I need a positive identification. Thank you.'

The young constable hurried off, and O'Dowd browsed aimlessly through the names for a few minutes. He felt in his pocket and produced the list of passengers who'd disembarked at Queenstown.

He rang Mrs. Lily Odell and arranged to see her the following day.

That evening he waited until the meal was over and the children put to bed.

'Can we talk?' he said as he sat down by the fire. 'There's something I've been meaning to say.'

Gracie was rinsing teacups in the sink. Her back stiffened.

'We should have had this talk a long time ago,' he said. 'I'm sorry.'

Gracie sat in the fireside chair that used to be his mother's and repeatedly folded a tea towel on her lap. Michael pulled over a chair from the table. They didn't say a word.

'I shouldn't have let this drag on. It's about the house.'

Michael leaned his elbows on his knees. 'We thought that's why you came all right. I thought that you were coming to, well, sort something out.'

O'Dowd sat back and ran his fingers through his hair. 'I gave it a lot of thought. At the end of the day, I felt that if I didn't take your father's name when he was alive, then I really couldn't take half his house. I'm never going to live here, and I'd never ask you to sell the only home you've ever known. I've seen too much of that in Ireland – it's heart-breaking. This was your father's house and now it's yours and Gracie's as far as I'm concerned. I'll sign anything you like to make that official. I'm sorry – I should have done that before now.'

Michael swallowed hard. 'You could have said something, could have written. What would it have taken? A few lines, that's all.'

'I sorry – I was –'

Michael held up his hand. 'No, I know you were busy.' There was an edge to his voice, and his eyes had filled. 'We've been on tenterhooks since we got your letter. You've no idea …'

'I'm sorry, genuinely sorry. There's no excuse. I'll try to be a better brother to you in the future.' He hadn't intended to make this promise, but something pushed him to it. Maybe it's Mam making me talk this way, he thought.

Gracie was on her feet, and O'Dowd knew there would be hugs to endure.

'Never mind all that,' she said as she leant down and embraced him where he sat. 'What's past is past. There'll always be a bed for you here, Lorcan. We can't thank you enough.'

It was worth it to see her flushed face and shining eyes.

'Why don't the two of you go to the Dog and Duck and drink to it?'

Michael blew his nose and nodded his head at the same time. 'We'll try to be better brothers to each other.' He wiped his eyes and glanced around the kitchen. 'Are you sure you can manage, Gracie? We'll only be an hour. I'll bring you back a bottle of milk stout.'

'Go on then. It's certainly something to celebrate.'

❦◊❧

They took the seats they'd sat in the previous night.

'Tell me how you got on in Scotland Yard. What's it like?' said Michael.

O'Dowd was glad to be back on firm ground. 'I'll tell you all about it, but first things first. There must be something better to drink than the cat's piss we had last night. Do they not have any Guinness?'

Michael was on his feet. 'I'll get you a Paddy.'

'No, don't get me started on whisky – a pint will be fine.'

Michael returned, triumphantly bearing two glasses of the dark porter. O'Dowd sipped apprehensively. It was often said that Guinness didn't travel well but he risked a large gulp.

'Very good,' he declared. 'I'd better not have too many of those. Early start in the morning. I have to find my way to Wimbledon to meet the Odell family. They were on the ship and got off at Queenstown.'

Michael raised the eyebrows on his large round face. 'You think they can identify him? Bit of a long shot, isn't it? Any other developments in the case?'

'Yes and no. The only first-class passenger with the initials T.B. is Terrence Bennett. But, somehow, he was first reported as a survivor and later as "missing". That man may be in hospital in New York.'

'I see your problem.'

'A big problem at that.' He tapped his fingers on the side of the glass. 'To tell the truth, I can't be absolutely sure who the man in the mortuary really is.'

CHAPTER NINE

O'Dowd made his way to Charing Cross train station, sat in one of the first-class compartments on the train to Wimbledon, and reviewed the list of passengers again. Mrs. Odell had said she would do anything she could to help, and he had asked her to be so kind as to ask all the members of her *Titanic* party to be there: her two brothers, her sister-in-law Kate, and her son Jack.

It was a thirty-minute journey out of London city, but when he left the station it felt as though he'd travelled to another part of the country entirely. He was struck by the size of the houses and the broad tree-lined road running alongside Wimbledon common. Well-tended gardens competed for his attention, and he almost walked past the house. It was as large, or even larger than its neighbours, double-fronted, with expansive bay windows. Tall trees and shrubbery seemed intent on hiding the house and protecting it from prying eyes.

As he walked up the driveway, he heard the sound of a bouncing ball, shouting, and hoots of laughter from the rear of the house. He rang the bell and heard it echo through the hallway on the other side.

A butler admitted him in silence, led him through the large hallway, the light-filled drawing room, and out the French doors to the garden.

Although the day wasn't hot, it was still April, and the family sat outside in chairs watching two men play tennis.

Mrs. Odell came forward to shake hands. 'Apologies, inspector. You must think we're awful playing a silly game when there has been so much tragedy. We thought the match would be over before you got here. Are you in a hurry?' She didn't wait for an answer. 'If Stanley can get this point, that will be the end. I can't get them off the court until the winner is decided. They're so competitive.'

She was tall for a woman. O'Dowd guessed her to be about forty, the sort of woman who always knew what to say and when to say it. She shouted at the men to 'get on with it' and stood with her hands on her hips, watching the rally. Her shouts seemed to produce the desired effect as the winning point was scored. A cheer went up from the onlookers as the two players shook hands, one a little more enthusiastically than the other. They looked to be in their forties, wore white trousers and jumpers, and the ladies wore long white dresses pulled in at the waist and buttoned to the neck. They might have been at a tea party rather than playing tennis. They all looked quite jolly and delighted with life – as well they might be, thought O'Dowd.

'Come along, everyone! Inspector O'Dowd wants to talk to us.'

Lily herded everyone toward the large drawing room, and they arranged themselves on the sofas and chairs. She introduced each of them. The two tennis-players were Rupert May and his brother Stanley. The brothers looked remarkably alike. O'Dowd tried to fix each of them in his mind. Kate Odell, Lily's sister-in-law, was an attractive girl in her early twenties. Finally, Lily's son, Jack, looked to be barely into his teens.

'Now what's all this about, inspector?' said Stanley. 'You realise that we were on the ship barely twenty-four hours. We've been trying to guess what on earth we can do to help.'

'Yes, if there was a crime committed, we don't see how you can solve it,' said Kate.

'We're in the early stages of a murder enquiry and you're quite right, it's extremely difficult to carry out an investigation under the circumstances, but we must try. Can you tell me why you chose the *Titanic*? It would have been quicker to go directly from Southampton to Queenstown rather than crossing to Cherbourg in France to pick up passengers on the way.'

'Too good a chance to pass up,' said Rupert. 'It was Herbert's idea – he bought all the tickets as a surprise, though in the end he couldn't go.'

'Herbert?' asked O'Dowd.

'My husband,' said Lily. 'He can't be here today – he's at work. I didn't think you'd mind – seeing as he wasn't on the boat. So you're stationed in Queenstown, inspector?'

'Well, in Youghal which is about 23 miles from Queenstown. I'm the District Inspector for the area. The body of this man was found the day after you disembarked at Queenstown.' He produced the photograph of the drowned man. 'Could you look at this, please, and tell me if you've seen him before.'

'How awful!' Mrs. Odell barely glanced at it. 'I hate to see pictures of the deceased. I know it's very popular nowadays but, really, I feel it's so intrusive, don't you?'

'Indeed,' said O'Dowd. 'We haven't put a name to him yet, but we have reason to believe he was on board the *Titanic*. I'm afraid you are the only people I can ask. Do any of you recognise him?'

They handed the photograph from one to the next.

Stanley passed it back to his sister. 'It could be anyone really. The dining room was very full – unless he'd been right beside us, we wouldn't have noticed.'

'Can I see?' said Jack.

'No, darling – it's too gruesome,' said his mother.

'I'm old enough, and maybe I can help. Please, Mother!'

He took the photograph from her hand, and O'Dowd saw his eyes narrow as he studied the features.

'I ... I think it's him. I saw him smoke a cigar on the deck after dinner. It was getting dark. I went out to see if I could photograph the sunset. I took a few snaps of the deck, but I don't know if he was in them. He was leaning over the edge, looking down into the water. The next time I looked, he was talking to a woman. I don't think I saw him again after that.'

O'Dowd held his breath.

The room had gone quiet. Everyone focused on the boy.

'Are you sure, Jack,' O'Dowd asked, his voice a little shaky. 'Are you sure this man was on board the *Titanic*?'

Jack looked again at the photo. 'I think it was him.'

'Goodness,' said Mrs. Odell. 'I can't believe it!'

'Jack, what was the man on the deck wearing?' O'Dowd asked.

Jack lifted one shoulder. 'Same as everyone else.'

'A jacket?'

Jack nodded.

'And the woman. Can you describe her?'

Jack looked stumped for a moment then his face lit up. 'She had a hat with a veil over her face, a black one, and a coat. I think that was black too.'

'You think it was black?'

'I might be mixing it up with the woman on the tender the next day. She had the same hat.' He looked at O'Dowd, wide-eyed.

'Though, you know, it might be the same woman. I think it was.'

O'Dowd looked at the boy's excited face. 'Now slow down. Are you saying that the woman who was talking to this man on deck is the same woman who got off the ship with you in Queenstown? Think carefully now. It's very important.'

Jack's face turned serious as everyone in the room watched him. He nodded. 'Yes, I really and truly think it was the same woman.'

'Can anyone else remember what she looked like?' O'Dowd looked around the room.

'I remember something,' said Mrs. Odell. 'Though I don't think it will be of much use to you, inspector. When we waved to the people on the boat deck, she did the same. I remember she raised her arm and waved. Her coat had a fur collar and cuffs and Jack is right – she wore quite a thick veil attached to her hat.'

'Who was she waving to?'

'Oh, unfortunately I have no idea.'

O'Dowd scribbled in his notebook. 'Father Browne, who was on the tender with you, mentioned you had cameras. May I see the photographs?'

'Yes, Jack and I both had cameras,' said Kate. 'You think she could be in one of our photographs? Mine haven't been developed yet. I don't know why – it felt morbid to look at all those happy snapshots. I wasn't sure I'd ever get them developed. But if you think they might be of use …'

'I haven't finished the roll,' said Jack. 'I think there's a few left. I took some at the tennis court just now.' He ran into the garden to fetch his camera and returned moments later carrying it by its strap and showed it to the inspector. 'You look in there, see? Then you click this and roll on to the next one. It came with 100 negatives, and I have to use them all up and send the camera back to Kodak, and they send the photographs back to me with the camera loaded up again, ready to go.'

'Ingenious,' said O'Dowd, turning the camera over in his hands. 'Do you think you could send them off immediately, both of you? Anything taken that day or on the ship could be very helpful.'

Jack and Kate nodded, and Jack disappeared back into the garden to use up the last of the camera roll.

Lily stood up. 'We'll let you know when the photographs are back. What station can we ring you at, inspector?'

He gave her the phone number for Scotland Yard and asked her to leave a message if he wasn't there when she rang.

As the butler escorted him to the door, he felt he was getting closer to the truth. Tomorrow he would visit the seventh passenger on his list. Who was, according to young Jack, the woman who spoke to the murdered man on the deck of the *Titanic* and was possibly the last person to see him alive.

He was coming down the stairs when he heard Michael's key in the front door and Gracie calling, '*Is that you?*' which he found annoying on a daily basis. Was there anything more irritating than living with a happily married couple? He knew it was irrational, that the fault was in him. Though he'd never been jealous of other people's good fortune, lately he was aware of a feeling of resentment that surfaced when he caught those moments when the couple's eyes met and a wordless communication was made.

He'd only ever had that sort of relationship with one woman. It had been during his posting in Ennis. Penelope was the only daughter of a landed Protestant family in the area. They got on so well together.

She was a first-class horsewoman, had a great sense of humour, and a face that smiled easily. He'd never been in love before, and perhaps he'd been a bit reckless and rushed into proposing. He'd asked, and she said yes. He'd thought, foolishly as it turned out, that his status in the R.I.C as District Inspector Grade 3 would put him in good stead with his prospective in-laws and outweigh his Catholic religion. He even fancied himself as a bit of a catch. Her father lost no time putting him straight, and when Penelope stood up to her father, she was told she'd have to choose between her inheritance and the young inspector. She didn't choose the young inspector.

O'Dowd paused briefly before continuing his descent, but Michael was already on his way up, taking the stairs two at a time. They met mid-staircase.

Michael handed him the newspaper. 'Look what I found. Page four. Come down and look.'

In the kitchen O'Dowd spread the newspaper across the table and turned the pages, scouring for whatever had caught Michael's interest. The story was tucked away halfway down the fourth page under the small heading: **Nottingham Woman Escapes Titanic**.

The article said Amelia Nelson, whose mother still resided in Nottingham, had disembarked the ship at Queenstown. The story went on to say the reporter had asked Mrs. Nelson why she had come to Ireland, and she'd told him that she was joining her husband, Frederick James Nelson. The newspaper exclaimed how delighted everyone was that she was safe and sound.

'I plan to visit Mrs. Nelson first thing in the morning. She's the last name on my list.' O'Dowd cast his eye over the article again. 'She was there to join her husband, the newspaper says. So that's why she got off at Queenstown. I hope they're both back by now.' He wondered what Mr. Nelson was doing in Ireland. Couldn't have been military;

they would have mentioned his rank. He turned to Michael. 'If Mr. Nelson is still in Ireland, I can interview him there.'

He knew he should hand the investigation over to Scotland Yard, but he couldn't bring himself to let go of it. Not quite yet. He imagined meeting with the Chief Inspector in the Yard and revealing the solved case to him with all the loose ends neatly tidied up.

'Why are you smiling?' said Michael.

'Was I smiling? Just thinking the case could be closed soon, and I can go home.'

'And you'll be happy to go back there?'

Will I really be happy there? He pushed the thought aside.

'Yes, of course.' He forced a smile. 'It's my home. It's where I'm needed most.'

CHAPTER TEN

Elm Lane, near Peckham Rye train station, was the sort of small, slightly dejected side street where strangers didn't go unnoticed. Inspector O'Dowd knocked at the door of Number 18, which compared favourably with most of its neighbours. He noted the very small, neat garden, snow-white net curtains, the shining knocker and letterbox on the dark-blue front door. The sound of hurried footsteps came from within, then the front door opened wide to reveal a young woman struggling into her coat. She glanced at him and called back into the house. '*Mother, it's for you! I won't be long!*' She gathered her belongings from a hall table, brushed past him and hurried away.

He was still staring after her when a small auburn-haired woman appeared in the hallway and met him with a frown he felt he didn't deserve.

'I'm looking for Amelia Nelson,' he said.

She looked out the front door and watched the young woman disappear down the road. It was as though she hadn't heard him.

'My daughter,' she said, then rolled her eyes. 'She'd be late for her own funeral.'

O'Dowd smiled.

'I'm Amelia Nelson,' the woman said and with a sweep of her sharp eyes took in everything, from his polished shoes to his hat. 'If you're looking for a room, I've none available. Anyway, I only take ladies.'

She began to close the door but he placed his hand against it.

'I'm Inspector Lorcan O'Dowd,' he said. 'I've come from Scotland Yard.' He'd decided that was neither a lie nor the truth, but he knew it would get her attention.

She went a little pale and opened the door wider. 'Come in, inspector.'

He removed his hat and followed her down the narrow hallway, decorated in a deep purple-and-beige flock wallpaper. She opened the door to a small parlour and stood back to allow him to pass.

'Go on in and sit down, inspector. Will you have some tea?'

'That would be most welcome.'

She withdrew and he heard her murmur to someone in the kitchen and then the sound of teacups, saucers, and cupboard doors opening and closing. The air was heavy, as though the room wasn't often used and had been standing ready for some time. He looked around for somewhere to put his hat – the black lacquered cabinet seemed too grand to be a makeshift hat-stand, so he kept it in his hand. Two dark-green armchairs and a sofa with plumped cushions filled the room; they seemed a little tired but well-kept with lace antimacassars. Brass swags held the heavy green curtains in a graceful swoop, and the white lace curtains provided protection from inquisitive neighbours. He felt that neither the furniture nor the curtains belonged in this room, in this neighbourhood. He thought it likely that Mrs. Nelson had come down in the world.

The mantelpiece was covered with lace doilies and photographs. He carefully examined each one, hoping a face would match the one in the picture sitting in his top pocket. There were several photographs of Mrs. Nelson, some taken of her alone and others with a bearded man he took to be her husband. One was of two men in Royal Navy uniforms with the young woman he'd seen briefly moments before. Her brothers, he thought. He was drawn back to the lacquered cabinet, exquisitely decorated with gleaming red and orange flowers, an arched bridge over a pond with fish peeping through the reeds. Japanese or possibly Chinese? The two doors in the cabinet bore ornate gold wings at each corner. He put his hand out to touch them just as Mrs. Nelson returned to the room.

He tried to dismiss the feeling that he'd been caught doing something improper but knew his cheeks had flushed. 'It's a wonderful piece, Mrs. Nelson. Are you a collector of oriental art?'

'You'll have to speak up. I'm rather deaf, particularly in one ear.' She tapped the ear. 'From the noise working in the mills when I was young.'

He pointed to the cabinet, raised his voice and asked the question again.

'No. It was a gift. Bit too gaudy for my taste, to tell you the truth. What's wrong with a nice piece of English mahogany, I say. Easy to polish. Half afraid to touch that thing in case I wipe a flower off. Sit down, I know why you're here. It's bad news, isn't it?'

She sat and he took the chair opposite. For the first time, he got a good look at the woman. She was small and neat, her auburn hair pulled back from her face. She wore a high-necked blouse with a cameo brooch at her throat and a dark-coloured skirt – the picture of respectability and prudence. He guessed her to be about mid-forties though he often found it challenging to put an age to women, and the deep frown between her eyebrows might make her seem older. Her accent suggested she came from the north of England.

'You say you know why I'm here.' He balanced his hat on the arm of the chair and took out a notebook. 'Mrs. Nelson, I'm here –'

The drawing-room door opened, and a dark-haired woman came in, carefully carrying a tea tray. She looked to be in her thirties, hair pulled tightly back and spectacles that threatened to fall off her face when she set the tray down on the small table between them. Though she wore a long black dress, O'Dowd guessed she wasn't a maid, so he stood.

'Oh, please sit down, inspector,' she said and glanced at him shyly as she poured two cups of tea. She placed one in front of him. 'Help yourself to milk and sugar.'

'Thank you, Miss …?'

'Henrietta Harper.' She held out her hand and blushed as he shook it gently. It felt like a tiny bony bird.

'You live here, Miss Harper?'

Amelia Nelson cut across him. 'She's a lodger here, inspector,' she said. 'Thank you, Henrietta, I'm sure you have lots to do.'

'Of course.' Miss Harper continued to blush. 'I'll leave you to your chat. Call if you need anything else.'

She had a lilting accent which O'Dowd thought might be Welsh. He watched as she scurried out and pulled the door gently behind her. Though he listened for her footsteps returning to the kitchen, he heard none. Probably listening at the other side of the door, he thought, but no matter.

Mrs. Nelson rolled her eyes and tasted the tea. 'Not bad,' she declared. 'She can be a bit odd – Welsh, you know. Poor as a church mouse. But she does know how to make a good strong cup of tea. I'll give her that.'

He noticed Mrs. Nelson's hands were not the soft white of the gentry – they bore the signs of washday hands: bony knuckles, and a rawness around the base of her fingers. He remembered his mother's hands, and for a fleeting moment he softened toward the woman.

'Mrs. Nelson,' he began his rehearsed introduction, 'I'm investigating the death of a man who was on the *Titanic* who –'

'Yes, I know. Terrence, of course.' Her hand shook slightly as she replaced the cup on the saucer.

O'Dowd felt the hairs on the back of his neck stand up.

'I looked at the lists in the papers, but how would I know if they were right? I went to the police station myself to see if I could find what happened to him but, as I'm not a relative,' she rolled her eyes as though the police had been pedantic, 'they said they couldn't tell me anything, but I left my name and address. One newspaper had him on the survivor's list. Then his name was on the missing list. How could that be?'

'You knew Mr. Bennett?' The woman sitting in front of him had been on the *Titanic* and knew the victim. She instantly became a person of interest. He tried to hide his excitement. Tread softly here, he thought.

She was looking at him curiously and didn't appear to be nervous or suspicious of him.

'Yes,' she said. 'I know – knew Terrence very well. We go back years, since Nottingham. He was a salesman for the lace mill I worked in. Isn't that why you're here?'

'We seem to be at cross-purposes, Mrs. Nelson. I've come to ask for your help in identifying someone.' He took the photograph and the cufflinks from his pocket and held them in his hand for a moment. 'Mrs. Nelson, this is the photograph of a man found in the waters off Youghal. I have to warn you – it was taken post-mortem.' He passed it to her.

Her fingers quivered as she took the photograph and pressed her handkerchief to her lips.

'It's Terrence Bennett,' she said quietly. She looked at the cufflinks in his hand. 'Yes, I've seen him wear those many times. Is Youghal in Canada? The newspapers said some bodies were taken to Canada.'

'No, Mrs. Nelson. Youghal is in Ireland. Terrence Bennett's body was found off the Irish coast three days before the *Titanic* sank. His body was taken to Queenstown in east County Cork. I am overseeing the investigation in conjunction with Scotland Yard.'

'I don't understand.' The lines in her forehead grew deeper. 'Three days before ...'

'Mrs. Nelson, when exactly was the last time you saw Mr. Bennett alive?'

'What difference can it make when I saw him?'

O'Dowd sat forward, his hands on his knees. 'Really, Mrs. Nelson, there is no point in denying it. You accompanied Mr. Bennett on the *Titanic* as far as Queenstown, in Ireland.'

'*I most certainly did not!*' She stood up. 'I've no idea what you're talking about, inspector. Terry gave me the ticket, but of course I didn't go.'

'Mrs. Nelson, we both know that you and Mr. Bennett boarded the *Titanic* in Southampton. So perhaps we can get straight to the truth. I need you to tell me when exactly you last saw Mr Bennett alive?'

Mrs. Nelson looked furious. 'I told you I most certainly did *not* spend the night on the *Titanic!* She grasped the cameo brooch at her throat.

'There are witnesses that can identify you, Mrs. Nelson.' This was not the truth, but there was still hope that someone might come up with a photograph that would prove that she was on board. 'You were seen disembarking the ship in Queenstown. It's even in this newspaper article. Here!' He took the folded page from his inside pocket and handed it to her, trying to keep the triumphant note out of his voice.

'Perhaps I can speak with Mr. Nelson? Has he returned from Ireland yet?'

She took the newspaper page and opened it. As she read she lowered herself into the armchair.

He waited. 'Do you remember talking to a reporter in Queenstown? I expect you thought it wouldn't matter what you said to a provincial newspaper reporter in Ireland. If the *Titanic* hadn't sunk, you might have got away with it. But, of course, with the tragedy comes public interest in everything and everyone who had any connection to the ship.'

She stood and took the photograph of the middle-aged, bearded man from the mantelpiece.

'Now listen to me, *inspector!* She almost spat the word '*inspector*'. 'I was nowhere near that ship, and I could *never* have said I was meeting my husband.' She held out the photograph to him. 'That's the only sighting you'll have of Frederick Nelson. He's been dead for twelve years. I would never claim to be meeting him. Everyone who knows me knows that I am a widow. This woman was most certainly not me and was definitely *not* meeting my late husband. Now, inspector, I would like you to leave my house with your ridiculous accusations.'

O'Dowd felt his stomach knot. He tried to cover his confusion. Could she be telling the truth? She certainly looked shocked enough for him to believe her but, then again, she might be a practised liar.

'That doesn't prove that you were not on the ship, Mrs. Nelson. Though, I concede, there is obviously some mistake in the article. I would ask that you come to the police station tomorrow morning and make a full statement so we can get to the bottom of this.' There was clearly no point in trying to question her further at the moment.

She drew herself up to her full height. 'I will do as you ask, inspector. And I'll want to read it before I sign, mind. I never sign anything without reading it thoroughly first.' She gave him a warning look.

'Mrs. Nelson, it would be very helpful if you could bring a photograph of yourself tomorrow. It could help me eliminate you from our enquiries.'

She picked up a photograph of herself from the mantelpiece, quickly removed the frame and handed it to him. 'Be careful of that, I'll want it back,' she said.

'Thank you. I'll send a cab for you tomorrow.'

'You will not. I'll make my own way, thank you very much. I won't have policemen calling to my door in broad daylight. Good day to you, inspector.'

He found himself outside the house with the door closed firmly behind him.

CHAPTER ELEVEN

Amelia didn't usually encourage Henrietta to sit in the parlour, but this was not a usual sort of day. Although the two women were on good enough terms, there was still the lodger/landlady relationship to keep in mind. Henrietta was always careful not to step too far across the line and Amelia was, by nature, very cautious with her words.

But the events of the afternoon had blurred the edges of the unwritten rules and, so, when Henrietta tiptoed in and asked if she'd like a nice strong pot of tea, Amelia said, 'I've had such a shock. I think I need a brandy, Henrietta, and do have one yourself – to keep me company.'

'Thank you, Amelia. You're very kind.'

She went to the Chinese cabinet to fetch the brandy and two glasses. Sitting, she poured the brandies.

'And he seemed like such a nice man!' she tutted as she handed a glass to Amelia. 'You can't be too careful who you let into your house, Amelia. You're far too willing to see the good in people. Now, tell me, what has he done to upset you?'

Amelia hesitated for a moment. 'He wanted me to identify a post-mortem photograph of Terry. Drowned. It was him all right.' She shuddered.

Henrietta gasped. 'How terrible!'

'Then he began to accuse me of all sorts. It's some sort of terrible joke or a mistake. I really don't know why someone would say I was there.'

'Where?'

'On the *Titanic*.'

Henrietta's mouth dropped open. 'The *Titanic*?'

Amelia nodded. 'He said they had witnesses. But I can prove it wasn't me. You were here with me, weren't you?'

'Was I? What night was it exactly?'

'Wednesday the tenth of April. They said I got off the *Titanic* the next day, Thursday.'

Henrietta clasped her bony hands together. 'Well, dear, now let me think. Wasn't that the week I went to do the brass rubbings in Winchester? I got such a good impression of Jane Austin's grave – it's rather large. It's upstairs. Shall I fetch it? I'm sure you'd like it.' She caught the slight sagging of Amelia's face. 'No, not now of course. We must concentrate.' She frowned at her small black-slippered feet. 'I remember you suffered a severe headache that week. I was going to cancel the trip to stay with you, what with Claire being away, but you insisted that you would recover, that it would pass quickly.'

'Yes, I did, didn't I? Well, you saw how sick I was. I couldn't even go to the bottom of the road let alone set off to Southampton to board the *Titanic*!'

'Yes, Amelia, you were not very well at all – but you said you'd be all right once you had a good night's sleep. So I went.'

'Yes, of course, that's what I said.' Amelia rubbed her temple with the heel of her hand and took a sip of brandy.

'Let's calm down, we have to think about this,' said Henrietta. 'There must be a reasonable explanation.'

Amelia glanced at the chirpy spinster, whose only interest was in brass rubbings and lectures on the architecture of the cathedrals of Great Britain. However, besides the histories of cathedrals, Henrietta had a small collection of well-thumbed books that Amelia took to be romantic novels. Titles like *Tess of the d'Urbervilles* and *Anna Karenina* and books by Jane Austin didn't interest Amelia. She was happier with a 'penny dreadful'. You knew where you were with them. She could see that Henrietta was almost bursting with questions.

Henrietta sat forward, ready to hear everything, but Amelia couldn't even begin to describe her relationship with Terry. However, the urge to talk about him was overwhelming. Of course, she couldn't tell everything, certainly not to Henrietta. Nor could she speak of it to Claire, who thought Terry Bennett was the most wonderful and sophisticated man in the world. She glanced at Henrietta and wondered how much she could be trusted. Well, certainly not with the whole truth.

She gave in to the temptation of talking about her past.

'I met him when I worked in the lace mills in Nottingham,'

Henrietta sipped her brandy and gazed at Amelia over her glass.

'It's funny the little things you remember. Just before I met Terrence for the first time, I felt a breeze from the door circle my neck. The commercial travellers were cutting through on their way to the floor above. Most of them didn't even see me, too busy telling their stories, trying to outdo each other. You know what men are like.' She glanced at the wide-eyed Henrietta. 'Perhaps you don't. Anyhow, Terrence Bennett stopped – just stood and stared at me.'

'Oh Amelia, how romantic! Was it love at first sight?'

'I believed in such things at the time. I really did. He looked as though he was about to say something and then thought better of it. He shook his head and smiled. Such a handsome face.' She sighed at the memory. 'I was eighteen and he was barely into his twenties. He always attracted a lot of attention from the girls – even the older women dallied in the hope of a smile from him. But what made it unusual was that I was never pretty, with this –' she touched the furrow between her eyebrows, 'I always looked cross. So, his interest in me didn't go unnoticed. For weeks, even months afterward, the atmosphere in the winding room changed the moment he stepped in. Like March hares on their hind legs, the women watched as he passed the end of my bobbin machine. Watched to see if he glanced at me again. He didn't. They watched as he progressed down the length of the room through the spill of light from the high windows. Watched me to see if I blushed. I did. Always.'

'Oh, you poor dear!' Henrietta refilled Amelia's glass. 'You must have been devastated.'

'I was. Completely. But life goes on, and what choice did I have? Well, it can't be helped, can it? The winding room in the lace factory wasn't the worst place to work but, even so, all us girls were glad to escape into the cool evening air. We walked arm in arm through the gates, faces to the sky. That's why I didn't see him. We were talking too loudly, the factory din still ringing in our ears. That's why I didn't hear him call my name. He tapped me on my shoulder.'

Henrietta put her cup down and clapped her hands together. 'What did he say?'

'He had such a lovely voice – even then he'd lost the London accent and spoke like a gentleman. My friends winked at me and walked on into the stream of workers. More people surged through the gate, buffeted against us. He placed his hand under my elbow to steady me. I didn't pull away.'

Henrietta swallowed audibly.

'He introduced himself, then said, "Would you do me the honour of having tea with me on Sunday afternoon? I watched his mouth make the words I'd wanted to hear, but I still couldn't believe it – I panicked. It was too much for me to take in. Going to tea was out of the question. Of course, he had all the answers. "Not alone, Miss Lee. Perhaps your mother could accompany you? I thought we might go to the tea rooms.' Another wave of workers surged around and past like we were a little island in a sea of lace weavers. I made the decision that was to change my life. "Not tea," I said. "But I will be by the bandstand in the park at four o'clock on Sunday." "Perfect," he said. "Four o'clock." He released my arm, replaced his hat, and disappeared into the crowd. And that was the very first time I spoke to Mr. Terrence Bennet.'

Henrietta pulled a lace-trimmed handkerchief from her sleeve. 'It's the most romantic thing I've ever heard,' she said as she dabbed the corners of her eyes. 'And what did your mother say when you told her? Was he there, waiting for you on Sunday?'

'I didn't tell Mother. I knew she would be full of unanswerable questions. On the Sunday, I pinched my cheeks and bit my lips to raise their colour, then checked myself in the mirror. This was the very best I could be. My serious face, with its awful frown, wasn't going to get any prettier.'

'I'm sure you looked very pretty indeed,' said Henrietta, eyes glowing.

Amelia barely heard. She'd never told this story to another living being, and somehow the words bubbled up and spilled out like milk coming to the boil.

'The park was bustling that bright Sunday afternoon. I could hear the music before I saw the bandstand: a military brass band was playing. Half of Nottingham was seated in the circles of wooden chairs facing the musicians. He stood at the entrance to the rose garden. Tall and so handsome in his dark-blue suit and a shirt so white it could have been woven from snow. I could barely believe he was waiting for me. *Me!* Plain Amelia. As soon as he saw me his face lit up. He smiled. My heart sort of turned over. We spent a pleasant half-hour strolling, admiring the blooms. Neither of us mentioned my missing mother. I didn't talk much, not having much experience with roses. Terry, he insisted I call him that, chatted about all sorts of things, including the mills of Nottingham. He told me he was from London, the son of a publican, but had no intention of working in a public house. As we walked and talked, I noticed the envious stares of some of the women in the park. I had never been happier.'

Henrietta hung on every word, handkerchief at the ready.

'From the other side of the bandstand, a man hurried toward us, his hand outstretched. Terry shook the man's hand enthusiastically. "What are you doing here?" He turned to me. "May I introduce my friend Frederick Nelson – Miss Amelia Lee." Frederick tipped his hat and leaned toward me. I wondered if he was short-sighted. He appeared to have something of the soldier in his bearing. Straight back and a large ginger moustache. "Frederick is a commercial traveller too. We often bump into each other in hotels up and down the country," Terrence told me. I decided not to say a word – I really didn't want to encourage Frederick to stay, but Terrence seemed delighted with him – even asked him if he'd like to come to the tea rooms with us. I didn't feel comfortable. I mean, what would I have to contribute to the conversation? And I'd probably fumble and spill the tea or say something ridiculous and they would see how foolish and unsophisticated I was. I have to say I was disappointed that Terry agreed so readily. I began to dislike Mr. Nelson very much indeed.'

'But you ended up marrying him.' Henrietta's voice was soft.

'Yes, well, that's a story for another day.'

'I never felt such a fool,' said O'Dowd. He kept his voice low enough not to be overheard by the other customers in the pub. 'Rule number one: don't jump the gun. I was like a constable on his first case.'

'It's a right mess all right. Perhaps you could bring her in?' said Michael who was sitting opposite him.

'She's coming in tomorrow to make a statement. That will give me a chance to ask more questions.'

'And maybe arrest her?' said Michael.

'On what evidence? I'll have to double-check the story. Should have done it before I went to see her. The worst is that I'll have to tell the C.I. Any bit of confidence he had in me will go up in smoke.'

'Lorcan, have you thought?' said Michael. 'What if Mrs. Nelson *was* the woman in Queenstown and said that to the reporter on purpose to cover herself?'

O'Dowd raised his eyebrows. 'I'm impressed that you should come up with something so devious.'

'Thank you … I think,' said Michael.

'I'll make a detective out of you yet, Michael Sudbury.' O'Dowd grinned and stubbed out his cigarette. 'It's simple really: a woman spent the night on the ship with him and if it wasn't Amelia Nelson then who the hell was it? I should have just let her talk. Why couldn't I have kept my big mouth shut for once.'

'Know when to keep your big mouth shut. Is that not one of your Number One Rules"?'

'It is now.'

CHAPTER TWELVE

The next morning O'Dowd wished he'd not had that last pint the previous evening. He stood, feeling increasingly queasy, in front of Chief Inspector Atkinson in Scotland Yard. That is to say, he stood in front of the Chief Inspector's desk. He wished the Chief would open the window that he was standing in front of, instead of just staring through it across the Embankment. The office was warm and stuffy, but he didn't feel he could remove his overcoat. He felt sweat gather in his armpits. The *Nottingham News* was open on the desk.

'And you didn't check the story before you barrelled in? That's not the way we do things here. You should have checked this thoroughly before you opened your mouth.'

'Yes, sir. Sorry, sir.'

The Chief shouted for Barker, who came in immediately, the hint of a smirk on his face. O'Dowd guessed he must be the talk of Scotland Yard, for making a fool of himself.

The Chief handed the newspaper to Barker. 'Find out who wrote this and get him down here. We need him to identify someone. Don't go into detail, just get him here asap. Got it? And find out the next-of-kin for *Titanic* passenger Terrence Bennet.'

'Yes, sir.'

Barker left the room, and O'Dowd continued to sweat.

The Chief sat down. 'So, she could have boarded at Southampton, and waited for this Bennett chap to arrive.'

O'Dowd pressed on. 'Yes. But as yet there is no motive. They were obviously on good terms, even intimate terms. Unless they had some sort of disagreement we don't know about.'

'And she just happened to have a bag full of poison in her luggage?' The Chief shook his head. 'Bit farfetched, to say the least. How would she have got him over the side after she poisoned him? She couldn't have dragged him across the deck and dumped him overboard without help.'

'Mrs. Nelson is coming in this afternoon to make her statement. I will try to get this sorted out, sir.'

The Chief nodded absently. 'See the desk sergeant – he'll sort out an interview room for you.' He picked up a letter from his desk and waved it. 'Well, I have a bit of news for you.' He looked very pleased with himself as he pushed a letter across the desk toward O'Dowd.

O'Dowd scanned the letter from Mr. Eliot Gordon, a solicitor of Jerome Street London.

'From what Mr. Gordon says, your Mr. Terrence Bennett has left almost everything he owns to someone called Sadie Bradshaw,' said the Chief.

'He's not exactly *my* Mr. Terrence –'

'Through a legal firm in Dublin, he contacted the residents at the address given to him by his client – her uncle and aunt, Cecil and Prudence Bradshaw – they don't know her whereabouts. They are very anxious to make contact with their niece. Probably even more so now that she's about to inherit a tidy bit of money. Over seven thousand pounds, according to Gordon.'

O'Dowd whistled.

'Look at the address.' Atkinson leaned back in his chair and watched O'Dowd's face.

'Highfield Road, Rathgar, in Dublin. I know it. Very nice area. But you say she's not there – only her aunt and uncle?'

'As far as the solicitor could find out. I thought I'd leave that to you to follow up, seeing as you're already knee-deep. No point in Scotland Yard wading in. Of course, anything we can do and all that. Goes without saying. But it looks like you've been looking in the wrong country. Amelia Nelson may not have a financial motive for doing away with Terry Bennett, but Sadie Bradshaw certainly has.'

'Could she have been on the *Titanic*?' O'Dowd wondered. 'I'll have to check the passenger list to see if she was on board.' His mind raced through the possibilities. 'Do they have a telephone – I mean the Bradshaws?'

'No, Mr. Gordon communicated with them through the Dublin legal firm only.'

O'Dowd held the solicitor's letter in his hands, already wondering if he should return to Dublin immediately to interview the Bradshaws. He thanked Atkinson, even though he knew he hadn't done much, but it cost nothing to be civil and, in fairness, he'd sent someone to find out about the reporter and Terrence Bennett's next-of-kin. The information came back more quickly than he expected.

O'Dowd took a cab to the Pig and Whistle pub in Camberwell. The sign outside displayed a fat-faced pig and a flute. This must be the place. The small public house occupied a large corner site and even though it was not a warm day some customers sat on the window ledge sipping and watching the world go by. He pushed open the door and murmured conversations stopped suddenly. Several pairs of eyes watched him approach the bar.

O'Dowd showed his credentials to the man behind the bar who leaned across and studied the badge briefly.

'Not the usual one, then,' he said.

'I'm with the Royal Irish Constabulary.' O'Dowd tucked his wallet back into his pocket. 'I'm looking for Mr. George Bennett.'

The man nodded. 'That's me. What can I do for you?'

George Bennett could hardly deny his kinship with Terrence Bennett. He bore a striking resemblance to his brother and had the same hair and eye colour but lacked height. He stood looking at O'Dowd, shirtsleeves rolled up to his elbows, hands spread on the wooden countertop.

It wasn't long past one, but O'Dowd felt it had already been a long day. The pub looked comfortable and smelled of timber and whiskey. He was tempted but he swallowed and told himself not to have a drink and, in reward, he could have one, at least one, later. He drew himself up to his full height.

'I have some bad news, Mr. Bennett. Is there somewhere we can talk privately?'

He took his time coming back from Camberwell. He wasn't due to see Amelia Nelson for another hour so he walked along the Victoria Embankment. He didn't like the idea of returning to Dublin until he could find out more about Sadie Bradshaw. He stopped on the bridge to look at the river traffic beneath; it didn't seem to stink as much today. Must be the breeze. He rested his elbows on the wall. The grey clouds trimmed in opal white were almost over the bridge now. The same cool breeze that took away the smell also made the tip of his nose red. He pulled up his collar and walked back toward Scotland Yard.

As he went inside, the desk sergeant called him over. 'Woman waiting to see you, inspector. I wasn't sure if you were coming back anytime soon. You really will have to get used to letting us know your comings and goings. Said she'd wait.'

'Sorry, sergeant. Where did you put Mrs. Nelson?'

The sergeant checked his register. 'Not Mrs. Nelson, sir – it's a Miss Claire Nelson. Interview room B.'

CHAPTER THIRTEEN

Inspector O'Dowd listened carefully to Claire Nelson as she explained her reason for coming to see him. Then he asked if her mother knew she'd come here today.

'Well, no. I didn't discuss it with her. To be truthful, I don't think she would approve. I wouldn't have thought of it, coming to see you, I mean, if she hadn't made such a fuss about your visit yesterday. By the time I got home, I couldn't get any sense out of her or Henrietta. I shouldn't say this, but they'd had a brandy. More than one. I gather you're not exactly her favourite person at the moment.' A mischievous grin flitted across her mouth. She had the same sharp features and auburn hair as her mother but had escaped the frown. 'If you could see your way to helping me find Charles Morley, inspector, if there's anything at all you can find out, I'd be very much obliged.'

'I'll see what I can do, Miss Nelson. Though it's not a crime for someone to leave and not get in touch. Now I suggest that if you'd rather not bump into your mother in the hallway, perhaps you should leave now.' He looked at his watch. 'She's due here in half an hour.'

Exactly twenty-five minutes later he watched Amelia Nelson stride toward the entrance. For a small woman, she could undoubtedly cover ground quickly. She was smartly dressed in a maroon-coloured jacket, skirt, and matching hat. As she neared the entrance to Scotland Yard, she glanced up at the building. He knew she couldn't possibly see him, but he found himself taking a step back. His heart quickened as though he'd been discovered spying.

A few minutes later, he sat opposite her with a young constable ready to take notes. Typed pages containing their conversation from the previous day lay on the table in front of them. They waited while she removed her gloves, one finger at a time, smoothed them out, and carefully placed them on the desk.

He pushed the pages toward her. 'Basically, it's a record of your identification of Mr. Terrence Bennett. It states you recognized the cufflinks and the photo –'

'I can read, inspector.' She pulled the pages toward her and read, her finger following the text.

The inspector and constable watched her progress and both released a silent breath of relief when she nodded.

'I wanted to be sure you put in that I wasn't on the *Titanic*.'

'I think you'll find the wording says "Mrs. Nelson stated that she was not on the *Titanic*".'

'Same thing,' she said. 'But I want it to show that the newspaper article was wrong.'

'That's being looked into by Scotland Yard.'

'Well, shouldn't it say that here?'

O'Dowd met the constable's eye. 'Constable, would you include an addendum to state that an investigation into the contents of the newspaper article will be carried out as soon as possible.'

The constable stood. 'Five minutes, sir.' He took the pages and left.

Once the door closed behind him, Amelia lifted her chin and stared at O'Dowd.

'There was no need to send a constable to my house to remind me. I had every intention of keeping the appointment. I'm sure the neighbours saw. You've ruined my reputation, you know. They probably think I've done something awful.'

'There could be any number of reasons why a constable might come to a person's house. Not usually bearing good news, I'll grant you that. Why would your neighbours immediately assume that you had done "something awful"?'

'That's easy for you to say. It's hard being a widow, you know. People treat you as though it's your fault that your husband has passed on. All of a sudden, you become a threat to be dealt with. We suddenly don't fit into their world anymore, and they ...'

'They what?'

She dropped her eyes. 'Well ... they watch. You know, if you stop to talk to a man, any man, even the postman, they concoct stories in their heads, they do.'

He nodded in that comforting way he'd learned over the years. 'And that's why you only take in female lodgers, is that right, Mrs. Nelson?'

She put her small hand on the table. 'That's exactly why. A woman on her own can't be too careful.'

'If that's the case, perhaps you can explain why you allowed a man to live in your garden for the past six months.'

She looked startled and her face flushed. 'Who told you that? It's nobody's business. One of those nosy neighbours, was it?'

'You're not being accused of a crime, Mrs. Nelson.' He opened the notebook he used when speaking with Claire Nelson. 'A Mr Charles Morley is the name I've been given. Apparently, he hasn't been seen for several weeks. Do I have that right, Mrs. Nelson? He's been living in some sort of outbuilding? So, tell me, who exactly is Mr. Charles Morley?'

She folded her arms and glared silently across at him.

'I have all day, Mrs. Nelson.' He leaned back in his chair, linked his fingers behind his head and whistled the opening notes of a popular music-hall tune.

'It's not what you think,' she said.

He stopped whistling and leaned toward her. 'How do you know what I think?'

'It's all perfectly innocent. He was Frederick's brother-in-law from his first marriage.'

'Your husband has been dead for twelve years. Are you telling me that you kept in touch with his brother-in-law from his first marriage for all that time?'

'No, of course not.' She fixed her eyes on him. 'He arrived at the door a few months ago, at the beginning of winter. He didn't even have a warm coat to call his own. I felt sorry for him. I was the nearest thing he had to a relative. I couldn't just turn him away, so I took him in. There's a small building, more of a shed, really, at the bottom of the garden. Said he didn't mind that, was grateful for the bed. That's all.' She cast a challenging look across the table. 'He does a bit of work around the house and tends the vegetable plot. He planted it himself to help out – the garden is too big for me to tackle. It was an arrangement that suited us both. The cost of lodgings in London is shocking, you know.'

O'Dowd watched the self-satisfied look cross her face. He guessed that she'd told this story many a time – of how she'd rescued a poor unfortunate man and had put a roof – even a draughty shaky roof – over his head.

'You said it was an arrangement that suited you both, Mrs Nelson.'

'Yes, it was.' She nodded her head firmly.

'In the past tense. What changed? Why is it not a suitable arrangement now?'

'That was just a figure of speech,' She picked up her gloves and straightened the fingers again. 'Of course it's still a good arrangement for both of us.'

'I think I'd like to have a word with Mr. Morley.'

'He goes off from time to time. I'm not there to keep an eye on him. He has his own life to lead.'

'You just said he knows no one in London. Could he have relatives in another part of the country?'

'No.'

'You seem very certain of that, Mrs. Nelson.'

She put her hands on the table. 'Look, I know very little about Frederick's first wife or her family. The only thing I know is that her name was Elizabeth Morley, and she was the daughter of a convict deported to Australia. It's not surprising, really, that he wouldn't want people to know he married the daughter of a convict. Elizabeth's father never returned from Australia. He remarried and had a second family there. Charles Morley was one of his children. He would have been Elizabeth's half-brother, a much younger half-brother.'

O'Dowd sat back in his chair and observed Amelia. He believed what she said; he could see no point in her lying about it. It would be easy enough to check the facts. However, though she gave the appearance of being open and honest, he had a suspicion that Amelia Nelson had something to hide.

The constable returned and placed the amended statement in front of her. She spent quite a while reading it. Eventually, she dipped the pen in the ink and signed the document.

'Thank you, Mrs. Nelson,' O'Dowd said. 'I'll arrange a cab and accompany you home.'

'Why? There's really no need for that, inspector. I'll be quite all right alone.'

'I'd like to see if Mr Morley has returned, if you don't mind?'

Her shoulders slumped a little, and she nodded.

Away from the formality of the interview, he felt her relax a little beside him as the horse-drawn cab turned to cross the river and head south.

'How long have you been a widow, Mrs. Nelson?'

'I told you already. Frederick has been dead twelve years.'

'And the circumstances of his death?'

She sighed heavily. 'I don't see what that has to do with anything, inspector.'

'Humour me.'

'If you must know, Frederick was cleaning his gun and it went off. It was a terrible accident.'

'Was there an inquiry at the time?' O'Dowd had read the case notes. He didn't think Amelia had anything to do with his death, but he wanted to unnerve her and stir some emotion. It wasn't working. Amelia seemed to have recovered her composure and turned to look him in the eye.

'The inquest said it was "accidental death", which it was, inspector. I may as well tell you, you probably know already, that it turned out Frederick had lost all his money. I'll never forget the solicitor coming to see me after the funeral, all sweaty hands and shifty eyes. Deadly serious though. "I must inform you, Mrs. Nelson," he said, "that your husband has amassed a considerable amount of debt. He invested heavily in unsuccessful train routes, both here and in America, and in a series of failed ventures that have eaten away all his resources." He tut-tutted at Frederick's foolishness. I asked him about the house. I felt sure that Frederick would have taken care to at least leave us with a roof over our heads. I had three children to think of.'

O'Dowd was inches from her; he watched the vein in her forehead throb.

'But I was wrong. The solicitor, Mr Edgecumbe, had a self-satisfied look on his face, a look that said "I told you so" except that he hadn't ever told me anything. Now he was saying that the house had been re-mortgaged a year previously. I wasn't sure what that meant, but I knew it wasn't good.' She sighed. 'Such a lovely house, three storeys. It had steps up from the garden to a veranda. Frederick said he bought it because it reminded him of the houses he'd seen in the Far East. We had a maid, a cook, a kitchen girl, and a gardener who came once or twice a week. When the children were small, we had a nanny. But it all collapsed to nothing. Mr. Edgecumbe said that if Frederick's investments had turned a profit, all would be well. But it seems he threw good money after bad, the way gamblers do, trying to recoup his losses.'

'He left you with nothing at all?'

'Very little. Some pieces of furniture. He had stopped paying his life insurance policy. All I had was some nice jewellery, but you can't eat gold, inspector. I sold it for less than it was worth, but I didn't have a choice. The money didn't last long.'

She'd turned her face away from O'Dowd and looked out the window; she didn't seem inclined to talk any further. He felt a grudging admiration for her. She'd managed to pull the pieces of her life back together, somehow run a boarding house and bring up her children.

As they made their way out of central London, he followed her gaze to the streets full of hawkers and pedlars pulling or pushing wagons piled high. Everyone on a mission, somewhere to go, the hum of the city, the trams, the voices, the weaving in and out of narrow streets.

The further they got from the city, the cleaner the air became, and soon the smell of the river and the stench of the city were behind them.

'I could have just as easily taken the train,' Amelia said. She appeared to have buried her emotions again for the time being. 'You really didn't have to accompany me all this way.'

'I'm happy to see you home safely and, of course, I want a word with Mr. Morley.'

The carriage crossed the bridge over the Grand Surrey Canal and minutes later turned into Elm Lane.

She looked along the empty street. 'Good,' she said. 'Quickly now, I don't want the neighbours seeing you.'

Unfortunately for Amelia, her neighbours seemed to sense that something untoward was happening. O'Dowd was aware of twitching curtains and the sudden opening of doors as neighbours found an urgent need to be outside. He helped Amelia out of the cab, and she hurried to the front door, key in hand.

The smell of beef broth filled the hallway. O'Dowd breathed in the aroma and realised he was hungry.

Henrietta and Claire stood at the kitchen table, heads close together while folding clean laundry. They were deep in conversation. O'Dowd guessed that Claire was confiding her worries about the missing Charles Morley. For a moment, they seemed unaware of him and Amelia. Then Henrietta turned suddenly and greeted them while Claire looked at O'Dowd with hope in her eyes.

'Hello, Mother. Hello, inspector,' she said.

'How do you know –' began Amelia

'Would you like some tea, Amelia?' Henrietta was reaching for the kettle. 'How nice to see you again, inspector – you'll have a cup?

'No, thank you, Henrietta,' said Amelia. 'I'm going to lie down. Thank you for doing all the laundry today, I appreciate it.

'Oh dear, I hope you didn't overdo it today.' Henrietta glanced accusingly at O'Dowd.

'The inspector wants to see where Charlie sleeps when he's here,' said Amelia. 'Claire, I'd like a word with you upstairs.' She began to remove her hat as she left the kitchen.

'Yes, Mother.' Claire didn't seem particularly upset or fearful of what that conversation would reveal. 'I'll see to the inspector first. Do you want me to show you, inspector?'

He declined her offer with a smile. 'I've had years of training – I should be able to find a garden shed. Is there a key?'

Henrietta selected a key from several hooks on the kitchen wall and handed it to him.

He went through the back door, aware of the two women watching him from the kitchen window. He followed a well-worn track through the sodden grass toward a cluster of apple trees. One of his socks was damp and getting wetter with each footstep. He made a mental note to ask Gracie to take his shoes to the cobbler. The grass hadn't been cut in a while. Mr. Morley seemed to be neglecting his duties. A tangle of blackberry bushes, heavy with raindrops, showered him as he pushed past. The vegetable patches were neatly dug, and bright green shoots, possibly carrots or potatoes, had poked through the soil – he pulled at one of the weeds that had sprung up. This did not have the look of a well-tended garden. He stood and faced the thicket of bushes and glimpsed the corner of a wooden building. He called the man's name. No response, which didn't surprise him. He took a few steps nearer and called again. There was only birdsong.

He unlocked the door and stepped inside the small cabin. It was neat and clean and draughty. A low makeshift bed lay bare in the corner near the wood burner. O'Dowd looked around. It was basic, but a man could live here in the summer without too much hardship.

The winter, however, would be an entirely different matter. The wooden floor seemed to have been swept, gardening tools stood in the corner. There were no clothes or shoes. Mr Morley had taken time to tidy everything and had left. Or that's how it appeared. Of course, someone could have been here and tidied up. There was no way to tell. The only thing for sure was that Morley was gone, and it didn't look like he had any intention of coming back. Poor Claire, he thought as he locked the shed door.

The inspector's shoe squelched as he retraced his steps to the kitchen.

'Tea, inspector?' Henrietta hovered at the kitchen door. 'Or there's some hot beef broth if you prefer?' She tapped her fingertips together, as though itching to be of service in some small way.

He would have liked a bowl of broth but didn't think he could face the inquisition. On the other hand, he'd not eaten since morning.

'Thank you, Miss Harper,' he said. 'A small bowlful of broth would be very welcome.'

Henrietta quickly filled a bowl and put it on the table as Claire pulled out a chair for him beside her.

'Did you see, inspector?' she said. 'I told you he was gone. He'd never have left without telling me – I mean us.' She flushed.

He took a spoonful from the steaming bowl and blew on it gently. He didn't want to get into conversation with Claire again about Charles Morley. He very much doubted that he would be able to locate the missing man and his intention was to get advice from Michael on how to proceed.

Claire looked at him intently; he knew she was full of questions that he couldn't answer. He took a spoonful of broth and tried to avoid her eyes.

It was Henrietta who came to his rescue.

89

'I was just saying to Claire, inspector, how difficult it is for a woman on her own, as opposed to men, I mean. Men can go anywhere they like. Charles can go off on a whim and no one will bat an eyelid. A woman on her own, no matter what her station in life, has only so many choices. In many ways, we're at the mercy of men, of society, of the Church. We're not allowed to decide for ourselves, and we're frowned on if we try. Women like me and Amelia, without a husband to share the load, must make decisions for ourselves and learn to live with the consequences. Whatever your mother did, Claire, I know her well enough to think that she must have had a good reason.'

O'Dowd was intrigued. 'What is it Amelia has done?' he asked, feeling the comfort of the warm food travel to his stomach.

Claire looked abashed. 'Henrietta thinks Mother has sent Charles away because I was becoming infatuated with him.'

O'Dowd absently stirred the broth while he thought. 'This is a little delicate. Let me get this straight. This Charles Morley is the brother of your father's first wife. Is that right?'

Both women nodded their heads in unison.

'Doesn't that make him an uncle to you?'

'I suppose he'd be a sort of a distant uncle,' said Claire. 'If there is such a thing. His only connection was to my father's first wife, do you see?'

'Yes, I see,' he said, watching her pained expression. She seemed to desperately want him to tell her everything would be all right, but he had a horrible feeling that it wasn't.

'Nothing improper has occurred between us.' Her blush deepened. 'I'm worried about him. That's all.'

'As I've said before, it's not strictly my area, but I'll see what I can do.'

'Thank you.'

He finished the broth and set his spoon down.

'Thank you for the broth, Miss Harper. It was very good indeed.' He stood. 'I must be on my way now. Goodbye for the present, Miss Nelson.'

Henrietta scurried after him as he walked to the door.

'It's all right, Miss Harper. I can see myself out,' he said.

However, she still followed him out the front door.

'Can I have a word, inspector?'

His heart sank. 'Certainly,' he said.

She placed her hand on his arm. 'I don't think he's coming back, inspector.'

He waited for her to go on, as he knew she would.

'I saw him the day before he left. Amelia didn't see me and really it was none of my business, but I was stuck there. I'd been hanging sheets on the washing line. They didn't notice me behind the sheets, so I decided to wait until it was all over. I wouldn't like to upset Amelia, you see.'

'Why is that, Miss Harper?'

She dropped her voice even lower. He had to stoop to catch what she said.

'I come from a poor, but respectable family, inspector. I know what it's like to do without and it's not easy to find decent lodgings. I can afford the rent here and Amelia keeps a good clean house.'

'But?'

'She has a temper. I wouldn't like her to turn against me for telling.'

He saw her frightened eyes and understood the fear of being alone, the threat of eviction, and finding oneself without a roof or shelter. Not for the first time, he felt kindly toward Miss Harper.

'Mrs. Nelson won't hear it from me, I promise you,' he said. 'What exactly happened?'

She seemed to relax a little, but her eyes travelled back toward the empty hallway, just in case.

91

'They argued,' she said quietly. She put her palm on her chest as though begging for forgiveness for what she was about to do. 'I do not know what it was about, but she told him to leave and not come back. Then he said something that I didn't understand.'

'What exactly did he say?'

'He said he knew about the photographs.'

'And what do you think he meant by that?'

'Well, inspector, I don't know. I don't know whose photographs he was talking about, but she looked afraid when he said it. She said it was none of his business. He was very angry – I thought he might have struck her. In fact, I looked around for the yard brush, just in case.'

O'Dowd hid his smile at the thought of Miss Harper tackling the handyman with a sweeping brush. 'And what happened then?'

'Nothing. He just left.'

'Thank you for that information, Miss Harper. I'll call back tomorrow to speak with Mrs. Nelson.'

'And you won't tell her about what I said?'

'You have my word.'

Once he'd dried his feet, changed his socks and stuck some rolled-up newspaper into his shoes, O'Dowd put his slippers on and sat down to talk with Michael about the case. They'd fallen into the habit of reliving their day over a glass of beer in the kitchen instead of the pub. Here they discussed how investigations were going without fear of being overheard. Michael's day tended to be routine, and he preferred to focus on what was happening in O'Dowd's case. They enjoyed the puzzle to solve, the chase, putting together the story, and the 'what ifs'.

This is why he'd become a police officer, O'Dowd thought. Pieces falling into place with a click in his head. He'd spent the last few years tracking gunrunners, though catching them in the act was almost impossible, especially in County Cork with its million coves and inlets, rocky harbours, and hidden caves. He was enjoying this case in a strange sort of way.

In Ireland, the people's resentment of the R.I.C. was deeply set. O'Dowd realised that he'd become so accustomed to it that he'd thought it normal. Being in London had opened his eyes. Here no one hated him for being a policeman. He wondered if attitudes would change with Home Rule almost in the bag. Everyone was waiting; he could practically feel the country hold its breath, believing that this time it would happen without a drop of blood spilt. It seemed too good to be true, though how it would affect the R.I.C. hadn't yet been explained. Who would fund the force, and how would it be managed? Would he still fill in the Register of Crime, Warrant Book, and Pedlars' Licence Book? The list was endless, the future unclear. If there was one thing O'Dowd didn't care for, it was uncertainty.

CHAPTER FOURTEEN

Lily Odell introduced O'Dowd to her husband, Herbert, before breaking the news that she and Kate and Jack had gone through the photographs, and not one of them contained the woman in the veiled hat or the murdered man.

'I'm sorry, inspector,' said Lily. 'I feel I've let you down.' She poured him another cup of tea as he scoured through the photographs from Kate and Jack's cameras. 'As I said to you before, I was more concerned that Jack didn't fall overboard, camera and all, trying to get a better photograph than his aunt.'

'Perhaps you could look at this.' He handed her a photograph of Amelia Nelson. 'This woman is an acquaintance of the deceased.'

Herbert Odell, small, dark-haired, was a man who'd come up in the world since his days as a porter in Billingsgate market. He looked at the photograph over his wife's shoulder and shook his head.

'Acquaintance, is that what you really mean? I wouldn't have put the two of them together. Of course, I wasn't there, inspector. I'm no use to you, am I?' He hooked his thumbs into his waistcoat and rocked back on his heels. 'Pity about Terry though.'

'*Terry?*' said O'Dowd. 'You knew Terrence Bennett?'

'Knew him as a kid in Camberwell. His parents ran the pub, mine ran the butcher's and fish shop. We would have been about the same age, ran around together as young 'uns. Can't say I saw much of him as we got older. I was just starting off in Billingsgate market as an empty boy – collecting empty fish crates, that is – and he was working in the pub. I stopped in the odd evening for a drink and a chat. A good listener, I can say that for him. He always managed to steer the talk around to pounds, shillings and pence. I suppose it was only natural after what happened with Delia.'

O'Dowd leaned forward. 'Delia?'

'Made for each other they were, always together. I don't know the ins and outs of it, but her head was turned by another chap. He had a bob or two and didn't mind splashing it about. Terry's father had the pub, but he drank most of the profits. It had never bothered Terry before – or didn't seem to – but, when Delia started wearing fancy gowns and handmade gloves and going off in what's-his-name's carriage, Terry didn't stand a chance. Became obsessed with money – anytime I saw him he wanted to talk about profits and investments and how to get rich quick. Except there ain't no such thing – not legal anyway. Next I heard, he'd upped and gone to Nottingham. Said there were 'opportunities' there. I ask you, opportunities in Nottingham!'

'Lace,' said O'Dowd. 'It was the lace mills in Nottingham. He worked as a travelling salesman. How long ago was that, Mr. Odell?'

He puffed out a breath. 'Long time, maybe twenty years. Can't say for sure. That's the last time I saw him.'

'Thank you for that. Just one more thing – may I ask why you didn't travel on the *Titanic*, Mr. Odell?'

'Business. A minor dispute, that's all, with some of the porters. Had to get it sorted out there and then. If the porters weren't there to move the fresh stock coming in, it would be a disaster. I had no choice but to stay and get it sorted. It meant missing the trip, but that's how it goes. It was all right in the end.'

'It was such a shame,' said Lily, 'but couldn't be helped.'

Odell took a cigar from a box and offered one to O'Dowd, who resisted.

Odell lit his cigar. 'So, the woman you're trying to find, any clues yet?'

'Not yet, Mr. Odell. These things take time.'

'You'll probably find a dozen beautiful women lining up. From what I heard of him over the years, he didn't treat women very well. But you know what women are like.'

O'Dowd wasn't sure how to respond to that in front of Odell's wife.

Odell went on. 'Always thought they'd be the one to tame him, to make him fall in love with them. What they didn't understand was that he was a one-woman man, and she'd turned her back on him. How could they compete with the woman who'd turned him down?'

O'Dowd left shortly after. The mental image he was building of Terry Bennett was of a charming though heartless man. What didn't make sense to him was his relationship with Amelia Nelson. She wasn't rich, and she certainly wasn't beautiful. Yet there was something between them that had lasted. She was obviously in love with him and had been for years. But what made him keep coming back to her?

CHAPTER FIFTEEN

O'Dowd was beginning to value the telephone in a way he'd never have thought possible. He was able to phone his old friend, David Forde, in the Dublin Metropolitan Police force in Dublin Castle. They'd been cadets together twenty years earlier. O'Dowd explained the situation to David and asked him to visit Cecil and Prudence Bradshaw and find out what he could about their niece Sadie.

The next day he returned to his small desk in Scotland Yard and flicked through the newspaper while he waited for the return call.

Titanic. Page after page of articles and reports from the tribunal in New York. It somehow seemed surreal, as though it was a made-up story and hadn't really happened. Except that it had, and the newspapers showed the photographs of survivors on the *Carpathia* to prove it. He jumped when the phone rang.

'They seemed to be genuinely concerned about the niece,' said David. 'They haven't seen her for some time. She was in St. Patrick's Asylum when she came back from China – they said her nerves were bad – whatever that means.'

China? O'Dowd sat up straight. 'Tell me everything, Dave. Don't leave anything out.' He could hear him flick through the pages of his notebook and recognised the tune he whistled while he searched for the information.

'Yes, here we are. Sadie's mother died shortly after she was born, and her father passed away when she was nine years old. Her aunt and uncle, Cecil and Prudence Bradshaw, were left the house on condition that they looked after Sadie and that she'd inherit the house from them when they passed on. I'd say there's not much in the way of cash. The house looked like it needed a bit of attention. It was spotlessly clean but, you know, shabby.' Another page turned. 'Nothing much else about her childhood. Her aunt said Sadie was a determined optimist. They said she was an easy child, always willing to help.'

'What did she mean by "determined optimist"?'

'I asked her. I'll read what she said. "Sadie wouldn't countenance any sort of bad outcome to a situation. Not only would she not dwell on any sort of negativity, she ignored it completely." Her aunt thought she'd had so much unhappiness, with her mother dying so young and then her father, that she couldn't bring herself to face the possibility of any further upset.'

'So not fully in reality.' O'Dowd tapped his pencil lightly on the desk. He knew that feeling. That feeling of being slightly out of sorts with the real world, floating along half a second behind everyone else. His reaction had been to bury himself in work. Sadie chose to banish the darkness and live only in the light. That only works in a world where everyone loves you. It seemed that Sadie tried very hard to make everyone like her. How did she cope when someone didn't like her? That would be an itch that would bother her immensely.

O'Dowd heard a page flick over.

'I saw a photograph of her, not recent obviously,' said Forde. 'The

Bradshaws gave it to me along with her letters to them "just in case", they said. They're willing to do anything to help.'

'But they've no idea where she is now. Not even a guess. What did you mean when you mentioned China – could she have gone back there?'

'It's a possibility. She was obsessed with China – her aunt seems to blame herself for that. Mrs. Bradshaw told me that when Sadie was about sixteen, she took her to hear a missionary speak in the local church. Man by the name of Tom Pigott – his family has an estate in Leixlip. He spoke about his time as a missionary in China. Sadie was "transfixed", is the way that Mrs Bradshaw put it. She'd always been shy, so when Sadie asked if they could wait at the end to speak to Mr. Pigott and his wife Jessie, Mrs. Bradshaw was pleased to do that.'

'What sort of missionaries?'

'I didn't think to ask. To tell you the truth, I don't know the difference between all those Protestant religions. Definitely not Catholic anyway.'

Another page flicked over.

'From that day on, Sadie was convinced that she should go to China and work as a missionary. She was a changed person, and threw herself into raising money for the missions – sales of work, Christmas fairs, cake sales, all that sort of thing. They were pleased that she had some focus, and they didn't really think that Sadie would ever actually go herself, but when she was twenty years old she applied to the China Inland Mission in London and went there to study Chinese and the scriptures. They didn't try to stop her. In fact, I get the impression that they encouraged her. Off she went to London and then two years later to China.'

She might have met Terrence Bennett in London, thought O'Dowd.

'I got the name of her best friend, Sarah Britton. She wasn't as forthcoming, but, as soon as I mentioned Scotland Yard, she told me she had letters from Sadie and handed them over. I'll send them straight away. Apparently things didn't go too well in China.'

'Wasn't there some sort of uprising in Beijing? That was at least ten years ago,' said O'Dowd. 'She might have got caught up in that. I'll do a bit of digging here. Thanks a lot, Dave. I'll buy you a pint when I get back.'

'More than one, I hope. I'd like to hear what this is all about. Give me a shout when you're home. Good luck!'

O'Dowd hung up. Nothing to do now but wait. If I'm lucky, he thought, the letters from Dave will get here by the second post tomorrow.

There wasn't anything else to be done. He walked toward the train station. He needed to think it all out and decided to go home.

When had he started calling it home? 'Give me a shout when you're home,' Dave had said. But, at the moment, home was Michael's house. He checked his watch; his brother would be there soon. He was one of the best listeners he'd ever known. He would sit and not interrupt, take in all the information and ponder on it before asking one or two considered questions. He thought that Michael would make an excellent detective if he set his mind to it.

The next day luck, or at least the postal service, was with him. The small package arrived in the afternoon post. O'Dowd sat at his desk in the corner of the incident room. Most of the men assigned to help with the initial aftermath of the *Titanic* had been sent back to their usual duties, their desks abandoned. The sound of a clacking typewriter used by one of the constables echoed around the room, the cheerful ding at the end of each line at odds with an unsettling feeling of desolation. Two policemen crossed-checked lists of names, their voices barely above a whisper.

O'Dowd carefully untied the twine and pulled out the contents. Two separate bundles of letters and one photograph. He picked this up first. A young fair-haired girl, her hair in ringlets, looked shyly into the camera. Maybe fifteen or sixteen years old. Plump cheeks and a broad smile that didn't show her teeth. Her dress was buttoned up to her throat, and she had draped a shawl across her rounded shoulders.

He stared at the photograph as though it might hold a clue, but he could see nothing extraordinary about the young girl. He put her photograph aside and chose the bundle of letters addressed to *Mr. & Mrs Bradshaw*. There weren't many, perhaps six or seven. He selected the one with the oldest date stamp and sat back in his chair to read.

January 1899

Dear Uncle Cecil and Aunt Pru,

As you can see, I am on my way at last. I'm sorry I couldn't come home to say goodbye properly before I left, but in the end it was all a bit of a whirl, and speed was of the essence.

The China Inland Mission introduced me to a lovely lady called Pao Chu. She was born in China, and her family moved to London long ago. Pao Chu is what they call a 'Bible woman'. She travels to remote villages and preaches the word of God, especially to the women. She tells me she also tries to dissuade them from having their daughters' feet bound.

Pao Chu had been visiting family in London and was about to make the journey back to the missions when the C.I.M. asked her if she would take over my training. Wasn't that lucky? They feel I am ready. I'm so thrilled to be on my way and, with Pao Chu to guide me, I'm sure I won't go far wrong.

The ship has docked in Marseille and if I hurry I can catch the post before we go on to the next leg of the journey. I'm so looking forward to travelling down the Suez Canal. I've heard so much about it.

With best wishes

Your niece,

Sadie

❖

O'Dowd glanced at each of the letters to Sadie's uncle and aunt. They were short. Sadie always seemed to be 'running to catch the post' and talked of the weather and the missionary stations she stayed at while waiting to make a connection to another ship. She praised Pao Chu's efficiency in organising the passage. In short, he'd seldom read anything more tedious than Sadie's letters to her relations.

O'Dowd put the last letter on top of the pile he'd finished. Getting up from the hard wooden chair, he stretched and rolled his shoulders. The room was empty, the typewriter silent, the list-checkers gone. Outside, the clouds still threatened rain but had held off releasing its deluge just yet. O'Dowd wondered if he should leave now and hope to be home before the worst of it. Too late – the first sprinkles landed silently on the windowpane. He knew he was going nowhere.

He fetched a cup of tea from the canteen, brought it back to the desk and opened Sadie's first letter to her best friend. It contained charming and amusing descriptions of her fellow passengers on the ships. He read through it quickly then picked up the first letter written after changing ships in Macau.

❖

Macau, April 1899

Dear Sarah,

As Pao Chu and I got to the dockside we were relieved that the ship we'd booked passage on was still there. I could see some passengers already on the deck looking down to where we stood surrounded by our luggage. I have to confess when I say 'our' luggage, I really mean <u>my</u> luggage. I pretended not to notice Pao Chu's disapproving look. She travels with just one carpetbag! Can you believe it?

A lovely man whose name turned out to be John Robinson helped us with the luggage. He is attractive in a quiet sort of way. Light brown hair and a beard. We met him again at dinner – Sarah, it was so embarrassing. He'd kept a seat beside him for me, and there was no other empty seat! He'd assumed that Pao Chu was my servant. He was mortified. The table was full, but I refused to sit down until a seat was found for Pao Chu. Luckily, another Englishman and an American man made room between them, and Pao Chu sat there. As it turned out, the American (his name is Mr. Parker) is a cartographer, and he was delighted to talk with Pao Chu about the mountain passes. I sat beside Mr. Robinson (I've never seen a man blush like he does). There was a French couple and a German couple at the table. They were polite enough but kept themselves to themselves. The other Englishman was a tea trader. His name was Terrence Bennett.

'Yes!' O'Dowd exclaimed and thumped his desk.

Each time I looked up from my plate, he seemed to catch my eye. I couldn't quite help myself. He has such an attractive face, sort of angular and strong. His shirt was starched to perfection – even Aunt Pru would have approved of his shirt, and you know how fussy she is.

The thing that I couldn't help but notice was the colour of his eyes. Pale grey. They stood out so against his tanned skin and dark hair.

John was telling me something about his time at London University, but I have to say I missed most of it. I covered up by asking what brought him to China. You'll never guess in a million years! He'd been offered a post as tutor to the son of a missionary family. Do you know whom he meant? Yes, he was to be tutor to the son of Tom and Jessie Pigott. I almost dropped my soupspoon.

If that wasn't enough, a little lady, I'd say she was at least forty, who was sitting at the far end of the table, between the Germans and the French, piped up that she was also on her way to join the Pigotts' mission in Shou Yang. Her name is Miss Duval, and she asked why we were travelling to China, so I told them that Pao Chu and I were travelling to one of the missions but that I didn't know exactly where as yet. Well, Sarah, you could have heard a pin drop. I don't think they expected me to be a missionary. I think Terrence Bennett actually <u>laughed</u>. He pretended to cough behind his napkin and took a long drink of water, but I saw the look in his eyes. I've enough experience to know when people are making fun of me. I've never forgotten how the other schoolgirls laughed when I was the angel in the nativity play, and the costume was too small. Anyhow, he definitely found it very amusing. Well, maybe a lot of people do. I know I don't look like a missionary, but it doesn't say anywhere that a missionary has to be thin and severe and only wear dark, boring clothes. It doesn't matter to the Lord that I am plump and like frills and flounces and colourful ribbons in my hair.

The four of us met after the meal when the men began smoking. John accompanied us onto the deck, and I got a chance to speak to Miss Duval. She told me she'd always wanted to work on the missions but had to tend to her mother, who'd recently passed away. She'd applied to several missions, but they all said she was too old to be of any actual use. In desperation, she wrote to Mr. Pigott, who told her to come out, that he could find work for willing hands no matter their age. Isn't he wonderful? I wish I was going to his mission in Shou Yang, but I must wait. Patience, as you know, Sarah, does not come easily to me, but I will pray for it if I have time.

As for the attractive Mr. Bennett, I shall keep a very wide berth. There is something about him, something dangerous, that I can't quite describe, for there was no aggression whatsoever in his manner. Perhaps it is just his maleness that puts me on edge. I've never met anyone quite like him in my life.

Our next port of call is Shanghai. I'll write during the voyage and post a batch of letters to you from there. There is little else to do on board the ship except read and write.

Best wishes,
Your friend,
Sadie

There it was, in her own hand. Sadie Bradshaw met Terrence Bennett on a ship in the South China sea. He, probably on his way to trade, and she on her way to becoming a missionary. An unlikely pairing, thought O'Dowd. Did they fall in love? What became of Sadie? And why did Terrence Bennett leave her every penny he owned?

He opened the next letter.

The following day O'Dowd went to the offices of the China Inland Mission. He showed his credentials and asked to speak with whomever was in charge. A Mr. Osbourne came to his assistance, and O'Dowd asked for help finding Sadie Bradshaw or Pao Chu.

Mr. Osbourne nodded and shuffled some papers on his desk. 'As a matter of fact, I've had an inquiry from a Mr. Gordon, the solicitor looking for the whereabouts of Miss Bradshaw.'

'She's not in trouble and it appears there may be some good news for her if you should happen to know of her whereabouts.'

'Really? I haven't seen or heard from Miss Bradshaw since she returned from China. I did hear that she was in an asylum in Dublin at one point. I assume she's still there.'

'She isn't. Perhaps you can tell me where Pao Chu is?'

'Now that is something I can help you with. Pao Chu lives in London now. She preaches among the people in Chinatown. I can give you her address.' He checked an address book and wrote down the address for O'Dowd. 'She might have kept in touch with Miss Bradshaw.'

'I appreciate your help. We know so little about Sadie Bradshaw,' said O'Dowd.

'In that case, Pao Chu would be the best person to speak to. They spent a lot of time there and went through some very troubled times. I'd rather not get into the details, inspector. Pao Chu can explain everything to you. By the way, in China the family name comes first. You would address her as Miss Pao, not Miss Chu.'

O'Dowd thanked him for his help and looked at the address in Chinatown, relieved that Pao Chu hadn't returned to China. There wouldn't be any way of getting expenses to pursue a witness to the other side of the world. The chance of progress lifted his spirits.

Outside the impressive building, he put the card in his pocket and looked toward the sky. No sign of clouds today, the breeze was fresh, and the air smog-free. If he closed his eyes, he could almost be on the strand at Youghal.

Back at Scotland Yard, he opened the next letter.

Dear Sarah,

It's an hour before dawn, and I've just come back to our tiny cabin. I'm trying to write quietly, but the scratch of the pen on paper fills the cabin. Pao Chu is sleeping, not exactly quietly. It's a bit of a surprise that someone so quiet when awake can be so noisy when she sleeps. But that is not why I feel the need to put this scratchy pen to paper.

I often go to the deck during the night. There is so little freedom on board during the day, constantly bumping into the other passengers, and there's only so much small talk I can manage when every day is exactly as the one before. The slightest shift in the wind gives a half-hour discussion over dinner. But at night the deck is mine. The barque barely makes a ripple as it cuts through the dark water of the East China Sea. I tie my shawl around my shoulders and lean my elbows on the wooden bow and squint at pinpricks of light in the dark; I often think they are surely too low for stars. Sarah, I know you love stargazing, but you can't imagine the blanket of diamonds in the night sky here. Sometimes I think I can smell land. You wouldn't think that land can smell, but we're skirting the coastline and during the day I sometimes spy a brief thin streak of green or black on the horizon and fancy I catch the scent of damp earthiness. Perhaps it's my imagination.

A little while ago, I was on deck, stargazing and trying to figure out the constellations, when I smelled not land this time but cigar smoke, and I realised that I was not alone. I would have been pleased to talk with John or Miss Duval (she hasn't told me her Christian name yet), but I knew neither of them smoked cigars.

Terrence Bennett must have realised that he had been discovered, and he stepped out of the shadows and made a slight bow.

'You shouldn't lurk in the shadows, Mr. Bennett,' I said to him, quite primly. I hadn't forgotten how he had laughed at me, but this time he was so charming.

'Please call me Terrence, and perhaps I could call you Sadie? I wasn't lurking. I saw you come on deck and wanted to give you some time and space to yourself. I see you're looking at the stars. Perhaps you're looking for Orion or the Plough?'

Well, he had me there – I couldn't think of anything to say except 'Yes'.

'You're looking in the wrong place, Sadie. You should be looking further north.' He put his hands on my shoulders and steered me around until I faced north. He left his hand on my shoulder and, with the other, took my hand in his and pointed toward the sky. I think he said that the constellations had been named differently, something about a Purple Forbidden Enclosure. He pointed my finger toward Ursa Major and some others whose names I don't remember. Did you ever feel a rush of blood to the head, like when you jump out of bed too quickly, and there's a noise in your ears? I stepped away from him and turned, expecting to see a grin on his face, but he wasn't even looking at me. He was engrossed in the stars. Sarah, it was the strangest thing. The whole world shrank into the ship, the glow of lamps swinging from the hooks of the masts, the water swooshing, the creak of the boards underfoot, and the absolute darkness of the night. We were a moving island.

I can't say how long we stood like that. Then he said, 'I never get tired of looking at them, do you? You know how hard it is to see the sky in London'. I didn't answer because I'd never given it a moment's thought. Then he looked deep into my eyes and said, 'It's a perfect view from here'.

I should have been haughty and walked away, but it seemed silly to take offence. After all, he was just doing exactly the same thing as I was. It's all completely innocent. I don't know why I felt – in fact still feel – uneasy about it. Uneasy and a little excited.

It's so late, I must sleep. Pao Chu and I are meeting Miss Duval and John for prayers before breakfast. Though I have never felt less like eating in all my life.

Your friend,
Sadie

CHAPTER SIXTEEN

Even after two weeks O'Dowd still found it disconcerting to wake in the bedroom he'd slept in during those unhappy years after his mother had married Mr. Sudbury. He tried to push those years to the back of his mind, but they came spilling out at odd times. He was mortified to think how uncomfortable he'd made his mother's life with his cold stares, folded arms, and tight lips.

Now he heard Michael and Gracie talking in the kitchen. He paused on the landing to eavesdrop on their conversation. Even though he hadn't been aware of any urgency for him to leave, he was still sensitive to the intrusion his staying there could provoke. But their conversation was not about him, just the ordinary chat of a couple sorting out their day. What Gracie was going to cook for dinner, what time he would be home. One of the children had a runny nose and a wheezy cough that she didn't like the sound of – all this against the background noise of pots, spoons, and plates, the smell of boiling milk and porridge.

He trod heavily on the stairs to warn them of his approach though there was no change in their conversation nor the feeling that he had interrupted anything. Everything went on as before. Gracie stirred porridge and, over her shoulder, asked O'Dowd if he'd slept well. Michael tried to wipe the snot off his son's face. 'For God's sake, where does all this stuff come from?' He folded his hankie and threw it into the ever-present pile of laundry in the corner.

O'Dowd realised he'd become part of the family; there was no standing on ceremony, no show of special attention.

He sat at the table. Young Henry edged toward him and helped himself to one of the bread soldiers that accompanied his uncle's boiled egg and grinned guiltily up at him.

'What are you up to today, Lorcan? Any new developments?' said Michael.

'Couple of things to check out. Terrence Bennett's apartment – though I don't expect to find anything of interest there. I also need to speak to Amelia Nelson again. About something that Henrietta Harper told me.'

'I can come with you if you like. I'm not due in until this afternoon.'

'Thanks, Michael. Come with me to Terrence Bennett's apartment, if you've time. You never know what another pair of eyes will spot.'

The solicitor provided O'Dowd with Terrence Bennett's address and a set of keys. According to the housekeeper, Mr. Bennett was polite and kept himself to himself when he was here, but he'd always travelled a lot and was away for long periods.

The two men walked around the neat rooms.

'Looks like he intended staying a long time in New York,' said Michael, pulling up the corner of one of the dust sheets that covered the furniture.

There were no personal items, photographs, letters, or correspondence. O'Dowd looked in drawers and cabinets and found nothing of interest.

'He must have taken all his personal papers with him,' he said. 'There's no evidence of his past in the apartment. It was almost as though he knew he wouldn't be coming back.'

'Could be anybody's,' said Michael. 'Not even a photograph. Sad way to live, that.'

O'Dowd nodded. As he pulled the door behind him, he thought of his rented room in Youghal. I suppose the same could be said about me, he thought.

Amelia Nelson answered the door at his third knock. She stood defiantly, head raised, and asked him what he wanted.

'I have a few more questions, Mrs Nelson, and I also have some news that you may find distressing. Is there anyone else here? Your daughter perhaps?'

She opened the door just enough to allow him entry, and her eyes swept along the houses opposite before she closed the door firmly behind him. He followed her to the drawing room where they sat facing each other.

'You mentioned that there was some confusion over the identity of one of the survivors. I'm sorry to have to tell you that a stewardess mistook one of the survivors for Terrence Bennett. There is absolutely no doubt that the body found off the coast of Ireland is that of Terrence Bennett.'

'Yes. I knew when I saw the photograph that it was him. It was silly of me to cling to any sort of hope.'

'I've been going over the passenger list in more detail, and I've found something, or should I say someone, that might surprise you.'

'Who?' She snapped her mouth shut quickly and seemed annoyed with herself for falling into the trap.

'Charles Morley.'

Her eyes narrowed. 'I don't believe you. He has no money to speak of. Certainly not enough for passage on the *Titanic*.'

'Be that as may, the fact of the matter is that he went aboard the *Titanic* in Southampton and was supposed to disembark in Queenstown, but it appears he stayed on board.'

She let out a short gasp. 'Did Charles … I mean, is he … alive?'

He let a beat pass. 'He survived and was taken to hospital in New York for treatment.'

'Oh, what a relief! I'm so glad.'

She seemed to paste on a smile, but the quick look of something like fear had crossed her eyes.

'I've asked Scotland Yard to request his return for questioning.'

'Why? He has nothing to do with anything. I don't see why you would drag the poor man back across the ocean to ask him questions.'

'Charles Morley was mistakenly identified as Terrence Bennett. That's too much of a coincidence for my liking. He doubtless has information relating to this case. I also think that you know what that is. Mrs. Nelson, you can tell me yourself, now, or we can wait for Mr. Morley. What's it to be?'

'I've told you already, inspector. The man arrived here saying he was the brother of Elizabeth Nelson. He didn't know she'd been dead for many years. He was distraught and I let him stay.'

'In the shed.'

'Yes, in the shed, inspector. I run a clean, respectable guest house. All the rooms were occupied. What should I have done, let him sleep in the parlour? I have Claire to think of and my own reputation. A person can sink or swim on the strength of their reputation. People talk, as well you know.' She pulled in her chin and clasped her hands together beneath her bosom as he'd often seen women do when headed for the high moral ground. 'Charles understood that completely.'

'Do you know anything about photographs? He seemed to be concerned about particular photographs,' he said.

'Who told you that? I don't know what you mean,' she said with a sniff. 'You'll have to ask him.'

'Yes, I certainly will. By the way, Claire was concerned about Mr. Morley's absence. You might let her know that he is safe and well and in hospital in New York until he recovers.'

'She'll be relieved to hear it, though I can't fathom how he got there,' she said.

'Indeed.' He held her gaze for a few moments until she blushed and looked away. He chose his next words carefully and tried to speak casually. He hadn't intended to go down this route, but it seemed as good a time as any to break the news, and it might be just the thing to surprise her into revealing something.

'You may be interested to know that Terrence Bennett has been proclaimed dead in the eyes of the law and his solicitor is in the act of carrying out his wishes in accordance with the late Mr. Bennett's last will and testimony.'

She looked up quickly and this time held his eye.

'Apart from a small bequest to the housekeeper who kept an eye on his apartment while he travelled –'

'Just like Terrence to be so considerate,' she interrupted, dabbing her eyes, though he could see no sign of tears. She held her handkerchief as tightly as her breath.

'He left everything to a Miss Sadie Bradshaw.'

She twisted her good ear toward him. Her mouth hung open.

'What?' She seemed to mistrust her hearing and watched his lips carefully.

'He left everything to a Miss Sadie Bradshaw,' he repeated. 'Have you ever heard of Miss Sadie Bradshaw, Mrs. Nelson?'

She shook her head a fraction.

'The solicitor is searching for her,' he said. 'Hopefully, she'll turn up soon. There's quite a bit of money involved.'

She blinked. 'Are you telling me that Terrence's money is going to a stranger?'

'Irish, I believe. Apparently they met in China.'

'China? Terrence hadn't been in China for years. Swore he'd never go back.'

'I was wondering about burial, Mrs. Nelson. I've been in touch with Mr. George Bennett, Terrence's brother. He's still at the Pig and Whistle. Do you know him?' She didn't respond so he continued. 'There will be some cost to having the body brought back to London and interred here. George has said he won't be in a position to pay for the repatriation, but will pay for burial in Ireland. I thought I'd let you know, in case you might be prepared to assist him with the cost of having Mr. Bennett returned and buried here.'

She looked at him coolly. 'I expect Sadie Bradshaw will help take care of the arrangements when you find her.'

'That could take some time. As far as I can tell, Miss Bradshaw might have returned to China.'

A faint hope crept into her eyes. 'What if you don't find Miss Bradshaw? What happens then?'

He pursed his lips and considered for a moment.

'Frankly, I don't have an answer to that. I'm sure Mr. Bennett's solicitor would be able to tell you.' He paused. 'You had expectations, Mrs. Nelson?'

'I wouldn't say that.' She shrugged slightly. 'But we were close. We go back … went back a long way.'

'And yet you're not mentioned in his will.'

Amelia didn't reply. She stood and said, 'Well, if that's all, inspector, I have work to do.'

She let him out with a sour expression on her face.

As the door closed behind him, he gave a satisfied grin. Just good friends, my eye, he thought. The woman was seething with jealousy but, apart from the emotional factor, she'd expected to benefit from Terrence Bennett's death, that was certain. And the mention of another woman had been a blow she hadn't seen coming. He decided he'd pushed her as far as possible, and now he'd have to wait until Charles Morley returned.

On the train home, he reread the letter he'd received from the Cork District Inspector asking how much longer he intended to stay in London. He couldn't reply straight away. The truth was he didn't know how much longer this case would take. Perhaps when he'd spoken to Charles Morley everything might be resolved and he could return to Youghal. Leaving London meant leaving Michael and Gracie and their noisy children. Somehow, he didn't look forward to returning to the large, bare room he rented in Youghal. Its best feature was that he could hear the sea at night when he tried to sleep. It was his only companion. He thought of the small brown office in the barracks with the endless lists and registers. The silence when he walked into the station or went into a public house hadn't bothered him before. But was it any kind of life? Maybe a fresh start would do him good.

The train chugged slowly to a stop, passengers got off and were replaced by new faces. He brought his mind back to the case, took out his notebook, and scribbled a few questions he wanted to ask Pao Chu about Sadie Bradshaw. Where was she most likely to be? Somewhere in Ireland without her aunt and uncle knowing? He looked around. She could be on this train for all I know, he thought, or she could be in the middle of China.

It was early evening when he got off the train and began walking to Michael's house. The evenings were getting longer, and even at seven o'clock the sun still had the strength to warm his face. She might be enjoying the same lingering evening here in London or possibly in Dublin. He doubted she would be in China, not after the revolution two years ago when all foreigners had to leave. Though, he thought, China is a vast country – it would be easy to hide there. But why would she do that? No, far more likely that she would return to her people, whomever she considered them to be. He looked forward to meeting Pao Chu soon and hearing about Sadie. He'd become curious to find out more about the girl from Rathgar and felt a kinship with her that he couldn't explain. Both fish out of water, he thought. He walked past the neat, red-bricked houses, hedges trimmed, and brasses shining. Children's voices, carefully counting each other's skipping, echoed along the street.

There was a peacefulness here that he'd never noticed when he was young. Too intent on getting back to what I was determined was 'home', he thought. Is that what Sadie Bradshaw was trying to do at that very moment? He reasoned that it didn't really concern the case: she hadn't committed a crime. Falling in love was not a crime, nor was not wanting to be found, but he wasn't prepared to have any loose ends. With a bit of luck, Pao Chu would have the answers. Having read some of Sadie's letters, he felt he knew the Chinese woman intimately. He even knew she snored.

The next day, before he left Scotland Yard, O'Dowd went through the remaining letters that Sadie had written to her friend Sarah. He was sure Sadie would have written more about Terrence Bennett to her friend. He took out the final two letters and settled himself with his feet on his desk in the empty *Titanic* investigation room.

Dear Sarah

Tonight we didn't talk about the stars. I can't say I didn't notice them. It's like trying not to see a basket of diamonds. Terrence told me about his life and his past. He's done wonderfully well. I was amazed to find that he's the son of a landlord in a public house. He has such funny stories to tell. I had to stuff my hankie into my mouth to stop laughing out loud. Well, people were trying to sleep. After all, it was the middle of the night. There is something magical about whispered words in darkness. It's easier to tell the secrets that you store in your heart. Like Catholics tell their sins in those confessional boxes.

He asked me about my childhood, and I told him about Uncle Cecil and Aunt Prudence and about Mother and Father, and I found myself talking about them. I realised that I hadn't spoken about them for so long. I told him about my mother dying so young and how my father read me stories about faraway places like China. Terrence didn't interrupt me once. He listened carefully to everything I said. I told him about the house in Dublin, and how Cecil and Pru tried awfully hard to give me a good childhood but, bless them, they were already old when I was landed on them. Their idea of good parenting was to make sure I had clean clothes, enough to eat – far too much to eat really – and attend school.

I so enjoy the chats with Terrence. He still holds my hand, points to the stars, and whispers the name of each star in my ear. I don't pull my hand away the way I used to. Finding someone so lovely is the most beautiful feeling, and I enjoy our time together.

It's not all stargazing though. During the day I meet with John, Miss Duvall and Pao Chu, and we have a prayer group. We all have dinner together. Terrence said that it would be best for me and him not to sit together as this would give rise to gossip. He worries so for my reputation. Nothing untoward has happened between us, at least not on the outside. Inside I am a different person when I step onto the deck and see him waiting for me.

I will write to you from Beijing,

My very best wishes

Your friend

Sadie

O'Dowd threw the letter on the desk and snatched up the last one.

Dear Sarah

Tientsin is the name of the port where we will disembark. Isn't it a lovely name? Like the tinkle of a little bell. This is the nearest port to Beijing.

I think Pao Chu knows about Terrence and me. She is a taciturn person, very still, and is awfully patient with me during my Chinese language lesson. She notices everything but has said nothing. Terrence and I always sit together at dinner now. He said he wants me near him every minute to the end of the journey. Have you ever heard anything so romantic? We try not to search each other out during the daytime, so by the time we sit together at the table I can barely look at anyone else. I'm positive he feels the same way about me. I've never been happier.

We haven't spoken yet about what will happen when we get to Tientsin. I know the missionary, Mr. Armstrong from Beijing, is coming to meet us from the ship, and Terrence has said he has business in Tientsin to attend. I'm sure Terrence will find a way that we can be together.

I will write again as soon as I can.

Your friend

Sadie

CHAPTER SEVENTEEN

O'Dowd passed under the red gateway to Chinatown. He wondered if the real China was like this. Coloured ribbons and balloons tugged at their strings, eager for the celebration to begin. The smell of unfamiliar spices came to him as he passed open windows along the street. He looked at the street signs, relieved to see they were in English, and went up the steps to the entrance of the three-storey building. The hall door was ajar and, when he pushed gently, it swung back. He stepped into the cool dark hallway and knocked on the first door.

When O'Dowd asked for Pao Chu, a man in a shiny blue tunic pointed upstairs.

The Chinese woman who opened the door on the second landing was small and neat. It was hard to tell her age. From the lines around her eyes and mouth, he guessed her to be in her fifties. Her black hair was pulled back in the traditional style, but the jacket and skirt she wore were western. This woman appeared to straddle two cultures. He knew how that felt.

'Are you Pao Chu?' He took his badge from his pocket and showed it to her.

He was surprised that she took it and studied it carefully. People weren't usually so fastidious. Still, she did not speak.

'Are you Pao Chu?' he asked again.

She bowed slightly and stood back to let him into the sparsely furnished room. Although the room was practically bare of furniture, every inch of wall space was covered with scrolls and paintings. Drawings of animals and birds drew his eye and black-and-white sketches of long-stalked reeds and bamboo. Chinese figures in rich reds, delicate green, and blue flower scenes brought the drab room to life.

She pointed to an old armchair, he sat into it, and she took a chair opposite. Usually, people asked why he was there, but Pao Chu watched and waited.

'I'm here about Sadie Bradshaw,' he said.

She returned his steady stare.

'You travelled to China together.'

She nodded once.

'You stayed in Beijing with her at the Armstrong's mission house.'

She nodded again. 'I thought you had questions for me, inspector.'

He found her dark eyes disconcerting and shifted a little in his chair. 'Yes, I do have questions for you, Miss Pao.'

'I'm waiting.'

'Do you know where she is?'

'No. I have not seen Sadie for several years.'

'Have you any idea where she might be?'

'Possibly in Ireland, in Dublin with her aunt and uncle? But I don't know for sure.'

'No, Miss Pao. They haven't seen her in several years.' Her

expression didn't change. 'May I ask if you know, or should I say knew Mr. Terrence Bennett?'

'He is dead?'

She asked the question calmly and showed only a raised eyebrow of curiosity without emotion.

'Yes. Miss Pao, he is dead. You don't seem surprised by that.' He watched the straight-backed woman but could not read her face.

'Would you come here to say Mr. Bennett is alive and well, inspector?'

He gave a brief smile. 'Of course you are right, Miss Pao. Mr. Bennett has died in suspicious circumstances. I'm looking to find out more about him.'

'You suspect that Sadie Bradshaw had something to do with his death?' It was a question more than a statement.

'Perhaps, Miss Pao, it would be easier if you told me what you know about Sadie.'

Pao Chu nodded once. 'I will tell you what I know. I spent a lot of time with her but can anyone say they really know someone? Especially when one's life is threatened. How can we say we will act honourably in that moment of decision when the choice is to save one's own life or to save the life of another?'

'I don't understand – whose life was in danger?'

Pao Chu looked down at her red-painted fingernails. She seemed to be considering the situation. Finally, she met O'Dowd's eyes. 'I will tell you what I know about Sadie Bradshaw, but I don't think you will like it.' She stood up. 'It is a long story. I will make tea.'

O'Dowd felt unusually comfortable in the plum-coloured armchair. Sunshine slanted through the window and shone on the black dragons in the green-tiled fireplace. The everyday noise of horse-drawn carts and barrows rumbling along cobbled streets came into the room. Chinese voices talking, shouting, and laughing came and went. The family in the room above moved about, and the smell of fried food made O'Dowd wonder what Gracie was making for dinner – he was starting to feel peckish, and she'd turned out to be an excellent cook. Michael had fallen on his feet there, but then he always had been lucky.

Pao Chu brought tea and placed it on the table between them. He wrapped his hands around the small teacup and waited while she sat in the armchair opposite.

'I didn't particularly like Sadie Bradshaw the first time I met her, inspector. She appeared to have that silliness that young western girls have, perhaps all girls have. I didn't think she was cut out to be a missionary. I said so to the C.I.M. but they insisted that she was worth investing in, that she would apply herself diligently.'

'And did she?'

Pao Chu nodded slightly. 'In her own way, yes, she did. Sadie told me she'd heard a talk by an Irish missionary named Pigott, and it was as though she'd been struck by lightning, or the Lord had spoken to her. It all sounded to me like St. Paul on the road to Damascus. A bit too dramatic. I felt, and I still feel, that she was lost. Looking to belong to someone or something. She wanted people to like her – I could tell by the way she chatted to everyone we met.'

O'Dowd was about to say that chatting to strangers was a national occupation in Ireland, but he decided to hold his tongue and let Pao Chu continue.

'The China Inland Mission asked me to take her under my wing. It's a long journey to China – endless weeks on board ship, bound to the other passengers. I've always found it trying, but Sadie drew people to her. Don't misunderstand me, inspector, she wasn't looking to be the centre of attention – she just went out of her way to make everyone's journey less tedious. We had booked passage from Macau to Beijing on a barque. We met with two people, John Robinson and Miss Duval, on their way to work at Tom and Jessie Pigotts' mission. It was also the first time that she, well, both of us, met Terrence Bennett.'

'Yes, she wrote to a friend about that.'

'Did she? Yes, I suppose it was a situation that young girls might romanticise about in letters. A tall, dark, handsome stranger in the South China sea. I preferred the company of John Robinson. He was a serious young man but kind and thoughtful. I could understand how Sadie was attracted to Terrence Bennett. I've seen the type over the years. He dressed well, spoke well, had interesting stories that I'm sure he has repeated at dinner tables across London. His eyes seemed to take in everyone at the table and judge their worth to him. Beside him John looked like the boy that he was, just twenty-three years old. By the time we were halfway through the journey, Sadie and Terrence were inseparable. They tried to be discreet, but everyone knew. It's hard to keep a secret on a ship, Inspector O'Dowd. She was in love with him or thought she was, which is, I suppose, the same thing.'

She paused and he waited.

'Now I must tell you of something I regret, inspector. I wouldn't usually interfere, but ...' She looked uneasily around as though someone might overhear. 'We were to disembark at Tientsin. I'm afraid I'd lost patience with Sadie alternating between crying and moping in the cabin. I knew the fairy-tale romance between them would end now, and real life with all its annoyances and joys must start again. But Sadie hadn't even made it out of bed. I knew the ship would dock soon and Mr. Armstrong would be waiting – it was important that Sadie make a good impression on him. But she was inconsolable. I know I shouldn't have interfered. I'm ashamed to say, inspector, that

I was concerned that I would be blamed for not chaperoning her correctly. I did the only thing I could think of.'

'What?

'I went to Terrence Bennett's cabin. He didn't appear to be uncomfortable in my presence. In fact, when he opened the cabin door he was only half dressed, bare-chested with a towel over his shoulder and a shaving razor in his hand. Everything was a joke to him. He seemed quite amused by my reaction to him and said, "I'd invite you in, Miss Pao, but it would be quite improper". I asked what he'd said to Sadie. He shrugged and said Miss Bradshaw understood that their paths must separate now. I told him that was not good enough and that a man of his experience should know better than to begin an affair with a young girl when it cannot survive. I told him that Sadie was utterly devastated and that she was about to meet Mr. Armstrong, who was known not to stand for any nonsense. A blubbering tearful girl – for that is what he had turned her into – is what he would see. Sadie would be useless to him – he had no patience for love-struck women. He'd send her back to England in disgrace. I told him all this as plainly as I could.'

'How did he react to that, Miss Pao?'

'He took a step back from me. To be fair, he did seem concerned. He said he couldn't ask her to marry him. I didn't ask why – there was no point.' Pao Chu looked down at the tea leaves in the bottom of her cup. 'Perhaps it was the wrong advice to give. I thought of only the immediate problem. I told him he didn't have to propose marriage, that all she needed was a little hope. You know, inspector, women will cling to the tiniest thread of hope, even women who should know better. I told him he had to give her reason to believe that he would come to her. I thought that as time passed she would begin to realise that his promise was false, and she would forget. I told him to go to her there and then.'

126

O'Dowd wondered if Pao Chu had ever been in love. 'And did it work?'

She shivered and moved to close the window. The colourful Chinese lanterns were ready to be lit later in the square outside. O'Dowd joined her, and together they looked at the festive red balloons bobbing in the square below. She drew the curtain quickly, her hand shaking.

On impulse, he reached out and touched her arm. She snatched it away. She looked frightened.

'Pao Chu, are you all right?'

It took her a moment to regain her composure. 'I'm not feeling very well, Inspector O'Dowd. Perhaps we could continue this tomorrow.'

'Have I said something to upset you? I'm sorry if I have.' He went over their conversation in his head. No, he felt sure he hadn't said anything to frighten her. That was the expression on her face: pure fright. He'd seen it often enough.

O'Dowd pulled the curtain back slightly and glanced outside at the square where people had begun to gather in groups, drinking and talking. No one appeared to take any notice of the window he was looking through. He couldn't see what could have upset her.

'As you wish, Miss Pao. With your permission, I will return tomorrow if that is all right and you can take up the story. You understand that Miss Bradshaw is not in trouble, she's not implicated in the death of Mr. Bennett, but I would like to find out a bit more about him. Perhaps you can help.'

Pao Chu nodded.

'I'd also like to get in touch with Miss Duval and Mr Robinson – do you have their addresses by any chance?'

'No, it's impossible.'

'They're still in China?'

'No, inspector.' She lifted her black eyes to his. 'They're dead.'

CHAPTER EIGHTEEN

Pao Chu quietly closed the door, glad to be rid of the inspector. She looked at the cold teapot and empty cups and found she couldn't find the energy to tidy them away. She sat in the plum-coloured velvet armchair and saw the people from her past appear in the shadowy twilight. She had held them back for a dozen years, and now they seeped into the corners of her room. She allowed the memories to come to the front of her mind. I should have known they would flood back, she thought, that they would swamp me. She let her head rest on the saggy armchair, pulled her legs up beneath her, and felt her body relax.

'I remember you,' she spoke to the darkness. 'I remember you all.'

She let her mind slip back again to the morning the ship docked in Tientsin.

Hubert Armstrong seemed barely able to wait for the gangplank to be lowered before he rushed on board. The sprightly man blustered toward Pao Chu and she braced for a collision. He came to an abrupt halt, lifted his hat, and took the carpetbag she was carrying in one swift movement.

'Pao Chu.' He bowed deeply. 'Delighted to see you again.' His eyes searched the deck. 'And where is Miss Bradshaw?'

'She will be with us shortly, Mr. Armstrong. She's just giving thanks to the Lord for our safe arrival.'

Mr Armstrong seemed pleased but still looked anxious.

'Very good. But we must be away soon, or we'll miss the train. I've engaged sedans. Is this all your luggage?' He held up the carpetbag.

'Yes, that is all my luggage. However,' she pointed to a large trunk surrounded by a cluster of smaller bags, 'that is Miss Bradshaw's luggage.'

At that moment, Sadie arrived, her face a little swollen and her eyes and nose an unbecoming shade of red. She managed a weak smile as Pao Chu introduced her to Mr. Armstrong.

'My poor dear, have you been ill? Sea sickness? Terrible thing, sea sickness. I remember –'

'The train, Mr. Armstrong?' said Pao Chu.

Mr. Armstrong raised his bushy grey eyebrows. 'Of course, ladies. The train. Leave it to me. You go to the sedans.'

Sadie held the handrail tightly and seemed a little dizzy when they disembarked. They climbed into the sedans – a chair inside a wooden box attached to long poles that went on the shoulders of the bearers. Pao Chu watched Sadie settle herself and knew she was masking her feelings. She wondered what Terrence Bennett had said and hoped he hadn't overstated his intentions. She prayed she'd done the right thing. Sadie will be distracted by her new life, she thought. There are so many new experiences ahead of her that soon the memory of her attachment to that man will fade and become a bittersweet memory. She watched the pale face of the young girl sitting alone. Yes, she thought, I was right to intervene. He is not the man for her.

Pao Chu leaned her head out of the sedan to look for Mr. Armstrong and caught sight of Terrence Bennett still on the deck of the ship, staring at Sadie's sedan. He wore the face of someone who thinks they are unobserved, sadness naked across his features. Pao Chu sat back quickly. She recognized that look but told herself it was too late, and even if he did have real feelings for Sadie he was not the man for her.

They reached the train without incident. As they took their seats several passengers moved quickly away from them. Sadie smiled and asked Mr. Armstrong why they were pointing at her.

'Don't worry about that, dear girl.'

'But what are they saying, Mr. Armstrong?'

Pao Chu knew what she was thinking – Sadie was very proud of her long fair hair and had often been complimented, but she had to tell her what they were really saying. She thought it would be for the best.

'They're calling you a "foreign devil",' said Pao Chu. 'You'll just have to get used to it.'

CHAPTER NINETEEN

The following morning the desk sergeant greeted O'Dowd and looked pointedly at the wall clock.

'Chief Inspector Atkinson has been looking for you. You better look sharp and report to him right away.'

'I'll just hang up my –'

'I'd go straight there if I were you.' The sergeant returned his attention to the desk diary.

Moments later, O'Dowd tapped gently on the door of the lion's den.

The Chief Inspector glanced up and pointed to a chair. He picked up what looked like a telegram. 'Who the hell is Charles Morley and why are we paying his passage to return to London?' The bulging eyes fixed on O'Dowd.

O'Dowd decided to keep his voice low and his sentences short.

'Charles Morley is the brother-in-law of the late Frederick Nelson. He arrived from Australia some months ago, and Mrs. Nelson put him up for a time.'

Atkinson sat back in his chair, a look of exasperation on his face. 'And why is this important?'

'Well, sir. It seemed an odd coincidence that Amelia Nelson's lodger should board the same ship as her 'friend' Terrence Bennett and possibly herself. She is reluctant to talk about Charles Morley. I feel there is more to this than she's saying, and I'd like to hear his side of the story. According to Miss Harper, Mr. Morley and Mrs. Nelson had an angry exchange of words just weeks before. When I told her he'd survived the disaster she didn't seem as pleased as I would have expected.'

'But you didn't tell her that he was prepared to return to speak to the police, did you?'

'I told her.' He heard the Chief Inspector's sharp intake of breath but went on. 'I hoped that the threat of Morley returning would be enough to get her to tell her side of the story before he came back. I don't think she will try to run, Chief Inspector, if that's what you're thinking.'

'I wouldn't be so sure, O'Dowd. But at least this makes sense now.' Atkinson pushed the telegram toward him.

O'Dowd read the printed words.

'CHARLES MORLEY HAS DISAPPEARED FROM THE HOSPITAL. WE HAVE LOST TRACK OF HIM.'

The Chief Inspector leaned on his elbows. 'I doubt we will ever see the man again. If he's the only witness you have against Mrs. Nelson, I would say your luck's just run out, along with Charles Morley.'

After a late supper, O'Dowd and Michael sat each side of the hearth.

'So, don't you think it's likely that Mrs Nelson and Morley were in it together?' said Michael. 'I agree there doesn't seem to be an obvious reason for Morley to do away with Bennett unless there's something that Mrs. Nelson isn't saying.'

'I've never felt like she's told me the absolute truth – they could very easily be in it together. She's a tricky customer, is our Mrs Nelson,' said O'Dowd.

'You're starting to sound more English than I am,' said his brother.

'Really? I'd better knock that on the head before I go back.'

'Do you have to go back, Lorcan? I don't see why you can't get transferred here.'

The fire shifted in the grate, and a brief display of sparks flew up the chimney.

O'Dowd wriggled his toes and noticed a slight tear in his sock. He sighed. 'I have to go back. My life is there.'

'I haven't heard you talk about anyone, about missing anyone. At least here you have family,' said Michael.

'We'll talk about it when I've got to the bottom of this case. Now, just listen to me. We know that Amelia Nelson and Terrence Bennett were very close. Go back a long way. Why aren't they married? There's a reason, could be anything. Maybe he was already married, or he was leading her on and has been for years. Then she somehow hears about this other woman, Sadie Bradshaw. She'd see her as a threat to her position in Terrence's life and possibly a threat to her inheriting all his money.'

'She might not have known about his will though.'

'Let's say she did. She's furious. And when she hears that he's going to America she sees her chance. She gets to Southampton with Charles. Terrence suspects nothing but that night she poisons him. Charles is there to help her dispose of the body and she gets off the ship in Ireland.'

Michael raked the dying fire. 'But what does Charles get out of all this?'

O'Dowd sat back. 'What *does* Charles get out of all this? Why would Charles help Amelia?'

The two men sat in silence, watching the embers glow as they weighed up the possibilities. Yes, it was plausible, but O'Dowd remembered Amelia's face when he confirmed that Terrence was dead. There was genuine grief there. He was in no doubt that Amelia had loved Terrence, but there's a fine line between love and hate, and when you add jealousy into the mix it becomes even more toxic.

Michael nodded. 'It looks like she did it all for nothing. Risked everything, and now Sadie Bradshaw will inherit. Lorcan, what would you do if you were her?'

'You think she'll run,' said O'Dowd, 'but I don't. Anyway, I don't have enough evidence that ties her to the *Titanic*. Not one single person can link her to the ship, except for the reporter she spoke to. He's another one who's disappeared.'

'Really? Didn't they send someone to the newspaper in Nottingham?'

'They did. Turns out he's freelance and the editor said he's spoken about going to America. They're still trying to trace him.'

'Doesn't leave you any option. You're going to have to bring her back in. She might crack under pressure.'

'I'll send a constable for her tomorrow afternoon. That will annoy her enough to stir things up.' O'Dowd pictured her deep frown. 'It's going to be a long day.'

CHAPTER TWENTY

It was warm outside, but Inspector O'Dowd felt an involuntarily shiver ripple down his spine. He wasn't sure if it was the building itself or the stare from Amelia Nelson that chilled him as he took a chair opposite her. A constable sat beside him, foolscap pages, pen and ink ready to take notes of the interview. O'Dowd waited while the constable carefully wrote the date and the names of the people present.

'Mrs Nelson …' He risked looking into her eyes; she looked coldly back at him. 'Thank you for coming in.'

'I didn't have much of a choice, did I?' She leaned toward him and dropped her voice. 'I'm mortified. In broad daylight the constable came, and the whole street stood standing on doorsteps watching me. I'll never forgive you. I answered every question and this is how you treat me.'

'There are still a few things, Mrs Nelson, that need clarifying. So can we go over the facts and perhaps get a clearer picture of the events leading to the death of Terrence Bennett?'

His words hung in the air as she produced a lace-trimmed

handkerchief. He let a moment pass while she settled herself. Then he opened the file in front of him.

'Let's start by looking at what we know.' He gave her a brief smile and hoped it might warm the chill that seemed to surround her. 'Sometime early this year, Terrence Bennett bought a first-class ticket to travel to New York on the *Titanic* at the cost of twenty-six pounds. He was assigned a cabin on A deck. At the same time, he purchased a first-class crossing ticket in your name at a cost of four pounds.'

She shrugged. 'There's nothing wrong with that. Terrence was a very generous man.'

O'Dowd went on. 'Several boat trains carrying the passengers left Waterloo station throughout the morning. There were several boarding registers, depending on which deck you boarded. You had to show your ticket to one of the clerks, then your name was entered onto one of the passenger register lists.'

'I wouldn't know because I wasn't there.'

'I've seen the register that includes your name.'

'Well, it's a mistake of some sort. I was at home, with a bad headache.'

'So you say. And the ticket that Terrence Bennett gave you?'

'There was a ticket, but I can't seem to find it. I'm sure it'll turn up ...'

O'Dowd let the silence drag on for a few moments. She didn't fidget or look around.

'Whose idea was it for Charles Morley to go with you to Southampton?'

'I didn't know he'd gone anywhere. Not until days later.'

'You didn't know he was gone, even though you claim to have been in the house alone for two days. You're saying that it didn't strike you as odd that he wasn't around.'

'I was ill. I ...'

'I suggest that you and Charles Morley planned this whole thing together. Terrence Bennett had been using you for years. Treating you as someone to, let's say, fulfil his desires. Perhaps you were in love with him until you found that he was deeply involved with another woman.' Amelia looked as though she'd been slapped across the face, but he continued. 'The solicitor told me that Terrence Bennett had mentioned changing his will previously. He intended to wait until he returned from New York, but something changed his mind – what that was we may never know – but, the fact is, he visited his solicitor the day before he sailed. He changed his will and left everything to Sadie Bradshaw. I suspect you didn't know that you were already too late.'

'I don't know what you're talking about.' She appeared calm, but the vein in her temple throbbed.

'You must have felt such a fool,' said O'Dowd. 'Waiting for him to return from whatever jaunt he was on. Sleeping in your bed. While you waited for a proposal that would never come. *Hell hath no fury.* Tell me, how did you find out about Sadie Bradshaw?'

'If you remember, inspector, it was *you* who told me. I'd never heard her name before.'

O'Dowd ran his finger around his collar; the temperature in the small room was rising.

'And there was penniless Charles Morley who you somehow convinced to help you get rid of Bennett. You produced the poison, enough to make him drowsy, easy to handle. If anyone saw the three of you on deck they would think he'd had too much to drink or was seasick. No one would have looked twice. That was the plan, wasn't it? Charles could heave him off the ship – it would look like a drowning.'

'No, none of that's true. You can't really believe that I'd –'

'You disembarked at Queenstown and, as luck would have it, you had only to wait an hour or so for a ship travelling to Southampton.

The *Agatha Maria*, as it happens. I spoke to the captain. He doesn't remember you specifically, though he remembers a woman in a black veil. He showed me the ship's register, and there you are again, Amelia Nelson. You arrived back in Southampton that evening. You'd been gone only thirty-six hours. An early train back to London and you slipped back into your house on Friday morning.'

He saw the colour deepen in her cheeks, but her eyes were steely. 'Inspector, you're going to feel such a fool when Charles gets here and tells you that you're completely wrong.'

The interview continued. Amelia said very little. She repeated that she'd been at home with a severe headache on the 10th of April. Time ticked away without progress. O'Dowd asked the constable to bring some tea and water. They sipped the tea silently; a bluebottle flew around their heads and landed on the window. The buzzing sound echoed around the room. The constable tapped his pen against the glass ink bottle as he read over the notes he'd taken.

O'Dowd cleared his throat.

'Now, where were we, Mrs. Nelson?'

'You were concocting a ridiculous story, a fairy tale. I was at my house the entire time.'

'So you say, but you don't have any witnesses. Not one single person can vouch for you during those forty-eight hours.'

'Not one single person can say they saw me on board that ship because I wasn't there.'

'Had the ship not sunk, we could have had many witnesses.'

'Are you blaming me for that too? I wouldn't put it past you.' She threw her eyes to the ceiling.

'You spoke to a reporter at Queenstown. Don't you remember that?' He produced a copy of the *Nottingham Herald* and pushed it across the table to her. 'The article says that a local woman, Amelia Nelson, née Lee, escaped the sinking of the *Titanic* as she disembarked at Queenstown.'

'I've already told you I'd never have said I was meeting Frederick, inspector.' She lifted her chin as she spoke, but O'Dowd saw the shadow of fear in her eyes.

'You might have said that purposely to divert our attention from you.'

She pursed her lips and sat in silence. The buzzing bluebottle flew around their heads and returned to the window. The buzzing increased as it banged frantically against the glass.

O'Dowd waited while the constable blotted the page.

'Tell me again where everyone was for those two days.'

She sighed deeply. 'Again? How many times ? All right. Claire was visiting my sister in Leeds. She left on the previous Saturday and wasn't due back for a week. Henrietta went to Winchester to do the brass rubbings that she's so interested in. How she doesn't catch her death in those draughty old churches I'll never know. I'd told Terrence I wouldn't use the ticket. I get severe sea sickness even just stepping onto a boat. Going on the ship seemed a waste of time. I told him to give the ticket to someone else, or get a refund. Typical Terrence – never could take 'no' for an answer. I'm sure he fully thought I'd arrive at the last minute.' She lifted her face to the inspector. 'I didn't though. I'd planned on giving the house a good spring clean. The cat is such a nuisance at this time of year, shedding everywhere and clawing at rugs. But she's a good mouser, that's why I keep her. I wasn't so well on Tuesday and Henrietta offered to stay. I was sure I'd be all right after a good night's sleep but I wasn't. I couldn't lift my head from the pillow. I slept most of the time, I had no idea of night or day. The curtains were drawn. Ask the neighbours.'

'We did. According to many of them, your curtains were drawn. They assumed you'd gone away for a few days.' He leaned in for the kill. 'Amelia, time is not on your side. Charles Morley is being escorted back to England as we speak. Today he is mid-Atlantic and each hour that passes brings him closer. In a matter of days he'll be here and I, for one, will be very interested to hear what he has to say.' He stood and hooked his thumbs into his waistcoat. 'If I were you, I'd get my side of the story in first. That is, unless you are absolutely sure of what Mr. Morley is going to tell us.' He leaned forward and brought his face close to hers. 'Are you absolutely sure that Charles Morley will back you up, Amelia? Your very life might depend on it.'

The blue veins stood out in her white neck as she silently swallowed. She held his gaze for a moment. He could almost see her brain working furiously, looking for a way out. He'd witnessed this panicked reaction before as criminals felt the net tighten around them.

She asked for another glass of water, and O'Dowd retook his seat and nodded to the constable. When the door closed behind him, Amelia surprised O'Dowd by stretching her hand out as if to touch him. He kept still. She left her hand on the table and searched his eyes with hers.

'Inspector,' she whispered, 'you're right. There is something.'

The door opened, and the constable came in and placed the glass in front of Amelia. Her hand shook as she reached for it and brought it to her lips. She barely took a sip.

'You were saying, Mrs. Nelson?' said O'Dowd.

The constable took up his pen, dipped the nib carefully into the ink, and waited.

'I want to tell you, just you. I don't want this written down.' She looked toward the window. 'Can't you get rid of that terrible buzzing?'

'What do you want to tell me, Mrs. Nelson?'

'I'll tell you everything, the whole truth. I swear I will. But does he have to be here?' She nodded toward the constable, who sat solidly in his chair.

'The constable must write down everything you say. That's his job.'

She glanced at the young constable with narrowed eyes. 'Make sure you get it the way I say it.' She tapped her fingernail on the table as she spoke. 'Don't go adding anything else in. I can read, you know.'

The constable nodded, his pen poised.

'It was all Frederick's fault,' she said, watching as the constable wrote the words.

'Your husband has been dead for twelve years,' said O'Dowd

'Do you think I don't know when my husband died? Thank you very much. What I'm saying is that he started it all.'

'Started what?'

'Everything. I'll have to tell you from the beginning, or it won't make sense.'

CHAPTER TWENTY-ONE

O'Dowd rubbed his forehead. 'All right, if that's what you want.' It was easier to let her tell the story her own way. He'd often found that suspects gave away more details in a free-flowing interview than in a question-and-answer session.

Amelia paused and fiddled with her handkerchief.

'Of course, a blind man could have seen it, inspector, but I didn't. It should have been so obvious but I missed it. I'm far better at seeing the goings-on in other people's lives. It wasn't until the following week when Terrence hadn't been in touch, that the penny, and my heart, dropped. Has that ever happened to you? It doesn't drop like a stone, does it? It slides slowly like spit down a wall.'

'I'm sorry, Mrs Nelson,' said O'Dowd. 'You said it was obvious, but what is it that was obvious? Can you elaborate? What exactly am I missing here?'

'Terrence asked me out, and then introduced me to Frederick – as if it was accidental. I should have known that Terrence Bennett wouldn't be bothered with a shadow of a girl like me. What had I got to attract him, small and plain and tongue-tied? He was out in the world meeting people high-up in business. He stayed in hotels, for heaven's sake. Hotels! I'd not been across the threshold of a hotel in my life.' A grimace crossed her face. 'So how did I come to realise that things were not as I hoped? It was when Frederick appeared at the gate of the mill. I saw him before he caught sight of me in the sea of faces swarming out into the warm smoky dusk. He held a handkerchief across his mouth against the smut from the chimney. He looked out of place against the red-brick wall. I thought he must be waiting to meet Terrence, and I looked around the crowds in hope, but there was no sign of him. Then Frederick saw me and tipped his hat. He didn't even try to pretend it was a coincidence. It was obvious that bumping into me and Terrence in the park had been a farce. It was arranged between them. Frederick's moustache and sideburns were trimmed. He looked fresher, still not young – he was forty but not unattractive. His suit was made of fine tweed, and his oxblood leather shoes gleamed. He carried a silver-topped cane, though he didn't lean on it. He offered me his arm and asked if he could escort me home. He had a shy smile, just visible through the reduced moustache. I didn't know what else to do so I took his arm, mortified at the comments of my passing workmates, which he seemed not to hear. I was both flattered and unsettled. What girl wouldn't be flattered to have a man waiting for her? Especially in Nottingham.'

'Why especially in Nottingham?'

'Girls outnumbered men eight to one. And it was for exactly that very same reason that I was unsettled. Why me? Why did he choose me from so many?'

O'Dowd was wondering the very same thing. 'And your parents agreed to this ... arrangement?'

'Frederick could be a very persuasive man. The first time he came to our cottage he brought tea from China. Even years later, my mother often commented on the extravagance – it was something impressive to tell the neighbours. He said it was no trouble at all, that he "still had connections in the trade". I swear my mother's smile went from ear to ear when she took in the polished leather shoes, the tweed suit, and the silver-topped cane. She decided to overlook his lack of youth. What was youth compared to a man "who had connections"?

'And then you married him.' O'Dowd tried to gently hurry her along.

'Not the first time he asked. We'd only been stepping out two months the first time. I might never have married him except for … well, two things really.'

'What two things were those?'

'I wasn't over Terrence. Word in the mill was that he'd left, but nobody knew to where. I was desperate to find out, and one evening I asked Frederick. He looked a bit uncomfortable but told me Terrence had started a new job as a tea trader – in fact, he'd recommended him for the job. Terrence had been sent to India to learn the trade, and Frederick didn't know if he'd ever be back.' She pressed her lips together and looked embarrassed that she'd given herself away. 'I'll never forget that moment. I felt as though he'd died. Terrence was gone, and my heart broke.'

She threw her head back and gave a harsh laugh that startled the constable. The laughter, the inspector knew, was at herself, her younger self's foolish dreams. He saw the deep sadness in her eyes; she lifted her chin and struggled to pull her mouth into a straight line.

'That was the first reason,' he said. 'What was the second?'

She took a deep steadying breath. 'The mill,' she whispered. 'Frederick was clever – he found my weakness and worked at it.'

'Your weakness? What do you mean?'

'Have you ever been to any of the big mill towns like Manchester or Nottingham, inspector?'

'Can't say I have.'

'It was as though he was obsessed with the mills. Though not about how they worked, or what they made, or how much they were worth.'

'I don't understand.'

'He asked about the accidents. Every time I saw him, he'd say, "Tell me, any accidents this week?" There'd always be some accidents with so many people packed in together. It can't be helped. If you're ever in a mill town, you'll see people begging on the streets, missing an arm, maybe a hand, or a leg. He was very good at giving money to beggars. I think he made a point of it when I was with him. Then one day he said to me "Amelia, I worry about you". That caught my attention, no one had ever said they worried about me before. He nodded towards a one-legged beggar. "I see people like him, women too, all over the streets of Nottingham and Manchester," he said. "Casualties from a war fought indoors. The merchants' war. I see them every day, begging for bread. There's no help from the mill owners. Only whatever their family can spare. Amelia, what if something were to happen to you? Have you ever thought about that? What if you lost a hand, an arm maybe? Who would look after you?" It was as if he'd looked into my mind, into my darkest fears. I told him my family would take care of me. I made my voice sound surer than I felt, but he had an answer for everything. "Of course, they would, at first," he said. "I'm sure they'd do everything they could. But as the months and years went on, your brothers and sisters would marry, and your parents become tired and old ..." His hand tightened over mine. 'You're a young woman, Amelia, your whole life before you. You deserve to enjoy it, not risk it for a few shillings. I will look after you, always. If you will let me?' I hoped he'd finished. But he went on. "I don't mean to startle you, Amelia, or rush

145

you. Perhaps you feel I'm too old for you?" You can see what he was offering me, inspector. An end to any worry over money, a life of ease, and my family secure. Do you know what that's like, to have the fate of your family in your power?'

O'Dowd didn't respond. The room was dimmer, the corners bathed in forgiving darkness.

Her voice dropped to a whisper. 'We'd known each other barely three months. I remember how tightly he held my hand. He begged me to think about it, and I said I would. He made me promise, and only then he loosened his grip. I was so young and inexperienced. I didn't know what to think or how to act. You see, it wasn't only me that worked for the mill. Mother and Trinny took in piecework. The Missus brought a load every couple of days. We never knew her real name – there were many women called 'The Missus'. Mother and Trinny spent their day sewing tiny embellishments onto gloves. Trinny already needed glasses, and she was only fifteen. It seemed to me that even if the mill didn't get a finger or hand from you, it would still take your hearing or eyesight – it got a piece of everyone. But I had a way out for all of us. Trinny wouldn't have to ruin her eyesight, mother could stop the piecework. And for me too. I wouldn't ever have to hear the morning whistle of the factory, the shuffle of the clogs on the cobblestones all heading towards the mill, or the sound of the doors bolted when we got inside. I would never have to worry again.' She found his eyes. 'At least, that's what I thought at the time.'

She paused, eyes downcast.

'And did your family encourage you?' O'Dowd prompted.

'Of course. Mother wasted no time in informing the neighbours, and people looked at me with new eyes. I was no longer the plain, slight girl going to and from the mill daily. Now I was 'the intended' of a man of some worth. How much worth was unclear – to everyone, including me. I'd known Frederick only six months altogether when we were pronounced man and wife and moved to his new house in Reigate.' She leaned toward the constable. 'That's in Surrey,' she said and watched as he wrote it down. 'It was bigger than the whole row of cottages in Nottingham and three times as high. We had a cook and a maid and a kitchen girl. I was as wary of them as they were of me, but I got on well enough with the housemaid, Nancy – mainly because she didn't seem to expect me to know much about the running of a house and planning meals and the like. Cook was happy enough to do all that. Are you married, inspector?'

She caught him unawares, and it took him a split second to hide his surprise. 'No, Mrs. Nelson, I'm not.'

'Funny thing, marriage, isn't it? Women spend all their time wanting to be married and when they are they're …'

'They're what, Mrs. Nelson?'

She shrugged. 'I don't know really – disappointed isn't what I mean. Everything settles into a routine. Not unpleasant exactly, but every day seemed to be the same as the one before. Like in the mill, only more comfortable. Frederick took the train to London every morning and I quite liked the novelty of being in our new house. I took up lacemaking by hand again, bought all the coloured bobbins and threads, and would spend an hour or so every day making little doilies and the like. Everything was fine until the dresses arrived.'

'I'm sorry, did you say dresses?'

She nodded. 'Boxes of them. At first, I thought they were new dresses, but when I pulled them out and examined the necks and cuffs, I could see they'd been worn. I knew at once whose they were, and I told Nancy not to unpack them.'

'And whose were they?' asked O'Dowd.

She rolled her eyes as though he was a simpleton. 'For heaven's sake, inspector, they were Elizabeth's – the *first* Mrs. Nelson's. Had to be. I challenged him as soon as he got home but he wasn't in the least sorry. He asked what was wrong with them – they'd hardly been worn. I could see what he meant – they were almost new. I hadn't been brought up to throw away decent clothes, and I was a new wife. I didn't want to upset Frederick. I asked how long they'd been in storage – there wasn't a smell of camphor from them. "Since Elizabeth died," he said from behind his newspaper. I knew there was something not right. You see, I'd assumed that he'd been a widower for a few years. I hadn't wanted to talk about the woman I was replacing and he didn't offer much information. When I asked him the question again, he put down the newspaper and said "Eight months". Eight months, inspector! That meant he'd begun courting me only a few weeks after she died. I felt a bit odd, I can tell you. I asked him to tell me about her. "Too painful," he said. And he wouldn't talk about it again, inspector. Not ever. I decided to make the best of it and made some new lace collars and cuffs to change the look of the dresses but I never felt right wearing them. People admired the lace, but I didn't admit that I'd done it myself. No, that would have been frowned on. All these strange little rules that polite society lives by. I suppose we all have those, don't we? Things we don't allow ourselves for whatever reason.'

'And then?' prompted O'Dowd.

'Well, a few weeks later, Frederick said he wanted us to have our photograph taken. I didn't care one way or the other, but I was glad for a day out in London. He said I should wear the pale-blue dress and jacket and a hat with a veil. He knew more about these things than I did, as he said. He'd made the appointment at a studio in Shepherd Street. The camera stood high on a tripod, aimed at a small table and an upright chair. Fred was all business. He spoke to Mr. Jerome about how the photograph should look. He wanted me to wear the veil pulled down slightly. He fussed and changed my pose, the tilt of my head, the direction of my gaze, saying it would look so much better this way and that. He began to tease out some of the nettings on the side of my bonnet across my face – I thought it must be because my face wasn't pretty enough for the photograph and felt embarrassed – and he twisted the pearls at my neck to show the ruby clasp. "That's better, isn't it, Mr. Jerome?" The photographer must have taken a dozen photographs, some with both of us but most of me alone. Arrangements were made to collect the pictures in a few days and, before long, we were outside, blinking in the bright sunshine. Frederick seemed calmer now that we had left the studio. He was back to his usual self. He pulled my hand through the crook of his arm as he told me of the lovely restaurant he'd booked – a table by the window. I tried to work out why he would take such trouble hiding my face in a photograph and minutes later display me in the restaurant window for all to see.' She sighed. 'We were married ten years and had three children when he died. He was only fifty-two. It took a long time for me to find out what he was up to. A very long time it was. It was only after he was dead that the whole thing came out.'

After a long pause where she didn't seem inclined to continue, O'Dowd said, 'What exactly was it that came out after your husband's death, Mrs. Nelson?' He couldn't decide if this woman was telling the truth or fabricating a complete lie. He had always found questioning men easier – though perhaps not in Cork, where they always answered a question with a question. But in fairness, usually, you knew where you were with men. There were no fluttering handkerchiefs, quivering lips, and definitely no swooning. Sometimes there were tears, he'd concede that, but men didn't cry for effect, didn't cry prettily or dab at their eyes.

'This is very hard for me, inspector.'

'Perhaps another cup of tea?' said O'Dowd.

She shook her head and said she'd carry on. He felt the beginning of a headache and ran his palm along his forehead. The room was stuffy so he asked the constable to open a window and was glad of the gentle breeze.

'It was only after he died that I realised how little I knew about his finances. Frederick had taken care of everything, and it never occurred to me to ask. After all, he'd promised me a life free of concern and I believed that he would have made any arrangements necessary.' She sighed and looked down at her hands folded in her lap. 'I had no idea that he was losing money hand over fist.'

'I'm sorry,' said O'Dowd. 'How did you manage?'

'Frederick was dead and buried three weeks when Terry Bennett knocked on my door. He said he was just back from India and had only just heard about Frederick. He said he'd be going to China in a few months. I think he was genuinely sad about Frederick's passing, and he asked how I'd manage. I hadn't given any real thought as to what my life and my children's lives would be like without their father. I assumed my life without Frederick would go on much as it had with him. I was still in shock, not thinking at all. Terry asked several times if I'd seen the solicitor and when he was coming. I was a little peeved that it had taken him so long to come and told him I didn't need his help. He didn't like that at all. Terry wanted to be in control. He became pretty snippy with me. He said that I might feel quite differently after I'd spoken with the solicitor. I thought he was being petty. He commented on the pearls I was wearing. He sort of smirked and asked if I knew that they'd belonged to Frederick's first wife. He could be a bit cruel like that. Then he asked if I'd ever seen a likeness of the first Mrs. Nelson? I didn't know what he was trying to get at. I told him that Frederick felt it was too painful for him and unfair to me. He circled the room, picking up things and putting them down again as though he was trying to make up his mind about something. Eventually, he sat beside me. He was all charm and sympathy again. "Let me make a guess. I would put money on it that Frederick took you to a photographer's studio every year. Maybe in London?" He knew, inspector, he knew all about how Frederick was particular about how I looked in those pictures. He suggested I should find a photograph of Fredrick's first wife. He bent his head to my ear. I felt his breath on my neck. "I'll come back tomorrow after you've spoken to the solicitor. We'll talk then," he said.'

O'Dowd began to get an inkling of where her story was heading.

'As soon as he was gone, I went into Frederick's study. It was the first time I'd ventured in since his death. The desk drawers held piles of bills, letters from the bank, and files of documents that looked important, but I could find nothing that made any sense to me. But the safe held the strangest things of all. Photographs that had been taken of me and Frederick while we were married. Why would they be at the back of the safe? Then I found an envelope with even more photographs. Frederick with his first wife, Elizabeth. She was seated beside a small table, with her head turned toward the camera. I recognized her. She had the same smile, the same frown on her face, the tilt of her chin, the shape of her body. She looked almost exactly like me. I recognized her dress – it was the green-and-gold dress that hung in my wardrobe. Her hair was dark, but the likeness was extraordinary. She looked like my twin sister.'

O'Dowd watched her face as she told the story. The words tumbled out of her, without hesitation, as if she were simply telling the truth.

'Inspector, I didn't know what to think. Had Frederick married me because I looked like his dead wife? Was his grief so great that he couldn't bear to be parted from her? Was I taken in as a living memory, a replacement? All those years he had pretended he loved me. Then I thought of him playing with the children, his joy apparent. I'd given him the only thing that Elizabeth couldn't. His children made him happy. But did I make him happy? Did he love me even a little? And why the photographs? The only thing I knew for sure was that my whole marriage had been a lie.'

She looked at O'Dowd questioningly but he didn't know how to respond.

'Terrence came back the next day. I produced the photographs and spread them out on the table. Of course he wasn't in the least surprised. Clearly, he knew more about what was happening in Frederick's life than I did. I asked him to tell me everything. He made himself comfortable on the sofa. "I was only trying to help a friend," he said. "Frederick was so grief-stricken I had to do something. I'd seen you in the mill before Elizabeth died. I'd mentioned the likeness between you and Elizabeth to him. It was only afterward, after her death, that I thought of it." I asked, "Thought of what?" Terrence shrugged. "That he might like to spend some time with you and it would ease his suffering. You know, console him in some way. I'd never seen a man so distraught as he was when she died." He flicked at his sleeve as though brushing away specks of dust, then lifted his head and smiled at me. That smile still made me tremble a little. But years had passed, and I was no longer the innocent mill worker who took him at his word. I'd often noticed that he flicked at imaginary dust when playing cards. It usually meant he was bluffing. I told him I didn't believe a word of it and that he'd better come up with the truth straight away.'

'And did he?' said O'Dowd.

'He was very good at reading people. He seemed to be able to find any weakness, any need, and supply the answer. He did it all so charmingly, as though he had my welfare at heart. Even though I thought I knew him so well, he was already one step ahead of me. He gave the impression that I'd got the better of him, sat beside me, and said he'd tell me everything. "Frederick and Elizabeth were childhood sweethearts in Gloucester," he said. "They both came from working-class families, but her father was arrested when Elizabeth was just a baby. He was sentenced to twenty years hard labour in Australia. It might as well have been a death sentence – for him and his family. When he was released, Mr. Morley wandered around New South Wales. Gold had been found there, and he tried his hand at it. Turned out to be a lucky strike for him. He wrote to his wife and told her he wouldn't be coming home, but he intended to provide for her and Elizabeth as long as they lived. He asked that a photograph of Elizabeth be sent to him every year, and he would arrange for money to be sent to them. That was the deal. By then, Elizabeth had married Frederick. Each year her photograph was taken, and it was sent to her father, and the money arrived. Frederick was able to buy into the tea trade and become a tea merchant. He began investing in railways and other schemes. For a long time, he was lucky, seemed to have a gift for it – making money, and their lives would have been perfect except for one thing.'

'Elizabeth's health?'

'She was in her mid-thirties when she died but had never been in the best of health. She couldn't have children. Things had already begun to go badly with Frederick's investments. He was reckless. Several railways in America went under, and he quickly lost a great deal of money. Without the money from Australia, he wouldn't be able to cover his debts. Frederick was desperate, then he remembered what Terrence had said about me and how like Elizabeth I was. Between them, they put together a plan so that Frederick could continue to get the money from Elizabeth's father by putting me in the photographs with Frederick.'

'That was a terrible thing to discover, Mrs. Nelson. I'm sorry.'

'Yes, it was. But actually better than learning he had an unhealthy obsession with his first wife and used me to indulge it. And I now firmly believe that Frederick loved me in his own way.'

'So it was only after Frederick's death that you realised what was going on. Is that what you're telling me? Why did Terrence tell you about it? He must have realised that if it came out you would be implicated in the crime of fraud.'

'But I knew nothing!'

'So you say. But you'd been swindling someone for years.' O'Dowd leaned toward her. 'Did he attempt to blackmail you in return for his silence?'

The frown on Amelia's forehead deepened. 'No,' she whispered. 'Terrence would never do that to me.'

CHAPTER TWENTY-TWO

O'Dowd's instinct told him that Amelia Nelson was still hiding something, but she had said all she was going to say. As far as Chief Inspector Atkinson in Scotland Yard was concerned, that was tantamount to pleading guilty, but O'Dowd wouldn't charge her.

Amelia's defence was flimsy, and there was the question of motive, or to be exact, lack of motive. Amelia stuck to her story or at least the part of the story she chose to reveal. O'Dowd tried to get to the bottom of it, suspected it was something to do with Charles Morley, but she remained tight-lipped. That was why he'd refused to arrest her, which landed him in front of Chief Inspector Atkinson.

'There is enough evidence to bring Mrs. Nelson to trial for murder,' the Chief Inspector said.

'I'm sorry, sir, I don't think it will stick. Unless the Americans can find Charles Morley and have him brought back, then we just don't have enough.'

'Well, I'm not prepared to let a murderer walk free – even if she is a woman. What sort of message will that send? If we can't get Charles

Morley there must be someone who saw her in Queenstown. She had to make her way back to London. Somebody must have seen her.'

'There are people who saw a woman. But no one can absolutely swear that it was her. There's still no sign of the reporter.'

Atkinson puffed on his pipe for a moment. 'I think you've taken it as far as you can, O'Dowd. I'm going to assign more manpower to this. After all, the victim is English and the suspect is English, the fact that the body was found in Ireland doesn't affect the case one way or the other. We'll take it from here. You've done your best, no hard feelings.'

He held out his hand, and O'Dowd could do nothing but take it. The Chief called in D.I. Peter Lyons, made the briefest of introductions, and told O'Dowd to hand over everything to do with the case to him. An hour later, he was on the street outside Scotland Yard with no reason to stay in London.

O'Dowd looked over the rail of the ship into the depths of the sea. He was on his way back to Ireland, which he felt should please him, but the case still niggled at him. He turned it over again in his mind but still couldn't see how he could have handled it differently. Perhaps if I'd had more time, he thought. The seagulls flew alongside, but there was no sign of land yet. He used his coat to shield a match from the wind and managed to light a cigarette. What is it that she wouldn't tell me?

Michael had raged at the injustice of it all. 'They shouldn't have taken the case away from you. You'd have found a way to make her confess, wouldn't you? You're not thinking of going back, are you?'

'I don't have a choice. I told you before – that's where my life is.' As he spoke, he thought of the reception he'd receive.

He had no option but to return to Youghal, to the questioning eyebrows of his men and the whispering women gathered in the washhouse, sideways glances, probably wondering if he'd fallen in love with the woman and wouldn't see her hang for her crimes. That'd be the sort of thinking they'd come up with.

The night before he left Michael took him for the last drink in the Dog and Duck. He said he had a proposition to make. He tried to persuade O'Dowd to give up the Royal Irish Constabulary and come to London.

'To do what exactly, join the London Met?'

Michael rested his elbows on his knees and looked around the almost empty pub. 'I was thinking more in the line of us joining forces, maybe in a private capacity. We'd work well together. I know we would. *Sudbury and O'Dowd, Private Investigators.* What do you think?'

O'Dowd put his hand on Michael's shoulder. 'We would make a good team, but it's not the right time. The Home Rule bill is in jeopardy and that will cause a fair bit of unrest all over Ireland. It's not the time for me to pull out of the police force. But you know, Michael, maybe sometime in the future it might be an option for us. Who knows?'

Michael seemed happy enough with that. He said he'd write if he heard anything about the case and would keep an eye on the news and send him the clippings. Either way, they were going to keep in touch.

'Let me know as soon as you hear the trial date. I'd like to come back for it.'

'But they haven't even arrested her,' said Michael.

'Only a matter of time, I'd say. The chief is convinced she's guilty and she really doesn't have any sort of alibi to speak of.'

That morning he wrote a short letter to Pao Chu, explaining that he had to return to Ireland and thanking her for her cooperation. He said goodbye to Michael, Gracie, and the children and took the boat train to Holyhead, wondering when he'd return.

Pao Chu waited quietly in her apartment for the knock on the door. When it came, it was not the inspector. A constable handed her a note. She could feel his curious eyes on her as she read.

'He's most terribly sorry, ma'am. He's had to return to Ireland.'

She saw his eyes stray to the interior of her flat.

'I said I'd call to make sure you got the note and his apologies.'

'Thank you, constable.' She closed the door on the eager young policeman and sat at the table strewn with photographs she hadn't been able to look at for several years. She picked up one of two women. Edith and Ruth stared back at her, their eyes fixed on the camera, a slight smile on Edith's face. She picked up another taken in the hospital compound in Taiyuan. A group of missionaries, doctors, Chinese converts, and patients had gathered before an outing. She thought she remembered it being a summer picnic. She ran her finger across the smiling faces; some shielded their eyes from the sun. The pain in her chest grew until she couldn't look at them anymore. She put the pictures back in the tin box with the other small mementos, disappointed that he wouldn't be coming today. She'd decided to be truthful, but there were some things that she'd never before put into words, never spoken aloud. Awful, terrible things that sat in the back of her mind. The time had come to pull them from the darkness.

PART TWO

CHAPTER TWENTY-THREE

Beijing 1899

They sat close together in the rickshaw as it bumped along the uneven ground. Mr. Armstrong followed in the rickshaw behind, and yet another behind him bore their luggage. Sadie knew Pao Chu didn't like to be touched, but she linked her arm anyway, silently grateful that she didn't flinch. She felt the need for comfort from another person, a person who knew she was suffering. She was still shaken by the conversations with Terrence and struggled to understand why he'd seemed to want to distance himself from her, but the next morning was back to say he hadn't meant it, that he would write and, in time, would come to see her. She looked blankly at the passing streets as her mind's eye returned to those scenes yet again. She tried to pinpoint where she'd gone wrong, how she'd disappointed him.

The walls of the Forbidden City seemed to stretch forever. As they passed the monumental Meridian Gate, Pao Chu and Sadie leaned forward to catch a glimpse of the palaces with their colourful tiled roofs. Richly dressed people passed toing and froing through the open gates. Staunch Bannermen held impossibly high poles with long red flags flapping in the breeze. Pao Chu turned to her with a rare smile. 'Much better than Buckingham Palace,' she said. Sadie had to agree, but her thoughts were elsewhere. What is he doing now? Has he disembarked? Has he even given me a second thought? Her eyes filled again, and she turned away so Pao Chu couldn't see her distress. She knew Pao Chu saw through her like no one else ever had and for that she was grateful. She didn't think anyone had ever really tried before. Sadie always made an effort to be bright and cheerful. It was easier that way.

They continued through the streets of Beijing, and eventually turned in through an open gate into a large compound with a long low, single-storey building to one side. They went past a few green shrubs struggling to become a garden to the door of the Armstrong's mission house.

Mrs. Armstrong waited at the entrance to the house, her hair the same wiry grey as her husband's. One hand shielded her eyes, the other rested on her hip. She began calling hello before they were within earshot. She greeted Pao Chu as an old friend and then turned her attention to Sadie.

'My dear girl! Come in, come in! You must be exhausted.' Doris Armstrong hadn't lost her Scottish accent though she'd lived in Beijing for more than twenty years. She was a big-boned woman with a broad forehead and a face lined by years working in the sun. She led them into the cool of the house. 'Praise the Lord you're here. I very much want to hear all about your journey and all the news from home.' She clasped her hands together. 'But I know you must be tired, so I'll show you to your rooms and let you freshen up. Come down in an hour, we'll have a prayer of thanks for your safe delivery to us then we can talk over luncheon.' She signalled to the servants to see to the luggage and walked briskly ahead down the long cool corridor, her silk skirt swishing as she went.

Pao Chu had told Sadie that she'd known the Armstrongs for many years. They led a comfortable, busy life running the mission and had several servants: a cook, some housemaids, a handyman (Mr. Armstrong couldn't put a nail into a wall, according to his wife). Sadie could tell that Pao Chu admired the Armstrongs, particularly Doris. She could see why – Doris had an energy about her that suggested she was not a woman to be meddled with.

An hour later they sat in what could have been a parlour in any part of England, or Scotland for that matter. Mrs Armstrong poured tea and offered buttered scones and jam. Sadie felt herself relax. This she could do. She'd thought up questions to ask in case there was a lull, but mainly she thought that all that was needed was to be as charming as possible. Usually, people were so anxious to get their own stories told they only wanted a willing ear. She was well-practised in hiding her insecurity behind a bright smile.

They told Sadie about their early years in China and about the girls attending the mission school. They were especially keen to offer an education to girls as most parents didn't see any need to educate their female children. As the school was funded by donations from the Mission Society, there was no cost to the parents but they were suspicious of anything free of charge. Doris and Hubert translated Bible stories into Chinese and used the stories to teach the school children how to read and write.

'Often, the little ones go home and repeat the Bible stories to their parents, and their curiosity is raised enough for them to come to find out more,' Doris told them.

Sitting around the table, drinking tea, listening to Doris and Hubert talk about their work, was like a balm to Sadie's soul. What have I been thinking, she wondered. This is why I came here; this is what I've studied to do. No, more than that, this is what I am meant to do. Listening to their experiences made Sadie want to start work with the Armstrongs straight away.

Pao Cho put down her teacup. 'I expect Sadie will stay here for some time to study with you before she is placed in a Mission House?'

'Oh no, dear. I'm afraid we don't have the luxury of time.' Mrs Armstrong raised her hand before Pao Cho could say anything else and turned to Sadie. 'You've studied in London for two years, isn't that right?'

Sadie nodded.

'Usually,' said Doris, smiling, 'we have a settling-in period while new missionaries acclimatise to the customs and the weather and the language, but there's a particular mission that is desperately in need of help. We hoped you can go immediately. After you've had a little rest, of course.'

Sadie's new-found confidence waned. How little is 'a little rest', she wondered.

Hubert turned to Sadie and asked, 'Shansi region, Sadie. What do you know of it?'

Sadie's brain snatched for fragments of information. She glanced at Pao Chu who seemed to be willing her to remember. She felt her neck and face flush.

'I know the name Shansi means "West of the Hills". There's mountains to the east and to the west and in the middle the land is rich and fertile.' She stopped. 'Em ... oh dear ...'

Hubert spoke kindly. 'Never mind, go on. You're doing well so far.'

She relaxed a little. 'The Yellow River is also to the west of it. Oh, and it's about the size of England and Wales together.' She let out her breath and looked to him for affirmation.

'Anything else? Anything about the people?'

'The people.' She paused. 'The capital is Taiyuan Fu, it's one of the main trading routes.'

She saw Pao Chu raise her eyebrows and remembered that it had been Terrence who'd told her that and not Pao Chu. She bit her lower lip as she searched for any more facts but her mind was blank.

'That's enough to be going on with,' said Hubert, and patted her hand. 'About three days south-west of Taiyuan Fu is a large town called Hsiao. Two women are already out there doing a fine job. They're looking for someone to help. That's where we think you'll be needed most. What do you say, Sadie? It's not the easiest place to get to – you'll have to go through the mountains to get to the Shansi plains, mostly by mule.'

'Mule?'

'You'll be fine. Pao Chu has been over and back countless times. An old hand and all that.' He smiled at Pao Chu. 'I'd go myself, but I'm afraid my days of negotiating mountain passes are behind me. It'll take about six weeks to get there, but at least it's not winter – no snow to contend with.' He smiled and sat back in the chair as though he'd just given her a present.

'You're coming with me, Pao Chu?'

Pao Chu looked down at her plate for what seemed to Sadie to be an extraordinarily long time. The grandfather clock ticked in the silence.

Pao Chu lifted her head. 'The mission you are talking of, is that where Edith and Ruth are?'

'Yes, that's the one.' Hubert seemed abashed. 'I'm sorry I didn't have time to discuss this with you before now, Pao Chu. I shouldn't have presumed.'

Pao Chu let Hubert's words hang in the air. Sadie prayed inwardly that she would come with her. She crossed her fingers under the table.

'I did not return to China to teach children,' said Pao Chu. 'I intended to work with the women in the villages.'

'Of course, of course,' said Hubert. 'Wherever you feel you can best do the Lord's work. I've often thought mixing with the people is an excellent way to gain trust and share the Bible. I'm sure that Edith and Ruth can provide you with whatever help you need.'

'If that is agreed then I will take Sadie to the mission in Hsiao.'

Sadie uncrossed her fingers and picked up her teacup. She felt like a foolish child sitting with the grown-ups. The Armstrongs and Pao Chu had moved on to chatting about people they knew and changes to the city since Pao Chu's last visit. Sadie smiled and nodded, but a dreadful feeling that she was out of her depth began to rise inside her.

Before they left, Mrs. Armstrong tackled the problem of Sadie's wardrobe.

'The clothes you brought with you won't be suitable for Shansi,' she said without apology. 'We'll have to get you kitted out in Chinese clothes.'

'Not bring my dresses? Oh Mrs. Armstrong, I really don't think I could go about in a tunic and trousers!'

'You'll be surprised what you will "go about" in. For a start travelling on a mule or in a litter is much easier in loose-fitting trousers. More importantly, you won't stand out as much. You really will need to get some suitable headwear and several pairs of the shoes the Chinese wear. They're made of tree bark – don't last very long but they're very cheap. You'll need a dozen pairs to start. And for the winter you'll need a padded jacket. Nothing keeps out the cold like duck feathers. I'll bring you to Mr. Chang's shop and we'll get you sorted out.'

'Will my hair be a problem, Mrs. Armstrong?'

'It could be. One never knows how people will react. Even here, where there are quite a few foreign traders, fair hair can cause – let's say a bit of a stir. Sometimes good but more often bad. In Shansi many people haven't seen a person from outside China. You might be a curiosity to them, but I doubt that you'll come to any actual harm.'

After a trip to Mr. Chang's clothing emporium, Sadie and Pao Chu said their goodbyes to the Armstrongs. It had been arranged that they would travel with a muleteer taking a train of mules to the Shansi region. He would take them directly to the mission.

As the mules waited patiently on the grounds, Pao Chu overheard Sadie remind Mrs. Armstrong about forwarding any letters that might come for her.

Sadie and Pao Chu set off on the route that would bring them through the mountain pass known as the Niang Tzu. From there, they would descend to the plateau of central Shansi. It was a busy route used by traders carrying goods between Taiyuan and Beijing or Tientsin.

The time passed quickly – Sadie made up stories about other travellers' reasons for being on the road. Pao Chu tried to study her Bible, but the mules made it impossible for her to read the words and, despite herself, she found Sadie's stories amusing. It won't last, thought Pao Chu. She knew the worst of the journey lay ahead, and Sadie's good humour would probably diminish with each mile.

At the end of the first day, they stopped in a large town. The muleteer led his mules through the narrow streets straight to a gate leading into an inn.

'Am I reading the sign right?' Sadie asked Pao Chu. 'Inn Where Everything Runs Smoothly.'

Pao Chu nodded. 'Let's hope it lives up to its name.'

Pao Chu hadn't talked to Sadie about the inns. She didn't see the point. What can't be changed has to be endured. She suspected Sadie was looking forward to a warm bath and a good meal. She'll just have to get used to it, there is no other way, thought Pao Chu.

In fairness, Sadie seemed to at least try to hide her disappointment at the sight of the one large room for eating and sleeping on one side and directly opposite a stable for the horses and mules. However, she couldn't hide her feelings when she found she was expected to share a communal kang – a sort of long wooden bed raised off the floor to allow the warm air from the oven to flow beneath and heat them.

Pao Chu was getting on with staking her place on the kang by putting her blanket there. She took Sadie's blanket and put it beside hers.

Sadie was at her shoulder. 'Can't we go somewhere else?' she whispered.

'There is nowhere else. The town gates are closed now. All the inns will be full. This is the best one in the town. The food is good.'

Pao Chu caught sight of a group of locals gathering at the open door. News of her companion must have spread. Before Pao Chu could warn Sadie, she turned to smile at them and they scattered as though scorched by an invisible flame.

Sadie looked as though she might cry, but Pao Chu didn't try to comfort her. 'Come eat,' she said and led Sadie to the end of the bench to eat the rice and vegetables. Pao Chu ate silently while her eyes scanned the room. Apart from the few people who'd come to look earlier, no one paid much attention. Pao Chu told Sadie to keep her eyes on her plate and her head down. The other guests seemed more used to outsiders. Apart from an occasional glance, they didn't seem to find her in the least interesting.

'I can't understand what anyone's saying. It's too fast.'

'Just be grateful they're not talking about you. Now finish your meal and we'll get some rest.'

'Where will I get changed?' Sadie whispered back.

'Everyone will sleep in their clothes. If you want to undress, you can do so under your blanket. But I wouldn't recommend it.'

Sadie followed Pao Chu's example and lay on one of the hard kangs. None of the Chinese people joined them.

'Will all the inns be like this?' Sadie asked.

Pao Chu shook her head. 'Most will be worse.'

'It's going to be a long six weeks,' said Sadie. She bit her lip and joined her hands. 'I'll pray for strength to get through this ordeal, but I don't think I'll be able to sleep a wink.'

She somehow managed as Pao Chu had to shake her awake just after dawn. Sadie's nose wrinkled as she opened her eyes to the sights and smells of the communal room. 'Oh dear God, what on earth is that smell?'

Pao Chu chose not to answer.

People were beginning to awaken. They stretched, then yawned, and immediately took up their shoes from the floor and turned them upside down.

Something fell from one of the shoes and scuttled under the kang.

'Scorpions,' said Pao Chu. 'They hide in shoes. Always check your shoes.'

The journey began early every morning. Each town or village was surrounded by a thick wall with one gate in and another out. The gates closed each evening, and it was the responsibility of their muleteer to make it to the next town before the gates closed so they could get accommodation at one of the inns.

The further they travelled, the worse conditions became. Sadie found the communal latrines filled with human waste particularly difficult. When Pao Chu told her that the landlord sold the contents at a premium to farmers for compost, she went as white as a sheet and swore she could never eat a single thing ever again. But, somehow, she managed. When they crossed the mountain passes and descended into the Shansi region, the stony scenery was replaced by green hills with terraces of crops.

Slithery noodles replaced rice and were served with beans or cabbage and if they were lucky steamed dumplings. They didn't stay in any inn longer than one night. They knew Edith and Ruth were anxiously waiting for their help. Finally they reached the fertile central plain of Shansi, the Loess Plateau made from sand that had blown from the Gobi Desert for thousands of years.

Pao Chu and Sadie arrived at the walls of the large town of Hsiao on a warm dry day. The muleteer led them through the busy streets to the open wooden gate of the mission house. He unloaded their luggage and quickly bade them farewell. They picked up their bags and went through the gate into a large square courtyard with buildings on each side. The centre of the courtyard was planted with a small copse of pomegranate trees, already showing their glossy green foliage. The main house was opposite, but they were drawn to the sound of children reciting phrases in sing-song voices. It came from a long low building along one side of the courtyard.

'*Hello!*' called Pao Chu.

The voices stopped. Two women, wearing blue Chinese tunics and long loose silk skirts, came out of the school building, followed by several pupils. Everyone seemed to be talking at once.

The younger woman clapped her hands together and rushed toward Pao Chu. They bowed deeply to each other.

'Pao Chu, we're so glad to see you again!'

The young woman looked as though she was about to hug Pao Chu, but the Chinese woman's stance made it clear that hugging would not be tolerated.

The young woman turned to Sadie and held out her hand.

'Ruth Whitechurch,' she said. 'You must be Sadie Bradshaw. Praise the Lord! We're so happy that you've come to help us.' She shook Sadie's hand vigorously.

Sadie looked into her deep-set shining brown eyes and felt she would get on well with this woman. Several young girls edged closer but kept a safe distance from the new arrivals.

The other woman looked a few years older than Ruth and approached more slowly. She seemed to be sizing up the newcomer with her eyes. Sadie noticed she had a slight limp and was about to move toward her, but a glance from Pao Chu kept her in her place. The woman still clutched the book she'd been reading to the class. Several children walked behind her in an orderly line. She raised her hand, and all the children fell silent.

Ruth smiled encouragingly at Sadie. 'This is Edith Searell. We've been so looking forward to your arrival. Haven't we, Edith?'

Edith held out her hand in a much less enthusiastic manner.

Sadie took it and shook it gently.

'You're very young,' said Edith, withdrawing her hand.

'I've just turned twenty-three,' said Sadie. She almost felt that she should apologise for her youth. She waited for Edith to continue, but she'd already turned to bow to Pao Chu. Then she started back toward the school, followed by a line of girls, who glanced back at the newcomers and giggled.

'We have another hour of schooling,' said Edith over her shoulder. 'Go in and see Shu Lan – she'll give you something to eat.'

'I'll show you,' said Ruth, picking up one of Sadie's bags. She said

169

something to the group of children, who smiled delightedly. 'I've promised them a treat in honour of your arrival.'

They all followed Ruth up the steps to the largest of the four buildings. Each building had pillars that supported the protruding tiled roofs which provided shade on the veranda. Their feet echoed on the floor as they ran ahead to the kitchen, giggling and chattering at their unexpected break from lessons. The hallway was bare except for a large mirror in a heavy-looking brass-coloured frame; small patches of brown spots marred the glass.

Sadie stopped to look at her reflection. She hadn't seen herself since they left Beijing. She poked at loose strands of hair that had become unclipped.

'It belongs to Wu Chow,' said Ruth. 'He's the merchant who owns the house.'

'It's quite handy to have a mirror there,' said Sadie, twisting her head from side to side in case of more stray hair. In the mirror, she saw Ruth and Pao Chu exchange a glance.

'It's the message it gives about us though,' said Ruth. 'He wouldn't take it down because the Chinese believe that it keeps evil spirits out. So, local people might think we believe that too. Do you see?'

'Oh yes, I see, I didn't realise.' She felt foolish and turned her back on the mirror.

'Don't worry, Sadie. It will take time to get used to all the Chinese customs and beliefs. Come along, your rooms are up here. They're a bit small, hope you don't mind.'

'As long as I don't have to sleep on another kang, I'll be perfectly happy.'

'Oh dear!' said Ruth. Then smiled when she saw Sadie's face. 'Only joking – it's a bed!'

Sadie laughed, and Pao Chu looked puzzled at the exchange. Even after all these years, Europeans sometimes befuddled Pao Chu.

'You're in here, Pao Chu. I hope you will be comfortable.' Ruth opened the door.

Pao Chu bowed, went inside and closed the door.

Ruth continued down the corridor past several doors on each side. 'Some rooms are not habitable,' she said. 'The roof leaks in parts.'

They came to the last door and Ruth opened it. Sadie followed her inside, went straight to the window and opened the shutters. A soft warm breeze swept into the room. They both leaned on the window ledge, overlooking the courtyard.

'Hope you like it,' said Ruth.

Sadie swallowed. 'It's perfect.'

'I'm so pleased,' said Ruth. 'All the bedrooms on this side face into the courtyard.'

At the far end of the courtyard stood the large open gates. People glanced in as they hurried past.

'We usually keep the main gates closed, but they were left open today for your arrival.'

Ruth pointed to the building on their right. 'You saw the school as you came in, just two classrooms at the moment. One for five to nine years and the other from ten years onwards. You'll meet the children tomorrow.' She leaned out further and pointed to the verandas that linked all the buildings. 'It's usually quicker to cut across the courtyard, but during the rainy season, you'll be glad of the shelter. Not sure yet what we're going to do with the building on the left. It would be a good space for prayer meetings with the Chinese Christians, but it needs a bit of work.'

Ruth walked out to the corridor and through the door opposite. Sadie followed her to the window.

'We're over the kitchen here. There's a smaller gate just there out to the laneway. Much easier to manage, and quicker if you're going into the town. We thought this room would be too noisy for you, though there is a nice view of the garden.' Ruth smiled. 'I say garden – I really should have said 'jungle'– you can see it's overrun with bamboo and lemongrass, even the stream is choked in parts. It's high on our list of things to do, but we simply haven't had the time. I'll show you the way to the far end of it – that's where the latrine is and a few rickety outhouses that aren't much used. You'll need to watch out for snakes on your way to the latrine and never go there at night. 'Don't worry – there's a chamber pot under your bed.'

'That's the best news I've heard in a long time.'

'I'd better get the girls from under Cook's feet,' said Ruth. 'Come down whenever you're ready and we'll show you around properly. Dinner is at six o'clock. Sharp. Edith likes us to keep to a routine.'

When Ruth was gone Sadie stood at the open window a little longer and began to feel at ease in this strange landscape. Perhaps this is where I'll fit in, so different from Ireland and England. Maybe this is where I'm meant to be. She leaned further out the window and could see the solid walls protecting the town, the tops of pagodas – red, green and blue tiles caught the afternoon sun. Terracotta pots in the courtyard were filled with herbs, she took a long deep breath and fancied she smelled sage. Children's laughing voices reached her ears. Carts rumbled past in the busy street outside. For a few moments she felt peace.

Sadie's thoughts, if left unchecked, tended to turn to Terrence Bennett – as they did now. I wonder if he's written? Has he called to see me and found that I'd already left? She hoped Mrs. Armstrong would remember to give him the note she'd written for him.

She knelt and prayed that Terrence would find her and they could be together, for she was sure that was meant to be. She didn't know how this could happen, but she was willing to leave those minor details in the hands of the Lord.

CHAPTER TWENTY-FOUR

When the school closed for the day and the pupils returned to their homes, Ruth and Edith showed Sadie and Pao Chu around the mission and at dinner told them how they'd arrived there three years before. Pao Chu had heard it all before, but Sadie was perched on the edge of her seat as she listened.

Edith's eyes shone as she talked about their work. 'The first task,' she said, 'was to clean the whole building, replace some of the windows and put a coat of lime on the internal walls. We caused quite a stir, I can tell you. We distributed posters around the town letting people know their children could come to be educated at the new school. We had to answer so many questions, didn't we, Ruth?'

'They were probably just nosy, wanted to see what was going on,' said Ruth. 'There was a constant stream asking, "*Can girls with unbound feet come to the school? Can slaves come to school? Will the children be taught to read Chinese characters or only foreign words?*" Each time we responded that any child wishing to learn to read and write in Chinese and in English could come to the school. As for the children's feet, I'm sorry to say many young girls still have their feet bound.'

'We employed a teacher,' said Edith. 'Chia Loh. Wonderful girl. She had converted years ago – she's married now, but she had been to a missionary school run by Mr. and Mrs. Pigott when they were in Taiyuan.'

'Is that Tom Pigott?' asked Sadie. 'I heard him speak at home. He was one of the reasons that I wanted to come to China. I hope I'll get to meet him in person while I'm here.'

'As a matter of fact, he's in Fen Chow Fu. Only about two days' journey away,' said Ruth. 'Practically next door. Here, have some more dumplings.'

Edith twiddled her thumbs and waited, a little impatiently, for the exchange to end so she could go on with her story.

'The Chinese are very wary of foreigners, and they were reluctant to let their children come. But they do value education highly, wouldn't you agree, Pao Chu?' She didn't wait for Pao Chu to agree or disagree before she went on. 'And we knew this was the way to entice them to allow their children to come. Chinese girls who are not engaged are kept in their houses from the age of about twelve years until a husband is found and they marry – often at the age of fifteen. We politely asked the families to allow us to teach their daughters the basics of English and maths and science. As an educated girl will attract a higher bride price, they usually agree. We hope that the children will be led by our example and become Christians as well as educated. They could become teachers themselves, like Chia Loh. On the first morning the school opened eight girls and four boys arrived. The number has risen slowly to twenty. More girls than boys. The boys start working early in life, unfortunately.'

'Did you take in orphans?' Sadie asked.

Ruth nodded. 'Before the school opened, when we were still

cleaning out the rooms an elderly woman came to the door. She had two small children with her. She told us their parents had died and that she couldn't look after them.'

'What could we do?' said Edith. 'The woman said she wasn't their grandmother, and I had no way of knowing if that was true. But she left the children and we haven't seen her since. We had no idea if she'd ever come back. We had no choice.'

Sadie began to feel a little warmer toward Edith as she heard the emotion in her voice.

'We didn't even know how old they were. Once we accepted them, other babies – always girls – were left for us to deal with.'

'But I didn't see any young children today,' said Sadie.

Edith looked a little uncomfortable. 'The house was becoming quite full and we didn't have the resources to look after young children – especially babies. You've heard, I'm sure, about the large numbers of girl babies that are abandoned or killed by their families?'

'Yes, I heard about it when I was studying at the China Inland Mission school. I couldn't quite believe it.'

'Well, you can believe it because it's true,' said Edith. 'We had no choice but to turn to the Catholic orphanage in Taiyuan for help. It's run by the Dominican nuns. They take the babies and find wet nurses for them, so the child lives with the wet nurse's family until they are about four or five. Then they are moved to the orphanage and go to school there until they are old enough to marry.'

'That seems to be a splendid arrangement. I'm glad it worked out.' Sadie turned her attention to the noodles.

Edith and Ruth exchanged a glance.

'It only 'works out' for a small percentage,' said Edith. She swallowed hard. 'Many don't make it to the orphanage – they are set adrift on rivers or abandoned in fields or –'

Sadie pushed her food away.

'We shouldn't have gone into all this so early in your stay with us,' said Ruth. 'Let's talk about you. How is your Chinese?'

'She needs to improve her Chinese before anything else,' said Pao Chu.

'Yes, I certainly do,' said Sadie. 'But I can be of practical help too. The building that needs cleaning and the garden. I can clean, and I'm good at gardening. I mean, if you think that would be a good place to begin?'

Edith met her eyes, and Sadie thought she saw the beginnings of a smile. 'Yes. Perhaps that is why God sent such a young, healthy girl to us.'

In the first weeks she awoke each day thinking: *This could be the day.* Each morning her heart beat faster whenever a messenger came through the small door in the wooden gate. She was pleased to receive letters from Aunt Pru and Uncle Cecil, from her friend Sarah and from Doris Armstrong. But it wasn't what she wanted. She felt helpless, imagined all the reasons why his letter was delayed, was silently furious and moments later desperately sad. All she could do was pray. Weeks turned to months. The light in her heart dwindled to a glimmer, but she couldn't extinguish it completely, couldn't give up hope. She thought that, perhaps, if she prayed each night on the hard wooden floor, surely He would grant this one blessing. Tomorrow might be the day.

They were halfway through the Chinese summer. Sadie had been at the mission for about four months, working hard on emptying and cleaning rooms. She'd also begun to tackle the jungle garden. She got Yuan Bo, the cook's husband, to help her clear some of the overgrown reeds choking the stream and little by little her efforts made a difference. Ruth said she was 'an absolute marvel' and Edith commented on how much easier it was to get to the latrine. The physical work took a toll on her body. She had to take in the waist bands on her trousers and skirts. Her back and shoulders ached, and her hands were covered in welts and cuts. Pao Chu made her soothing lotions from the wildflowers and plants she collected on her trips to local villages.

Every day Sadie studied the Chinese language, and when Edith gave the older students lessons in writing Chinese characters, she joined the class. Although she wasn't allowed to preach to the adult Chinese converts, her language skills improved and she was able to have conversations – albeit a little stilted at first – with the students. Sometimes Edith let her take the older girls for Bible study. She'd become a favourite with them, so they often sought her after class on the pretext of not understanding some text or Bible reference. The conversation always ended up with her telling them about life in Dublin and in London.

During one of these conversations, Sadie saw Edith storm across the courtyard toward the house. She guessed Edith's latest visit to Wu Chow had been fruitless, as had all the previous visits. A storm last winter had loosened roof tiles, and Edith had set out earlier, determined to get them replaced before the rainy season.

The students tried to keep the conversation going, until Sadie led them to the door and firmly said goodbye. She rushed to the house to see what the news was.

'He says it probably won't rain until the seventh moon,' said Edith. 'Insufferable man!'

Sadie totted it up in her head – about the end of July.

'He says he'll send someone, but you know what he's like.' Edith looked pinched and pale. 'He'll do nothing till the roof falls in – and then he'll probably blame us and try to get us to pay. We just don't have the money.'

'Sit down, I'll make you some tea,' said Sadie. 'Is that post you've brought? Anything for me?' She tried to make her voice light.

Edith threw the letters on the small table. 'I met the messenger at the gate. I was so annoyed I didn't even look at them.'

Sadie picked up the bundle. She recognized her Uncle Cecil's handwriting, and she tucked that into her pocket. The others were for Edith and Ruth. She flicked through them again, just in case.

'I'll get that tea for you,' she said. On her way out she passed Ruth and shook her head a little. 'She's not good,' she mouthed.

Sadie returned with the tea tray ten minutes later, surprised at the change in Edith's expression. Both women sat on the edge of the divan, heads together, reading one of the letters. They hardly noticed her struggling with the tray until she put it down in front of them.

Both heads looked up in surprise as though they'd forgotten she existed.

Ruth took the letter from Edith's hand and reread it as Edith watched her.

'Goodness, what's wrong? Are you all right?' said Sadie.

'Absolutely wonderful,' said Ruth. She looked at Edith, who reached across and reclaimed the letter.

'What on earth's going on?' said Sadie.

'It's a letter about a meeting of missionaries in Shansi. It's to be held in Fen Chow Fu in a few weeks' time. It would be a wonderful gathering, if we could attend – they don't happen very often ...'

Sadie looked from one to the other. Realization dawned on her.

'Of course you should go,' she said. 'Pao Chu will be here and I'm sure we can manage between us. How long will it go on for?' She smiled at them, delighted that she could be of use.

Ruth nodded vigorously. 'Five days,' she said. 'The school will be closed for the summer holidays, so it's only the prayer meetings that you would need to worry about.'

'And the evening Bible group on Wednesday, and the Sunday morning prayers, of course,' said Edith. 'It's quite a bit to take on.'

'We can manage,' said Sadie. 'It's only five days.'

'Plus four days there and back, so it's actually nine days,' said Ruth. 'Do you really think you can manage? It's a lot to ask.'

'What about Pao Chu? We should ask her before we make any plans,' said Edith.

'Oh, Pao Chu will be fine. I'm sure she'll be happy to help out. I'll talk to her when she comes back.' Sadie smiled broadly – a little less certain than her bright smile suggested – but delighted at the joy she was giving.

When Pao Chu returned from visiting a village a few miles away, she listened carefully to Sadie as she repeated what had happened and how they would be in charge of the mission station during Edith and Ruth's absence.

'I've told Edith and Ruth there wouldn't be a problem, Pao Chu. They were so happy. You don't mind, do you?' Sadie hadn't really thought it wouldn't be all right with Pao Chu but now she watched the other woman's face harden.

'Sadie, sometimes you forget that I have my own work with the village women. I am not tied to the mission house. Do you remember when we were on the ship, and the people thought I was your servant?'

'I remember, and I did everything to make sure people knew that wasn't the case.'

'Perhaps the fault is mine,' said Pao Chu. 'Perhaps I have protected you too much, but somehow you feel you have the right to answer for me. You don't have that right and please do not speak for me again.'

'But, Pao Chu, the ladies so want to go!'

'This time I will help, if I can, for their sake.'

Sadie pressed her lips together and hoped the tears in her eyes wouldn't spill onto her cheeks. 'You're right, Pao Chu. I have been taking you for granted. I'm sorry.'

Pao Chu bowed and left her alone.

For the next week, the only conversation to be had was about the trip and who would be there. They discussed Bible passages and tracts that they might bring to the attention of others. They talked of people that Sadie didn't know – Doctor and Mrs. Lovett, the Edwards, Stokes, and Simpsons – she soon lost track of the names. They chatted excitedly as they steamed their skirts – having decided they should wear their English clothes. Whose point of view would they align themselves with in disputes among the missionaries? That startled Sadie. She couldn't imagine a congress of missionaries would be anything less than harmonious. Even Tom and Jessie Pigotts' names were whispered as having a different view on the aims of mission houses and hospitals. Sadie avoided these conversations and tried to divert Ruth and Edith at any mention of a possible disagreement. She focussed on how pleasant it would be for them. She had told them about John Robinson and Miss Duval and asked Edith and Ruth to take letters she'd written to them and one she'd written to Mr. and Mrs. Pigott.

Just after dawn on the following Monday, the muleteer led his beasts into the main courtyard and Edith and Ruth's luggage was loaded. Edith checked the straps holding all their worldly goods in place, and declared them safe.

They climbed onto their mules, calling goodbye over their shoulders, and set out on the thirty-mile journey.

Sadie waved enthusiastically, shivering at the thought of staying at an inn. 'Rather you than me,' she whispered as she watched them turn the bend in the road. She swung the heavy gate closed and leaned against it for a moment. Quiet. Well, reasonably quiet – the odd rumble of a cart passing, the owner muttering to his mule. A warm breeze whistled through the gaps in the wooden gate, and the hens made their way to the courtyard to cluck and argue. She looked toward the main house. Pao Chu had gone directly to the kitchen. Breakfast could wait, thought Sadie. She wanted to enjoy the feeling of power, albeit a limited power and only for a short time.

Sadie strolled through the building she'd cleared out over the last few weeks and gathered some buckets of paint together. This was her chance to brighten things up while Edith and Ruth were away.

At the squeak of the small door in the gate, she returned to the courtyard. A woman stood there, looking unsure and distraught. Sadie watched as Pao Chu appeared and hurried toward the woman, put an arm around her shoulders and led her toward the main house. It was not unusual – many Chinese people came to Pao Chu when they couldn't afford to see the apothecary. Sadie followed them into the kitchen. The woman was still talking, and Pao Chu stood, head bent, listening to every word. She began to pull small covered jars from the medicine cabinet. She had several in front of her before she finally noticed Sadie.

'I'm sorry, Sadie. I must go and help this woman's husband. It's not too far – the next village. I'll be back as soon as I can.'

Sadie felt uneasy at the thought of being completely alone, except for the servants. 'Do you have to? Can't you give her the medicine to take with her?'

Pao Chu leaned her palms on the table and closed her eyes for a moment.

'It will be a tragedy for the family if he dies. I must go.'

Sadie lowered her eyes. 'I'm sorry,' she said. 'Of course you must.'

Pao Chu pulled on her straw hat and wrapped a light scarf over her mouth – protection from the grains of sand carried on the wind.

'I'll be back as soon as I can.'

Sadie watched Pao Chu and the village woman leave through the small door. She had hoped that Pao Chu would help her select the readings for the Chinese Christian group on Wednesday. She took a deep breath and decided the garden would be a good place for inspiration. *Gardens in the Bible*, she thought. She put on her hat, collected some tools and strode out through the bulrushes to the stream. The Garden of Eden and the Garden of Gethsemane – she was sure more would come to her.

Hours later Sadie removed her straw hat and wiped the sweat from her forehead, glad of the coolness of her long shirt and loose pants. She opened the collar buttons, peeled the material away from her sticky skin and flapped her tunic to feel the air sweep along her body.

She'd worked hard clearing ivy from a clump of black locust trees, and cutting down bamboo which she thought Yuan Bo might be able to make use of.

The heavy warm silence was broken only by the bird's evensong. Sadie stood and watched the sun graze the tip of the mountains on the horizon. Clouds were already gathering. Darkness would come quickly now, no lingering twilight – but the scent of jasmine reminded her of home. She fetched the balm that Pao Chu had made for her skin. The sun always found some part of her to redden. Her face felt taut and dry. She eased back into the old bamboo rocking chair on the veranda, rubbed the balm into her cheeks and lips and felt her skin absorb the soothing cream.

What was that noise? She sat up straight. Horses' hooves? They seemed to have stopped on the other side of the high wooden gate.

She picked up the broom and moved toward the gate.

Just as she leaned her ear to the gate, a loud knock came from the other side. She jumped back, her heart racing.

'*Hallo?*'

The voice of a man. Not a Chinese man. Her heart quickened.

She waited a moment.

'*Hallo!*' came the shout again from the other side.

She knew the voice. Her hands trembled as she slid the bolt from the gate, pulled it back, and looked out, still holding the broom.

He had turned his back to the door and was about to remount the horse. She shielded her eyes against the low sun and leaned on the broom.

He turned. 'Sadie,' he said. 'Is that really you?'

She could barely hear him over the sound of her heart thumping. 'Terrence?'

All her imaginings of this moment – falling into his arms, being swept into his embrace – fell away, and they stood facing each other.

The space between them seemed as vast as a galaxy.

'You didn't write,' she said.

'I wrote,' he said. 'Or at least I tried, but I couldn't ever seem to find the right words.'

'That's a poor excuse,' she said. He looked tired, and the sharp edge of her anger melted just a little.

The horse's sweat glistened in the evening sun and his two mules waited patiently.

'There's a stream at the back,' she said. 'The animals look like they could do with a drink.' She pulled the gate open and he led the animals into the courtyard then followed her along the passageway that led to the back of the house. She tried to think of something clever to say but ended up saying nothing at all.

'Sadie. A kind word would be welcome. I've come a long way to see you.'

'Have you really? Just to see me?' Hope seeped into her heart.

'You're not so easy to find, you know. China's a big place. I was with the Armstrongs a few weeks ago. I'm afraid I told them a little white lie.'

She put a hand to her mouth to hide her smile. 'You did? What did you say?'

'I told them I had letters for you and knew only roughly where you were. They told me where, but it's a devilish hard place to find. I said I'd bring your post with me. See what you've done to me, Sadie Bradshaw? I've never told a lie to a missionary before.'

She was glad the darkness hid the red blotches rising to her neck.

'It's through here,' she said, and pulled away the overgrown bushes that led to the garden at the back of the house.

The horse and mule seemed to sense the water and pushed through reeds to reach it. Lemongrass and jasmine grew wild along the banks and the air filled with their scent as the animals brushed past. She watched Terrence take his handkerchief, dip it in the flowing water and mop the back of his neck. When he turned to smile at her, she felt her stomach tighten, and her heart thump. He opened his arms, and she walked into them.

'I've missed you so much,' she whispered. 'I waited for a letter every day, Terrence.'

His arms tightened.

Someone called her name, and it took her a moment to recognise the cook's voice. She stepped away from Terrence, realising that the servants might have seen them from the kitchen.

'We should go in,' she whispered. 'It's dark.'

Terrence removed letters and parcels from his saddlebag and they walked slowly toward the lights spilling from the house.

The servants hovered at the kitchen door.

'Shu Lan, please bring some food and tea. Yuan Bo, will you look after the horse and mules, please, and check the main gate? I'm not sure I closed it properly.'

The servants were a little slow to respond. The cook and her husband exchanged a quick glance; he seemed to be waiting for his wife to decide. Shu Lan disappeared into the kitchen, muttering to herself, and her husband shrugged and went in search of the animals.

Sadie could have told the servants to bring the food to the dining room – it had a long table and hand-carved chairs, but instead she led him to the larger of the two rooms. It was sparsely furnished with two wide divans on each side of a low dark table. The divans were covered with rich green, blue and red brocade. She loved this room and often sat there and studied her Bible or daydreamed, depending on her mood.

He placed the letters on the low table while Sadie went around the room lighting the lamps.

There was a low rumbling sound. 'Is that thunder?' She looked toward the window.

'It's more likely to be my stomach.' He looked abashed. 'I haven't

185

eaten since breakfast. I wanted to get here as fast as I could, before the gates closed.'

'Please sit down, you must be exhausted.' He sat in the middle of the divan and leaned back. Even in the lamp light she could see how worn out he looked.

Sadie knew it was not the custom for a man to visit the house of an unchaperoned single woman after dark. It would probably cause the townspeople's disapproval, and she did not wish to give any reason to upset the delicate balance the mission maintained.

Terrence didn't appear to notice her discomfort, and gave her a broad smile as his eyes took in her fair hair and clothes. She remembered what she was wearing. The Chinese tunic and trousers. It was perfectly respectable if a little unorthodox. Too late now, she thought.

It had all seemed so natural on the ship but, now, in a house with walls and furniture, the trappings of another life, other people, she felt uneasy and wasn't sure how to be in the room with him. Should she sit beside him? They'd hugged in the garden. What did that mean? What was she to do? She wanted to sit beside him, but what would he think? Everything was different now. She had no idea how to act without other people around to enforce the unwritten rules.

'How are the Armstrongs?' she asked. She had run out of lamps to light and now sat down at the other end of the divan.

'They are remarkable, aren't they?' he said. 'So dedicated to converting the Chinese all these years. They don't seem to gain anything from it for themselves. Do you know, they haven't even been to the new horse-racing track? They don't seem to mix with other British people at all.'

'They mix with their own kind, with people bringing the Word of God. I doubt they would be interested in horse racing.' Sadie couldn't picture Doris and Hubert going to a racing track. She wasn't sure that any missionary would attend such an event.

'It's more about *being* there, meeting the right people. Maybe people who would donate to the missionaries' cause. I'd say the Armstrongs are missing out on an opportunity.'

Shu Lan swung the door open and carried a food tray into what she probably considered the wrong room. Sadie pretended not to notice her furrowed eyebrows and pursed lips as she placed food bowls on the low table. Terrence thanked her in perfect Mandarin, but if she was impressed she didn't show it. Neither did she close the door on her way out.

He patted the space on the divan beside him. It seemed silly not to sit close to him, so she did. He lifted her hand to his lips, and she felt his lips brush her fingers – then he turned to the food.

'I'm starving, do you mind if I …?'

'Oh no, help yourself. I've eaten already.'

He reached for the noodles.

'Aren't you going to say Grace?' she said.

'Why don't you say it for me? I'm out of practice.'

She noticed that he didn't close his eyes; they were firmly on the bowls as she recited a short prayer.

He didn't say 'Amen' when she'd finished. She felt a little put out by this, but he looked at the food so hungrily that she said it for him.

He picked up the chopsticks and began to eat the fish and noodles. He asked, 'How have you been getting on? Who lives here with you? Surely you're not alone? Tell me everything.'

While he ate, she told him about her journey across the mountain pass and her first few weeks at the mission station. He listened, though she realised he knew all about the route, the passes, and the inns. He nodded as she spoke and scooped food into his mouth. When finished, he sat back on the divan and patted his stomach.

'That was the best food I've eaten since I left Beijing,' he said.

He moved nearer and reached for her hand.

'Sadie, I hate to ask but do you think you could put me up for the night? I know it's an inconvenience. I should have been here earlier – now the gates are closed.' He turned her hand over and gently rubbed the inside of her wrist with his thumb in a strangely intimate way.

'Here? You want to stay here?' She tried to think what Edith and Ruth would say.

Again, the rumble of thunder carried to them from the mountains, the wind lifted the dust from the loess and swirled it through the open window. The small pile of letters and parcels he had brought slid to the floor.

She pulled her hand from his and rushed to close the shutters. Eyes closed, she asked for guidance from the Holy Spirit, but nothing came to her mind.

'There's a guest bed in the building on the other side of the courtyard. You are very welcome to sleep there – there's also a kang near the kitchen if you'd find that more comfortable – that's if anyone can be comfortable on a kang. I know I still prefer to sleep on a straw mattress …' She stopped abruptly and flushed.

'Is Pao Chu staying here with you?' he said.

'Usually, yes. But she's gone to the next village to help a sick man. Why do you ask?'

'Oh, no reason in particular. I wouldn't like to think of you here alone, that's all.'

CHAPTER TWENTY-FIVE

The muffled thunder was definitely getting closer. From her bedroom window, she watched a sheet of lightning reveal the outline of the mountains on the horizon. Soon it would be here. Sadie knelt and prayed that the roof would hold. But the roof wasn't her only concern. She felt uneasy, acutely aware of the electricity in the atmosphere, aware of the man asleep on the other side of the courtyard. Another low growl of thunder brought the first heavy drops of rain. She watched the pomegranate trees wave their branches as though beseeching the drops to fall into them.

She ran to the kitchen and was relieved to find Yuan Bo and Shu Lan already placing basins and pots strategically around the kitchen floor. Obviously not their first rainstorm in this house.

The back door opened and Terrence came in, already wet through.

'The animals are all right. I've secured them. Now, what can I do to help?'

Lightning lit up the room. The rain drummed onto the roof tiles and she already heard the sound of dripping water.

'Help me with these,' she said as she gathered a pile of bowls and jugs.

Between them they carried whatever they could find upstairs and ran the length of the corridor opening doors as they went. They pulled chamber pots from under beds and left bowls dotted around the floor. Flashes of lightning lit the rooms and their oversized shadows filled the walls.

Terrence took some jugs to his bedroom. He told her it wasn't too bad, but that he'd seen tiles slide off the roof of the schoolroom. They ran out with the last of the pots, but it was too late. Water was trickling through a large hole in the roof. Terrence didn't seem deterred and she watched him place the last of the pots and pans beneath the little waterfalls and found herself smiling in the middle of it all, thankful that he was here with her.

The storm raged and battered the buildings for more than an hour. They returned to all the rooms throughout the storm and emptied all the receptacles as they filled to the brim and so managed to keep the main part of the house reasonably dry. It was almost dawn before everyone finally crawled into their beds.

The sun was already high in the sky when she awoke. She washed and dressed as quickly as she could and went to the courtyard. Terrence was standing outside the schoolroom. Her heart sank as she picked her way carefully through the shards of broken roof tiles that littered the ground.

'Good morning, Terrence,' she said. 'Though it really isn't a 'good morning', is it?'

'I'm afraid the storm did quite a bit of damage to the school.' He stood back to let her brush past him into the school building.

Through the several holes in the roof, she could see straight up to the blue sky. The classroom floors were awash with water. Drawings and posters lay in matted clumps along the floor.

Terrence followed her in. She was acutely aware of his eyes on her, waiting to see what she would do. She felt her tree-bark shoes getting soggy. Where to start? she thought. What would Edith do?

'We'd better see to the bedding in the house first,' she said.

'I saw a hand-cart in the yard,' said Terrence. 'I'll fetch it. We need to take everything out into the sun and let the building dry out. If you send Yuan Bo for fresh straw we can start drying out the rooms. It won't take long if the breeze keeps up, then we can see how the bedrooms are.' He smiled down at her. 'Don't worry, Sadie. It will be all right.'

She watched him walk away. Despite the devastation around her, she felt her heart lift. She was willing to believe that everything would be all right. More than that, he'd said '*we*' – as though they were a team working together. Partners. She was filled with joy and silently thanked God for sending him to her.

They spent the next few hours moving furniture and mopping. Yuan Bo complained in a low voice to Shu Lan about doing woman's work but she rolled her eyes and took no notice. Wet clothes and bedlinen were hung on lines in the sunshine. Doors were flung open and the warm air flowed through, taking the dampness with it.

When they'd done as much as they could, Shu Lan made them a rice porridge. Sadie wondered where Terrence had got to and went back to the classroom. She found him looking up at the ceiling.

'I've checked all the rooms,' he said. 'The tiles that are still in place aren't going to last long. You must get the roof repaired before the rains come. Judging from last night, they might be starting early.'

'I was afraid of that. Edith and Ruth have been worried about the roof for months. I'll have to get in touch with Wu Chow to let him know.'

'Wu Chow. I've heard of him, but if what I've heard is true, I'd say Wu Chow knows already. He's not one to spend money until he absolutely must.'

Sadie lifted her hands to her cheeks. 'We don't have the money for big repairs.' She was about to say they barely had enough to live on but she didn't want his pity.

He took a step closer and put an arm around her shoulders. 'Poor Sadie,' he said. 'I suppose this isn't what you expected.' He smiled into her eyes and stroked her cheek for a moment. When he stepped away, she felt a little off balance.

'Where did I leave my hat?' he said with a sudden burst of energy. 'I'll go and have a word with Wu Chow.'

He left the classroom and crossed to the main house and out to the kitchen yard. Sadie just about managed to keep up with his long strides.

'*Yuan Bo!*' he called. '*Bring my horse and saddle!*'

Yuan Bo reluctantly went to fetch the horse.

'That would be so very helpful,' she said. 'If he thinks that we are under the protection of a man, then perhaps he will do as we ask.' A wave of gratitude made her suddenly want to hug him, but she turned away and faced the garden as though looking for Yuan Bo.

Terrence put his hands on her shoulders. 'But you are.'

'Are what?'

He whispered close to her ear. 'Under my protection, Sadie.'

She bit her lip to stop it from trembling and felt ridiculously happy. She could see the horse and the top of Yuan Bo's straw hat as they walked through the bamboo toward them.

Terrence took the saddle and reins from Yuan Bo, who didn't seem completely sure what to do with either contraption. Sadie watched as Terrence placed the saddle across the horse's back and then tightened the straps under its girth. He pulled the reins over the horse's head.

'What will you say to Wu Chow?' she asked.

'He's a merchant,' said Terrence. 'I'll talk to him about business. I should be able to put some trade his way.'

Yuan Bo held the reins while Terrence mounted the horse, then ran to open the gate.

'What sort of business?' she asked, but he wasn't listening.

He tipped his heels against the horse's sides, and they went through the gate. Yuan Bo closed it firmly behind him.

She looked at the closed gate for a moment before shaking herself. Pathetic, she thought. Get a grip on yourself and stop mooning around. There's work to be done. I still haven't found the topic for the Bible study group on Wednesday. But first I'd better see how the bedding is getting on.

Three hours passed before she heard his horse's hooves smack in the mud. The back gate creaked open. She rushed outside to see him lead the horse through the gateway and hand the reins to Yuan Bo.

'All sorted,' he said. He wore a smug smile. 'Is there anything to eat? I'm starving!'

She followed him into the kitchen.

'But what happened?' she said.

Shu Lan placed bowls of guangdong noodles with steamed buns on the table and Terrence sat down to eat. She felt he was deliberately teasing her, but she held her tongue for as long as she could. It turned out not to be very long at all.

'Well?' She put her hands on her hips.

'Everything is sorted out,' he said. 'The workmen will be here shortly.'

Sadie sat down slowly. 'But how? What did he say?'

Terrence grinned across the table. 'Nothing for you to worry about. All is taken care of.'

'But that's not good enough.' Her voice sounded sharper than she'd intended. 'I'll have to tell Edith and Ruth. I'll have to explain all this when they get back.'

'Explain what when they get back?' Pao Chu came into the kitchen. She opened her eyes wider than Sadie had ever seen them. '*You,*' she said. 'What are you doing here?'

Sadie saw the look that passed between them. 'Pao Chu, you remember Mr. Bennett,' she said. 'He's been very helpful. The rain damaged the school roof and he went to Wu Chow and the workmen are coming to fix it. Isn't that wonderful?'

'What have you done?' Pao Chu fixed her eyes on him.

He picked up a dumpling with his chopsticks, popped it into his mouth, and shrugged.

'Only what any good Christian would do.' He mopped his mouth with a napkin and stood up. 'That sounds like the workmen arriving. Now, ladies, if you'll excuse me, I'd better have a word with them.' He left the kitchen.

Sadie went to follow him but Pao Chu reached out and put a hand on her arm. 'What have you done?' Her voice was raw with tiredness.

'Nothing, I haven't done anything.'

Pao Chu rubbed her forehead. 'You think you've done nothing. *You silly child!* You've put us in debt to a man who cannot be trusted. Do you really think Wu Chow would come and repair this house without a murmur? He is a merchant, a man of business. A deal has been made.

You can be sure of that. Why would you trust such a man? What do you know of Terrence Bennett? Nothing, I expect. Do you even know what he trades in? Don't say tea – the nearest tea plantation is a hundred miles from here. You've let yourself be led by your heart instead of using your head. He's filled you with dreams and romantic nonsense. For all you know, he is already married or promised to someone.'

Sadie felt as though she'd been slapped in the face. The words 'married or promised to someone' ran around her head. She realised that Pao Chu was still talking.

'What are you going to tell Edith and Ruth?' she said. 'What deal has he done? If it endangers this mission, Sadie, it will fall on your head.'

The workmen said it would take a few days, but would not commit to a definite number, to repair the tiles. Terrence said he would stay for two days to keep an eye on them but then he would have to go. Sadie was quietly pleased that he stayed, convinced that Pao Chu would come around to liking Terrence as much as she did – well, maybe not quite as much – once she saw how diligently would supervise the labourers.

'You've been so kind to me, to us, I mean,' she said. 'I'll ask Shu Lan to prepare a special meal.'

He raised an eyebrow. 'What have you got?'

'Nothing really special!' she said with a laugh. 'Noodles and eggs and fish. I think we may even have some peanuts.'

'A feast for an emperor.'

Pao Chu did not come down for dinner. She said she would stay in her room, that she was tired and needed to pray.

Sadie knew the real reason and she didn't try to coax her. 'She's old enough to make her mind up and there's nothing I can do to change it,' she whispered to herself.

She wouldn't acknowledge that she was thrilled that she and Terrence would be alone together all evening. They could have eaten in the formal dining room but she chose to sit on the divans as they'd done the first evening and placed the food on the low table. She found herself pleased to be able to behave in this bohemian way without the disapproving gaze of Pao Chu. They were relaxed and easy in each other's company. She found him even more attractive than when they'd been on the barque.

He wore his hair longer than most men, and she noticed that he often ran his fingers through it. He said something about not trusting the barbers who set up at random on the streets of the cities. She nodded and smiled but wasn't really listening. The phrase 'married or promised' came to the forefront of her mind. She tried to ignore it. No, she told herself, he wouldn't have been so attentive to me on board the ship in the first place if there was someone else.

She suddenly realised he'd stopped talking.

'Sorry, what?' she asked. Was he still talking about barbers?

'I was asking if you'd like to try the huangjiu that Wu Chow gave me. It's a sort of rice wine.'

'We don't usually have alcohol …'

'A small glass,' he said. 'I've opened it now.' He poured two glasses and handed her one. 'As I was saying, the barbers are not for me but they always attract a crowd when they produce their bamboo pole. From one end hangs a brass basin and from the other a small wooden cabinet for the customer to sit on.' He pulled at the hair at the nape of his neck.

He'd never mentioned a fiancé or wife; she was sure about that. She sipped the rice wine. There was no mark of a ring on his third finger.

'They're more used to braiding men's hair than cutting it, so I'm not sure how I'd end up. I doubt that a pigtail would suit me.'

She laughed and said, 'I think the long hair gives you the look of a romantic poet. Byron, I should say.'

He raised his eyebrows, and seemed pleased at the comparison. She felt her face redden.

They ate the food, and he complimented Shu Lan when she came to collect the plates. She seemed to have mellowed over the last few days and smiled broadly at him.

He talked about his travels and mentioned missionaries he'd met since he left England. She recognized some of the names from the London Missionary Society, and was glad to note that not one of them was a single woman, as far as she knew.

Night had fallen, and darkness had crept in without either noticing. Only the candle on the table lit the room. They'd talked for hours as though they'd known each other for years. She'd never felt more at ease talking to a man. Usually, men looked over her shoulder at prettier girls with better figures, but Terrence seemed captivated by her. He's just being polite, she told herself.

He was now sitting close beside her. Perhaps too close. She took a deep breath, and a musky scent filled her senses. A pomade on his hair? She tried to concentrate on what he was saying rather than how he smelled. She thought she shouldn't have any more rice wine.

'The thing is,' he said, 'foreigners, even Englishmen, are not revered or even liked here. Tolerated, at best. Attitudes change from province to province and the people of Shansi seem to be, let's say, relaxed, considering that many already think we're devils.' He looked at her expectantly.

She sat up straighter. 'I know. Every now and then townspeople seem to be suspicious of us. All we can do is be pleasant and set a good Christian example that they will follow. In time they will set aside their spirits and ghosts and come to believe as we do.' She smiled and glanced at him, confident that she'd given the correct answer.

'What about the Holy Spirit?' A grin played around his lips.

'That's completely different, and you know quite well it is. It's irreverent to bring the Holy Spirit into this.'

'I'll bet you prayed to him to get your roof fixed, didn't you?'

'I prayed ...' She bit her lip, annoyed that she'd fallen into his trap. 'God moves in mysterious ways.'

They fell silent for a while as they sipped the wine.

'You're not like the others, Sadie,' he said.

She could just about make out his features in the candlelit room. She was tempted to lean closer so that she could see his eyes.

'What others?' Her heart almost leapt from her chest. Was he about to compare her favourably with women he'd met?

'Other missionaries,' he said. 'Maybe it's because you're still quite new here.'

He leaned back, she couldn't see his face at all, but she knew when she was being teased.

She straightened her shoulders and tried to ignore her disappointment. 'Everyone is different, you know, you have to concede that much.'

'I'm not saying that you're not devout in your beliefs. It's just, I don't know, the zealousness isn't there.'

'Of course it's there. Edith has said I will be able to preach to the adults soon. I've worked very hard to improve my Chinese and I am allowed preach and tell Bible stories to the girls every day.'

'And they understand?'

'Yes, they do. Even though they seem to be fixated on Noah rather than Jesus,' she conceded. 'They're rather taken with the Ark and the animals and with Moses parting the Red Sea. But I am always there, taking small steps in the right direction, albeit in the background, but as zealous as any other missionary, Mr. Bennett. I can assure you of that.'

'I see.' He seemed to be slightly amused. 'And what do you make of their beliefs and customs? Their idols and their customs are as important to the Chinese people as yours are to you. You mustn't disrespect them.'

'We don't actively disrespect them. We just point out that the idols are meaningless.'

'How can you say that, Sadie, in all honesty? You are telling the Chinese that they shouldn't worship their ancestors? Wu Chow told me that one of your girl students refused to burn the gold paper at her grandmother's funeral.'

'Yes, that's true and she refused to bow to their idols. We were so proud of her. We are –'

'That's a fundamental belief of the Chinese. What you're telling them to do goes against the beliefs they've held for hundreds if not thousands of years. They have their own culture and traditions, their own beliefs. Why would they change? You can't expect them to suddenly turn away from that. I expect that girl will be ostracised by her family or she may not be let return to the school.'

'We're not forcing anybody to convert, but if they would just listen to the word of God they could be awakened to the knowledge that Our Lord exists and wants them to be saved.' She sipped the wine. She was enjoying this exchange. Terrence would think her a woman of the world. A pioneer.

'You expect them to listen to you, but you don't listen to them?'

'What we need is to get more churches built.' She was quoting the Armstrongs but couldn't recall the reasoning behind it.

'Don't even think about it, Sadie. This is not the time.'

'When is it ever the right time? I don't think such a thing exists. We can't decide on the right time. It's in the hands of the Lord. He will guide us.'

Silence fell between them and, after a few moments, Terrence stood. 'I'd better turn in. Early start tomorrow.'

She quickly got to her feet, a little unsteadily, and tried to hide her disappointment at his sudden urge to leave. She held out her hand.

'Goodnight, Terrence, sleep well.'

This time it was Terrence who held her hand longer than was necessary. He brought it to his lips and kissed it lightly. 'You're a good woman, Sadie. Your goodness shines like a candle in the darkness. I've never met anyone so innocent yet beguiling – but you need to think for yourself and not leave everything to God's will.'

She pulled her hand away as though scorched. 'I will always rely on God's will.' She raised her chin in defiance.

He drew closer to her and whispered, 'It could be that God's will is that you use the brain He gave you.'

He pulled her closer and kissed her gently on the lips. She felt his arms tighten around her as the kiss deepened. She tasted the rice wine on his tongue. Her arms slipped about his neck, her fingers pushed into his hair. The earth seemed to tilt a little, and she lost herself in the strange feeling that flooded through her.

The kiss ended, and he slid his hands along her bare arms until he reached her trembling hands. 'I'd better say goodnight, my beautiful young Sadie.' His eyes were fixed on her, and she couldn't seem to look away. 'You know where I am. Goodnight.'

He moved away, and she immediately wanted his arms again, but she stood and waited. He didn't turn his head.

You know where I am. She watched the open door, hoping he'd return, but the corridor outside was empty.

In a trance, she walked around the house and locked the doors. Moments later, she returned to check that she *had* locked them. Finally, she blew out the last of the candles and tiptoed up the stairs to her room.

She looked across the courtyard – the glow of a candle in his room was visible through the blinds. *You know where I am.* His voice was in her head. Perhaps I'm a fool, she thought. She remembered all the people he'd talked about during the evening. He must know dozens of beautiful women all over the country and back in England. She took a deep breath and fought the urge to go to him. *Get a grip, Sadie, don't make a fool of yourself.* She went to her bed and tried to sleep. Tomorrow will be a day like any other. I'll say a dignified goodbye to Terrence Bennett, then occupy myself somehow. Goodness! I haven't written anything for the prayer meeting tomorrow night! God knows there's plenty to do.

Five minutes later, she went to the window again. His candle was still burning. He was waiting for her. She paced between the window and the door, each time looking to see if the candle had been extinguished. She knelt and prayed, and when she moved again to the window, all was darkness. She knew she should be pleased that she'd been resolute, but she couldn't help wondering how it would feel to give herself to Terrence, to be wrapped in his arms, to be Mrs. Bennett.

When Sadie woke, her room was already filled with light. Could he have left without saying goodbye? She dressed quickly and ran a brush through her hair. She didn't have time to pin it up. She wanted to run down the stairs, but her head throbbed.

Shu Lan looked up from the large pot she was stirring and smirked at her.

Sadie pulled back her shoulders and cast a cold eye at the cook. 'Where is Mr. Bennett?' Her voice was sharp.

Shu Lan pointed to the door.

Sadie went quickly to the garden at the back of the house. She heard the water pumping – then she saw him. He was carrying a bucket of water to his horse and wasn't wearing a shirt.

He casually waved to her, and she automatically waved back but wasn't sure of the protocol for talking to a man without his shirt in these circumstances. She tried not to stare at his body as he came toward her and wasn't sure where to look. His dark curly chest hair seemed to draw her eyes like a magnet.

'Shu Lan kindly offered to launder my shirts.' He grinned at her as though it was perfectly normal to chat without being fully dressed.

She blushed and nodded, and turned back to the kitchen.

He followed.

'Shu Lan, are Mr. Bennett's shirts ready?' There was an urgency in her voice.

Shu Lan went to the line and unpegged the laundry blowing in the breeze. She held up one of Terrence's shirts by the shoulders and waved it around, smiling. 'Big man shirt.'

Terrence laughed out loud. Sadie blushed.

'I'd better put this on,' he said. Though he didn't seem in too much of a hurry to do so. 'Good idea, that.' He pointed at the tunic Sadie had on. 'Wearing loose clothing. Some of the missionaries I've met insist on wearing the dresses from home. I don't know how they do it in summer. Must be stifling.'

Sadie swallowed and nodded.

'It suits you, that shade of blue, I mean. You look particularly beautiful in it.'

That's twice he's said I'm beautiful. She reached for a laundry pile and began folding the clothes as though they were exceptionally precious.

He pulled on his shirt and buttoned it up. 'I'm nearly ready to be off now. Is there anything you want me to take back to Beijing?'

'No. Sorry, I mean, yes … I've some letters. If you wouldn't mind taking them.'

She rushed back to her room. Still flustered, she pulled out drawers and looked under the table before finding them.

He was waiting for her at the foot of the stairs. She slowed her pace. It wouldn't do to tumble down and disgrace herself. She handed over the letters, head down without looking at his face. She knew her own face had flushed to bright red.

'I must get ready for our Bible readings this evening,' she said. 'Can't leave everything to Pao Chu.' She tried to sound jolly, as she always did when embarrassed. 'Thank you for taking the letters and for your help with the roof. Goodbye.' She held out her hand and felt his hand envelop hers. She wanted him to pull her toward him. His eyes met hers, but she couldn't hold his gaze. 'God bless you. Safe journey,' she managed to say. but couldn't seem to release his hand.

He pulled her toward him and kissed her softly.

'Goodbye, my beguiling Sadie,' he said. 'I'll be back before you know it. Perhaps December.' He released her and looked into her face. 'Christmas isn't too far away, is it?'

'No, it's not,' she said half-heartedly. 'Christmas would be lovely.' He may as well have said ten years not six months, and how could she be sure that he would come then? Would he even write to her? She couldn't find the courage to ask, nor could she see the point. If she asked, he would most certainly say that he would write, but he'd said that before. She was beginning to understand that Terrence wasn't always a man of his word – but she didn't care.

'I'd best be off now, I've a long way to go.' He held her close for a moment. His shirt smelled of lavender soap, his arms felt strong, and she was willing to believe she would see him again at Christmas. He released her and went back toward the kitchen, calling for Yuan Bo.

She couldn't speak. Instead of going to fetch her Bible, she went upstairs to a room that overlooked the yard. She watched him saddle his horse and managed to stop herself from running down the stairs for one more embrace. He mounted the horse and took the mule's lead from Yung Bo. He was really going. The pain felt like hunger in her stomach. He half-turned on his horse to look back at the house. She ducked out of his sight.

'I've fallen in love with him.' Even as she whispered these words, she wondered if it really was love, this overpowering feeling, this need to see him one more time, even for one more minute.

She heard the horse and mule move slowly away from the house, and when she peered through the window again he was completely gone from her sight.

CHAPTER TWENTY-SIX

Edith and Ruth returned from their meeting with the missionaries in Fen Chow Fu positively aglow with energy.

'Letters for you!' Ruth waved them above her head.

'Miss Duval and the charming young Mr. Robinson asked us to deliver them to you.' Ruth actually winked at her.

'Thank you.' She forced a smile. 'I'll read them later. Tell me all about your trip.'

'Wonderful, just wonderful. It was restorative and fulfilling. We had prayer meetings and discussions on the Gospels. There were visitors, missionaries we'd never met before, and doctors from the mission hospital in Shou Yang – we spoke with them quite a lot and they had some exciting ideas.'

Sadie was glad they were in good spirits and thought she'd let them finish before telling them about the roof. They talked for quite a while over several cups of tea. Eventually, there came a lull.

Sadie shifted in her seat and was about to launch into the version she'd rehearsed in her head.

'There is something –' Edith and Sadie said at the same time.

'You go first,' said Sadie, pleased to put off the roof story as long as possible.

Edith looked as though she'd drawn the short straw. 'There is something, dear, that we'd like to talk to you about.' She tapped the tops of her fingers together as she spoke. 'While we were in Fen Chow Fu, we spoke with Mr. and Mrs. Pigott.'

'They told us to call them Tom and Jessie!' said Ruth.

Edith raised her eyebrows in a 'what's that got to do with anything?' expression before she went on. 'The thing is, they're thinking of leaving Fen Chow Fu to build a school for foreign children in Shou Yang. They feel there is a great need for it. So many missionaries have children and this would mean they wouldn't have to send them all the way back to England for their basic education.'

'I see,' said Sadie, looking from one to another, not really seeing at all. 'That's excellent ... but ... that wouldn't affect us in any way, would it?'

'Well ...' Edith glanced at Ruth. 'You see, our pupils could be transferred to the Pigotts' new mission station if their parents agree to them going as boarders. That would have to be discussed with them. It's not going to happen until next year. Mr. Pigott will take charge of the building of the school himself. If he can organise the funding and the labour, he hopes to have it ready by March next year. These things take time, and money. Nothing happens quickly in this country.'

Sadie shook her head. 'You mean you'd close this mission? Why? And what would we do then? Where would we go?'

'It was when we spoke with the doctors in Fen Chow Fu that it came to us,' said Edith. 'You see, they try to help the opium addicts and they've read many articles about addiction in the medical journals. Even here we've become aware of the very real damage that's been done to so many Chinese, both physically and mentally, by their addiction to opium. Once the men get hooked on it they change completely. Men that had businesses, farms with families to support, just lose interest in everything. They don't want to work, they don't seem to care if their wives and children starve. All they want is another pipe full of the stuff to smoke and not a thought for their dependents. It's pitiful to see them wasting away. The doctors said that there doesn't seem to be any cure except abstinence from the drug. So we talked and prayed about it.' She took a deep breath. 'What we think is that if we can provide a refuge and support, there is every chance they can be saved from ruining their lives and the lives of their families and may in time come into the light of the Lord.'

'Oh, dear God!' Sadie stood up. 'You can't think of opening the mission to opium addicts! We couldn't, well, I couldn't cope with them.'

'Sit down, Sadie. It's all right. We did wonder. I mean Ruth and I wondered, if perhaps you'd prefer to help Mr. and Mrs. Pigott in their new school? If some of our pupils transfer there, it would help settle them to have a familiar face. What do you think?'

Sadie watched the two faces opposite her, filled with concern and apprehension. 'Yes,' she said. ' Of course I would be happy to work at the mission with the Pigotts. I would like that very much.'

The ladies clapped their hands together, and Sadie realised how much they must have worried and discussed this. Her heart warmed to them, to their goodness.

'It's my turn to give you some news,' said Sadie. 'The most amazing thing. Wu Chow has fixed the roof.'

She told them about the storm, the roof, and how Terrence Bennett somehow persuaded their Chinese landlord to make the repairs.

'It's a miracle,' declared Edith. 'He's been impossible with us, can't get him to do anything. So, who is this Mr. Bennett and why was he here?'

Sadie had deliberately skipped over any details about Terrence, but she realised that she had to give some sort of explanation for his visit. She also knew that Shu Lan and her husband would be happy, maybe more than happy, to give chapter and verse about the nights he'd stayed.

'We met him on the ship. Miss Duval and Mr. Robinson met him too.'

'I don't think they mentioned a Mr. Bennett, did they, Edith? Is he a missionary?' said Ruth.

'No, though he's a Christian. He's a tea trader.' Sadie picked her words carefully. She wouldn't lie, but she made sure to present Terrence in the best possible light. 'He knows the Armstrongs and he was kind enough to bring letters. It was a bit out of his way – he usually only comes as far as the capital. Wasn't that kind of him? Mr. Wu Chow did as he promised that very day and all the repairs have been carried out.'

'Good for you, Sadie!' said Ruth. 'I knew you'd be a great help.' She raised her teacup in a toast, but Edith didn't join her.

'And how much did it cost?' Edith had the look of a sparrow hawk who'd just seen a mouse.

'Not a penny.' Sadie's smile waned a little.

'And Mr. Bennett, would he have contributed to the cost in any way?' Edith looked stern.

'Mr. Bennett said that he might be in a position to put some trade Wu Chow's way? I think that's it, well, something like that.' She bit her lip.

'You said he was a tea trader?'

'Yes. Mainly – and he sometimes buys pieces of furniture or pottery.'

'That's all?' Edith held the girl's gaze. 'Are you sure that's all?'

'I … I think so.' Sadie tried to remember the conversation, but the details of what he traded hadn't been her focus of attention. She didn't like the way Edith was looking at her. Almost the same way that Pao Chu had.

'Perhaps it's all right,' said Edith after an age. 'It's just that Wu Chow is hard to deal with – he's promised to fix the roof before, but then he moans about the cost of the tiles and the labour. I wonder what it was that persuaded him this time?'

Sadie felt her skin grow hot. 'Terrence said I … we were under his protection. Wu Chow wouldn't want to upset an Englishman, I'm sure.'

Sadie caught the look that passed between the two women. She found her temper rising. 'I did the best I could in the circumstances. Mr. Bennett was kind enough to help us, and I think we should be grateful to him. In fact, I've invited him to come for Christmas.'

'Have you indeed?' said Edith. 'Well, that might be a good thing. I should very much like to have a chat with Mr. Terrence Bennett.'

CHAPTER TWENTY-SEVEN

It was still three days to Christmas when Sadie heard the crack of hoarfrost under boots. She lifted her head from her studies. Could it be?

She rushed to the room on the other side of the corridor and crossed to the window. The window she'd last seen him through six months ago. The morning sun danced on the ice and made the roofs glitter as he strode across the yard toward the back of the house, his horse and mule following behind as though it was the most natural thing in the world. She put her hand on her chest and felt her heart thump.

Sadie heard Shu Lan shout, '*Big Man! Why you back?*'

'*I came back for more of your cooking, of course. Is Miss Sadie here?*'

Sadie rushed back to her room where she brushed her hair and checked that her skirt and tunic were neat and stain-free. Then she pinched her cheeks and bit her lips to bring up their colour.

She went to the top of the stairs, her heart still thudding, but stopped as she saw Edith come bustling out of the drawing room, paper and pen in hand. Edith stopped abruptly – faced with the sight of Shu Lan mopping Terrence's footprints and complaining loudly.

Sadie pulled back around the corner.

'Can I help you?' said Edith.

Sadie could hear the suspicion in her voice.

'You must be either Miss Searell or Miss Whitechurch,' came Terrence's voice. 'I'm Terrence Bennett.'

Sadie risked a one-eyed peek around the corner.

She saw Terrence hold out his hand, and Edith take it, though only briefly.

'I'm Edith Searell,' she said.

Terrence had his back to Sadie, but she had a clear view of Edith's unsmiling face. Well, Edith's not one to waste a smile, she thought. I bet Pao Chu has turned her against him – probably told her about Terrence and me. That's really not very fair at all.

Terrence broke the silence. 'I was here some months ago. I thought I'd call in to ensure the repair work was done to your satisfaction.' He glanced toward the window at the thickening snow. 'I was concerned that you ladies would be exposed to the elements.'

Touché, thought Sadie. Edith will have to be gracious now.

'Yes, that was kind of you, Mr. Bennett,' said Edith in a grudging voice.

'Please call me Terrence.'

She has to invite him to stay now, thought Sadie. Time I went down and said hello.

She took a deep shaky breath and went down the stairs. 'Hello, Terrence,' she said. She held out her hand as she reached them.

His cold hand took hers and squeezed it slightly before letting go.

'How have you been, Sadie?'

She felt Edith's disapproving eyes on her – probably shocked that he hadn't called her Miss Bradshaw – but she avoided meeting them.

'I've been well, thank you. But you look frozen. Shall we have some tea in the kitchen? It's the warmest room in the house. We don't light the fires in the other rooms during the day. Have you time for tea, Edith?'

Much to Sadie's disappointment, she said she had.

They sat formally upright at the table. Sadie wished that Edith would leave but knew she wouldn't, not until she'd interrogated Terrence. Sadie tried not to be too bright and welcoming. She must treat him as though he were an ordinary visitor, though visitors were few and far between.

Shu Lan put a pot of tea in the centre of the table and Sadie began to pour.

'Will you be able to stay for Christmas?' said Sadie. 'It's the least we can do after all the help you gave the mission the last time you were here. Isn't it, Edith?'

Edith's thin smile didn't reach her eyes. 'Yes, of course, Mr. Bennett. You would be most welcome to stay with us for Christmas. I will ask Shu Lan to make up a bed for you.'

'No need,' said Sadie. 'I asked Shu Lan to have rooms ready in case anyone came.'

'Like who?' Edith looked sharply at her.

'I don't know, Edith, but I thought if anyone did call to the mission it would be nice to offer them hospitality and a bed for the night at Christmas.'

Edith turned her attention back to Terrence and watched him over her spectacles.

'How long have you been coming to Shansi province, Mr. Bennett?' she asked.

'Off and on about six years, I should say. It's hard to keep track of time here, isn't it?'

'We stick with the Gregorian calendar, Mr. Bennett. That keeps us on the straight and narrow. Isn't it odd that we have never met you before now? I myself have been in China some fifteen years. With so few foreigners around I'd have expected that we would have met at some point.'

'Usually when I come to Shansi on business the merchants offer me a room. They are very hospitable to me. But you're quite right. I keep to the trade routes and don't often venture further than Taiyuan. But the last time I was in Beijing Mrs. Armstrong asked me to call to see Sadie, I mean Miss Bradshaw, and it was only another two days' ride. Mrs. Armstrong seems to have taken a special interest in Sadie and asked me to find out how she was getting on.'

'There's a perfectly good messaging service for that. Mrs. Armstrong could have sent a telegram to Taiyuan if she was concerned for Miss Bradshaw.'

Terrence nodded. 'True, but there's only so much one can say in a telegram.'

Edith sipped her tea and watched him as though he were a dangerous snake.

Sadie held her small cup in two hands. She tried to behave normally but knew her face was flushed with happiness that was beyond her control.

'Christmas is the most wonderful time, isn't it?' she said.

Edith left a short pause before she answered. 'Quite wonderful.' Her voice was flat. 'It is the season of good tidings to *all* men, I suppose.'

There was no doubt about it: the house felt different with a man in it. Whistling. He whistled in the mornings when he shaved. In the evenings, a whiff of cigar smoke floated in certain rooms. Alien smells and sounds, though not unpleasant.

Sadie suspected that Edith and Ruth had a conversation about Terrence and decided she needed a chaperone. Edith or Ruth often appeared at odd moments to check 'how she was getting on'. Terrence seemed determined to outwit them at every turn. He invited her to go with him to the town in the cart he'd hired. He brought back practical things like logs for the fire, oil for lamps, fine writing paper and ink, and many large candles and scented oils. He bought rice wine, delicacies that made Shu Lan happy, and a goose that she plucked enthusiastically. Sadie thought this would be the best Christmas she'd ever had, and it was all because of Terrence. She didn't want it to end, and put the fact that it must out of her mind.

On Christmas morning, Terrence helped them push back the divans and the low table in the largest room. All the servants and Chinese Christians had been invited to prayers, readings, and carols. Everyone crowded into the house and wished a peaceful and happy Christmas to all. Terrence joined in and sang the hymns with gusto. Sadie read the nativity story from the Gospels with tears of happiness shining in her eyes. They prayed for all the people of China to find the one true God.

After the carols Sadie poured tea, and Shu Lan served sesame seed balls and butter biscuits. Pao Chu had been invited to the house of one of the Chinese Christians, and said goodbye to Sadie. After everyone had departed with the Word of the Lord ringing in their ears, the missionaries and Terrence sat down to eat the cooked goose, vegetables and dumplings. Terrence offered them a glass of rice wine. Edith refused, Ruth also shook her head though a little less enthusiastically and Sadie, seeing that, felt she shouldn't have any either.

She had to constantly remind herself not to stare at Terrence across the table. He listened to the stories of the three women missionaries, smiled, and nodded in the right places. He even asked some interesting questions that showed his knowledge of the country and its people.

Sadie looked fondly at him. She knew he was trying his best for her sake. The same could not be said for Edith. On the surface, she seemed perfectly polite to Terrence, but Sadie noticed that she answered his questions in short sentences. There were a lot of pauses in the conversation when the sound of heavy cutlery scratching across plates filled the room. Sadie had mentioned twice that the cutlery and plates had come with Edith and Ruth from England. Now she searched for something else to break the silence.

'Edith and Ruth are changing the mission house into a place where people can come to be cured from addiction to opium,' she said.

For a moment, she thought she shouldn't have mentioned that. It was, after all, not wholly finalized, but to her relief Edith turned toward Terrence and asked what he thought of the plan.

'I didn't think there was a cure for opium addiction,' he said.

'There isn't, as far as we know.' Ruth nodded in agreement as she sucked in the last of the noodles.

'So how do you propose to go about it?' said Terrence. 'You can't expect addicts to suddenly stop. They'll go mad. I've heard of men willing to sell their children for a pipeful of opium.'

'We're here long enough to know that!' Edith snapped. She pressed her lips together then spoke as though addressing a child. 'We will provide a place of safety, where those addicted can come. I've read articles in respected journals that say reducing the amount of opium little by little, day by day, can be very successful.'

More than anything, Sadie wanted Edith and Ruth to approve of Terrence, but she could see by his face that he was intent on arguing the point.

Terrence opened his mouth to respond to Edith, but Sadie cut across before he could speak.

'The locals had theatricals a few weeks ago. They all came out every evening and watched the performers act out plays. There was singing and dancing. The costumes and masks were spectacular, but it was so noisy we couldn't get to sleep. Isn't that right, Ruth?'

'Yes, absolutely right. Three days and nights it went on for, some of it very inappropriate, I could see over the wall if I stood on a chair. Absolute torture to my unaccustomed ears, a sort of mix between opera and folksongs but the locals loved it. Yes, the costumes and masks were most spectacular, and the dances were very graceful.'

'How long did you spend on that chair, Ruth?' He smiled across at her. 'They do love their theatricals. It's a competition between neighbourhoods to see who can have the theatre for longest. The longer the performers stay the more prestige the neighbourhood gains.'

'Yes,' said Edith. 'In fact, one of the townspeople came in here, to this very room, and asked me to contribute money to extend the whole thing by another three days.'

Sadie was pleased to see her engage.

'And did you?' Terrence asked.

'Of course not! It was a disgrace. The people became very raucous at night. We couldn't wait for it to go. I told him in no uncertain terms that I would be delighted when it finished and sent him on his way. He was not too happy about it, I can tell you.'

The women nodded in agreement.

Sadie looked at Terrence, expecting him to congratulate Edith on not being cajoled into giving a donation. After all, they were there to promote Christianity, not provide Chinese entertainment.

Terrence put his fingertips across his mouth the way people do when they hear bad news.

'What is it, Terrence? What's wrong?' said Sadie.

'You've made no friends there, Miss Searell,' he said quietly. 'In fact, I think you might have made quite a few enemies.'

'I'm not here to make 'friends', Mr. Bennett,' said Edith, and pulled back her shoulders.

'You must have known,' he went on, 'that to refuse to contribute to the communal festival would not go down well with your neighbours. It strikes me that if you do go ahead with this centre for saving opium addicts you may have to rely on the goodwill of your neighbours. It may not be the sort of thing that they would support on their street. Schooling children is one thing, Miss Searell – inviting opium addicts into the neighbourhood is entirely another. You might do well to reconsider.'

'What makes you think they are not already here?' said Edith. 'You may not see them lying about in the streets, but I speak to the women of this town every day and more and more they have the same story. It's getting worse, they say – their husbands, who used to smoke a pipe of opium socially, have become dependent. They will not attend to their work or labour in the fields. Slowly but surely the grip of the opium strangles them until they become ghosts of the men they once were. They are already here, Mr. Bennett, but hidden in their homes while their wives try to sustain the family. Believe me, any help we can give these people they will take and appreciate. I have no doubt of it.'

'You must do whatever you think is best, Miss Searell. But I don't think you will have much success.'

'There we can agree, Mr. Bennett. We will not have success until the people who bring the drug into the country and sell it cheaply can be stopped. They bribe their way in and out without hindrance. Why, Mr. Bennett, you probably meet many of them on your travels about the country, do you not?'

'I wouldn't know, Miss Searell – but it's not illegal to sell opium.'

'Perhaps not illegal, but it is most certainly immoral.'

Sadie looked from Edith's flushed face to Terrence's cool gaze. What on earth was going on? Why was Edith being so horrible to Terrence after all he'd done?

'It's time for gifts!' Sadie stood up quickly. 'Let's all go into the drawing room.'

'I'll go first,' Sadie said, when they were all settled.

She watched excitedly as each person opened the miniature painting she'd made for them. She'd used the last of her watercolours to paint some of the local scenery and plants.

Terrence's picture was of the little stream at the bottom of the garden.

'It's charming, Sadie, absolutely wonderful the way you've captured the water and stepping-stones. I shall have it framed as soon as I get back to Beijing.'

She watched with pleasure as he carefully rolled it up and tied it with the little ribbon she'd attached to it.

'Mine next,' said Ruth, clapping her hands together.

She handed out soft packages and they opened them to reveal knitted socks. They pretended complete surprise, but they'd all heard the fierce *clickity-clack* of knitting needles for several weeks coming from Ruth's bedroom.

Terrence's package contained just one sock.

'I'm sorry! But men have such big feet I'm afraid the other one won't be ready until the new year!' said Ruth.

Terrence held up the single sock and said he would look forward to receiving its mate in the new year. 'That's if you don't mind me staying till then.'

Even Edith laughed.

'Of course you must stay – if the snow continues the roads and passes will be closed,' said Sadie, avoiding Edith's eyes. 'Imagine! The year nineteen hundred. How will we get used to a new century?'

'We don't have a choice,' said Edith. 'Now, it's my turn.'

She gave each of them a pouch tied with a silk ribbon. Inside, Ruth and Sadie found dainty white collars that Edith had crocheted. Sadie strained to see what was in Terrence's pouch. It was a crisp white handkerchief with the letter 'T' embroidered in dark-blue silk thread.

'What exquisite work, Miss Edith! I very much appreciate your kindness.' He seemed quite moved by the gesture.

Edith nodded, and Sadie was relieved that a truce seemed to have been declared.

'Excuse me, ladies.' Terrence left the room, returned a moment later, and handed out presents.

'With thanks for this wonderful Christmas and good wishes for the New Year, the new century!'

Each of them unwrapped a small rectangular lacquered box.

Edith's box was bright blue and Ruth's pale green, each decorated with tiny blue and green hand-painted flowers. The edge of each lid was decorated with a swirling gold line surrounding the flowers. The interiors were painted in bright red lacquer, hard, smooth, and shiny.

The top of Sadie's box was a golden yellow with tiny purple flowers. She thought she'd never seen anything quite so exquisite in all her life.

'I don't think we can accept such gifts – they're obviously very expensive,' said Edith.

'Oh, you must, please! You've all been so kind to me.'

Terrence seemed determined and, in the end, Edith and Ruth

219

accepted the trinket boxes – a little uneasily, Sadie thought. She joined in the thanks, looked at the pretty lacquered box, and tried to reason why she felt somehow disappointed. It was a beautiful gift; she should appreciate it, she knew that. She watched Terrence's smiling face, obviously pleased with the reaction. Sadie forced a smile and said something about how lovely it was. She told herself it was ridiculous to be disappointed because he hadn't given her something different from the others, something that was just for her. She was sure she was special to him. Almost completely sure.

Every night she dallied at bedtime to ensure that she was the one dousing the candles and checking the locked doors. Every night Terrence hung back to help her. His eyes followed her around the room. Every night they spent these last few precious minutes together until she reluctantly pulled away for she knew that Edith or Ruth would come down the stairs if they did not hear her go to her room and he to his.

But this was his last night. Tomorrow he would leave for Beijing. She put a bright smile on her face throughout the evening while her heart fluttered with desperation. They would have just a few moments alone to say goodbye and tomorrow he would be gone.

He impatiently raked the fire and waited for her to cross the room to him.

'Sadie, come sit with me. There's something I want to talk to you about.'

Her heart raced. This was exactly how she'd thought it would be. The glow from the dying fire, through the window the glistening snow on the stark bare branches of the pomegranate trees. I will remember this for the rest of my life, she thought. She sat beside him on the divan.

He held her hand in his and looked into her eyes. 'Sadie,' he said, 'are you sure about all this?'

'All what?'

'Being a missionary, here.' He waved his hand toward the window. 'Is it what you really want to do with your life?'

'It is most definitely what I want to do,' she said. 'It's what I've always wanted. It doesn't have to be in this particular mission, but I was always drawn to China.'

'Could it be in Beijing? Could you come with me to Beijing? You know how I feel about you, Sadie.'

'I can't go to Beijing.' Why is he teasing me like this? Why so cruel? 'You've never actually said how you feel about me. Not in words.' I can't put it any plainer than that, she thought.

He pulled her to him and kissed her lips.

She pulled away. 'Terrence, what are you asking me?'

'To be mine. I want you to be mine. The sooner the better. Will you have me, Sadie?'

She felt his fingers stroke her neck, his breath fell on her shoulder.

'I could get you your own apartment, if you like.' His voice was low, desire in his eyes

She flushed deeply. 'What do you take me for?' She tried to pull her hand from his, but he tightened his grasp. 'You're hurting my wrist, Terrence.'

He released her. 'I'm sorry. I've handled this badly.' He stood and ran his hand through his hair. 'I should have been gentler, but my emotions took hold. I've never done this before, you see.'

'Done what?'

He took a deep breath and paused for a few moments as though gathering his thoughts. 'I'm a good deal older than you, Sadie, but fifteen years isn't too big a gap to bridge, is it?' His voice was softer now.

She rubbed her wrist, more for effect than actual hurt.

He sat beside her again, took her hand and brought her wrist to his lips.

'Sadie, I haven't always been a good person, and when I compare myself to you, how good and kind you are, so different from anyone I've ever met before, I see what a selfish life I've lived, up till now. If anyone can make me a better person, it's you. I'm asking you to save me. I'm asking you to be my wife.'

It hadn't the romantic air that she'd hoped for. Perhaps it was just nerves.

She looked into his eyes. 'Yes, Terrence,' she said. 'I'll marry you.'

From his pocket he produced a small black box, opened it and turned it toward her.

'It's beautiful,' she said.

He took the gold ring – a dark round ruby surrounded by pale opals – out of the box and slid it onto her finger.

'Well, that's settled then,' he said. 'I'll delay going to Beijing until the end of the week. That should be enough time to get your things together.'

'I can't go to Beijing,' said Sadie. 'It's out of the question. I can't just go off and leave Edith and Ruth. They are depending on me.'

'I'm sure if we explain, they'll understand. It will be months before I can come back.' He kissed her neck.

'No,' she said. 'Really I can't.' She leaned into him slightly. 'I have commitments and responsibilities that I must carry out. I've already written to Mr. Pigott to say I will teach at their school.'

They both heard the footsteps walking along the landing. They knew what it meant.

They rose and went quickly to the door.

'Come to me when everyone is asleep,' he said as he left. 'We have so much to talk about.'

Sadie closed the door behind him and went up the stairs, her tread heavier than usual. She sat on the side of her bed, waited and thought about what this would mean. She would be married to Terrence. *Married.* She could barely believe it and held her hand out in front of her to admire the ring. She went to the window. The full moon glowed like a pearl. The distant mountains looked nearer, their white peaks stark against the midnight blue sky. She twisted the ring on her finger. Opals, she thought. Aren't they bad luck? Terrence mustn't know about that. He's waiting for me. *We have so much to talk about.* She put her hand on her neck in the place where his lips had been.

A few minutes later she slipped quietly out of the main house and along the veranda to his room. They whispered their plans. He wanted her to come with him as soon as possible, but again she said she couldn't.

'Let's not tell anyone just yet,' she said. 'At least until you come back from Beijing. I won't wear the ring, though it is so beautiful. I'll look at it every day. Six months will give me a chance to break it to them gently.'

'It will seem like an eternity,' he said and held her to him.

She knew it was wrong, but in the heat of the moment, his body urgent, his lips on hers, she forgot everything. Nothing else mattered. It couldn't be a sin. They were engaged to be married. Promises had been made.

The next morning, she washed and dressed carefully. Combed and pinned up her fair hair. *Breathe*, she told herself, *just breathe*. She stopped to look at herself in the mirror in the hallway. Do I look any different? It must show on my face that I'm not the same person – that I can never be the same again.

She took a deep breath to steady her thumping heart and walked toward the kitchen, touching the ring in her pocket. I won't let my feelings ruin the last hours together. Anyhow, we won't be apart for long. We will be married in Beijing, A warm glow spread through her. Though in her heart she felt that he was already her husband and she his wife.

He stood when she came in and their eyes locked. She blushed and waved at him to sit down. Ruth was too busy pouring tea to notice.

'Good morning, Sadie. Terrence has just been telling me he ran into Doctor Edwards in the hospital in Taiyuan and –'

'Were you ill?' The words were out of her mouth before she could stop them.

He grinned. 'No, not at all. We had a little business to conduct, that's all.'

'Have some more eggs,' said Ruth. 'The chickens are laying well this week. How are things in Taiyuan? Had the doctor any news?'

'There was something that concerned him all right but it might be a rumour.' He helped himself to another egg. 'You know how things are here. Rumours, I mean. You're never quite sure if what you hear is the truth or someone's imagination. Doctor Edwards has heard there's a chance that the new governor of Taiyuan will be Yu Hsien.'

Sadie poured herself some tea, sat beside Ruth, and looked from one to the other.

Ruth had gone quite pale.

'No, it couldn't be.' Ruth pushed away her plate. 'Surely the Dowager Empress wouldn't do that. It can't be true.'

'Why?' said Sadie. 'What's wrong?'

Terrence spoke quietly. 'Yu Hsien is the governor in the Shantung Provence – he's well known for his anti-foreigner stance. Last summer, a missionary named Brooks was killed in Shantung. Did you know him?'

They both shook their heads.

'Although Yu Hsien didn't actually kill Mr. Brooks, he's let his feelings about foreigners be known. No one was arrested for the murder, which has sent an undeniable signal to anyone of the same mind.'

'Even if they did make him the governor of Shansi, the people here have never been violent – they've always been welcoming and peaceful,' said Ruth.

Edith came in just as Ruth spoke.

'What did you just say, Ruth?' she said as she sat down. 'Make who governor?'

Ruth looked anxiously at her. 'Mr. Bennett met Doctor Edwards in the hospital in Taiyuan and the doctor had heard that there's a chance that the new governor of Taiyuan will be Yu Hsien.'

Edith was visibly shocked but said quietly, 'We must pray that this man does not progress any higher in the regime.' She looked at Ruth 'What you just said is right – we've always been welcomed, but people are sometimes suspicious of us and what we stand for. But we are making progress with conversions. It's true that suspicion can turn to anger very quickly. We don't always know what's being said about us. But we can only do what we were sent here to do. Continue to spread the word of the one true God as He intended us to do. In fact, I think we will bring forward our plan to open the recovery centre.'

'Perhaps he won't be made governor ...' Sadie's voice drifted away. She hadn't paid much attention to the politics of China and had only the barest knowledge of how the country was run. She knew about the Dowager Empress in the palace in Beijing but had taken very little notice of the regional governors and prefects. Terrence must think me an awful dunce, she thought.

'Do you have any arms here for protection?' he said.

'Absolutely not,' said Edith. 'What sort of message would that send out to the people?'

'That you have the capability to defend yourselves, and even cause harm to those who might see you as easy prey. That would be a useful message to send. I could get you a small pistol, something easy to handle, if you like?'

Edith shook her head. 'We will never bear arms against the Chinese.'

'As you wish, Miss Edith. Let's hope you won't regret it.' He stood up from the table.

The morning was clear and bright, but the sun held no warmth against the biting breeze. Everyone wore their coats when they gathered in the kitchen yard and shook his hand.

Sadie was consoled, just a little, by the kiss on her cheek and the sadness in his eyes when he whispered goodbye in her ear. She was aware of the look between Edith and Ruth, but she couldn't worry about that now. She was having enough trouble keeping the shaky smile on her face while quietly dying inside.

He mounted his horse. Yuan Bo handed him the mule's lead, and Terrence rode to the gate. He turned to wave a final goodbye to the group, and they held up their hands in a last salute as he disappeared through the gate to the laneway. Edith and Ruth hurried back to the warmth of the kitchen while Sadie stood a few moments longer, listening to the sound of the hooves growing fainter until they disappeared completely.

CHAPTER TWENTY-EIGHT

China, 1900

At first, she thought she imagined it, was overly sensitive, but during the last few weeks there seemed to be a shift in the people's attitude and behaviour. Small things. The shopkeepers didn't look them in the eye or give the usual greetings. People who'd attended their evening Bible classes stopped coming and disappeared down laneways or swerved into shops if they met them in the street. More worryingly, many schoolchildren didn't attend class, and their parents closed the door in their faces when they went to enquire if something was wrong.

In the past, from time to time, mud would be thrown at Ruth, Edith, or Sadie by youths, but now it seemed to happen a little more often. The most frightening thing was the noise at night. Increasingly they heard the thud of stones banging against the wooden gate. It seemed to go on for hours. Edith and Ruth tutted and complained about boys being let run wild by their parents. At first, Sadie was comforted by their attitude, but as it continued, night after night, they all became less tolerant, their nerves frazzled. She tried to hide her growing fear. Edith said the locals might have heard about their plans to open the addiction clinic. She didn't mention that Terrence could have been right about that.

Red balloons tied to trees or buildings started to appear. They thought it meant the theatrical company was coming back. More sleepless nights. Sadie counted the days until she and Pao Chu would leave all this behind.

Early one morning in mid-March, as they said their goodbyes, Sadie felt she had failed Edith and Ruth, but she couldn't see how exactly she might have avoided that. Perhaps if she'd been more enthusiastic about accompanying Pao Chu to the villages and interacting with the women? She had offered but Pao Chu told her the women in the villages would not take kindly to her 'interfering'. Pao Chu was trying to convince them not to bind their little girls' feet and felt Sadie's presence wouldn't help.

Sadie and Pao Chu had a small cart with their luggage and supplies for the new school. They joined the muleteer's other travellers and he led them through the gate onto the road to Taiyan.

Sadie's lessons in Chinese had continued and she had learned the vocabulary quite well, but still found the tenses confusing. It often wasn't clear to her whether something had happened, or was about to happen though she could understand the language better than she could speak it. She prayed, and promised God that she would do better, try harder in Shou Yang. Things would be different there. She'd already written to Terrence to tell him when she expected to arrive at the Pigotts' mission. It was on the route between Beijing and Taiyuan, so he should have no trouble finding her.

They travelled through the loess. They wore scarves tightly about their heads and across their faces, only their eyes visible. Canyons surrounded by high pillars of brown compacted sand on each side brought a line to mind, though she couldn't remember if it was from the Bible or a poem she'd heard: *'into the valley of the shadow of death ...'* These pillars of sand had blown from the Gobi Desert to the plains of Shansi for thousands of years. She told herself that God would not let harm come to them while going about His business.

They travelled for two days to the capital, Taiyuan, the centre of commerce, politics and culture in Shansi. Sadie looked around the crowded streets in the faint hope of seeing Terrence. She knew it was a silly hope, but she still felt disappointed when there was no sign of him. Shou Yang was east of the capital, and it took them two more days to complete the journey.

When they reached Shou Yang, Sadie didn't notice the red balloons, not at first. It was only when she followed the gaze of Pao Chu that she became aware of small clusters of them bobbing cheerfully in the breeze. She turned to look for one of the theatrical companies and hoped they wouldn't be too near the Pigotts' mission.

As soon as they turned into the mission compound, they heard shouts of '*They're here!*' and people emerged from the buildings. Tom Pigott, who was head and shoulders above everyone else, his wife Jessie and a tall boy Sadie assumed was their son Wellesley, two girls and several Chinese people waited for their mules to stop before greeting them in the centre of the courtyard. She caught sight of Miss Duval and John Robinson hurrying to join the welcoming party.

Sadie eased herself down from the cart and walked slowly toward them. She had pins and needles in her legs and her bones ached. Before she could say anything, Jessie took her hand and said how pleased they were to have them and how much they'd been looking forward to meeting her. They'd met Pao Chu many times before, and Sadie was beginning to wonder just how old Pao Chu actually was; she seemed to know everyone in China – or at least every missionary.

People came to take bags from the cart. Tom Pigott was delighted that they had finally arrived. He shook them warmly by the hand and told them how pleased he was that they were there.

'We are honoured to have you. The school is much in need of your services.'

Sadie smiled and nodded as enthusiastically as she could, though all she wanted was to lie down for hours. She suppressed a yawn.

'I'll show you the new school,' said Tom. 'Wait till you see it, Pao Chu! We've got three separate classrooms each with –'

'Let them get their breath, Tom, for heaven's sake! They must be exhausted.' Jessie took Sadie's arm. 'You look quite pale, dear. I think you need a cup of tea. Oh my, you've brought books! How marvellous! We haven't got quite that far yet.' She turned and beckoned to two young girls. 'Girls! Come and say hello to Miss Bradshaw and Miss Pao.'

Two girls with serious faces came toward them.

'This is Ernestine Atwater, who's ten years old,' said Jessie. 'And her sister Mary, who's just turned eight. They've only just arrived too.'

Ernestine, wore her fair hair loose and long and was the first to smile. The younger girl Mary had very short dark hair and looked at Sadie with curious eyes.

'Good afternoon, Miss Bradshaw and Miss Pao,' they said in unison.

'I'm very pleased to meet you. Now where are you two from?' said Sadie. 'You don't sound English. Let me guess. I would say you are American. Am I right?

Their smiles broadened.

'We were born in Ohio, America, but we have lived in China with our parents for six years,' said Ernestine.

Mary took over. 'We have two younger sisters – they might come here next year.'

Sadie guessed they were missing their family. She put her hands on their shoulders. 'Well, you two have lived in China for much longer than I have. I shall have to come to you for lessons in Chinese.'

The girls' eyes lit up.

'Oh yes, we would be very happy to help you,' said Ernestine.

'Reverend and Mrs. Atwater are at the Fen Chow Fu mission,' said Jessie. 'It's quite far away. They were so pleased that we are starting a school that their children can attend.'

The boy who looked to be about twelve or thirteen came toward them, trying to carry more bags than he was able.

'And that is our son, Wellesley,' said Jessie. 'Put those down and say hello properly, young man.' She rolled her eyes at Sadie. 'Boys! Always trying to prove something.'

'Hello,' he said and shook their hands.

'I'm pleased to meet you,' said Sadie. She could see that Wellesley took after his father. He was already taller than his mother and Sadie and Pao Chu for that matter. He picked up the bags and lumbered towards the schoolhouse.

Ernestine said something to her sister in Chinese and they both looked after the boy.

'*I'm thirteen, if you must know!*' he shouted over his shoulder. '*And I speak perfect Chinese too!*'

The girls laughed and ran to help him with the luggage.

'John and Miss Duval are politely waiting to say hello,' said Jessie, waving them forward. 'I'll go in and get tea started.'

Miss Duval and John greeted Sadie and Pao Chu like old friends, and Sadie blinked back the tears – she seemed to do that quite a bit lately. She blamed the tiredness for all this emotion.

'Tell Sadie your news, John,' said Miss Duval.

Sadie looked at John expectantly. He appeared to be far more confident than the last time she'd seen him. Was it only a year ago?

'Tom has been guiding me. I've been studying to become a preacher. I'm to preach to a gathering soon – it will be my first one. I hope you'll be there.'

'Of course we'll be there. Won't we, Pao Chu? We've come just in time.'

He blushed. Some things haven't changed, she thought.

'You're still tutoring Wellesley?' she asked.

'He's only thirteen, so I expect to be here until he's ready to go to university in England. It's quite a houseful. Just as well Tom, I mean Mr. Pigott, had some more accommodation added. We'll certainly need it.' John smiled happily at her.

'Yes,' said Sadie. 'We certainly will.'

That evening, the fifteenth of March 1900, as the new arrivals of the mission in Shou Yuan settled into their surroundings, the Dowager Empress in Beijing appointed Yu Hsien the Governor of Shansi.

CHAPTER TWENTY-NINE

Sadie would not admit, even to herself, why she was pale and tired and listless. Waves of nausea twisted her stomach and left her sweating when she heaved into the pretty blue-and-white Chinese bowl under her bed. Then the vomiting stopped, and now she tried to convince herself that she'd been mistaken, that nothing was amiss. She did not feel as though another living being had taken up residence inside her. It was preposterous. The travel, the different food, the heat, all or any of these had interrupted her cycle, and now she was perfectly fine. Except that she wasn't, not even close to fine. Although she went to bed exhausted each night she couldn't sleep and by day she had bad headaches. She hadn't heard from Terrence since January. Though she'd written to him at the address of his office in Beijing, no reply came. She told herself that he was a freelance trader, travelling the roads of China; he could be anywhere. She didn't even know where he called home. When she thought about it, she realised she knew very little about him at all. It hadn't seemed important, his past, her past. She pushed her hair behind her ears. She didn't want to think about what the future would bring.

233

The only person she thought she could turn to was Pao Chu. She found her in the new classroom sweeping the wood shavings from the new floor. Sadie took a cloth to the window blinds. She spoke with her back to Pao Chu.

'I'm not feeling very well. Do you have anything I can take for a headache?'

'No, I haven't had time to forage but there is an apothecary not too far from here. I will come with you.'

'No, no need. I can manage alone.' Sadie ran the cloth along the window blinds.

'You don't know what to ask for,' said Pao Chu. 'You cannot take something that will harm the baby.'

Sadie spun around to face her. 'How did you know?' She'd been so sure that she'd acted and looked normal, but Pao Chu had seen through her. A moment of panic engulfed her. 'Oh, dear God! Who else knows?'

'I don't think anyone else knows. If Jessie suspects she has not confided in me. I think they have more serious matters on their minds.'

'What do you mean? Is it the new governor? They don't seem that concerned really.'

'What do you expect them to say?' Pao Chu snapped back. 'That we are in mortal danger?' She bit her lip. 'You will have to tell them you're pregnant.'

'I know, but not yet. I can't face it.' She put her hand to her head. 'I'm not sleeping, I have awful headaches. I'm so tired.'

Pao Chu shrugged. 'Perhaps it is punishment for your sin.'

'Then this is the start of my life as a sinner – it can never be undone. Will you help me, Pao Chu? I have no one else to turn to.' She dropped her eyes. 'I'm so ashamed.'

'I'll take you to the apothecary. I know him. He will give you something for the headaches.'

'Does he have to know I'm not married. I have my mother's wedding ring. I'll wear that. He won't know ...'

'That you don't have a husband? The apothecary won't know. But God knows.'

They thought the streets would be quiet but, as they turned the corner, they were confronted with a noisy melee. It turned out to be a theatrical company setting up for a performance. A shaky-looking stage was in the process of being erected at one end of the street, the surround painted black with red dragons. People came from their business and houses to view the work. They seemed to be in a good mood, shouting and laughing across from one to another. Pao Chu and Sadie didn't slow to watch; they skirted unobserved around a growing crowd.

The apothecary's shop smelled of wood and herbs but there was an earthy undertone to the aroma that Sadie couldn't identify. Shelves held labelled boxes, but there was space for candles, jars, and urns. Pao Chu told her to keep her large round bamboo hat on and wait just inside the door while she spoke with the apothecary. It was obvious that they'd had dealings before. Sadie watched Pao Chu lean toward him and whisper into his ear. His eyes narrowed and fell on Sadie. Neither the apothecary nor Pao Chu seemed happy with the conversation. Pao Chu turned from him and went to Sadie.

'He will give you something for the headaches. A special tea, he says. As for the sleeplessness, he can make you a tincture of opium and alcohol which you must use very sparingly.' Pao Chu glanced back at the apothecary. 'But he is charging you twice the usual price. He says he can't be seen helping a foreigner. He could get into trouble. He says he is risking a lot even by letting you into the shop.'

Sadie handed her purse to Pao Chu. 'I will take the tea but not the tincture. From what I've heard opium is far too dangerous. I'll manage without it.'

They walked back silently through the bustling crowds. Her mother's ring couldn't protect her from the shame she felt.

In her room, she sipped the herbal tea and prayed that Terrence would come soon and save her.

Weeks passed. The tea helped her headache but nothing could take away the gnawing anxiety that haunted her. She had committed a sin and, though she prayed on her knees for hours and punished her body by not eating, nothing could take away her guilt. When she did manage to sleep she saw the faces of her family and friends look at her in disgust, accuse her of her most dreadful sin and she awoke filled with self-loathing. There was only one solution, only one person who could rescue her. Terrence must come and marry her before the baby was born. Even then she would always be tarnished. But there was no reply to her letters. He may not have received them, she thought. He probably thinks I'm still with Edith and Ruth. Would Edith even tell him where I am? Ruth would, I know she would, if he got to talk to her, but Edith is a stubborn woman. She knew the older woman disapproved of him, but would she lie to him?

She would have to speak to the Pigotts soon. The very idea of that conversation made her feel weak. It wasn't a conversation that she wanted to have with anyone but especially not the Pigotts. She ran her hand over her stomach; it swelled a little more each day and began filling the loose-fitting pale-blue cotton tunic. She knew she couldn't conceal it for much longer. She went to Pao Chu's room and told her she was worried that Edith wouldn't tell Terrence where she was.

'It doesn't matter if he knows or doesn't know – he is not here. You must act alone. You must tell Jessie. There is no other way.'

'Can you tell her for me, Pao Chu? Please. I'm too ashamed.'

Pao Chu shook her head. 'You have to face the situation that you have got yourself into, whatever the consequences are. It won't be easy, you may be shunned.' She put her hand on Sadie's arm. 'I will help where I can, but you will be seen as a sinner.'

Sadie found Jessie in the garden cutting leaves from a comfrey plant. She knelt beside her and rubbed the soft green leaves between her fingers.

'You know so much about Chinese medicine,' Sadie said. 'It must have taken years to learn.'

'Would you believe, the first thing I learned about medicine was from Doctor Schofield at the hospital here. He taught me how to remove cataracts, but over the years I've learned much from the native herbalists and apothecaries. We must be able to receive knowledge from Chinese scholars and realise that we don't know everything.'

'Mrs. Pigott …' Sadie began.

'Why so formal, dear? Is there a problem?'

'I have to go back to England. Straight away. I must leave as soon as possible.'

Jessie examined the contents of her basket. 'I don't think you should go on a long sea voyage. I imagine it would be hugely uncomfortable. What did you plan to do when you got there?'

'I … I'm not quite sure. I thought I might find … someone.'

'The father of your baby?'

The words stung but she could only hang her head in shame.

'Is it that obvious? Does Mr. Pigott know?'

'Tom wouldn't notice, well, not at this stage. But I'd say you're about four or five months?'

'Yes, nearly five,' said Sadie in a very quiet voice. She'd practised what she wanted to say, but her mind was empty. She watched Jessie's fingers pinch the spongy leaf of an Aloe vera plant and catch the sap in a bottle.

'Hold that, would you, dear? Squeeze it a little bit and catch the drops. Very good, you're as steady as a rock.'

'I don't feel steady at all.' She felt encouraged by Jessie's kindness. 'I feel that the world is spinning too fast for me. I'm dizzy all the time.'

Jessie put a stopper in the bottle. 'Now, two questions. You expect to find the father in England – I take it that he is probably English then?'

'Yes, he is.'

'Well, that's something. We could have got into a tangle if you had to marry a Chinese man.' She looked up suddenly from the pile of bottles. 'I didn't know any English missionaries were staying with Edith and Ruth. Second question: when is he coming to see you?'

'He isn't a missionary. He's a trader. I've tried to get in touch with him. He doesn't know about …' She twisted her handkerchief through her fingers. 'I'm hoping he'll come this way. He will, won't he? This is a big town everyone passes through on the way to Beijing. So, he'll have to pass this way. Won't he?'

'Ah … He's a trader. What does he trade in?'

'Tea. Green and black tea. He returned to Beijing after Christmas. I've written but have heard nothing.' As she said the words aloud she realised how ridiculous it sounded. She produced the ruby-and-opal ring that she wore on a chain around her neck, hidden under her tunic. 'You see, we're engaged to be married. He wanted me to go with him to Beijing but I said I couldn't yet because of my commitments here. But now there's been no word ...'

Jessie glanced at the ring. 'I supposed that you had some sort of firm understanding with your intended and that a wedding would take place – sooner rather than later. This all seems very flimsy, I must say. No word from him in five months – it's worse than I thought. You'll have to tell Tom.' She brushed some of the clippings from her lap. 'You should have told us before now.'

'Do we absolutely have to tell Tom? I don't think I can bear the shame.'

'You'll have to get over that. You won't be the only one affected by this situation. What you've done by coming here is to confirm what most Chinese think if they see an unmarried woman staying at the mission. They will assume you are the concubine of my husband, and your current situation will confirm that.'

'I'm so sorry.'

Jessie stood and then stooped to pick up the basket of bottles and herbs.

'What am I going to do, Jessie? Will you tell Tom for me? Oh please, I can't!'

'I will tell him, but you must be there while I do it. He will have questions that I can't answer. Come on, no point in delaying this any longer.'

They found Tom as his desk. He looked up and initially seemed relieved at the interruption – until he saw Sadie's pale worried face slip in behind Jessie.

She got through it, red-faced and humiliated, but at least it was over. They agreed there was no point in trying to send her anywhere else. She could continue to work in the mission school, for the time being, but was not allowed outside the gates.

239

'Once the child is delivered,' said Tom, 'you can return to England, and it will be up to you to report to the China Inland Mission and return the money to them.'

'What money?' asked Sadie.

'The China Inland Mission has paid for your fare here and has been paying you a salary for your work here.'

'Well, yes, but I've no –'

'You signed an agreement, a contract, Sadie. Saying that you would work in China for five years. The usual agreement, if I remember correctly, states that if you do not stay for at least five years, you must refund the C.I.M. the cost of your travel and forfeit your wages. About £1,600, I recall.'

'I suppose I must have signed it, but I don't –'

'We can lend you the money for your return fare when the time comes.'

Sadie heard Jessie sniff.

'Thank you.' Sadie kept her head bent. They are desperate to be rid of me, she thought. 'You've been very kind,' she said, her voice low. For the first time she wished to God she'd never set eyes on Terrence Bennett.

CHAPTER THIRTY

More red balloons in the early morning sunshine. Sadie thought they looked so pretty flying over the city. She caught sight of Tom and Jessie looking toward the balloons from the small herb garden. She came through the kitchen door and was about to ask about the balloons, but something stopped her.

Jessie put her arm around her husband, looking into his face.

He pulled her to him and said, 'It will be all right.'

It wasn't his usual voice. It wasn't the booming preacher's voice she'd heard in the parish hall that first night in Dublin. It was the voice of a husband comforting his worried wife.

Sadie didn't ask; she couldn't face more bad news. She slipped back into the house, through the door to the courtyard, and into the school building opposite. It smelled of new wood and paper. Pao Chu was counting wax crayons, pencils, small paint boxes, and brushes. She didn't lift her eyes when Sadie came in.

Only when Sadie stood in front of her and asked her directly what the red balloons meant did Pao Chu look up from the collection.

'It's a sign from the Boxers to the people of Shou Yang.' Her voice was steady, but her eyes told Sadie there was something to fear.

'The Boxers? Who are they?'

'The Boxers are a society – a militant group – who have a powerful influence over the people. The balloons are a sign to let the people know they are here and to be ready.'

'Ready for what, Pao Chu?'

Pao Chu silently cast her eyes around the neat and tidy classroom.

'Pao Chu, what is it? Tell me, it can't be so terrible.'

'Ready to get rid of the foreigners.'

'To send us home, you mean? Well, that's not going to happen.' Sadie folded her arms. 'The Chinese Inland Mission told us that according to the settlement after the opium wars, foreigners are allowed to come inland and to preach. That new governor chap doesn't have a leg to stand on.'

Pao Chu looked exasperated. 'Are you so blind to everything except yourself? The Dowager Empress has not tried to stop them. She is aware that the mood of the people has changed. Everywhere there is talk against foreigners. The anger that the people felt when the English and French and Germans and Russians and all the others destroyed our defences and gave themselves privileges has been stirred up. They see the Boxers standing up for the Chinese ways, the old ways before the foreigners came. They say the foreigners have forced themselves on us, have ruined people with the cheap opium they sell. The Boxers have awakened a sleeping dragon, they have poked at it and made it angry and shown the dragon who the enemy is.'

Sadie was shaken by the anger in Pao Chu's voice.

'The Boxers attract crowds when they perform their drill,' said Pao Chu, 'and get the young men and women to join in. They create a show, an entertainment almost as good as the theatre. They tell them they are invincible, that the bullets of the foreign soldiers cannot harm them. The people are swayed – they want to believe. They want China to be as the Boxers tell them it once was. They feed the people the opium of dreams, they have them under their spell. They do not see foreigners as people who helped them. They see devils. Devils to be destroyed. I have said all this to Tom Pigott, but he believes that good overcomes evil. He doesn't see the danger.'

Sadie had never seen Pao Chu in such an animated state, and felt confused and upset. She walked across the courtyard, unable to focus on work – she was supposed to be helping put together leaflets to hand out to the people, but if the people hated the missionaries, what was the point? She could see people pass the open gate; they didn't seem to pay much attention to the mission and were going about their business as usual.

Pao Chu is probably exaggerating, though it isn't like her to do so, she thought. Anyhow the British soldiers will come and sort everything out. I've more important things to think about. I should write to Edith and Ruth and ask if they have any word of Terrence.

The certainty she'd felt months ago had dissipated; she could barely remember his face. Only his pale grey eyes and the feel of the stubble on his cheek move against her skin.

A red balloon floated carelessly over the mission, past the school, the large house, the herb patch in the garden, and the wooden doorway that opened out to a laneway beside the city wall.

Sadie opened the wooden door and immediately saw the poster with large black letters. She didn't know what it meant, perhaps something to do with the theatricals. She called Pao Chu.

'What does it say, Pao Chu? I don't know what SHA means?'

What little colour Pao Chu had in her face drained away completely.

'The Boxers left this. "*Sha*" means "*kill*". It says: *Kill all the foreigners.*'

Sadie took her meals in her room. It was easier that way. There would not have to be the stilted conversation – the elephant in the room could be avoided. She had become separate from the other missionaries and teachers and resigned herself to becoming an outcast within the group. She looked down at her growing stomach. The life within her, the fleeting fluttering sensation, turned to movements; she could feel him or her turn inside.

Miss Duval had been quite marvellous. She'd come to see Sadie earlier that day, handed her a brown-paper parcel, and stood by anxiously while Sadie opened it. Sadie pulled out the beautiful soft material and unravelled it. Yards of it. 'I thought it would make a lovely skirt,' she'd said, and Sadie felt tears sting her eyes at the act of kindness. In fact, everyone was kind to her, more than she thought she deserved. Except for John, who seemed to find it challenging to look at her, let alone talk to her.

'You can hardly blame him, Sadie,' Jessie had said when she mentioned it. 'People might suspect that he is the father. You've put him in such an awkward situation. He's not in a position to deny that he is the father, as it is never discussed. Any attention from him toward you could be misconstrued as evidence that he is responsible for your situation. He must find it intolerable.'

She hadn't thought of that. I'm despicable. I've brought nothing but trouble with me to these good people, and I can think of no way to repay them.

And there was no shortage of trouble already. The lack of rain and rising heat was of great concern to everyone, Chinese and foreigners alike. Drought would lead to famine as surely as night follows day.

The thud of marching soldiers brought the missionaries to their gate, and even Sadie came to see what was happening. She stood beside Pao Chu and asked what was going on. The missionaries covered their noses and mouths as they watched the troops of the Chinese army march past, hundreds of them, raising dust on the road to Beijing. There had been rumours that the Embassies of Britain, France, Italy, Germany, and the USA were under siege. They had hoped it was not true, but the sight of so many soldiers on the move made them think they'd been wrong. Even so, the disturbance was hundreds of miles away. Their work here had nothing to do with war and politics. They thought they would be safe – that this did not concern them and relied on the assurance of the Prefect that he would protect them.

Sadie and the others noticed some of the crowd try to pull the soldiers toward them, shouting that there were foreigners there; they seemed to want the soldiers to attack the mission. But the soldiers marched on. The missionaries knew they were not popular with everyone, but this was the first time they'd seen hatred in all its ugliness thrown at them. They felt their world shift beneath their feet.

Placards and banners were painted onto walls by the Boxers. *DEATH TO THE FOREIGNERS* in large red letters.

'We mustn't worry too much about that,' Tom told them after Sunday service.

It was easy to believe that this man could protect them. He was broad and strong and seemed confident that they would be safe, that it was all smoke without fire.

'It might last a few days and will certainly be a nuisance. But I think the worst that can happen is that we might run short of silver taels for a while. I'm going to write to Mr. Farthing in Taiyuan. They might know more in the capital.'

'I will take the message and go to the piaohao bank,' said Li Pai, one of the Chinese Christians who worked at the mission.

Tom thanked him and patted his shoulder as he handed him the bank draft.

The nights were humid. The drought had still not broken. The sky hung low with bulging clouds. Still, the rain did not come. The city felt quiet and brooding in the dark, with only an occasional murmur of thunder in the distance.

When Sadie managed to sleep, she dreamed of Terrence in a green field beside a stream, water dancing over the stones on the banks. He smiled and filled a jug with the clear water, but when she took the pitcher from him and put it to her lips, she tasted only the dry sand of the loess on her tongue, and she woke choking and coughing. Day by day she ate less and less. The oppressive heat had killed her appetite. She would take only water or tea.

Everyone was on edge, pretending to be busy with unnecessary tasks.

Li Pai returned with enough silver to pay all Tom's debts and money to buy supplies. It lifted the spirits of everyone in the group. Even

Sadie managed to take a little broth that Jessie had made for her.

On Sunday morning the missionaries and the Chinese Christians were all gathered in the room they used as a chapel. The children had already left for Sunday School with Lao An, one of their teachers.

Tom got to his feet. He'd chosen the 23rd Psalm. '*The Lord is my Shepherd –*' he began.

A loud knock on the door made everyone turn. John Robinson went and opened the door a little timidly. The messenger handed John a letter, bowed and left. He brought it to Tom, who put his Bible aside. All eyes were fixed on the letter as he opened it.

'You'd better read it aloud, dear,' said Jessie. 'Whatever is in it will affect everyone here.'

He glanced at the first paragraph then looked around the room. His eyes fell on Sadie.

Her thoughts immediately went to Terrence. *Please God, no. Please don't take him.* She put her hands to her face and waited for Tom to speak.

He sat down slowly as he read the letter to himself.

'What does it say, Tom?' said Jessie. 'Please tell me Edith and Ruth are safe.'

'They are with the Lord,' said Tom. 'They died at the hands of the mob, burned to death in the mission house.'

Sadie turned to embrace Pao Chu and, for once, Pao Chu didn't pull away.

Miss Duval stood up, a little shakily. 'We should pray for them.'

'We will,' said Tom. 'Sit down, everyone. That is not the end. There is more news in the letter, but I fear none of it is good.'

Sadie was ashamed to think that her first thoughts had been for

Terrence. Poor Edith and Ruth who'd done nothing but good! She dropped her eyes to the floor. Thanks be to God we left when we did. It could have been us burned to death. She said a silent prayer for Edith and Ruth and another asking forgiveness for being glad she'd escaped their fate.

Tom began to read the rest of the letter, though again not aloud. They watched his face and Sadie noticed his hand shake when he turned the page over.

A few minutes later he looked up to see the faces of his fellow Christians waiting for him to speak.

'It's worse than I thought,' he said. 'Doctor Lovitt writes that a few nights ago a mob gathered outside the hospital compound. He and his wife and child were there along with some others you may know – Doctor Wilson, Mr and Mrs Stokes and Miss Coombs.' They could hear the strain in his voice. He turned to Jessie. 'You remember them from the meeting last year?'

Jessie nodded and came to stand beside him. She put her hand on his back. 'Yes, I remember them well. Such good work they were doing,' she said.

Sadie looked around the room. Miss Duval held a handkerchief to her mouth and John Robinson looked at Tom with disbelief written across his face.

'The mob set fire to the building and Doctor Lovitt says it was only due to the fact that he and the other men had firearms that they managed to hold the mob back and escape.'

'Thank God,' people murmured.

But Sadie could see Jessie's eyes on the page that Tom was holding. She saw the look of fear spread across her face.

'I can hardly bear to tell you this,' he said. 'Three girls they'd been caring for who had become Christians tried to follow but they couldn't walk quickly as their feet were bound. It seems that Miss Coombs went back to try to help them, but the others didn't notice.' He swallowed and took another shaky breath. 'The mob pulled her away from the girls and threw her into the burning building. She died trying to save them.'

'Oh dear God, how could they be so brutal?' said Miss Duval.

'What of the girls, did they at least manage to escape?' said Pao Chu.

Tom shook his head. 'They have no idea where the girls went, or if they were taken. Doctor Lovitt and his wife and child have sought refuge with other missionaries and have asked to see the Prefect, but the Prefect has refused to see him.' He put the letter down for a moment. 'He was always on good terms with the Prefect in the past. This is very serious indeed. Serious for all of us.' He looked broken and confused.

Jessie took the letter and read the final paragraph aloud: '*We would like our dear ones to know we are being marvellously sustained by the Lord. He is precious to each one of us. We cannot but hope for deliverance (hope dies hard) and our God is well able to do all things – even to save us from the most impossible surroundings when hope is gone. There is not much time. We are ready. Arnold E. Lovitt.*'

The group was silent.

A loud knock came on the outside door, sending shock waves through the room. John let a moment pass before he went to see who was there. He returned with another letter and handed it to Tom. It was from the local magistrate and was a much shorter missive.

'He says that, in consequence of instructions received from the governor, he can no longer protect us. We must leave.' Tom looked at each person in the room . 'I will go to see the Prefect – he isn't going to stand by and let us –'

'He would, Tom, and we both know it,' Jessie interrupted. 'He will use the Boxers for his own ends. We need to go. He says we need to leave here before the sixth moon – when is that?'

'The first day of the sixth moon is next Wednesday,' said Pao Chu. 'We can't make it to the coast by then. It would take weeks.'

They sat in silence, each with their own thoughts.

Yen Lai Pao spoke. 'My village is in the hills about fifteen miles to the south. Many of its people are now Christians. You will be safe there.'

Tom put his hand on Yen Lai Pao's shoulder. 'You have been a true friend, but I cannot put your family at risk. You and the others should go to your villages. We will stay here, and I'll try tomorrow to see the Prefect. That would be best for everyone.' He turned to Pao Chu. 'You go with them. You will be safer there.'

'I will go with them,' said Pao Chu, 'but I have promised to look after Sadie. I feel that she should come with us.' She turned to Yen Lai Pao. 'Will your people take us? Are you sure?'

'Yes,' said Yen Lai Pao. 'I am sure.'

Sadie felt relieved, more than relieved. She felt as though Pao Chu had saved her life but when she tried to thank her Pao Chu swept the words aside.

'Go and pack only what you absolutely need,' she said. 'If you have any money or jewellery, you should bring that too. We will need it.'

Before dawn next morning Sadie, Pao Chu and the Chinese Christians – teachers and servants – packed what little they had and put it in the cart. Wellesley helped the cook add his pots and pans to the luggage. The Chinese promised they would return as soon as they knew their families were safe and well.

Sadie and Pao Chu said goodbye to the Pigotts, Miss Duval, and

John Robinson in the courtyard, not knowing if they would ever meet again.

Sadie waved up to Ernestine and Mary and felt a twinge of regret. Should she have taken them with her? No, she thought. The Pigotts would look after them better than she could.

Pao Chu grasped Sadie's hand and helped her into the cart. She owed so much to Pao Chu, who had never admonished her about the baby. She felt that Pao Chu would be her friend no matter what happened.

As Yen Lai Pao led the cart toward the street, Jessie locked eyes with Sadie. Jessie's arm was around her son's shoulders, and tears fell freely from her eyes.

CHAPTER THIRTY-ONE

Yen Lai Pao's village was one of the small cave villages typical among the loess hills of Shansi. It was dark when they arrived, and they were warmly but quietly welcomed by the Chinese Christian families. Pao Chu and Sadie were given a yangdon, a small cave room, one of several scooped out of compacted sand. It was warm and comfortable. On the walls around the kang someone had painted scenes from various Chinese fables in bright colours.

During the night they slept little; they prayed together quietly and waited for dawn.

'Sadie,' whispered Pao Chu, as the sky began to brighten, 'if we are to survive this we cannot always rely on the generosity of people.'

'They have been very kind to us.'

'What I am saying is that we will need money for the journey ahead. I have only a little, it will not stretch far. Do you have anything of value that we can sell?'

Sadie reached into her leather travelling bag and pulled out a purse and a soft drawstring bag. 'I have some silver taels,' she said and emptied the silver pieces from her purse onto the blanket. 'And I have these.' She untied the drawstring bag and poured the contents onto the blanket.

Pau Cho leaned toward the pile of jewellery. 'I've never seen you wear any of these.' She picked up a string of pearls. She gazed at the emerald and sapphire rings, and several brooches set with coloured stones.

'My father gave them to my mother, and so they came to me. I never felt they were mine to wear. They were between my mother and father, their story, their love. But these are mine. From Terrence.' She handed the package to Pao Chu who pulled the paper away. The yellow lacquered box gleamed in her hand. Sadie removed the ruby-and-opal ring from her neck and gave it to her.

'Terrence Bennett gave these to you?'

Sadie nodded.

Pao Chu turned the ruby ring and the box over in her hand. 'Your parents and Terrence Bennett may have saved our lives.'

The next day, at Pao Chu's request, Sadie did not venture outside; her appearance might not be welcomed by everyone. Yao Chien Hsiang and the others brought food to them and said goodbye. They were going to journey further, to their own villages, to ensure their families were safe. They said they would return as soon as they could.

Yen Lai Pao seemed disconsolate. He came to their yangdon and told them he was going to risk returning to Shou Yang in search of news of the missionaries. 'I might be able to help them,' he said.

It was the first night of the sixth moon. They heard thunder rumble toward them from the north and prayed the drought might be broken.

Soft, warm rain fell in heavy drops during the dark hours and was absorbed into the loess's sands. By dawn, all was quiet; the earth looked brown instead of yellow. It reminded Sadie of sand when the sea went out, how it wedged between her toes and clung to her bare feet when she walked along Dollymount strand.

The next day, Yen Lai Pao returned from Shou Yang. He came into the yangdon and closed the door behind him. He bowed his head quickly, obviously upset.

'They are in the Prefect's palace,' he said. 'I think they might be safe there. But I do not think you will be safe here for much longer. There are many rumours. I heard that the Boxers are killing foreigners in the villages outside Shou Yang. But the Prefect still has control of the city though he has not sent any soldiers to stop the Boxers outside.' Yen Lai Pao turned his eyes to Sadie. 'If the Boxers find you they will show no mercy. They are saying that the rain has come because the foreigners have left. The people seem to believe everything they are told. The Boxers tell them that they are invincible, that they cannot be killed by bullets. They are turning the people against the missionaries, saying the foreigners have poisoned the wells. They will come to this village soon. We must all leave.'

'What are we going to do, Pao Chu?' said Sadie.

Pao Chu put her head in her hands for a few moments. 'I think there's only one thing we can do.' She bit her lip and faced Sadie and Len Yai Pao. 'I think we have to go back to Shou Yang. I know we are taking a chance, but there's someone there who can help us. I think it's our only hope.'

Rainwater filled the warren of sand roads in the loess, making the floors of the canyons slippery. Sadie couldn't understand how Yen Lai Pao could know one canyon from the next; they all looked the same to her. Sadie and Pao Chu were in the small cart, but the wheels became stuck several times. Yen Lai Pao had to lend a shoulder to move it. Sadie and Pao Chu got out and led the mule, slipping and falling to their knees. Pao Chu asked Sadie to get back into the cart, but she refused. She couldn't bear to see her companions struggle while she sat and watched. They moved slowly, alert to every sound until they came out from the cover of the loess. The new moon was a sliver of silver in the darkening blue sky.

The gates of the city of Shou Yang stood before them. It looked as it always did; it didn't appear to have extra guards, and they could see people going freely through the gate. Too many people, but they were grateful that there was no sign of Boxers. Yen Lai Pao knew of a cave outside the city, and they waited there. The town's gates would be locked at ten o'clock. If they timed it right, they could pass through in darkness just as the gates closed.

When it was time, they dressed in dark padded jackets over trousers, with straw hats. Pao Chu smeared mud across Sadie's face to darken her skin. Sadie's heart thumped in her chest. She knew the others would not attract comment; if anyone gave the game away, it would be her. She wrapped a dark scarf around her head, pulled her straw hat low, and kept her eyes on the ground. Her hands were hidden by the long sleeves of the coat. She lay on the cart floor as Pao Chu and Yen Lai Pao led it past the guards already occupied with closing the towering gates.

As soon as they were through, they turned off the main road. Pao Chu told Yen Lai Pao to take the cart and meet her later. She turned to Sadie.

'Walk quickly behind me and don't look up,' she said.

255

'Where are we going?' whispered Sadie.

'To the apothecary.'

'I don't think he liked me.'

'He doesn't like anyone. But he does like money.' She patted the bag. 'And now we have some.'

They skirted the streets until they came to the back door of the apothecary's shop.

Pao Chu rapped at the door. He came, bearing a flickering candle stub. His thin, wrinkled face appeared around the wooden door. Grey hair fell over his shoulders, while the top of his head was completely bald.

Pao Chu pushed past him, dragging Sadie with her. He couldn't manage to shoo her out and hold the door and the candle simultaneously. He closed the door and talked to her in a hushed angry whisper. His eyes narrowed when he looked at Sadie. The whispering became more furious, spittle flew from his mouth, but Pao Chu would not back away.

Pao Chu produced the silver taels and waved them under his nose. He held the candle closer to the money. Silver and light reflected brightly in his black eyes; he reached out to touch the coins in her hands but Pao Chu closed her fingers around them and held her fist to her chest.

Sadie saw his shoulders drop in defeat; greed overtook all his reasons not to help them.

He led them into a storeroom at the back of the shop. Sadie breathed deeply and felt comfort in the smells, the smallness of the untidy room, and the darkness. She could smell a mixture of herbs and other less inviting aromas that reminded her of the butchers' shops on Moore Street in Dublin.

The apothecary pulled back the hessian cloth that covered a table at the end of the room. A shoddy straw mattress lay underneath; he looked at her and pointed a long fingernail toward it. Sadie obediently climbed under the table.

Pao Chu knelt beside her and whispered, 'He has promised to look after you. I will come later. I must see what has happened to the Pigotts and the others. You rest.'

Sadie held on to Pao Chu's arm, fastened her eyes on her and tried to interpret her mood, search out anxiety, but Pao Chu had long ago learned the art of concealment.

'Can we trust him, Pao Chu? He could give us away. Why can't I come with you?'

'I don't know who we can and can't trust,' said Pao Chu. 'Say nothing to him of the missionaries, or of our journey to Yen Lai Pao's village. Best if you don't talk to him at all. I must find out what has happened to our friends. Be strong, Sadie. I promise I will come back.'

Pao Chu turned to the apothecary and said she would return the next day. Sadie watched the apothecary follow Pao Chu out of the storeroom through the shop, muttering something she didn't understand. She heard the door open, then close and a bolt was slid across.

Sadie felt guilty that her first thought had been for herself, though she inwardly argued that she had to also worry for her baby. She was six months pregnant and her stomach was getting larger by the day. She lay back on the thin mattress, eyes scanning the room for rats. Nothing stirred. Open sacks filled with seeds of some sort lined the wall furthest away from her.

The apothecary returned and muttered to himself as he began to take items from drawers and assemble them on the table.

Why did I ever come here? she thought. Why did I ever meet Terrence Bennett? Are you looking for me, Terrence? Will you come to save me?

She peeked out from behind the tatty hessian and watched the apothecary go about the room, muttering and tutting among the lines of blue-and-white bowls and the leaves and stalks of plants. He didn't look at her. He worked in the small pool of candlelight, adding to his concoction in a large bowl. When the candle died, she heard him open and then close the door. A key turned in the lock. She was utterly alone.

She slept in a corner under the table, covered by her padded jacket, and woke before the sun had fully risen. She struggled out from underneath the table to see the workshop in the dull grey morning light. Bunches of fennel, birch leaves, and other unidentified foliage hung drying from hooks in the ceiling. A pile of unusual-looking mushrooms sat in a blue-and-white porcelain bowl. A sack covered something large on one of the other tables. She lifted the edge, looked underneath, and found two pairs of eyes looking back at her. She pulled back the cloth, and two dead monkeys stared at her, their claws missing. The apothecary came into the room and found Sadie in tears. He pointed to the corner, wanting her to return to the bed under the table.

She pointed out the window to the garden. He seemed to understand and led her to the door to the garden.

When she returned, she found him waiting with a bowl in his hand. It was the mixture he'd concocted the previous night. She'd watched him grate the husks of black walnuts, put them into a bowl, and stir in black tea. The top of the wooden spoon he'd left standing in the bowl had turned black but didn't smell too bad. He pulled out a three-legged stool and pointed at it. She silently prayed that she could trust him and sat down.

He put a tattered old shawl around her shoulders and began to circle her. He produced a small brush, put his hand on her shoulder and told her to sit still, and she was too afraid to ask why.

He dipped the brush into the bowl, took one piece of her hair, and painted it with the thick syrupy liquid which dripped down her neck and onto the old shawl. He continued, carefully lifting her tresses with his bony fingers until all of it was completely black. He moved the stool toward the window where the July sun rays came in and told her not to move until it was dry.

For an hour, Sadie sat on the small stool, her head as still as she could, hair piled on top of her head. Droplets of thick black liquid slid down her face, and she wiped them away with the shawl. She prayed that he'd come back quickly and help her. When he finally returned, he poured cold water into a basin, told her to kneel, and dunked her head several times until the water in the bucket looked as black as the hair on her head.

He opened the door to the garden, slowly this time. It smelled of recent rain, damp and earthy. He put the stool in the doorway and bade her sit on it. She turned her face to the sun and felt its warmth. A light breeze moved through her long hair. He handed her a high comb, the sort she'd seen Chinese women put on the top of their heads and wrap their hair around. She tried, but her hair slid back down around her shoulders. He put his hands to his head, and she thought it likely that the mumbling sound he made was actually swearing. The sound of customers knocking at the shop door sent him scurrying inside, beckoning her to follow. He waited until she took her place under the table, then she heard the door close. She was alone.

Out of boredom, she picked up the sweeping brush and began to tidy the drooping sacks of seeds. She pulled them away from the wall, swept in behind them and pegged the sacks closed. She emptied shelves, dusted, and straightened the pots and jars as she replaced them. Her back ached, and her legs began to complain. That was enough physical work for one day. She arranged herself under the table and waited for the apothecary to come in.

At the sound of his shuffling feet, she stood ready with a smile, hoping he'd brought food.

Instantly he saw what she'd done. He put down the bowl of food he'd brought and began talking so fast she couldn't keep up with him.

She caught the gist of it.

'Everything is mixed up!' He pulled at one of the sacks.

She remembered Pao Cho's warning and said slowly in Chinese. 'I careful. I help.'

He looked around and nodded, reluctantly it seemed to Sadie. Not even a thank-you, she thought but kept her demeanour submissive. She moved to the table and picked up a mortar and pestle.

He put his hands on his head and moved toward her.

She pointed to herself then mimicked the action of grinding the contents. She bowed low and held out the bowl, which he took and put safely on the shelf. He stared at her for a few moments.

She could almost hear his mind working. Free labour. Why should he not profit from the situation? He pushed the bowl of noodles toward her.

'Eat,' he said.

She didn't move.

He put the bowl of noodles into her hands. 'Eat,' he repeated and this time she took the bowl and looked at him, as though for confirmation that she was doing the right thing.

The following day he came to see her before he opened the shop. He put her standing at the table and she watched as he put seeds and shells into a small stone mortar, placed it on the table and handed her the pestle. She nodded.

He placed a second bowl with herbs and green leaves. She nodded again that she understood.

From high on a shelf he retrieved a thick white tusk. Some poor animal, she thought. Could it be an elephant like the one in London zoo? She'd brought it a bun one sunny day, in a past that seemed a hundred years ago.

The apothecary showed her a thick metal file and drew a mark on the tusk. 'Here,' he said, and put some rice paper under the tusk. He motioned that the filings should be caught on the paper. 'Very, very careful,' he said slowly. He watched her and narrowed his eyes to barely slits, and she nodded once again.

He seemed to be very pleased with himself as he went out the door to open the shop. Sadie looked at the tasks on the table, glad of something to occupy her while she waited for Pao Chu to return. She tried to stem the awful thoughts that circled her mind and thanked God that she didn't have to do anything with the dead monkeys under the sack.

CHAPTER THIRTY-TWO

Pao Chu went by the side streets of Shou Yang to the Prefect's yamen. She wasn't too concerned about being recognized. She'd never preached in the town; she'd always preferred to go to the women in the villages, sit in their circle, and talk directly to them. It wasn't likely that she'd be noticed in the city, just another woman in a blue tunic.

The yamen stood at one end of a busy square. There were people about, but she had no sense that they were bent on violence of any sort; they appeared to be going about their business the same as any other day. She listened to the chatter in the marketplace. Nobody talked of the missionaries, but she overheard several groups gossiping about strange happenings; some said the sea had receded so far that no foreign ships could land. Another claimed that a great trident had risen up in the sea to protect the Chinese ports against foreign invaders. When Pao Chu heard anyone mention the Boxers – she stood close by, pretending to examine the goods in the stall. Some said that the Dowager Empress would endorse the Boxers. Pao Chu shivered at the thought. The people seemed to believe that the Boxers had magic powers. They could not be killed by the foreigners' bullets, food multiplied in their hands, and they were never hungry. People swore they had seen these very things happen. That it was all true.

Pao Chu skirted through the shade towards the Prefect's yamen and waited in a corner. There was no sign of Boxers in the city. Only the Prefect's guards were in evidence. She recognised Lai Pi and walked slowly toward him with her head bent and touched his sleeve at the last moment. He flinched. The young man was always neat, tidy, and scrupulously clean. But she could see that he was dishevelled, dirty yellow marks stained his clothes and his eyes were red, as though he'd not slept for several days.

She pulled him around the corner. 'Be careful, Lai Pi,' she said. 'Don't show too much interest, or you will become a suspect yourself.'

'I've waited here two days.' His voice was raw. He slumped to the ground and leaned his back against the warm wall. She sat next to him and glanced around the courtyard.

'Tell me, Lai Pi, tell me what happened after we left the mission house.'

Lai Pi shook his head. 'Everyone was exhausted, but no one could sleep except the two American girls.'

'Mr. Pigott thought it would be safe in the Prefect's yamen and it is true that it's not so bad here as outside the city. The Boxers have no one in charge, there is no one to control them. Here the soldiers are under the orders of the Prefect. Mr. Pigott led the missionaries here. He said the Prefect would be obliged to protect them, but he was wrong.'

'How long have they been here?' asked Pao Chu.

'Since the first night of the sixth moon. I know one of the runners, I gave him fruit to take to them and to find out how they are. The runner says the rooms they are in are filthy. Mr. Pigott, John, and Wellesley are together in one room, and the women and children are in another. It was not the reception that Mr. Pigott thought he would get. I think all the Prefects in Shansi are afraid to confront the Governor.'

'Are they in chains?' she said, looking around to ensure they were not overheard. She inched closer to him.

'No, they are not in chains, not yet. The Prefect has told them that he will send them to the coast under armed escort and, to make it look as they are going to Taiyuan, they will put chains on the men. Mr. Pigott says they will only be for show, loose chains, so that if the Boxers stop them on the road the escort can say they are prisoners.' He shook his head. 'It doesn't feel right. I think the Prefect wants them off his hands but doesn't want to upset the Governor.'

'You think he'll send them to the Governor and not the coast?'

Lai Pi raised his shoulders. 'I don't know, but he won't want to hold them too long. He'll send them very soon to avoid trouble in the city. The only thing for sure is that once they leave this place and go through the city gates they will have no protection. None.'

They sat in silence, watching the shade creep and darken the wall of the Prefect's yamen.

'Have you seen Yen Lai Pao?' he asked.

'He is in the house of Wang Kei,' she said. 'Have you not spoken with him?'

'I will go to him. I have news of his family. Some of them escaped from their village, but the Boxers followed them into the hills. They showed no mercy. The villagers had no defence – they were hacked to pieces.' He wiped tears from his eyes with his sleeve. 'Even the children …'

'We will tell him together, Lai Pi,' she said. She took his arm and led him away.

Pao Chu returned to the apothecary's shop and he let her into the workroom. Sadie's feet protruded from underneath the table.

When Sadie's head appeared with her coal-black hair, Pao Chu knelt beside her and took her hand. 'Sadie, I spoke with Lai Pi. He had some very bad news for Yen Lai Pao. He says the Boxers found the people in the village where we sheltered. They have been –' Her voice faltered.

'Don't tell me! Please don't tell me! I can't bear to hear it!' She grasped Pao Chu's hand even more tightly.

Pao Chu nodded. 'I will leave it upspoken, but you cannot escape the truth.' She released Sadie's hand and stood up. 'Our friends are in great danger. I fear they made a mistake in putting themselves under the protection of the Prefect. I don't think there is anything we can do to help them. We must find a way out for you but for the time being you are safe. I will try to think of something, but for now you must stay hidden. Even with your black hair, your face does not look Chinese and I don't think the apothecary will have a potion to fix that.'

'What are we going to do?'

'I will talk to the apothecary and ask him for help. He knew my family, but was not an easy man to deal with, never had patience, and doesn't like any change to his routine. His weakness is that he's a miser: money is all he cares about. I am going back to the Prefect's yamen to keep watch. Rest and be sure to stay out of sight.'

Sadie knew she should cry about the murdered innocents, but it didn't seem real. She couldn't believe that while she'd been safely stowed away, the people who'd helped her were butchered. No, there must be some mistake. Surely someone was making mischief? Could Pao Chu be telling her fibs? No, of course not. But a whole village of people put to death? She remembered the faces of those people, the shy smiles, the children's heads peeping from behind their mothers' tunics. She forced herself to stop. I can only deal with one thing at a time. She put her legs out to straighten her aching muscles and lay down on the old straw mattress but did not dare close her eyes.

Pao Chu spent the night huddled like a beggar in the corner of the square near the Prefect's yamen. Just after dawn, two large carts were brought to the doorway. Pao Chu risked moving closer; she could see that only the yamen guards surrounded the carts, and there was no sign of Boxers or soldiers. She heard the rattle of chains grow louder and saw the prisoners as they shuffled through the doorway.

She barely recognised them. Tom Pigott and John Robinson looked stooped as though they had been beaten. As they slowly put one foot in front of the other, Pao Chu gasped and put her hand to her mouth. The men wore chains on their wrists and ankles, and their necks were also shackled. Tom tried to help his son get into the cart, but the guards lifted the boy roughly and threw him in.

As the women and children were led out, Tom's eyes squinted toward the door. Like the men they looked dirty and dishevelled, but Pao Chu was glad to see they did not wear chains. They put their hands up to shield their eyes in the early light. Jessie tried to run to Tom but was prevented by the guards. She heard Tom say something to his wife about staying with the little girls, and Jessie looked torn, but the guards didn't give her an option. She was firmly put in the cart with Miss Duval, Ernestine and Mary Atwater who tightly held hands.

The heavy carts shunted into movement. Guards on foot and horseback surrounded them as they made steady progress through the streets and the gates of the city walls. Pao Chu bowed her head as jeering shouts came from passers-by. A group of young men picked up stones and threw them at the passengers. The escort did nothing.

266

Pao Chu followed the carts to the city's edge and watched them disappear through the gates to the open roads. She'd heard the stories about groups of Boxers who freely stopped anyone who passed and asked their business. A woman travelling alone wouldn't get very far. No, she thought, I must return to the apothecary's shop and talk to Sadie.

CHAPTER THIRTY-THREE

Pao Chu came through the door of the apothecary's shop to a smell that she knew would stick in her nostrils long after she'd left.

The apothecary was talking to a customer. Pao Chu took a seat and waited as though she was there for a consultation. Her eyes browsed the lines of small drawers fixed into a tall orange cabinet, each with a shiny ring-pull at its centre. A carefully written bright-red label was on either side of the ring-pull. Row upon row almost to the ceiling. The apothecary stood in front of the cabinet and was separated from the customers by a gleaming pale-blue counter. A long bench for customers to sit and wait was against the opposite wall, and nearer the counter two wooden chairs, possibly to give the customer an illusion of privacy. Pao Chu could hear the entire conversation of the woman sitting in the chair, shoe and sock removed to show the apothecary a toenail that looked soft, loose, and yellow. He shook his head as he spoke, going along the drawers, occasionally pulling one open and removing a porcelain jar. He poured and mixed a concoction, talking all the time; the woman nodded as she replaced her footwear.

When the customer had left, the apothecary fixed his eye on Pao Chu.

'She cannot stay here any longer,' he said. 'You must take her away.'

'Just a few more days. I promise. I can pay you.'

'How much?'

'I can pay you in gold and silver jewellery.'

He didn't seem impressed by her offer.

'You've seen the painted signs on the streets. They are showing no mercy to the foreigners or anyone who is shielding them,' he said.

'I've seen the signs. The Prefect had a chance to kill the missionaries, but today I saw them being transported to the coast. He is helping them.'

'The Prefect may not want to kill them himself, but he is not going to risk his own position. He knows the Governor is determined to wipe out all foreigners. Perhaps the Prefect has sent the foreigners to Taiyuan, not to the coast.'

'No!' said Pao Chu. 'Why would he do that?'

'To save face with both sides. If the foreign soldiers come, he can truthfully say that he is not guilty of murder and that he sheltered the missionaries as long as he could. If the foreign soldiers do not come and Yu Hsuan stays in power, the Prefect will not get into trouble with him because he has sent him a gift of missionaries.'

Pao Chu sat down. It made sense. The Prefect wasn't stupid. The apothecary was wiser than she'd thought; she'd made the mistake of judging him by his greed, not by his words.

'What should we do?'

'We?'

'Please help us. You can see that Sadie isn't well enough to travel. Even with dark hair and a blue tunic, she doesn't look Chinese. Can we make her skin look more like ours?'

269

He raised his shoulders in a show of disinterest. 'You can't make her look like us. There is nothing to be done. She has blue eyes. The Boxers have posted a list of ways to know a foreign devil. Blue eyes is the first one.'

'Please, could she stay here until the baby comes?'

He shook his head. 'That is weeks away. I cannot hide her any longer. One night you told me. You must take her away from here. With each passing hour there is more chance of Blue Eyes being found.'

Pao Chu knew every word was true; the apothecary didn't have to lie. The truth was bleak enough. There was nothing left but to beg.

'Just a few more days, I ask you humbly. I must find out what has become of the others. I must find if they have been sent to Taiyuan. Please just give me a few days more. She is quiet, she will not be any trouble. I can give you some money now and the jewellery when I come back.' She pulled silver taels from her pocket and placed them on the counter. 'A few days – and you can save her life. She is not a devil. You know that is not true. I promise I will come back and take her away very soon. I must go to Taiyuan to see if I can help our friends.'

'You are putting yourself at risk. What if you don't come back? What am I supposed to do with her?'

'Perhaps you can move her upstairs to your apartment?'

'No. If she is found in the storeroom I can say she sneaked in without me seeing. If she is in my apartment that would look bad for me.' He picked up the handful of silver taels. 'Three days,' he said.

Pao Chu decided not to push the old man any further. She bowed deeply and went out to find Lai Pi.

The news was as terrible as she feared. The carts carrying the Pigotts, John and Miss Duval, and the children had not taken the road east. They were bound for Taiyuan to the yamen of the Governor, who hated foreigners.

Lai Pi had managed to rent two mules to take both him and Pao Chu to Taiyuan. They had no idea what they might accomplish, but they couldn't turn away from their friends in their hour of need. Before they left, they rid themselves of any sign that they were Christians. They knew they could be stopped and searched by soldiers or Boxers along the road.

They could travel thirty miles a day, but it was not quick enough for Pao Chu. The ground still held the weight of the rain, and the sand floor of the canyons was rutted by many wheels and feet. Even so, they travelled more quickly than the heavy carts they passed on the road. They reached the city gates to Taiyuan at noon on the second day and left the mules at an inn near the city walls.

They contacted Chang Ang, who had been an assistant at the hospital. He pulled them down a side street. His whispered words hard to catch. He told them he was leaving now, while he still could. 'It's only a matter of time before someone betrays me.'

'But what about Doctor Lovitt, and his wife and son and all the others,' said Pao Chu. 'Are they here?'

He closed his eyes as though the memory physically hurt him. 'Dead,' his voice dropped even lower. 'All of them killed yesterday by the Boxers on the order of the Governor. You shouldn't have come. You cannot save them. If you are suspected of even knowing them you will be put to death with them. Save yourselves. Go back to Shou Yang now, before it is too late.'

Pao Chu knew it was hopeless, that they could do nothing to help. She was about to tell Lei Pi to leave her, to go with Chang Ang but he spoke first.

'We will not abandon our friends in their hour of need. We will bear witness to whatever is about to happen and make sure we live to remember and honour them. Go, Chang Ang, you have been here too long already. Save yourself.'

Chang Ang hesitated a moment, then bowed and disappeared into the busy street.

All paths seemed to lead toward the giant dragon mural covering the entire wall of the entrance to the Governor's yamen. It occupied a site opposite the city's two huge pagodas and people had climbed up there to get a better view. The Boxers were everywhere, carrying out their acrobatic drills to the cheers of the people. In the main square, Bannermen stood to attention around the walls in front of the yamen.

Lai Pi and Pao Chu merged into the heaving mass. People around them talked of the prisoners captured while trying to escape. They laughed at the foolishness of the white people trying to outwit the great Governor who was going to restore the pride of China and rid their country of the foreign devils.

A door opened at the far end of the square, and guards marched out to the crowd's roar. Pao Chu was carried forward by the sway of the mob as they surged into the courtyard. She looked around wildly for Lai Pi but couldn't see him. Another roar from the crowd. Guards surrounded a sorry line of humanity led by Tom and Jessie Pigott, her arm around the shoulder of their son. The guards prodded them forward with spears toward the centre of the square, their clothes dirty and torn. John Robinson and Miss Duval held the hands of Ernestine and Mary Atwater. They huddled together and looked confused and frightened. Blood dripped from Tom's face and seeped through his shirt. He was unsteady on his feet and faltered as he became aware of the crowd. The manacles bit into his skin, and the sun beat on his sore head. Pao Chu watched the Boxers emerge from the mob and circle their prey. Again, the crowd cheered as if this spectacle was entertainment for them. The noise rumbled and grew. John stood in front of Ernestine and Mary who clung to the skirts of Miss Duval She put her arms around them as though she could protect them.

The Boxers played to the crowd. Pao Chu was repulsed by their strutting, their obvious delight in the degradation of her friends. The crowd drew in a breath as though they were one being. A Boxer dressed in red, with a bandana around his head, approached Tom Pigott and raised his sword. He tantalized the crowd by swirling the weapon above his head as he spun like a dervish. The Boxer was not going to grant his prisoner even the slightest kindness. He leapt, as though dancing, toward Wellesley, who clung to his mother. She screamed as her son was dragged from her arms.

The mob shouted '*Sha! Sha! Sha!*' and, with a malicious grin, the Boxer plunged the sword into the boy's chest.

Tears ran down Pao Chu's face. She felt a hand on her shoulder and held her breath. Lai Pi put a handkerchief into her hand.

'Be brave,' he whispered in her ear.

They saw Tom crumple to the ground at the sight of his murdered son and heard Jessie scream and hit out at the Boxer, but he twirled his sword in the air and sliced through her thin body. She fell beside her son, her hand outstretched toward him. Her eyes flickered and closed.

'*Sha! Sha! Sha!*'

The crowd urged the Boxers on. Pao Chu knew there was no hope for Tom and John and Miss Duval but prayed that Ernestine, only ten years old, and her little sister Mary might be spared. But no one was shown mercy. More Boxers joined the massacre to the crowd's delight. Within minutes, all the missionaries and the young girls lay dead.

Pao Chu's throat was dry, and tears flowed unheeded.

'Hide your face – you must not show grief, not yet.'

There was more space now as the crowing crowd had streamed into the centre of the bloody square to look more closely at the bodies.

Pao Chu and Lai Pi began to make their way back to the stable. People gathered in the streets, talking and laughing as though it were a festival. It was difficult to slip between the groups as they moved nearer the gates.

From behind came a cry and a surge of power. Lai Pi pulled Pao Chu to a side street to let the running mob pass. It was the piece of material she recognized. It was a piece of Ernestine's blood-stained dress. The crowd ran, arms aloft, carrying the near-naked bodies. Blood ran down their arms, but they ran like drunken men toward the gates, and when they got to the walled perimeter, they threw the bodies from the walls onto the waste ground below.

Pao Chu clutched Lai Pi's arm as they watched the people walk back from the gate, slapping each other on the back, congratulating themselves on a job well done. The murderers were filled with the joy of the righteous having completed a task for the greater good. They had got rid of the foreign devils.

'We cannot go,' whispered Lai Pi. 'We must bury them. They must have a grave, they must have prayers.'

'No,' said Pao Chu. 'We can only pray for their souls. They are already receiving their reward in heaven. Their bodies are lost to us. We can do nothing.'

Lai Pi looked distraught. 'Nothing? We cannot leave their bodies to the wolves. They deserve to be buried, to have prayers said over them.'

Pao Chu put her hand on his arm, her voice soft. 'We would have to wait until nightfall to retrieve their bodies. Then we would have to look for a place to bury them. We have no tools, Lai Pi. And, if we stay, we put Sadie at risk. Even if we leave now we might not get back in time. We must worry about the living, the dead will understand.'

She pulled his arm gently and led him back to the stable.

'There's still a few hours of light,' she said. 'We can make it to Luoyang before the gates close.'

As they passed through the gates of Taiyung, Pao Chu kept her head bowed to avoid any possible sight of the bodies, or even a snatch of their clothing. She had to concentrate on getting back to the apothecary's shop. He had said three days. Tomorrow night. She prayed they would make it in time.

CHAPTER THIRTY-FOUR

For Sadie, the outside world didn't exist. She prayed that Pao Chu and the others were safe and would return soon. She took solace from the hope that perhaps all the badness was over, and they could return to stay with Tom, Jessie, and Miss Duval (she really must find out her first name) and John Robinson. Even with the little jobs she was able to do for the apothecary, each hour felt like a day. She had to bite her tongue to stop herself talking to him and, even though she prayed, her spirits sank lower each night.

She knew the routine of the apothecary's day from sounds and smells. The shop opened early and stayed open while there was daylight outside. People came and went and she listened at the door, trying to decipher their ailments. She worked at grinding the potions but he wouldn't tell her what was in them, but she liked the smell of the herbs and having something useful to do. She waited hour after hour for the rattle of wooden shutters. Once the shutters were down she could open the door, just a fraction, and peek out into the shop. She saw the apothecary pull back the heavy brocade curtain that hid the stairs and make his way to the apartment above. She looked at the ceiling, could hear him walk across his rooms, the clatter of pots and soon the smell of food. Soon he would appear with a bowl of noodles for her. On the first two nights he left her to eat alone, but last night he'd brought his food too, and they sat on the floor, in silence at first, and ate together. In very simple sentences he asked her about her health and even looked at her teeth and asked about her baby – when it was due, how many more weeks? She answered in her simple Chinese and was pleased that he didn't seem to judge her. When they'd finished, he took the bowls and went back to his apartment upstairs. He pointed to the house across the road, and said they knew his routine, could see the candlelight through the shutters. She realised he was taking a risk; even buying extra food would be a cause for comment.

It had rained heavily all day but now the early evening sun broke through and Sadie sat with the Bible open on her lap. The outside world existed through several gaps in the window blinds that showed slices of the garden full of herbs and plants. She yawned and crawled under the corner table, pulling her black padded coat over her.

There was a tap at the window. She froze.

Another tap, and a voice she recognized said, 'It's me.'

'Thank God!' said Sadie, unlocking the door. 'I thought you weren't coming.'

Pao Chu came in followed by Lai Pi.

Rain dripped from their clothes. Their hair stuck to their heads, eyes swollen and red-ringed, but it was their air of desolation that said everything.

Sadie didn't want to ask, she didn't want to hear but slowly the words came from Pao Chu. Sadie sat and listened, her hand on the wall for support as she watched Pao Chu's lips move, making words she didn't want to hear. Words that crushed her soul.

Sadie covered her face with her hands and sat very still. She'd never seen Pao Chu cry before. She'd never even seen her become emotional. Sadie wanted to comfort her but couldn't find the words. Familiar words of comfort didn't seem right or enough. Not nearly enough.

'Has anyone escaped, anyone from the other missions?' she asked.

Lai Pi seemed to weigh up how much he should say. 'The Lovitts who ran the hospital mission and the family called Farthings from the Baptist mission are all dead. We heard the Boxers have killed Chinese who are Christians, or even Chinese who worked for the Christians. Hundreds who sheltered in the Catholic church have been slaughtered, all their priests and nuns. Everyone.'

Pao Chu shook her head. 'We don't know if everyone was killed. Maybe if people went toward the coast … except …'

Sadie let her hands drop. 'Except what?'

'We heard that the Empress has allowed the Boxers to fight with her soldiers in Beijing. They have surrounded the embassies. Foreigners and Chinese Christians are under siege there. It might be true, we don't know.'

'The Armstrongs – is there any word of them?'

'We don't know anything else.'

They sat in a circle and prayed for Tom, Jessie, Wellesley, John, Miss Duval, Ernestine and Mary. They felt a little comfort in saying their names; it kept them close.

Pao Chu slowly got to her feet. She put her hands on her back and rolled her shoulders.

'We should go.'

Sadie lifted her bag from under the table.

'No, Sadie, you cannot come now. I will come back for you tomorrow morning. I am going to meet someone now who may be able to help us. It's not dark yet. It's not safe for you to be out in the street.'

Sadie tried to hide her disappointment. 'It's all right. I think he's beginning to like having me here.'

Pao Chu looked down at her soiled clothing. 'We cannot stay like this – we must wash and change and I will come back early in the morning. Will you tell the apothecary? The shop is full and I must go now.'

Sadie nodded. 'Be careful. Please be careful. I couldn't bear to lose you too.'

They slipped out the door; she heard the rustle as they went through the garden. She sat with her back to the wall, clutching her Bible and prayed for Edith and Ruth. Poor Terrence. No wonder he hadn't come back. He must be caught in Beijing and, with things as they were, he couldn't write. She prayed that he was safe.

'Please let me see him again, dear God. He must survive this. *He must.*'

CHAPTER THIRTY-FIVE

As Sadie prayed, Pao Chu's and Lai Pi's descriptions of the murder of their friends replayed in her mind. She found not only anger rising but a deep desire for revenge. She paced the room, frustrated that she could do nothing to gain retribution. The months of pregnancy took their toll and the energy generated by her anger soon dissipated. She sat, drained and wretched.

She took deep breaths and tried to control the nausea. The baby stirred only slightly within her – she put her hand on her stomach, as though to soothe it. She whispered a prayer, asking God for forgiveness for her sins and to put these feelings out of her heart and soul.

I will think of the good Chinese people, the people who have cared for us, shown us kindness. Her mind turned to Pao Chu and Lei Pi. What better examples of Christianity could be given?

And if it wasn't for the kindness of the apothecary, where would I be? How kind he was last night, asking about my health, and the baby's health. She took a deep, cleansing breath and began to find some solace in her mind. She knew the shop was still open, she could hear people talking. She reckoned there was another hour of sunlight left. When the shop closes, I'll give him Pao Chu's message, and let him know how grateful I am to him. She began to feel better. Not better enough to forgive the murderers, she didn't think that could ever happen. But she would like to let the apothecary know how much she appreciated his help.

There was still some thin rice paper and an ink brush in the workshop. She rummaged through the drawers and found some black ink and brought everything to the window table. It would calm her. Perhaps I will leave it in the workshop for him to find when I am gone, she thought. It pleased her to imagine him opening the note and hoped he would laugh when he realised that she could speak and write Chinese.

It took Sadie some time to remember the correct Chinese symbols and use the ink brush to paint them onto the rice paper with a hand that wasn't quite steady. She blew gently over the page to dry the ink. The sun was almost gone. He would shut the shop soon.

A few minutes later she heard the sound of the shutters closing. She opened the door slightly, ready to stop him before he ascended the stairs. She had decided it was too dangerous to leave the note lying around.

She heard him speak quietly but wasn't surprised, old people often spoke to themselves – she found it endearing. She was about to open the door fully when she heard an answering voice. A low male voice, too low to hear what it said. She opened the door a fraction more, glad of the twilight. She saw the apothecary light a candle and motion to a tall, broad man to be quiet as he waved him through the heavy brocade curtain. Sadie's heart thudded in her chest as she listened to their footsteps disappearing.

He didn't usually bring anybody to his apartment. Why this man? Why so secretive? There was only her to hear. She bit the side of her nail. I need to get closer, she thought.

With the note in her hand, she crept through the shop barefoot, slipped through the brocade curtain gap leading to the stairs, and crept up the steps one by one. Voices, she heard men's voices murmuring and put her ear close to the door. They sounded as though they were arguing.

No, not arguing. Bargaining. The strange man was saying it was too much.

The apothecary said, 'It's two for the price of one.'

Were they talking about the monkeys?

The stranger's voice said, 'She's not young enough. They prefer them very young.'

One of them stood up and walked around, the stranger by the sound of the heavy tread.

The apothecary spoke. 'You drive a hard bargain but I will let her go to you. You can take her now.'

Sadie took a sharp breath and stepped back from the door.

The voices continued, 'No. Tomorrow. I will bring the silver tomorrow night. Give her something to make her sleep. I don't want any trouble.'

Sadie shook from head to foot. She wanted to run down the stairs and out into the street but forced herself to walk carefully down the stairs, praying they wouldn't creak, back to the storeroom. *Where is Pao Chu? I'm trapped. I can do nothing but wait.*

The key turned in the door. It was barely sunrise, the room still full of shadows. Sadie's stomach turned over. The apothecary poked his head in and swivelled his eyes around the room. They landed on her. His thin smile creased his face and revealed his blackened teeth. She hadn't seen him smile before. He left her some thin porridge and tea and withdrew without a word. and bile rose in her throat. She stroked her stomach. *Please, God, let Pao Chu come back soon!*

Her body needed rest, but she couldn't stay still. She paced around the small room in the grey morning light, angry at her helplessness. Her thoughts focused on revenge. How can I make him suffer? She felt powerless as she sat on her makeshift bed with her Bible in her hand. She'd heard the stories about girls and boys sold into slavery. For the first time in her life, she felt hatred for another person and didn't try to fight it. She let it take hold of her heart. She would not let him get away with trying to sell her and her baby. The very words made her retch.

There was a tap at the window.

Pao Chu climbed in and told her to get her things together quickly. 'Are you all right? You look awful,' she said.

Sadie picked up her bag. 'Pao Chu,' she said, trembling. 'Last night I overheard him making an arrangement to sell me.'

'*Bastard!*

Sadie had never heard Pao Chu swear before.

'We're going to P'ing Yang,' said Pao Chu. 'We must hurry.' She took out a pot of thick white liquid. 'We have to put this on you.'

She smeared the gooey paste onto Sadie's face and rubbed it until it became like a white mask. She put the high comb on her head and wrapped her hair around it, adding something greasy to keep it in place. She drew red lips and thin black eyebrows, then sat back on her hunkers to view her work.

Sadie felt the white cream tighten; it was uncomfortable. 'What are you doing, Pao Chu? I'll stand out even more, looking like this.'

'One of the travelling theatres is leaving this morning. If our cart goes among them it will look as though you are one of the performers.

Put these on,' she said and handed Sadie a long red embroidered robe and a pair of darkened round spectacles.

'No! Please! We'll never get away with it. You said they were looking everywhere for foreigners.'

'They are, but do as I say. You will look like an actress with the theatricals,' said Pao Chu, tidying the creams in her bag. 'You must walk slowly, as though you are old and hunched. Keep the glasses on no matter what. You must keep your eyes hidden.'

'Pao Chu, the apothecary would be in a lot of trouble if it was found that he hid me, wouldn't he?'

'If the authorities found out he hid a foreigner then he would be, but who would give him away? Put your coat on. It is early yet, but some people are around. Small steps, sort of hunched over as though your feet are bound.' Sadie looked down at her feet: the robe covered them but she wasn't sure if she could carry it off.

Pao Chu seemed to read her mind. 'We must try not to draw attention to them. Remember to walk slowly, always slow.'

The wind grew stronger. A stray branch brushed the shutters, and jasmine petals flew like summer snow.

Pao Chu peered out into the deserted garden. 'Hold on to me, Sadie. We will be safe soon. We should go now. Make sure you take everything. You must not leave any sign that you have been here.'

They went through the garden, as far as the wooden gate leading to the alleyway, where the cart and mules waited. Sadie held the thank-you note she'd written for the apothecary. She wedged it between the wooden lathes, making sure it was visible. It might blow away or be washed by the rain and never be seen again. It's in the hands of the Lord, she thought, as she closed the gate behind her.

Pao Chu helped Sadie into the cart and pulled a shawl and rugs around her, as though she were an old lady. She took the reins and the mules lumbered along the alleyway that led to the town gates. Sadie tried to pray, but her mind was on the note sticking out of the apothecary's garden gate. Who might find it? She prayed that someone would. She thought of Tom Pigott and how his whole family would have prayed, but now they lay dead in an unmarked grave. He, who had given his life to the preaching of Christ, had the cruellest of deaths and had to witness the murder of his wife and son before they took him. Poor Miss Duval, she only ever wanted to help. Her worst fear was that she would somehow be in the way. That's how she would remember Miss Duval, unassuming, apologizing for putting people out.

Why should God help me when He wouldn't help them? Is there any point in praying?

'Here they come,' said Pao Chu.

The rattle of the travelling theatre carts began to roll past them. When there was a gap, Pao Chu moved the mules into the stream of carts driven by the theatrical company through the gate and out into the countryside.

The long train of carts wove along the rutted road toward P'ing Yang with Pao Chu and Sadie somewhere in the centre of the caravan. Sadie lifted the dark glasses that pinched her nose and looked around. They were on a track with steep inclines on either side. She quickly replaced the glasses. Groups of squatting men with piles of stones neatly herded at their feet stood up fast and picked several rocks as the caravan approached. As they got nearer, the men were distracted by the scenery boards and boxes piled high on the carts. They lost interest as they passed and sat down to wait in case foreigners without protection came. Pao Chu's plan was working; as long as they didn't attract any attention, there was a chance they would make it to P'ing Yang, where they were to meet other missionaries and travel together to the safety of the coast.

That's if the others were still alive.

PART THREE

CHAPTER THIRTY-SIX

DECEMBER 1912, LONDON

The steps that led from the holding cells to the dock were steep and narrow. Amelia put her hand on the cold white wall to steady herself and briefly wondered how many prisoners had done the same before her on their way to the same dock, perhaps the same fate.

The court room was smaller than she'd expected, solid oak everywhere. Directly opposite the dock the upright red-leather judge's chair waited staunchly for its occupant. To her left several rows of gallery seats were full of gawping people backlit by a large window. They leaned forward to catch their first glimpse of Amelia Nelson and whispered comments to each other, perhaps disappointed by the ordinary-looking woman. Let them stare, she thought, and pulled back her shoulders. Let them think what they like.

Claire was up there somewhere but Henrietta had to wait outside. She would be called to give evidence – for the prosecution, for God's sake. Henrietta hadn't stopped apologising since she'd received the summons to appear, begged Amelia to forgive her, said she would refuse to give evidence. In that moment she knew that Henrietta didn't believe that she was innocent. Amelia had waved her away with a weary hand.

She felt dwarfed by the stone-faced policeman beside her as the solicitors and barristers entered the arena, shuffled papers back and forth and ignored the prisoner. She caught sight of Claire, her face pale, a crumpled handkerchief in her fist. Amelia wished she hadn't come, but she supposed that Claire would have to know the truth sooner or later. She'd hoped for later.

The news sheets were full of it, every detail of her life laid out in neat paragraphs for all to see. Her carefully constructed respectability torn from her, leaving her naked, open to abuse, fair game for tittle-tattle. And yet the trial hadn't even begun, though she felt it had.

She watched her barrister, Mr. Bosworth, and solicitor chat as more and more people crowded into the galleries. The audience, she could think of no other word that fitted them, had come to be entertained, to hiss and boo the villain – in this case her – and then go home to their safe little lives and continue on as though nothing had happened.

The judge arrived with due pomp to his throne and the crowd heaved themselves to their feet and tried to gain an extra inch of space as they collectively sat down again.

'Order! Order!'

The murmuring stopped.

The judge's wig was longer than the barristers, as was his face. He looked as though he'd prefer to be anywhere else in the world rather than here. As though the proceedings were intolerable to him, but here he was. As trapped as she.

Mr. Bosworth had reassured her that the prosecution's case was weak – 'circumstantial' was the word he'd used. 'Everything will come out in the trial,' he said, which seemed more a threat than a consolation. 'If there is anything else you feel I should know, now is the time. I don't want any surprises.' He'd paused a moment, in the cold interview room, looked at her with one accusing eyebrow raised and said, 'This is my business. I need to be sure you've told me everything.' And he was supposed to be on her side!

The prosecution barrister, Mr. Grimsby, began his opening statement. In his booming voice he said he intended to prove that the accused was neither honest nor virtuous and that Mr. Terrence Bennett had, in an effort to assist, become her victim. The court would hear compelling evidence as to the nature and character of this woman and the murder of Mr. Terrence Bennett.

The crowd looked at Amelia Nelson with fresh eyes.

Bosworth stood, one hand on his hip, and made his opening statement in a solemn voice, occasionally pointing to her and calling her 'the poor widow, making a living letting out rooms to boarders'.

She didn't like that. She pressed her lips together. He'd warned her not to let her emotions rise to the surface, unless it was to occasionally dab at her eyes, as though she were the victim in all this.

'But I *am* the victim,' she'd said sharply. 'And don't you forget it. The last time I saw Terrence Bennett he were hale and hearty, and it were on dry land. I never –'

'Absolutely, Mrs. Nelson. I understand that, but it will be in your interests to portray yourself as a still-grieving widow. A wronged woman, soft and harmless.'

'*Bloody hell!*'

'And no swearing.'

There he was, in full flow, in defence of the poor widow taken advantage of by Terrence Bennett. She took a lace handkerchief out and tried to look soft and harmless as instructed.

Bosworth sat down with a flourish, almost bowing to the audience.

In the gallery, District Inspector Lorcan O'Dowd watched the opening gambits and tried to decipher Amelia Nelson's face. He had written and asked to see her, but she'd refused. His meeting with Mr. Bosworth had been both fruitless and alarming.

'I can't make her see you,' Bosworth had said, 'She's impossible to deal with. She seems to believe that she knows best and, for some reason that she won't reveal, she won't take the stand. I'm sorry she won't see you, maybe you could talk some sense into her.'

O'Dowd watched Amelia intently. Why? he thought. Why won't you talk? What are you hiding?

CHAPTER THIRTY-SEVEN

'*Call Detective Inspector Peter Lyons!*'

In the gallery, O'Dowd sat straight and watched Inspector Lyons, the young detective in what looked to be a smart new suit, take the stand and swear to tell the truth in a strong, clear voice. What did he find out that I didn't, O'Dowd wondered.

The opening questions dealt with the inspector's experience as a detective before going through the details of the finding of the body and the work involved in identifying Mr. Bennett and moved on to the relationship between the deceased and Mrs. Amelia Nelson.

The gallery was quiet; their eyes travelled between Mrs. Nelson and Peter Lyons.

'Inspector Lyons,' said Mr. Grimsby, the prosecuting barrister, 'can you take us through the evidence on the circumstances surrounding the death of Mr. Terrence Bennett.'

Despite his youth, D.I. Peter Lyons looked confident. He spoke with authority, and O'Dowd knew he must have rehearsed this repeatedly as he, himself, would typically do. No one wants to falter on the big stage.

'Mr. Terrence Bennett boarded the *Titanic* on Wednesday, April tenth of this year, at Southampton. According to the White Star Line register, Mrs. Amelia Nelson, who had a ticket in her own name, had already boarded. Her name appears on the register kept by the White Star Line, along with the destination showing 'Queenstown'. The ship was delayed leaving Southampton and arrived in Cherbourg, France, at 6.30 pm, where more passengers boarded. The vessel left Cherbourg just after 8.00 pm toward the south coast of Ireland, where it docked outside Cork harbour the following morning at 11.30 am. Several first-class passengers, including Mrs. Amelia Nelson, disembarked at Queenstown and many third-class passengers boarded. The ship left Queenstown at 1.55 pm.'

'Does the register tell us anything else, inspector?'

O'Dowd leaned forward. What were they up to?

Inspector Lyons put his hand to his mouth, as though embarrassed. 'The register showed no cabin number for Mrs. Nelson – only for Mr. Bennett.'

Mr. Grimsby turned toward the gallery, eyebrows raised. 'So, we are left to assume that Mrs. Amelia Nelson spent the night in the room assigned to Mr. Terrence Bennet.'

'*Objection! Supposition!*' shouted Mr. Bosworth.

'Sustained,' sighed the judge.

But O'Dowd knew it was too late. The jury had already heard it. The damage had been done.

The gallery audience whispered and frowned at the woman in the dock.

'Did Mrs. Nelson speak to anyone in Queenstown?' asked Grimsby.

'She did. She spoke to a reporter at the quayside and told him her name and that she'd come to join her husband, Mr. Frederick Nelson.'

'To be clear, Detective Inspector. The woman spoke the name of her husband – Frederick Nelson. A detail that not everyone would be aware of.'

'She did, sir. It appeared in the reporter's article printed in the *Nottingham Herald*.'

Mr. Grimsby held up a copy of the newspaper. 'Exhibit B, m'lord.'

'And *was* Mrs. Nelson in Queenstown to meet her husband?'

Detective Inspector Lyons paused for a moment and assumed a stern expression. 'Mrs. Nelson's husband was not in Queenstown. He died in London in 1900. She told a blatant lie. If she lied about this what else did she lie about?'

'*Objection!*' said Mr. Bosworth.

'Yes, yes,' said the judge. 'Sustained. Inspector Lyons, you are not allowed to express your opinions. Facts only, please. Continue, Mr. Grimsby.'

'Inspector Lyons, let us move on to the discovery of the body of Mr. Terrence Bennett.' Mr. Grimsby made eye contact with every man on the jury as he walked slowly past them.

'Yes, sir. On Friday, April twelfth, a body was brought in to Youghal by a local fishing boat, and, following an investigation by the local R.I.C., was identified as that of Mr. Terrence Bennett. His body was subsequently confirmed to be that of Mr. Bennett by his brother, Mr. George Bennett. A post mortem revealed that Mr. Bennett had not died from drowning, but there is evidence that he had consumed a large quantity of opium and alcohol. The coroner's report states that the amount he consumed was more than enough to kill him.'

'Thank you, inspector. Can you explain to the jury how you know that Mr. Bennett was killed on the night of April tenth?'

'There was no water in the victim's lungs, indicating that he had stopped breathing before he entered the sea. The post mortem also identified the victim's last meal as being consistent with the menu provided by the White Star Line on the night. Roast duckling, to be exact, so we know Mr. Bennett was still alive on the evening of April tenth. Witnesses saw a woman of roughly the same size and height as Mrs. Nelson, and wearing clothes that could be hers, including a hat with a veil, during the voyage and later in Ireland.'

'Thank you, inspector.' The barrister hooked his thumbs into his waistcoat pockets. 'So a woman wearing clothes similar to Mrs. Nelson's, with her face covered, was on the *Titanic* and subsequently disappeared. How extraordinary! Now what possible motive had Mrs. Nelson? What could have driven her to end the life of a man who'd been a friend to her for very many years?'

O'Dowd looked down at Amelia Nelson, who stared straight ahead as though she couldn't hear the evidence against her.

'Our investigation revealed that Mrs. Nelson had very recently been replaced in Mr. Bennett's will as the main benefactor. According to Mr. Cranley, solicitor to Mr. Bennett, a few days before sailing Mr. Bennett had instructed Mr. Cranley to change his will immediately. He wanted all his belongings to go to a Miss Sadie Bradshaw, with an address in Dublin, Ireland. Mr. Bennett signed the new will the day before he left.'

'And if Mr. Bennett had not changed his will, who would have inherited the bulk of his wealth?

'Mrs. Nelson, sir.'

Grimsby let the name hang for a moment.

'Inspector,' he said, 'would you, by any chance, be aware of any other possible motive why Mrs. Nelson might want rid of Mr. Bennett?'

'We have reason to believe that Mr. Terrence Bennett had been blackmailing Mrs. Amelia Nelson for several years.'

A whisper went around the gallery.

O'Dowd looked down on Amelia. He knew this was her worst nightmare. He remembered when he'd interviewed her. She hadn't wanted the constable to write it down, hadn't even wanted him in the room.

The inspector went on. 'Mrs. Nelson has confessed that she impersonated her husband's first wife, Elizabeth Nelson, in order to benefit financially and receive money from the first Mrs. Nelson's family in Australia. She claims she did not know about this until after her husband's death. She admits that Mr. Bennett knew of the arrangement.'

'Thank you, inspector. No further questions.' Mr. Grimsby returned to his seat.

The defence barrister, Mr. Bosworth, stood and faced the young detective. 'Were attempts made to identify the unknown woman on the *Titanic*?'

'Yes, we sent a photograph of Mrs. Nelson to the Royal Irish Constabulary. They showed it to the local people. Our investigation was very thorough.'

'And not one person could positively identify the defendant. Isn't that so?'

'Yes, sir.'

O'Dowd sat back with a slight smile on his face. From his own experience, he knew that it was almost impossible to get Irish people involved in criminal prosecution. Unless land was involved, they preferred to stay out of the way of policemen and certainly wouldn't be persuaded to get involved with an English court of law.

'Mrs. Nelson runs a boarding house in Peckham. Isn't that so, Detective Inspector?'

'Yes, she does.'

'And what can you tell us about one of Mrs. Nelson's lodgers, a Mr. Charles Morley?'

'Mr. Morley also boarded the *Titanic* but we have no further information about him. We assume he did not survive the disaster.'

'You didn't send anyone from Scotland Yard to investigate his whereabouts?'

'We've been in touch with the Royal Canadian Mounted Police and with the American Police but so far we have not been lucky.'

Mr. Bosworth raised his eyebrows and looked around the gallery. 'You must have some concerns about Mr. Charles Morley's involvement in this case. After all, he was a sort of handyman for Mrs. Nelson and he would have met Mr. Terrence Bennett, a frequent visitor to the house.'

'We have no way of knowing that for certain.'

'But it's quite possible they would have met?'

'Yes,' the detective yielded. 'It's very possible.'

'What about the reporter, a Mr. Sanders, who spoke to the seventh passenger to leave the tender?'

'We are still searching for Mr. Sanders. We have information that he is in America.'

'So you haven't managed to find either of the two witnesses who could go a long way to throwing some light on this case.'

'No, sir.'

'No further questions.' Mr. Bosworth sat down.

The crowd murmured. O'Dowd watched the slightly dejected young detective leave the stand. He'd seen this ploy in trials before. Give the jury another suspect, which might introduce enough doubt to influence their verdict. Mr. Bosworth went up several notches in O'Dowd's estimation.

CHAPTER THIRTY-EIGHT

Michael arrived in full uniform and somehow managed to squeeze in beside his brother in the crowded gallery. He stared down at Amelia Nelson and seemed a little put out.

'She's not exactly the prettiest, is she?' he said in a low voice.

'What's that got to do with it?'

'Just saying. I thought she'd be, you know, prettier.' He rummaged noisily in a small bag of boiled sweets, chose a bullseye, and offered the bag to his brother, who shook his head. 'She's got a look about her, a frosty look, wouldn't you say? Not a patch on my Gracie.'

The prosecution called the next witness.

'Call Lily Odell!' echoed around the courthouse.

O'Dowd watched Mrs Odell walk gracefully to the witness box. She wore a black wool coat, and a fur stole loosely around her shoulders. She placed her gloved hand on the Bible, listened intently, and swore to tell the truth in a loud, clear voice. She looked elegant and composed, as though this were an everyday occurrence. She barely glanced at the crowd.

The prosecution barrister simpered apologetically at the lovely Mrs. Odell as though he were keeping her from much more critical tasks.

'Mrs. Odell,' he said with a smile, 'you were on the *Titanic* on the first leg of its ill-fated maiden voyage, isn't that so?'

There was a communal intake of breath from the gallery.

'Yes, I was.'

'And you disembarked with your family at …' he picked up a page from the pile, 'Queenstown, in Ireland.'

'Yes. We all disembarked together.'

'Excellent. Now, Mrs. Odell, could you look at the witness and tell me if this lady was on the tender that took you from the *Titanic* to the harbour in Queenstown on the morning of April eleventh.'

Lily Odell looked across at Amelia, who sat up to her full height.

'Take your time, Mrs. Odell.'

'It's hard to say. The woman on the tender kept very much to herself. Most of her face was covered by a veiled hat, her coat collar was up and she wore a scarf around her throat and mouth.'

'You're saying she covered her head with a hat and scarf. As though she were hiding herself.'

'It was a cold day. We all wore hats and scarfs. It wasn't out of place.'

The prosecutor nodded to the clerk. 'Exhibits C and D,' he said.

'Please look at this hat, coat, and scarf and tell me if these were the clothes worn by the woman on the tender from the *Titanic*. Take your time.'

Lily Odell looked carefully at the coat and hat and glanced at Amelia.

'They are certainly similar in style and colour to what the lady was wearing. The hat had a black veil attached, as this does. The coat she wore also had a large fur collar, as this has, which she had pulled up around her face. But myself and my sister-in-law, Kate, had pulled up ours in the same way. The wind was piercingly cold.'

'Thank you, Mrs. Odell. For the record, m'lord, these items were found in a wardrobe in the home of the defendant, Mrs. Amelia Nelson.'

The crowd muttered.

The barrister slid some pages along the desk. 'Your sister-in-law, Kate Odell, and your son Jack took many photographs on board the ship and, indeed, on the actual tender and even at the harbour.'

'Indeed they did.'

'And not one of the photographs, which have been examined by the police at Scotland Yard' – he paused briefly to let those words sink in – 'includes any photograph containing the woman who disembarked with you.'

'No, there wasn't. Not one.'

'Odd, wouldn't you say, Mrs. Odell? Would you say that the woman must have deliberately avoided the camera lens?'

'*Objection.* The prosecution is asking the witness to make a supposition.'

'*Sustained.*'

The prosecutor bowed slightly to the judge. 'Let me rephrase the question. Did everyone else on board the tender appear in the snapshots taken by either Kate or Jack?'

'Well, yes, they did. There were only seven people disembarking in all.'

'Thank you, Mrs. Odell. No further questions.' The prosecution barrister sat, obviously pleased that he'd managed to put his point across.

'Questions, Mr. Bosworth?' said the judge.

Mr. Bosworth smiled pleasantly at Mrs. Odell.

'The coat and hat, Mrs. Odell. Would that style of coat and hat be popular, would you say?'

'The hat was, well, up to recently, a very popular style, especially among older ladies – the veil is flattering. The wide collar on the coat would also have been popular, and a fur trimming is always fashionable.'

'So both these items would have been popular. Bought by many, would you say?'

'Yes, they probably would.'

'You wouldn't be surprised to see these items or, as you say, something very similar, in the wardrobes of many women across England?'

'Not in the least,' said Mrs. Odell, who seemed quite relieved.

'Thank you, Mrs. Odell. No further questions.'

'*Call Jack Odell!*'

Inspector O'Dowd watched as the young boy was led into court. The boy immediately looked around to check that his mother was there. O'Dowd couldn't see her face, but guessed that she smiled encouragingly at him. Giving evidence in a court of law was not an easy thing to do at such a young age.

'So, Jack,' Mr. Grimsby smiled at the boy, 'you are a keen photographer, are you not?'

Jack nodded.

'You need to say it out loud, Jack. For the court record,' Mr. Grimsby said in a pleasant voice.

'Sorry. Yes, I am, a keen photographer,' he said.

'How many photographs did you take on board the Titanic?'

'I took thirty.' He looked at the jury. 'I counted them when I got them developed.'

'Now, Jack,' said Grimsby, 'tell us about the photograph you took at sunset, the one that shows a man looking over the edge.'

Jack raised his eyebrows. 'No. It doesn't show him. I was photographing the sunset. He just happened to be there.'

'And was he alone?'

'There was a lady beside him at first, but she left while I was taking my shot.'

'But you did see her?'

'I did.'

'And you saw her again on the tender bringing you from the *Titanic* to Queenstown.'

'I think it was the same woman. She had a hat with a veil hiding her face, but she's not in any of the photographs.'

'And can you tell the court if the woman in the dock is that woman? Was this woman on the *Titanic*?'

Jack glanced at his mother again. 'I can't be sure it's the same woman. It might be, but I couldn't swear to it under oath.'

Grimsby pursed his lips. 'But you do think the woman with Terrence Bennett on the *Titanic* disembarked at Queenstown. Can you say that?'

Jack paused for a few moments. 'I would say the woman on the tender is the woman I saw with the man on the deck.'

'Thank you, Jack. No further questions.' Mr. Grimsby sat down.

Mr. Bosworth stood up.

'Is it more correct, Jack, to say that it was the veiled hat that you recognized, rather than the woman who was wearing it?'

The crowd in the gallery seemed to hold its communal breath.

Jack looked at Amelia in the dock. 'Yes,' he said. 'It was the hat I noticed.'

'No further questions,' said Mr. Bosworth.

The judge called for lunch.

The brothers went to the nearest public house. A solid building with oak beams and stained-glass windows that gave a false twilight effect. The brothers had a glass of beer and some bread and cheese.

'Mrs. Odell is a good-looking woman, for her age,' said Michael. 'She looked relieved that she could say the clothes could be anybody's.'

'No one wants to be responsible for sending an innocent person to the gallows,' said O'Dowd.

'And you're sure Mrs. Frosty is innocent?' said Michael, biting into a large piece of cheese.

'I still don't think she did it,' said O'Dowd. 'But I've been proved wrong before.'

'Is it because she's a woman? I always think women are better at lying than men.'

Can it be as simple as that, thought O'Dowd. Is Amelia Nelson a better liar than most? He put that thought aside – he'd interviewed many men and women during his career and was usually able to break down their stories if they were lying. No, he would be able to spot a lie. He was sure of it.

CHAPTER THIRTY-NINE

The oak-panelled room was warm in the afternoon sun as everyone retook their places. The twelve men of the jury looked comfortable after their meal, and the judge asked for the windows to be open as he cast his eye over them. He'd been a judge for many years and knew the post-lunch jury might be a little weary and prone to dozing off.

'*Call Miss Henrietta Harper!*'

Amelia had that slightly irked feeling that she often experienced when she saw Henrietta, especially if she hadn't seen her for a while. It was not so much what she wore – today it was her best black double-breasted coat and a hat that was in fashion when the old queen was on the throne. It was the look on her face. The same look that a mouse has when you strike a match in the dark and find it eating your food – the thing never knows whether to run or finish the cheese and dithers there looking at you until you hit it with a heavy pan.

Henrietta clutched her handbag and followed close on the heels of the court clerk as though afraid she might lose her way to the witness box. She looked starry-eyed at the gallery, and they looked directly

302

back at her. She risked a shy smile at them before placing her hand on the Bible and listening carefully to what the clerk said.

'… *to tell the truth, the whole truth and nothing but the truth, so help you God?*'

'I do,' she said, and then unexpectedly, '*Amen.*'

The clerk looked uncertainly at her. 'What?'

The crowd tittered.

'I'm so sorry,' she said to the clerk. 'I thought there was an "Amen" there. I haven't done this before.'

'It's quite all right, Miss Harper,' said the prosecutor. 'I'm sure God won't mind an extra Amen.'

She beamed a smile at him and at the crowded gallery.

Amelia's heart sank. *Silly woman will say anything they want to hear. She's the centre of attention and loving every minute of it.*

'Now, Miss Harper, can you tell me about Wednesday April tenth this year. Where were you and what transpired?'

'Transpired? Do you mean in Winchester?'

'Yes. Your trip to Winchester. You almost didn't go. Why was that?'

'Mrs. Nelson' – she nodded and smiled across at Amelia – 'wasn't feeling very well. She suffers terribly with severe headaches. The only thing is to lie down in a darkened room and wait for it to pass. On the morning of April the tenth Mrs Nelson was very pale and obviously not well. I offered to stay to look after her. I told her I wouldn't mind postponing my visit to Winchester. Excellent cathedral for brass rubbing, you know.' She fiddled with her lace handkerchief. 'Mrs. Nelson wouldn't hear of it. She said she would go back to bed and draw the curtains and rest.'

'So, you didn't stay,' said Mr. Grimsby.

'I felt I should stay, but she insisted I go. I'd seen this happen to her before and thought she would be right as rain in a few hours. Of course, I wish now that I'd stayed. She was obviously unwell. Far too unwell to do anything except lie down. I made her some camomile tea and left the house at about eight o'clock. It's very good, Mr. Grimsby, the camomile tea, in case you ever suffer with headaches.'

'Well, thank you, Miss Harper. I'll be sure to pass that on to my wife.'

A small murmur of good humour passed through the crowd.

'When did you return from Winchester, Miss Harper?'

'Friday afternoon. April the twelfth.'

'And how was Mrs. Nelson?'

'The picture of health, I'm delighted to say. She was in good spirits.'

Amelia tried not to glare at her.

'So, Miss Harper, you didn't see Mrs. Nelson from early on Wednesday morning, April tenth until Friday twelfth in the afternoon. In fact, you have absolutely no idea what Mrs. Nelson did during that time.'

The crowd began to murmur, and the judge called for order.

Henrietta tried to raise her voice above the crowd. 'She was so ill she couldn't possibly have taken herself off to Southampton.'

'Thank you, Miss Harper. I have no further questions, m'lord.'

'Mr. Bosworth?' The judge looked at him.

Bosworth got slowly to his feet and moved some papers around on his desk.

'Miss Harper. You've been a tenant of Mrs. Nelson for about a year, isn't that right?'

'Yes, sir.'

'And what about Mr. Charles Morley?'

'Charles Morley? What about him?' She narrowed her eyes.

'What was your impression of him, Miss Harper?'

'I don't think he had anything to do with this at all. Though …' She took in a deep breath.

O'Dowd leaned forward. She looked a little confused. He guessed she wasn't prepared for this.

She blinked several times, then seemed to recover her composure. 'There was something about him. A restlessness or uneasiness. Amelia, I mean Mrs. Nelson, was very good to him. He arrived out of the blue, without a penny to his name, and Amelia took him in, gave him a hot meal and a bed for as long as he needed it. There's not many women would be that charitable to a stranger.'

The gallery nodded in agreement.

'He stayed in the house?'

'Oh no! Of course not. There was an outbuilding at the end of the garden. It was a little bockety – it needed a bit of work done to the roof, which he did. It ended up being quite a comfortable little room.'

'I see. So, it's quite likely that Terrence Bennett and Charles Morley met during the course of Mr. Morley's stay?'

She rubbed her temple with her finger. 'I expect so. Perhaps they met ...'

'Did Mr. Morley ever mention his intention to go to America?'

'He might have. I really don't remember.'

'And you didn't think it odd that Charles Morley and Terrence Bennett both boarded the *Titanic*?'

'How could I think anything? I had no idea that Charles, I mean Mr. Morley, was gone.'

'How do you think Mr. Morley might react if he found that Mr. Bennett was, let's say, taking advantage of Mrs. Nelson in some way?.'

'*Objection!*' The prosecution barrister was on his feet. 'The defence is leading the witness and asking her to make a case against Mr. Morley, who is not on trial here today.'

'*Sustained.*'

'No further questions.'

O'Dowd watched Henrietta step down from the witness box. Something she'd said didn't sit right, but he couldn't quite put his finger on it just now.

He scribbled a note to Amelia Nelson. The case wasn't going well. In the note, he pleaded with her to see him.

A short time later, the reply came. She said yes.

CHAPTER FORTY

She sat at the table, very still, as though any movement might break the protective bubble she'd surrounded herself with. She must have heard the footsteps coming toward her, but she did not move her head or her eyes toward them. He asked the constable to wait outside the door in the hope she might speak more freely.

'Mrs. Nelson,' he said, taking the seat opposite, 'how are you?' He need not have asked; her face was lined with worry.

She let her cold eyes meet his and waited for him to go on.

'Amelia,' he tried again, his voice low, 'thank you for seeing me. I hope you got my letter explaining my sudden withdrawal from the case.'

She nodded once and waited for him to go on.

'Have you heard anything from Charles Morley?' he said.

'Not a word. Should I have?'

'You've got to tell your side of the story.'

She closed her eyes and let her head fall back slightly. 'You don't understand, inspector. If I tell the truth about Charlie it will look even worse for me. You're not on my case, that's right, isn't it?'

'Not officially but I've tried to find the reporter who spoke to the woman who got off the *Titanic*. He's in America. I've been leaving messages with every newspaper I can contact. But nothing so far.'

She smiled the way you would at a child digging holes in the sand for treasure.

He looked her in the eye. 'Amelia, your story doesn't add up. Was Terrence Bennett blackmailing you? What is it that you're not telling? What has Charles Morley got to do with it?'

'It wasn't blackmail,' she said, 'but Terrence didn't let me forget that he knew. I never felt I could refuse him anything. He had a side to him that wasn't kind. People who are too good-looking can be like that, don't you find? They can be mean-spirited.' She sighed as though finally surrendering. 'You remember the dresses? I told you about the photographs and the dresses.'

'Yes, I remember.'

'Well, the truth is it didn't end there. I let you think that once Frederick died that was the end of it. Terrence let a few weeks pass, probably waiting for the reality of my situation to hit home, before he came to see me again.' She leaned back in her chair and looked at O'Dowd as though trying to find the right words. 'Have you ever been married?'

'What? As a matter of fact, I haven't.'

'So you probably don't know.' She paused for a moment. 'I noticed it, when I was married, the way married men flirt with married women in small ways. Terry flirted a little with me when Frederick was alive. When he took my hand before leaving he'd squeeze it a little, or he'd catch my eye and smile without a word. He never said anything untoward. You'll think this silly, but I thought Terry might offer to take care of me and the children. Then he started speaking and I realised how far off the mark I was. He said there might be a way that I could come out of this with enough money to set me right. He said that Elizabeth's father in Australia was probably unaware that his daughter had died. I knew straight away what he was thinking. "Where's the harm, Amelia?" he said. "He's happy in Australia sending money to his daughter. He can't have many years left. What's the point in upsetting him now? Not to mention the fact that you don't have a penny to your name. You could get enough to buy a little house. Provide a home for yourself and the children." I felt myself wavering. I told him I'd think about it. But he pressured me. "You don't have time to think, Amelia. You have to leave this house at the end of the month, and you'll walk out that door with nothing but your clothes." It was clear he wasn't going to put his hand in his pocket to help me. He was strange like that: he liked to show off by giving expensive gifts, but when it came to handing over cash he could be quite stingy. He said that I didn't really have a choice, that he'd arrange everything, and all I had to do was to have my photograph taken in the same way as before. He made it seem so simple, not really wrong at all, and, of course, it was for the children's sake. So I said yes, I'd do it. He knelt in front of me and took my hands in his. "Don't worry, Amelia, everything will be all right. I'll take great care." And fool that I was, I believed him.'

O'Dowd sat back in his chair. 'Tell them, Amelia. Just as you've told me. It's a bit of a gamble, admitting to fraud, but it might be your only way out.'

O'Dowd sat in the gallery as Amelia told her story. She was telling the truth and was taking a risk that the jury would believe she'd been led astray by Bennett. He's seen this in trials before, especially in murder trials. Blame the victim.

Amelia was explaining in her matter-of-fact voice. As though the bizarre situation was perfectly normal. 'The truth is that Frederick had married me because I looked like Elizabeth. Long before she died Terrence Bennett had seen me in the mill, had even remarked to Frederick that he'd seen someone who looked like his wife's double. It was an innocent remark, but after Elizabeth died and things were going badly for Frederick, he bribed Terrence to introduce us.'

'Bribed?' said Mr. Bosworth.

'Frederick wrote a letter of recommendation for Terrence to the tea merchants he'd worked for in the past. It opened many doors for Terrence. Frederick married me and brought me to the photographic studios and had our photograph taken, year after year. I never knew why, nor asked why. It seemed a harmless thing to do, not important at all.'

'And for how many years did you carry out this pretence, Mrs. Nelson?' said the defence counsel.

She clutched her dry handkerchief, 'Ten years, sir. One photograph every year in May, on Elizabeth's birthday.'

'And lead us through what happened next.'

'When Frederick died Terrence persuaded me to continue with the photographs and I had no choice. Frederick had left debts that I had no way of paying, I had children to bring up. Terrence said he would organise everything and he was as good as his word. He organised the photographer, arranged for a commissioner of oaths to sign the paperwork that stated the photograph was of Mrs. Frederick Nelson, which technically it was. And then it was sent to Australia. I don't know exactly where. About three months later he would bring a cheque to me for £200.' She dabbed her eyes the way the solicitor had suggested.

'And you squandered this money on jewellery and furs, Mrs.

Nelson?' said Mr. Bosworth, looking to the gallery.

She smiled and paused, as she'd been instructed to do. 'No, sir. I have three children. All the money went to schooling and clothes. You know how quickly children grow.' She let her eyes linger for a moment on the jury. 'And it went toward the small house we have.'

Her barrister looked along the jury. 'So you put this money, freely given money, to the welfare and care of your children. But you lived a life of ease, no doubt?'

'No, sir. I took in boarders and washing and sent my sons to a school for the education of the children of deceased commercial travellers. They learned a trade there. They're in the Royal Navy now. Done very well for themselves.'

'And are you still in receipt of this yearly stipend?'

'No, sir. The money stopped. There was no explanation, no letter, nothing. Terrence thought it best to let sleeping dogs lie. He said that if we went digging for answers we could stir things up. He said it was best to leave things as was.'

'And that was the end of the incident, Mrs. Nelson?'

'Unfortunately, no. It wasn't.'

She took a breath and seemed to struggle with the words for a moment.

'One day last year a young man came to my door. He asked if I was Elizabeth Nelson. I knew there was no point in saying no – he had my photograph in his hand. He said his name was Charles Morley and that he was my half-brother. From Australia. I felt a little dizzy and he was concerned he'd given me such a shock. Which he had, but not for the reason he thought. As far as he was concerned, I was the woman in the photograph. He thought I was his half-sister.'

'And what brought Charles Morley to your door at this particular time?' said Mr. Bosworth.

'His father had passed away. He made his sons promise that one of them would go to England and make sure Elizabeth was all right. That's why he'd come. It was his father's dying wish.'

'So, Charles Morley thought you were his half-sister. What did you tell him?'

'The truth.'

'How did he take it?'

Amelia swallowed. 'Badly. I told Charles I knew nothing about it until Frederick died, and that was the truth. He went through the handful of photographs and picked up one of me, standing alone – it had been taken after Frederick died. He said, "I see it didn't stop you, though." I tried to explain that I had been at my wit's end, that I'd had no choice. We had no house, food, or any other way of getting money. But that meant nothing to him. "My dad went short," he said. "When things were starting to dry up he wouldn't stop sending you the money. He went hungry so that his daughter could have a good life. That was all that mattered to him, that he gave his daughter a better life." I asked if his father would have preferred to know that his daughter was dead all those years ago? At least he was happy, thinking she was still alive. Didn't that spare him the pain of losing a child? But it was the wrong thing to say. He shouted at me. He said we'd lined our pockets at his father's expense. His fists were clenched he was so angry. For a moment I thought he might hit me. I told him repeatedly that we were sorry, that we'd thought his father was wealthy and wouldn't miss two hundred pounds a year. That's when Charles looked really confused. "*Two hundred?*" he said. "*What do you mean? It was over a thousand pounds every year!*" I couldn't believe it – *one thousand pounds! One thousand pounds, every year!* In the heat of it all I'd slipped up. I'd said 'we'. He realised that someone else must have been involved. Someone was doing a lot better out of it than I was. He asked for the name of the other person involved but I wouldn't tell him.'

Bosworth held a hand up. 'But, Mrs. Nelson, why would you not tell Charles that Terrence Bennett was the other person?'

Amelia let her head fall. The jury leaned a fraction forward to hear her answer.

'I didn't tell him because… I thought he'd kill Terrence.'

'Thank you for your candour, Mrs. Nelson,' said the barrister. 'The defence rests.'

CHAPTER FORTY-ONE

The prosecutor flicked through his notes as he rose to his feet. O'Dowd guessed that by Amelia admitting her guilt in deceiving Charles' family she'd taken the wind out of his sails and pre-empted much of his arguments.

He asked her again about her relationship with Terrence and if she'd realised that he'd changed his will.

She told him she'd never had, at any time, any inkling of what was in Terrence's will. She thought it none of her business, and he had never discussed it with her. O'Dowd observed her face. She didn't blink. He knew that she was lying. He remembered how she'd reacted when he told her that Sadie Bradshaw would inherit. The look of shock on her face. She'd known because he'd told her so himself. Not a big lie, but nonetheless she was under oath, and if he hadn't known, he'd have believed her.

The door to the courtroom opened and O'Dowd caught sight of Michael scanning the benches of the public gallery. Their eyes met, and Michael motioned for him to come out.

Outside the doorway, a man waited.

'Lorcan, this is Mr. Sanders. He came to the house looking for you. He's the one –'

'I know!' O'Dowd scribbled a note and asked Michael to give it to Mr. Bosworth.

O'Dowd grabbed Sanders' arm. 'Come with me.'

He hurried the small, portly man along the corridor to the witness waiting room.

Notes passed furiously between the defence team. Mr. Bosworth asked for a few minutes' recess because of new evidence. There was a quick conversation between Amelia and her defence council. O'Dowd watched as she nodded. That simple nod, without hesitation, convinced him she was innocent.

'What is going on there?' said the judge. 'You've had months to prepare your case.'

'Your Honour,' the defence council looked slightly flushed, 'I'd like to call a witness who has just become available. He is the reporter who spoke to the woman who disembarked at Queenstown.'

'I haven't finished with Mrs. Nelson, Your Honour,' said Mr Grimsby.

'Well, get on with it,' said the judge. 'With the grace of God this man can settle the whole thing.'

'I'd like to remind you that you're still under oath, Mrs Nelson.' Grimsby's chest swelled, signalling the importance of his next question. 'I would like to put it to you bluntly, Mrs Nelson, that Terrence Bennett was blackmailing you, was a drain not only on your finances but on your good name and reputation. He came and went to your house freely at all hours of the day and night. When Charles Morley revealed how much Terrence Bennett received from his father you were furious. The only way to get revenge and be rid of him was to murder him. And the opportunity came when he invited you to accompany him on the *Titanic*. You murdered him in cold blood before returning to your home in London.'

'No. I did no such thing. None of that is true.' Amelia looked around the courtroom at the faces staring at her.

'That's all for now.' Grimsby raised an eyebrow. 'But I may need to re-examine Mrs Nelson following the reporter's testimony.'

A moment later, the balding, middle-aged reporter made his way to the witness box under the eyes of the gallery who watched him like prey.

O'Dowd prayed silently that he hadn't made the worst mistake of his life as Mr. Bosworth rose, glanced once at Amelia, and began his questioning.

'Kindly introduce yourself and your occupation.'

'I'm Bernard Sanders. I'm a freelance journalist. I've been in the west of America these last few months. Sorry, I had no idea you were looking for me.' He looked around apologetically, his hat in his hands.

'That's quite all right, Mr. Sanders. You were at the harbour in Queenstown when the passengers disembarked from the *Titanic*.'

'I was.'

'And you spoke to a woman claiming to be Mrs. Amelia Nelson, supposedly there to meet her husband?'

'Yes, I did.'

'Can you tell me if that woman is in the courtroom today?'

The reporter's eyes went straight to the dock. He studied Amelia's face. O'Dowd held his breath, as did everyone else.

'Well, Mr. Sanders, is the person in the dock and the woman you spoke to in Queenstown one and the same?'

He continued to stare across to the dock. 'I can't say. I'm sorry. It could be. But I can't be certain.'

'Well,' said Mr. Bosworth, 'can you at least say it's definitely *not* the same woman.'

'I … I can't say that either. I'm sorry.'

The crowd murmured, and O'Dowd couldn't be sure if they were pleased or disappointed. He hung his head. Tomorrow would be the final day.

He'd failed to save Amelia.

CHAPTER FORTY-TWO

It was the last day of the trial. O'Dowd left the house in the quiet of the early morning. He pulled up his collar and shivered briefly as he walked toward the omnibus. Michael would finish night duty shortly, and they were to meet at a café near the Old Bailey.

Rain drizzled against the fogged-up window on the omnibus, matching his miserable mood. He'd pinned everything on finding the reporter. He'd thought the case would be settled one way or the other, but it hadn't. He feared that he'd never know the truth. No matter what the verdict. He'd never know for sure if Amelia Nelson was guilty or innocent.

The café was crowded, but Michael had secured a comfortable corner. A pot of tea sat ready for him on the table. They talked about the reporter again and Amelia's testimony. O'Dowd had been impressed with her. She'd never wavered, not once. She'd told her story without a flicker of hesitation. Her solicitor had instructed her well. She was back on the stand this morning to finish her questioning by the prosecution.

Michael poured the tea. 'I expect that Grimsby chap was pleased to have a break after Amelia's testimony. It certainly put the cat among the pigeons, didn't it? I suppose now that she's admitted to posing as the first Mrs Nelson, the prosecutor might be content with that.'

'She says Bennett wasn't blackmailing her, but the prosecutor could still go for that angle,' said O'Dowd. 'He could still argue for a murder conviction. Someone who's already admitted fraud and thought she had a lot to gain from Bennett's death isn't going to sit well with the jury. It could go either way.'

O'Dowd didn't finish his tea. He felt restless and uncomfortable in the steamy tea shop. The fogged-up windows turned the passing people and traffic into a soft blur. He decided to get to the court early. He said goodbye to Michael, who was buttering yet more toast and headed out into the dull morning.

The doors to the public gallery in the Old Bailey were just opening. Even on this cold, wet morning, the crowds queued to listen to the closing statements and gawp at Amelia. He hadn't got over the disappointment at the reporter's testimony. They'd spoken afterwards. The reporter was apologetic, to a point. 'I couldn't be sure,' he'd said. 'In all conscience, I couldn't swear she was or wasn't the woman.'

The crowds were growing denser as they were funnelled towards the large arched doors. He realised he was behind Henrietta Harper. His instinct was to slow down, but seeing her had brought something to mind. He tapped her on her shoulder. Loose ends will be the death of me, he thought as he raised his hat to her.

'Oh, inspector!' She didn't seem at all pleased to see him.

'Miss Harper, how have you been? I expect you found the experience of giving evidence very trying.'

'Yes, indeed. Poor Amelia. It's not going well now, is it? I must hurry along to get a seat. The gallery is so full.' She pushed into the crowd, and he squeezed in behind her.

'Have you spent any time in Ireland, Miss Harper, visiting relatives perhaps?'

'No. I've never travelled overseas.'

'I see. My mistake.' He waited to see if she would enquire as to why he'd asked.

She didn't.

'It's just that,' he saw a flicker of annoyance pass across her face, 'you said the shed was "bockety". It's a word I've only ever heard used in Ireland. So I wondered …'

'We had an Irish cook,' she said quickly. 'When I was a child. You know what children are like for picking things up.' She was already moving towards the door.

'Yes, I see. That must be it.' He stopped walking. 'Excuse me. I've left my umbrella in the café. I must go back for it.'

She was already gone.

Michael was still there, reading the paper. O'Dowd sat down beside him and wrote down a name and address. 'Michael, can you fetch this woman and bring her to the court as quickly as possible? Tell her it really is a matter of life or death.'

Michael read the name. 'How is …'

'Just go, please. I'm going back to the court. I'll try to delay things as long as I can. Tell her she's the only one who can help. Here's money for a cab. Please hurry."

'All right. You know I shouldn't be doing this in my uniform. If I get into trouble …'

But O'Dowd was already headed for the door.

O'Dowd walked quickly back to the old Bailey. He hoped that Amelia would be called. It would kill some time. Once the barristers started their closing statements, it would be too late.

O'Dowd squeezed through to the front of the crowd. The judge hadn't come into the courtroom yet. He showed his identification and was allowed through to the defence council's room.

'Have you anyone else to call?' he asked Bosworth, who shook his head. 'No, and the prosecution have sent word that they're not going to call Mrs. Nelson again. They must be pretty confident. We'll go straight to the closing statements.'

'There's something you should know. I've sent for someone who has crucial information.'

'You said that about the reporter and you were wrong,' said Bosworth. 'We've run out of time.'

'Ask the judge to delay for a little while. *Please.* She's on her way. She'll be here any minute.'

'Are you sure about this, O'Dowd? I'm warning you, I don't want a repeat of the reporter incident.'

O'Dowd didn't want a repeat of the reporter incident either, but it was a chance he'd have to take. He realised he could be completely wrong, clutching at straws, but if he didn't try, he knew he'd spend the rest of his life haunted by Amelia Nelson.

The judge agreed to delay for half an hour but no longer. 'This is becoming quite a feature of this trial. But this is the last time I'll delay.' He took up his morning newspaper and looked at them over the top of it. 'Half an hour.'

Grimsby began to object on the grounds that he hadn't had the chance to see the new evidence.

The judge peered over his glasses and looked at Mr. Grimsby. 'This is a murder trial, and a guilty verdict will result in a sentence of execution. We cannot risk an incorrect verdict. I'm sure you wouldn't want to win a case in that way.'

O'Dowd took short puffs from a cigarette on the damp pavement outside of the Old Bailey. He saw the carriage coming towards him. Michael's head protruded out the window. When he saw O'Dowd, he gave him a thumbs-up sign.

'*Call Miss Pao Chu!*'

The small neat woman wore a dark-blue coat buttoned up to her throat. Her shiny jet-black hair framed her pale face. She walked quietly, eyes down, to the witness box, and the entire courtroom watched her take the stand. A ripple of interest ran through the gallery.

She laid her hand on the Bible and swore to tell the truth.

Mr. Bosworth seemed a little unsure where to start. He looked at the note in his hand. 'You are Miss Pao Chu?'

'I am Pao Chu.'

'Are you in any way acquainted with Mrs. Amelia Nelson?'

'No, I am not.'

'Could you tell the court what you know about the murder of Mr. Terrence Bennett?'

'I know nothing about the death of Mr. Bennett,' said Pao Chu.

Mr. Bosworth sent an exasperated glance toward O'Dowd before continuing. 'Is there anything relevant that you can tell me? I must remind you that a woman is on trial here for her life.'

'I don't believe Mrs. Nelson is responsible.'

'Who do you think *is* responsible, Miss Pao?'

Pao Chu looked along the faces of the jurymen. 'I suspect that Sadie Bradshaw can tell you more than I,' she said.

The judge looked at the defence counsel. 'Wasn't that name mentioned a few days ago? Remind me of the context.'

'Sadie Bradshaw is the sole beneficiary of the victim's estate,' said Mr. Bosworth.

'Miss Pao Chu, are you accusing this Miss Bradshaw?' said the judge. 'I hope you can substantiate it.'

'I will try to explain, sir.' She took a moment to gather herself together and looked Mr. Bosworth in the eye. 'Sadie Bradshaw and I worked in the missions in China. She was a charming young girl, and a very willing worker, but naive in the ways of the world. We met Mr. Terrence Bennett on the voyage over and Sadie fell in love with him. He came to see her several times but when the Boxer Rebellion spread, all foreigners were sentenced to death and most of the missionaries we knew were massacred. We barely managed to escape with our lives.'

The gallery was deathly quiet.

Mr. Bosworth spoke softly to Pao Chu. 'Can you tell us how you escaped? We all remember the terrible stories of the siege of Beijing.'

She pressed her lips together, as though trying to gather her patience. 'The people trapped in Beijing had some sort of protection. We, I mean the missionaries in Shansi, had nothing, no one to protect us. We had to rely on our own resources to escape.'

'And how did you escape?' said Bosworth.

'We were smuggled out by a group of travelling theatrical players. At first we were in our cart, but Sadie became very ill. She was carrying Terrence Bennet's child and had been frail for months. When they realised what was happening, the theatrical players hid us in their carts under scenery boards they use in their plays. There was a very real danger that we would be betrayed. They saved our lives. They tried to get us to safety before the baby was born.'

'And did they?'

'No, they could not. Sadie gave birth on our way. The baby, a boy, didn't survive beyond a few hours.' Pao Chu's voice cracked, and she took a sip of water. 'We couldn't let Sadie rest. If we stayed at an inn we knew we'd be discovered. Our only hope was to move quickly. It was unbearably hot under the scenery boards and uncomfortable on those stony roads – but it was the only way. Her mind was not right. I thought she might give us away. She often didn't know where she was and banged on the wooden scenery. By the time we got to Beijing, the city had been ransacked by the soldiers from many countries.' She paused and swallowed.

'Are you able to carry on, Miss Pao Chu?' said Bosworth.

Pao Chu nodded. 'It wasn't a safe place for women. I got us passage on a ship to England. I hoped Sadie would be able to rest, that she would recover, but she could not settle. She was awake day and night.'

'Was she ill?'

'I can't explain it to you. She wouldn't listen to me, to anyone.' Pao Chu looked along the gallery. 'She was obsessed with looking for her baby. She thought the child was alive.'

The judge looked at Pao Chu and then at the defence counsel. 'This is indeed a very sad story, but what has it to do with the murder of Terrence Bennett?'

Pao Chu didn't look at the council or the judge. 'Mr. Bennett contacted me early this year. He told me that Sadie had come to see him, that he had been surprised – he thought her to be in an asylum in Dublin. He asked me about our escape from China, about the baby. I told him the truth.'

'How did he react?' said Mr Bosworth.

Pao Chu closed her eyes for a brief moment. 'Relieved,' she said. 'Terrence Bennett looked relieved.'

The people in the gallery shifted and whispered behind their hands.

'Relieved?'

'He had seen Sadie, had listened to her story. Perhaps he was relieved that he was not tied to her. She was delusional when she spoke about China. I told him that I had tried to reason with her but she wouldn't listen. She was convinced that the child was alive somewhere in China. Terrence seemed to think that he could walk away from Sadie, despite the suffering she'd gone through. I argued with him that he was responsible for her. He had seduced her, had put her life in danger. She had lost what was most precious to her. She'd lost her baby and she'd lost him.'

'*Objection!*' said the prosecutor. 'Mr. Bennett is not on trial here. He is the victim in all this.'

Mr. Bosworth turned to the judge. 'I propose that the case be adjourned while we contact Miss Sadie Bradshaw.'

'Sir,' said Pao Chu, 'I thought you knew. Miss Sadie Bradshaw is in this courtroom.' She looked again at the sea of faces in the gallery until her eyes came to rest on one.

Everyone followed her gaze and turned to look at the flushed face of the woman at the end of the row.

Michael moved to where Henrietta Harper sat and held his hand out to her. She took it without a murmur and allowed him to lead her down the steps and to the front of the court.

'Hello, Sadie,' said Pao Chu.

Gone were the smiles and fidgets. Henrietta was still and composed.

O'Dowd watched her shed the skin of the dotty, irritating spinster she'd portrayed herself as and step into her real skin. The skin of Sadie Bradshaw.

The watchers in the gallery leaned forward as one body to catch her words.

'Do you mind if I …' She untied the black bonnet and removed it. 'It's sweltering in here.'

325

Her voice sounded different, O'Dowd realised.

She looked at the barristers and solicitors and took a deep breath. 'There is no point denying it. Yes, I am Sadie Bradshaw, though I think of myself as Sadie Bennett in the eyes of God. Terrence and I married in the only way we could at the time. We exchanged our solemn vows before God.'

The judge fixed his bulging eyes on her. 'Let's stay with the earthly, Miss Bradshaw. You can sort out your status in God's eyes at a later stage.' He addressed the two barristers. 'I'm adjourning this case until Miss Bradshaw and Miss Pao Chu can be interviewed by the police.'

CHAPTER FORTY-THREE

It took some time for the court to clear, and even now small groups of reporters clustered around the steps as the crowds made their way into the drizzly street. O'Dowd hung back, hoping that Michael was still around somewhere.

He felt a tap on his shoulder and turned smiling, only to face D.I. Peter Lyons, who didn't seem too happy with him.

'You kept all that about Sadie Bradshaw quiet. Why wasn't it in your notes?' said Lyons.

'It wasn't really part of the investigation. For all I knew she could have been dead. I had no idea that Sadie and Henrietta were one and the same. The only photograph I had was of a blonde-haired, plump, smiling young girl – nothing like the woman in the court today. The black hair, and her face seems years older than it should be.'

Lyons bit his lip. He seemed irritated but was professional enough not to let that interfere with the job in hand. 'I'm about to interview Miss Bradshaw now,' he said. 'It might be useful to have you there.'

It wasn't the most gracious invitation he'd ever received, but

O'Dowd quickly followed Lyons back into the courts.

'What's happened to Amelia?' he asked. 'Has she been released?'

Lyons nodded. 'She's been charged with fraud, but released for the time being. She's on her way home with her daughter.'

They took several flights of stairs to one of the many interview rooms. It was much cooler there. O'Dowd decided against removing his coat.

D.I. Lyons sat opposite Sadie, and O'Dowd took a seat beside him.

She seemed relaxed, her hands resting in her lap. She stared at a blank wall, her thoughts seeming to be engaged with something far away.

'Inspector,' she said when she finally noticed him, 'I must apologise for leading you on.' She smiled as she spoke, as though she was apologising for playing the wrong card in a hand of bridge. 'I wasn't very truthful. But you can see now that I really had no choice.'

He was struck again by how different she sounded – the Welsh accent discarded and now a soft Irish tone to her voice.

'I think it's Mrs. Nelson that you should apologise to, Miss Bradshaw. An innocent woman was very nearly convicted of a crime that you committed,' said O'Dowd.

'Innocent! You think she's innocent? Oh no, inspector, I was there many evenings when she thought they were alone and you wouldn't believe the carry-on of them. I could hear them whispering together. I know what they were up to – he was unfaithful to me.'

He watched her struggle to get her emotions under control. Surely she wouldn't have let Amelia go to the gallows. Would she?

D.I. Lyons smiled at Sadie. 'Perhaps we can start from when you returned from China.'

'You can start there if you like,' said Sadie. 'But Pao Chu is lying. I know that she sold my son. He's alive somewhere in China. I must get back to find him. You do see that, don't you?'

O'Dowd resisted the urge to glance at Lyons.

Lyons nodded and spoke quietly. 'We'll come to that. Perhaps you can explain how you came to live with Miss Nelson.'

She sighed. 'All right then, if you like. After the Boxer rebellion, I was brought back to Dublin to my Aunt Prudence and Uncle Cecil. They were horrified that I had a child as if that was the worst possible thing that could have happened to me. I told them I had to return to China to get my son but, instead of helping, they put me in an institution. I was prescribed laudanum to keep me quiet. I learned to fade into the background and be silent until they couldn't see me at all. After a while, I don't really know how long, I was released back to my aunt and uncle, and I kept up the pretence. The laudanum made it easier. I didn't mention my son or China. I spent my days doing embroidery, reading, and pretending I'd forgotten all about it. That was the only way I could get my allowance, such as it was, by pushing down the real Sadie and becoming a smiling helpless shadow. Time moved slowly until finally I had enough to take the boat to England to search for Pao Chu. It didn't take me long to find her. I asked her to come with me to China, to bring me to the village where my son was. Do you know what she said? She held my hand and told me that my son had died the night he was born. Well, I knew that was not so. How could it be? I'd held him, I'd heard him cry. He was there, he was alive somewhere. I could see it in her eyes. She'd sold my baby, probably to a farmer who would need a son to help in the fields, or maybe to the theatrical company.'

'Do you have any proof of that, Miss Bradshaw?' said Inspector Lyons.

Sadie's face froze.

Inspector O'Dowd leaned across the table. 'It must have been harrowing for you. How did you manage?'

Sadie gave Lyons a long stare before turning back to O'Dowd.

'My only option was to find Terrence. I suspected he was in London, but it's such a big place, isn't it, inspector? Compared to Dublin.'

O'Dowd nodded.

'Terrence had mentioned Amelia Nelson to me when we were in China. It was an easy name to remember. I knew he had helped her set up a boarding house somewhere in Peckham. I was worried that Aunt Prudence would have the police looking for me so I invented Henrietta Harper, from Wales. I put on my black clothes and bonnet and started to look for Amelia. People will talk to you if you seem harmless. Post offices are the best places to ask if you're looking for someone. That's how I found her.'

'You lodged there and waited for Terrence to turn up,' said O'Dowd.

'I didn't know for sure that he would, but he'd never mentioned anyone else – he wasn't a man with many friends. I knew they corresponded, and eventually, one day, Amelia was so excited she couldn't stop talking about the letter she'd received from her 'special' friend. When she finally put it out of her hands, I found his address at the top of the page.'

'And you went to see him?' said D.I. Lyons.

'The very next day,' said Sadie. 'When he opened his door, he looked puzzled. I know I looked very different from the girl he remembered. I wasn't that fluttering young blonde girl anymore. He seemed pleased enough to see me, but I couldn't forget that he'd left us there to die. He tried to put a good face on it. "Poor Sadie," he said. "I should have tried harder to find you. I heard about Ruth and Edith and then the Pigotts. I asked about you, but nobody knew. There was no word of you. I thought you'd been killed." There might have been a grain of truth in there, but I know that if he'd really wanted to find me he could have. Then I told him about Arthur. Although I didn't get a chance to christen him that's the name I picked for my son. I hadn't told anyone else that, I wanted him to be the first to know.' Sadie suddenly stopped talking and her eyes filled with tears.

O'Dowd leaned across and gave her his handkerchief. 'It must have been awful for you, Sadie,' he said.

She bent her head and held the handkerchief to her eyes. After she'd stilled herself, she blew her nose and looked at the two men. 'You see, it was going so well. I shouldn't have told him everything.'

'What else did you tell him?' said D.I. Lyons.

'I told him about Pao Chu. I told him that she'd sold Arthur. I remember how he sat back in his chair and seemed to weigh everything up. He said "Really, Sadie," speaking to me as though I were a child, "Pao Chu would never do such a thing. Why would she risk her life to save yours, but sell off your baby into slavery? It doesn't make sense." I told him I wanted to go to China and search for Arthur, but it would cost a lot. We'd need professional guides, money for bribes, money that I didn't have. He said the Chinese border was closed, but I knew the real reason. He was terrified. I could see it in his eyes. I told him God would protect us. He looked at me as though I'd lost my mind. I saw pity in his eyes where there used to be love. He must have felt guilty because he began to ask about money. Did I have enough to get by? He said he would go to his solicitor and set up a monthly allowance for me. He sat down at his desk and asked me for my address – I gave him the Dublin address. As he wrote, he said, "You'll receive a small amount every month, and I'll make sure that you will be looked after, when I'm gone." I didn't think much about that. After all, he was only forty-seven. He might live for another forty-seven years.'

'So you decided to murder him,' said D.I. Lyons.

'No, of course not. Not immediately, anyway. I went back to Amelia's. I hadn't told him I was staying there. I thought I'd bide my time. Stay in the background. Whenever he was due to call I pretended to go out, but I hid quietly in my bedroom and listened to whatever they talked about.'

'You spied on them,' said DI Lyons.

'Of course. How else could I find out what they were talking about?' she snapped. 'One day I heard him talk about New York – he planned to go for at least two years. He told her about the *Titanic* and he asked her to go with him. She got very excited, as though he were proposing to her. But then things quietened down, and I don't mean in the way they quietened when they were in the bedroom. The parlour door opened and he came out saying he didn't understand what he'd done wrong – that he thought she'd enjoy a luxurious overnight trip. She shouted something that I can't repeat and he slammed the door on his way out. Then Amelia stormed upstairs and banged her door closed. I slipped down and found the ticket. It was in her name all right, but only travelling as far as Queenstown.'

Sadie sat back, a smug look on her face.

O'Dowd thought how pleased she looked with herself. Finally able to tell how she'd planned all of this, how she'd overcome obstacles, how she'd managed to pull the wool over everyone's eyes. He could see she expected some acknowledgement of her cleverness, but he couldn't bring himself to do it.

'Is this when you began to involve Charles Morley in your plans? Did you tell him everything?' he said.

She shifted in her seat. 'No, not everything. Enough to keep him on my side.'

Ah, yes. Sides, he thought There are always sides, though everyone thinks theirs is the right one.

'Charlie had taken to Claire, and she seemed to be very fond of him. I planted the idea that he should think about going to America, that he could send for Claire once he got a job – plenty of jobs in America. I told him that I would help him. I gave him four pounds to buy a first-class ticket to cross to Ireland. It was important that he was able to access the first-class section. We boarded. There were people everywhere, making themselves familiar with the ship. I'd hoped that I could 'accidently' meet Terrence, but it was so big he could have been anywhere. I hadn't thought of that so I asked at the purser's office for the number of Mr Bennett's cabin, making sure that Charles could overhear. We had planned that he would come at midnight.'

'So Charles Morley knew what you intended to do?' said O'Dowd.

'Yes, he knew. Though he said he wouldn't be part of it, only to help afterwards. I needed him to help me get the body over the rails.'

She paused briefly, a half smile on her lips. 'Terrence was such a vain man. He thought I'd come to seduce him, and it was easier for me to go along with that idea than to argue again. You're probably shocked, Inspector O'Dowd.'

'I am a little surprised,' said O'Dowd, aware of the colour rising to his cheeks.

She went on. 'We stayed the whole day in the cabin, only coming out in the evening to walk around the deck. A few people were strolling around, looking at the sunset. A boy taking photographs made me feel a bit uneasy. I suggested that Terrence order dinner in the cabin.'

'And wine, I suppose. You poisoned the wine?'

'Three spoonfuls of laudanum is a lethal dose, but I added a few extra drops to each glass, to be sure.'

O'Dowd put his head in his hands. 'Henrietta, sorry, I mean Sadie. You admit you went with the intention of killing Terrence. That you took the laudanum for that purpose.'

'I always carry laudanum, many people do. It wasn't my choice, inspector. I wouldn't have had to kill him if he'd agreed to give me the money to go to China. It was entirely his own fault. At midnight Charles tapped on the cabin door. He was quite pale, you know, that sort of greenish tinge that people get when seasick. I wondered if he was having second thoughts. It's one thing to sit in your kitchen over a cup of tea and make plans, quite another to take a man's life in the flesh. Terrence had pulled off his jacket and lain down on the bed. He was in a deep sleep. I watched, waiting for him to draw his last breath. It was very peaceful, he didn't suffer at all. Just drifted off. When his breathing became so shallow that I had to lean over him to hear, he opened his eyes and fixed them on me. I looked into them and saw life slip away. Charles fell to pieces. "What will we do?" he said over and over again. I told him we'd bury him at sea exactly how we'd planned.'

'Why not leave him in the cabin?' said O'Dowd.

'I considered that, but I read that the *Titanic* was to have excellent medical facilities and doctors on board. They could easily carry out an examination and see signs of poisoning. No, best to let him arrive on a beach somewhere in a couple of weeks. We waited until the ship was quiet, till all we could hear was the waves and the icy wind. It was just a few feet to the rail. Over in seconds, I didn't even hear a splash. Later I imagined his white face in the black sea looking at us disappear into the night without him. Sometimes I see that white face in my dreams. I worry that he hadn't had a proper burial, that his spirit might be restless.'

'You said Charles was uneasy. But still he helped you.'

She looked down at her hands for a moment. 'I lied to him.' Her voice was so low he barely heard.

'What did you tell him, Sadie?'

'He wouldn't have gone along with it otherwise. He's not a bad person.'

Sadie took a few sips from her glass of water. She replaced the glass and twisted it slowly round and round with her thin fingers.

'I told him about Terrence and how badly he'd treated me, and I intimated that Terrence liked pretty young women, like Claire, and perhaps he'd become fixated on Claire, and that was why he came to the house so often.'

O'Dowd leaned back in his chair. 'I can see how that might affect a young man. So, he went along with it and was going to stay in Mr. Bennett's cabin?'

'Where else could he sleep? He put on Terrence's jacket. It fitted well enough. The key to the trunk was in the pocket. Clothes, papers, money, and watches.'

'You forgot to search his trouser pocket.'

'The badge. Yes, I couldn't believe it. He'd already been to the barbershop on the *Titanic*. I had no idea until you showed it to me. Had it not been for the badge you'd never have linked him to that ship, would you?'

'I wouldn't say that, Miss Bradshaw. But it certainly helped.'

She sat back in her chair and looked at the ceiling. 'Barbers, he loved barbers. He was always so meticulous about his hair,' she said.

Lyons had heard enough and seemed to want to bring the interview to a close. 'And the next morning you put on your veiled hat and left the ship, knowing that Amelia Nelson would be under suspicion.'

She shrugged, as though that was of no consequence to her. 'Charlie promised he'd keep his head down on the ship. As long as the bed looked slept in, and he left some clothes around every day, no one would pass comment. He would arrive in New York with all Terrence's belongings, papers, and bank drafts. He was to send money to my bank as Terrence Bennett. Meanwhile, I was to return to Dublin as soon as possible and wait. No one would make any connection between us. But I wanted to go back to Amelia's. I wanted to hear what was going on, what the police were saying.'

'And that's where I came in,' said O'Dowd. 'You had me hook, line and sinker.'

'He was meant to die, inspector. On the *Titanic*. It only happened a few days earlier than God intended.'

'Have you any idea where Charles Morley is now?'

'I have no idea. Even if I did, I wouldn't tell you. That's all I have to say about Terrence Bennett and Charles Morley. Can we talk about the reason I asked to see you?'

'Oh,' he glanced at Lyons, 'I wasn't aware that you'd asked to see me.' He paused. He usually would have said, 'How can I help you?' but he didn't think he could help Sadie Bradshaw.

'Inspector, somewhere in China is my twelve-year-old son. He probably wonders every day why his mother abandoned him.'

O'Dowd had a bad feeling about this. He knew what she was going to say.

'Could you help find him for me, please?'

'She really expected you to go to China?' Michael shook his head. 'The poor woman must be demented. It's a very hard thing to lose a child, but to have it drilling in your head that he might be alive … that would create all sorts of demons.'

'Despite the fact that she murdered a man in cold blood, it's hard not to feel sorry for her,' said O'Dowd. He took a large swallow of porter and wiped his mouth clean of the froth. 'I expect she'll spend the rest of her days in an asylum.'

'How did you figure out that Henrietta Harper was Sadie

Bradshaw? You never mentioned any suspicions.'

'I'd none to mention, not until the day she was on the witness stand and mentioned that the shed was 'bockety'. I particularly noticed it because I heard someone behind me ask what that meant and no one seemed to know. And then, on the last day of the trial, I found myself walking behind her. I asked her if she'd any relatives in Ireland to visit and she said she'd never been there. And when I asked her about 'bockety' she said when she was a child their cook was Irish.'

'So?' said Michael. 'Lots of Irish servants in England.'

'Yes, I know, but she had mentioned several times how poor her family was. Didn't sound to me like it was the sort of family that could afford a cook. I realised she was either lying about coming from a poor family or lying about the cook, or lying about never having been in Ireland.'

'She had something to hide, at any rate,' said Michael.

'Exactly! After that it was a flash of inspiration, I suppose.'

'More like a shot in the dark!' said Michael. 'Lucky it paid off! She nearly got away with it. But for you, Amelia Nelson could have hanged.'

'Did I tell you Amelia's coming over to Youghal?'

'Are you serious?'

'She wants to see where Terrence Bennett is buried. I said I'd take her to see his grave.'

'That'll set tongues wagging.'

'Let them wag,' said O'Dowd.

CHAPTER FORTY-FOUR

Youghal Police Barracks, 1913

District Inspector Lorcan O'Dowd came into the station, shaking raindrops from his tweed coat.

Sergeant Mulcahy was holding a blue envelope as Constable Flanagan read the letter it apparently had contained. The young constable tried to put the pages away, but O'Dowd told him to carry on.

'It's from a woman,' said Flanagan. 'Someone called Maggie. She was on the ship with Patrick, she says she danced with him.' He bit his lip to stop it trembling and handed the letter to O'Dowd.

Dear Liam,

You don't know me, but I feel I know you very well.

I met Patrick on the Titanic, and he talked about you a lot. You and, of course, your mother and brothers and sisters. He told me how you'd taken time off work to go to see him off. He was very proud of you and told me where you were stationed and I hope this letter reaches you in Youghal.

On the night of the accident, we'd danced together to the sound of fiddles and bodhráns and had a fine time. Later during the night, after the ship hit the iceberg, he went along all the corridors calling my name, looking for me to get out. I thought it was a joke, but then I saw how serious his face was. He made me put on my coat and the other girls in my cabin too, and he argued with the guard at the gate to let us through. The guard tried to get us to go back and wait, but Patrick would have none of it. He pleaded until the guard gave in and said women only could go to the decks. Patrick stayed behind but called out to us as we went to make sure we got straight into a lifeboat.

I looked for him for days but never saw him again.

I wanted to tell you that the six girls in our cabin probably would not have survived if it hadn't been for Patrick. We owe our lives to him.

You told him that he was to write to his mother, but now he can't so I thought I could do that much for him and it might be good for her to know how brave her son was.

We will never forget him.

Yours truly,

Maggie Fitzpatrick

THE END

Author's Note

I very much hope that you enjoyed the story. I know some of it is a tough read but those were probably the bits that were true and needed to be written. Although this is a work of fiction, it is based on fact. I thought you might like to know what the truth is and what I invented.

Seven passengers did indeed disembark at Queenstown. The Odells and Father Browne were real people, as was John Coffey who hid on the tender. This information is part of the excellent tour at the *Titanic Experience* in Cobh (formerly Queenstown).

Amelia Nelson is fictitious, though she is loosely based on a real passenger, a woman who became my 'Amelia Nelson'. Following the sinking of the *Titanic*, a newspaper reported that a woman had disembarked at Queenstown to join her husband. When I researched this, I found that her husband had passed away several years previously. The newspaper may have misreported, and she may have been there to meet her son, but I cannot be certain. The rest of Amelia's story is my concoction.

Terrence Bennett, Sadie Bradshaw and Pao Chu are all fictitious.

The missionaries mentioned in the book were all real, as was their fate in China. Their names haven't been changed except for one – Ruth Whitechurch was based on a missionary called Emily Whitchurch, who ran an opium refuge with Edith Searell. As Emily and Edith's names were so alike, and they appear together in several chapters, I thought it easier for the reader to change one.

A total of 239 missionaries were killed in China during the Boxer revolt, including the Pigott family, John Robinson, Miss Duval, and Ernestine and Mary Atwater. Many Chinese Christians were also murdered or sold into slavery. Some were recovered afterwards.

The Boxers were known in China as the Yihequan – the 'Righteous and Harmonious Fists'. Non-Chinese used the term 'Boxers' and I've kept it at that in the text to avoid confusion.

Here is a list of the main sources I used to research the China section. NB: some of the placenames in these books and articles are different from those in use in China now.

Anderson, Emma Marie Thompson (1920) *With Our Missionaries in China*

Davin, Delia. (1992) *British Women Missionaries in Nineteenth-Century China*. Women's History Review, 1:2, 257-271.

Edwards, E.H. (circa 1901) *Fire and Sword in Shansi; the Story of the Martyrdom of Foreigners and Chinese Christians.*

Hudson Taylor, J. (1895) *Three Decades of the China Inland Mission.*

The Society for Promoting Female Education in the East. (1847) *London History of the Society for Promoting Female Education in the East*

Stoddard, John L. (reproduced 2015) *China – John L. Stoddard's Lectures.*

Angie Rowe